S0-BNK-231

"Kimberly Cates writes with a unique blend of beauty, magic, and power that never fails to touch me deeply."

—Linda Lael Miller,
author of *The Last Chance Café*

PRAISE FOR

KIMBERLY CATES

AND HER POWERFUL CONTEMPORARY NOVEL

OF LOVE, FRIENDSHIP, AND FAMILY

Fly Away Home

"Kimberly Cates is one exceptional storyteller. . . . Her stories are just as riveting and unforgettable in a contemporary setting as they are in a historical one."

—*Romantic Times*

"A beautifully written romance that shimmers with the haunting magic of Ireland."

—Kristin Hannah, author of *On Mystic Lake*

"Relationship drama fans will want to fly away with this warm, contemporary romance with a bit of the supernatural. . . . A stirring tale of love."

—Harriet Klausner, Bookbrowser.com

Magic

"Cates uses Celtic lore and Irish tradition laced with humor and shimmering sensuality to produce an engaging, well-written story."

—*Library Journal*

"Fun to imagine . . . Cates' books always have an enchanting quality."

—*The Pilot* (Southern Pines, NC)

Morning Song

"Cates writes eloquently and emotionally. Her complex, riveting plot makes this a one-sitting novel, impossible to put down!"

—*BookPage*

"The perfect entertainment for a stormy summer night."

—Minneapolis *Star Tribune*

Stealing Heaven

"Kimberly Cates has the talent to pull you into a story on the first page and keep you there."

—*Rendezvous*

"Stunning in its emotional impact, glowing with the luminous beauty of the love. . . . Another dazzling masterpiece from a truly gifted author."

—*Romantic Times*

Books by Kimberly Cates

Published by Pocket Books

KIMBERLY CATES

The Mother's Day Garden

POCKET STAR BOOKS
New York   London   Toronto   Sydney   Singapore

10307031

This book is a work of fiction. Names, characters, places and incidents are products of the author's imagination or are used fictiously. Any resemblance to actual events or locales or persons, living or dead, is entirely coincidental.

An *Original* Publication of POCKET BOOKS

 A Pocket Star Book published by
POCKET BOOKS, a division of Simon & Schuster, Inc.
1230 Avenue of the Americas, New York, NY 10020

ISBN: 0-7434-1886-7

First Pocket Books printing April 2002

10 9 8 7 6 5 4 3 2 1

POCKET STAR BOOKS and colophon are registered trademarks of Simon & Schuster, Inc.

For information regarding special discounts for bulk purchases, please contact Simon & Schuster Special Sales at 1-800-456-6798 or business@simonandschuster.com

Front cover design and illustration by Tony Greco

Printed in the U.S.A.

The Mother's Day Garden

1

TRAPPED LIKE A RAT, Hannah O'Connell thought as the screen door slammed and all too familiar footsteps sounded briskly in her back entryway.

"Hannah?" her best friend, Josie Wilkes, called out. "Don't get up. It's just me."

Hannah clutched the handles of the wicker laundry basket as if it were full of drug money instead of mounds of damp things fresh from the washing machine. You'd think most people would consider hanging out wash pretty harmless. But she had a funny feeling Josie Wilkes wouldn't see it quite that way.

Hannah looked for someplace to ditch the evidence, but there was no retreat. Reckless, her nineteen-year-old daughter Becca's grizzled black Lab, blocked the way to the laundry room, immovable in his unfailing hope that anyone at the door might be his girl home from college. And Josie was already rounding the corner into the kitchen, a bulky plastic baby carrier clasped in both hands.

"Just when you think you're indispensable, you find

out the world can get along just fine without you." Josie sighed without looking up as she settled her five-month-old, Tommy, in the middle of Hannah's kitchen table. "You should see those eager little volunteers we trained at the community garden taking over while the two of us are on leave. By the time we get back to work they'll have pasted their names over ours on the manager's doors. When I stopped by to pick up the veggies they wanted to send you as a get-well present, I told Steve to quit looking so happy about being in charge or I'd rip his heirloom tomato vines out by the—whoa there!" Josie's green eyes widened in disapproval as they locked on Hannah. "Exactly what do you think you're doing, buddy old pal?"

Hannah's cheeks burned, but she clutched the basket even tighter in spite of the ache radiating from the angry red scar on her abdomen. "It's been four weeks since my surgery."

"And by my count that leaves at least two more weeks before you're allowed to lift anything at all, let alone something as heavy as that basket."

"But all this sitting around is driving me crazy, Josie. I can't stand it."

"Civilization as we know it won't come to a crashing halt if you let someone help you for once in your life, Hannah," Josie insisted, grabbing the basket's rim.

"Easy for you to say!" Hannah tried to hide a grimace of discomfort as she released her hold on the basket. "If people don't stop telling me to sit still, take it easy, you won't have to worry about my incision anymore. I'll just be stark, raving mad."

"I know you're not used to sitting around. But the more you obey doctor's orders, the sooner you'll be yourself again."

If only it was that simple, Hannah thought. Six weeks

of rest, and everything back to normal. But things hadn't been "normal" even in the months before she'd gotten sick. How could she begin to explain how much deeper the trouble ran than recovering from surgery?

That her life didn't fit anymore? That for the past year and a half she'd felt out of place in the world she'd always been so at home in? How could she explain her struggles in the months since Becca had left home for college, Hannah trying with all her might to find her way in a life that was utterly changed?

Even working in the garden, one of Hannah's most cherished pleasures, was denied her now. Since she'd started getting sick five months ago, the physical exertion was impossible.

Impossible for now, Hannah reminded herself, trying to be firm. Hadn't she promised herself that just for today she wasn't going to think about everything she couldn't do? That she'd find out what she *could* do instead?

But even if she did find the words to explain that much, she couldn't tell Josie the whole truth—that sometimes she got so sore, so tired, so worn out she feared if she didn't force herself she might never move again.

Josie's freckle-spattered face crumpled in a frown, making her look like a disgruntled, red-haired elf. "Hannah, you know darn well the doctor would have a fit if he saw you lifting something this heavy. Not to mention Sam."

Hannah's cheeks burned as she imagined her husband's reaction to this little mutiny of hers. Sam's blue eyes filling with worry and confusion, looking at her as if he expected her to shatter at any moment.

But she was tired of people hovering over her, whispering about how pale she was when they thought she

wasn't listening. She was tired of feeling sick and fragile and helpless. She was tired of Sam watching for
every nuance of pain or discomfort, the slightest tightening of her jaw, a stifled moan or wince when she
moved the wrong way.

"I know everyone is worried. I gave you all a scare.
But the crisis is over," Hannah said more sharply than
she intended. "And near as I can tell, having a hysterectomy doesn't transform you back into a child. I
can still make my own decisions, and if I want to hang
out a load of laundry, not Sam, nor you, nor anyone
else has the right to stop me."

Surprise flared in Josie's eyes. People were always
telling Hannah she'd feel better if she just let her frus-
trations out once in a while. It didn't make her feel better. It left a rotten taste in her mouth. And taking it out
on Josie was inexcusable. Josie had been terrific these
past weeks, running to the grocery store, filling the
freezer with casseroles so Hannah just had to stick
them into the oven for dinner. It wasn't as if Josie
didn't have a full enough plate of her own, either. A
new house, a new baby, a new husband, adjusting for
the first time in her life to being a stay at home mom,
and helping her nineteen-year-old adjust to sharing
mom's attention.

"I'm sorry," Hannah apologized. "You've been amazing, helping me through all this. I . . . I'm just tired.
Tired of being shut in, tired of feeling useless."

"You? Useless? That's a laugh. You're constantly
running around at warp speed doing something for
someone else. But the instant anyone wants to do
something for you—oh! The horror! As your best
friend, I've got to warn you that it's a really annoying
personality trait."

Josie had forced Hannah to be on the receiving end

once in a while no matter how uncomfortable it made Hannah. Sometimes Hannah had even managed to enjoy it.

"Hannah, so many people love you." Josie's tone gentled. "Don't make it impossible for us to show you how sorry we are you had to go through this. How glad we are you're going to be okay."

But I'm not okay, Hannah wanted to cry. *That's the problem. I'll never be okay again. Are you still a woman after they rip that part out of you? Are you still a woman if you can never have a baby again?*

Hannah turned away, but it didn't help. Her gaze fell on the portable baby carrier/car seat on the middle of the scrubbed oak table, Josie's red-haired baby boy sleeping in it like a cherub. Hannah tried to stifle a jab of envy. She was glad for Josie. God knew, Josie deserved this chance to be happy.

She'd met Josie when they'd been joint room mothers the year their daughters were in third grade. And they'd been inseparable ever since. After years of struggling as a single mom after her divorce and raising her oldest alone, Josie'd gotten a second chance when Hannah and Sam had set her up with Sam's best friend, Tom Wilkes. The bearlike cop had made Josie forget her vow never to trust a man again. They'd married and Josie had finally been able to have the second child she'd always dreamed of. Little Tommy was a miracle to both his parents, and Hannah and her husband Sam had been along for the whole journey.

That had been before the distance had crept between Hannah and Sam. Before they'd learned to be careful around each other. Before the looming shadow of Becca's leaving home and Hannah's illness had changed everything between them.

"Hannah, don't shut out the people who love you,"

Josie pleaded. "You and I have been through hell together. Marriage, divorce, chickenpox. We've told each other everything. Talk to me, Hannah."

Not quite everything, Hannah thought. Her eyes filled with tears she'd bottled up in the time since she'd fought the doctors, argued her last, surrendered to surgery because there was no other choice. Sick for months, she'd nearly managed to put herself on the critical list, believing—hoping—that the changes in her body weren't signs that something was very wrong, but maybe, just maybe, the pregnancy she'd secretly hoped for so long.

"I wasn't finished," Hannah admitted brokenly. "I thought I still had time. . ."

Josie squeezed Hannah's hand.

"I know it sounds crazy. I mean, I'm healthy, aren't I? It wasn't cancer. Like the doctor said, *'You're forty-four years old, Mrs. O'Connell. What are you saving your uterus for?'* "

Josie made a face. "I'd love to see just how blasé that doctor would be if you went after *his* reproductive organs with a scalpel!"

Hannah couldn't help but chuckle. She knew Josie's tactics, diffusing anything that hurt too much with that cynical humor that had protected her for so long. From bullies who'd teased her about her fiery hair, through the rocky parts of her first marriage, to the tough stuff she'd witnessed day after day in social services until she'd quit to raise her new baby.

Josie's eyes glistened in sympathy. "It stinks. You should have had a dozen kids. I've seen so many in rotten circumstances and their parents have litters of kids. But you, you're the best mother I've ever seen, and—" Josie broke off. "It's just not fair."

Maybe it was *fair.* Wasn't that what terrified Hannah

the most? The possibility that the empty spaces in her life were exactly what she deserved? She'd spent the past nineteen years hoping against hope that maybe, just maybe, if she was the best mother in the world to her little girl, God or fate or whoever was in charge would give her another chance. But the surgery had brought an end to even that faint hope.

The finality of knowing she would never have another child had brought memories flooding back, mistakes she'd made, prices she'd paid, regrets as real, as raw, as vivid as if they'd happened yesterday instead of a lifetime ago.

She'd worked so hard to make up for the past. Hadn't Hannah earned one more chance? But maybe there were some debts that no amount of regret or reparation could ever pay in full.

Hannah brushed back a strand of the black, wavy hair that cascaded halfway down her back. She held on tight to her morning resolution that today she would be stronger, do better, hold back shadows inside her.

She forced a smile, shrugged. "What was it my grandma used to say? Life's not fair?"

Josie made a face. "I always hate it when people say that. But from what I hear around town, it would have been worth listening to a few minutes of her words of wisdom for a slice of her raspberry pie."

Hannah sighed. "I can still taste it every time I walk into this kitchen." Hannah looked around her, taking in the red and white checked wallpaper, the white curtains with their blanket-stitched edges in cherry red embroidery floss. Scrubbed white cupboards with windows cut into them displayed time mellowed stoneware and bowls in which five generations of her family had mixed biscuits and cookies and pie dough.

When she and Sam had bought the house from her

grandmother just before Becca was born, she'd told Sam this kitchen would always mean "home" to her. But homes were supposed to be full of life and laughter and commotion. Children's school books sprawled across the table, their cast off shoes cluttering the entryway, the music from CD players drifting down from their bedrooms.

Even after seven months with Becca in college, Hannah couldn't get used to the silence of her daughter being gone.

In spite of her best efforts, Hannah's eyes burned. "I'm tired, Josie. I'm so tired. I don't know . . ."

"Don't know what?"

"What I'm supposed to do now. It's like I've lost something I never even had."

"What about Sam? You have Sam."

What about Sam? Hannah choked back the words. Truths she couldn't even share with her best friend. How could she tell Josie that she and Sam hadn't slept together for months? How could she explain he'd moved his things into Becca's room—his wooden hairbrush, the bottle of cologne Becca had given him for Christmas, his slippers and robe? She'd had so much trouble sleeping in the months before the surgery, he hadn't wanted to disturb her when he got up early.

And as for sex? He hadn't dared to touch her since the night her pain had gotten so bad she'd cried out. She could tell he still hoped things would be better between them as soon as she finished healing from her surgery. But she knew the truth. It was as if the doctor's knife had slipped. Cut away any spark of desire, any flare of sensuality she'd ever had, and thrown it out with the rest of the surgical debris.

How could you still be a woman if you couldn't even respond to your husband when he touched you? Fear shuddered through her. What if she could never find that part of herself again?

She closed her eyes, remembering all too clearly Sam's face—the hurt, the confusion her subtle rejections cost him. The pain that haunted his eyes—asked over and over again in silence. *What have I done? Don't you love me anymore?*

Questions she knew cut him far deeper than they would have wounded anyone else.

It isn't you, she'd told him. *It's me. Just me.*

But he didn't believe her.

"Hannah?"

She opened her eyes to see Josie staring at her, worry creasing her freckled face.

"There's one more thing I thought I should mention. Hey, it's not like it's that big of a deal. I just don't want you to, you know, be surprised."

"By what? The last shocking thing that happened in Willowton was when Mrs. Carney accidentally put salt instead of sugar in her fair-day pies."

Josie's smile didn't quite reach her eyes. "You probably didn't hear that old Mrs. Blake fell a few weeks back."

"No," Hannah said. "That's too bad."

"Well, seems that her son's come back to town to take care of her for a while."

"Tony?" Instinctively, Hannah crossed to a chair, sank down. She fought back a tiny flutter of panic.

"I remember that airhead ex-cheerleader at PTA once making a big deal about how you two had dated back in high school. I don't know, there was something in your eyes that—well, I just thought it wouldn't hurt to warn you. I heard from Maria down at the court-house that he's handling his big-city cases from here. He's going to do some temp work down at the courthouse to break up the monotony. Just thought you should know."

She'd been so unnerved by the mention of Tony Blake that Josie had noticed? Remembered all this time? She'd have to be more careful.

"Don't worry. It was a long time ago," Hannah said. *Then why didn't it feel that way? Especially now?* She pressed her hand to her tender scar.

"Why don't you lie down," Josie said. "Take a nap. From the looks of you, you could use one. I'll hang these clothes out for you before I go."

Hannah didn't feel like fighting anymore. Maybe Josie was right. Things would look more manageable after some extra sleep. "Thanks."

She wandered into her favorite room for napping, the sun porch that stretched along the east side of the house. She lay down on the white wicker swing with thick cushions she'd always found so comforting. But today, the room didn't work its usual magic. She peered out the window to the backyard, and watched Josie deftly pinning the sheets along the swoop of white line while Tommy kicked and waved his arms from his baby seat.

But this time it wasn't Josie's affection or Tommy's baby antics that pulled at her heart. It was the garden that lay just beyond the two of them, silhouetted against the ravine. Three lilac bushes, heavy now with buds, formed a backdrop for the riot of bulbs and perennials jostling for every inch of space at their feet.

Hannah swallowed hard, remembering the day Sam and Becca had dragged her from the house to see her "surprise."

"It's a Mother's Day garden!" Four-year-old Becca had chirped. "See, there's one lilac for you, one for Daddy an' one for me! An' there's lots of room, too, so when I get a brother or sister like Rachel or Jana, we can put more lilacs in for them, too!"

Hannah had cried, delighted, hugged them both—Becca, smelling of fresh dirt and baby shampoo, Sam woodsy and warm, his body hard, his hands callused from work. So familiar, so strong every time they brushed her skin, they left a trail of sparks in their wake. She'd been so sure then, about everything. She and Sam would be crazy in love forever. They would fill the garden with lilacs. She'd been so sure—

But as the years passed by, with no sign of the brother or sister Becca had spoken of, Hannah had filled the empty spaces they'd left in the garden with other flowers, trying to hide them. And Sam—Sam's smiles grew uneasy, as if her love were water he was trying to hold in his hands, helpless to keep it from slipping away.

Now, there would never be another lilac bush, full of blossoms tucked into that garden. There'd be no more babies. No more chances.

And Tony's come back, a voice inside her whispered. Wouldn't that make things even more strained, reminding her of things she'd tried to forget? *What if he—*

No, Hannah told herself firmly. It didn't matter. Nine months of high school—that's all she'd known him. He might as well be a stranger. Just a wispy memory from a long time ago.

Let the past stay where it belongs, Hannah resolved. Where it can't hurt you.

She was hurting enough already, she thought as she drifted off to sleep. There could never be an ache more painful than her Mother's Day garden, and all the blossoms that should have been.

* * *

The afternoon sun was streaming across Hannah's face when she finally woke from her nap, and for a split second, she was well again. Strong. The house was still bursting with kids and chaos and there was nothing she couldn't do. Then she moved.

Hannah pushed herself up on her elbows, hating that moment when it all came flooding back to her. The weakness, the sense of frustration and the pressing loneliness. That was always the hardest part, when she woke up and remembered what was real.

Shoving herself upright, she rubbed the sleep from her eyes, paused for a moment to catch her breath, let the tenderness in her belly subside. No, she wasn't going to let either her emotions or the aches and pains of recovery ruin things today. She was better. And she was going to prove it to everyone. Especially herself.

Maybe Josie had intercepted her on the way to hang out the sheets, Hannah thought. But she could still take them down and fold them by herself.

She stood and made her way out to the backyard. Odd. There weren't as many clothes on the line as she remembered. Sam's blue shirt was missing, and those peach towels she had tucked into the basket were nowhere to be seen. Maybe they had blown off the line. And where was the basket? It looked like Josie had set it in the shade of the lilacs.

It was an odd place to leave it, considering the fact that Josie had wanted Hannah to take as few steps as possible. She trudged over to the wicker basket. Maybe Josie had hoped if she stuck it far enough out of the way, it would discourage Hannah from taking the laundry down. Josie should have known better.

With a smile, Hannah bent down to grasp the worn wooden handles. She froze. The missing clothes lay in a soft puddle in the bottom of the basket. Pillowed on a drift of peach towels was a tiny bundle wrapped in the soft folds of Sam's favorite blue shirt. Suddenly, the bundle moved. Had some animal gotten into the basket and not been able to get out? Hannah wondered. Maybe she should just tip the basket on its side, let whatever it was scamper away?

But as she touched the basket's rim, the creature whimpered, rustling something white and crisp. A folded bit of paper safety-pinned to a corner of the fabric the way Hannah had pinned important school notes to Becca's shirts to make sure they made it to kindergarten. "What in the world?" Hannah breathed, nonplussed.

Heart hammering in her chest, she reached down to touch the bundle, ever so carefully drawing a corner of Sam's shirt aside. Her knees buckled. She sank to the ground, barely feeling the jarring pain that went through her body. Round blue eyes gazed up at her from a red, wrinkly pixie face. The tiny rosebud of a mouth sucked fiercely on a tightly clenched fist.

A baby. Far tinier than chubby Tommy Wilkes.

Hannah blinked hard, swiped her hand across her eyes, but the baby was still there. Dear God, had the poor little thing been crying? How long had it lain out here alone? With trembling fingers she tore loose the note, unfolded it.

I always thought if I could pick anyone in the whole world to be my mom, it would be you, Hannah read. *Please take care of her for me. Her name is Ellie. Eleanor Rose.*

Hannah gasped, stunned. Eleanor Rose? That was her grandmother's name. A coincidence? A sign from God? Or had the girl who left the baby here known how much Hannah had adored her grandmother? Had the girl given her baby that name on purpose?

Don't hate me. The letter ended. *I'm just so scared.*

Hannah dropped the note back into the basket. Who had left the baby here? Obviously some girl who knew Hannah. One of the army of Becca's friends who had made the farmhouse their second home? Or one of the "satellite kids" who'd only drifted in and out of Becca's circle of friends?

Instinctively, Hannah's mind sorted through dozens of mental pictures, faces and laughter, hair and eyes, trying to remember any changes in the kids who'd come to see Becca off that last day before she left for college. Who on God's earth could this baby belong to? And where was she? Trying so hard to hide what had happened to her? Desperate? Despairing? Too young and naïve to know how many things could go wrong after childbirth? Or with a fragile new life?

Oh, God, Hannah thought, what was she going to do? She'd need to get the baby to a doctor, make sure the little one was healthy. And she'd need to call the authorities—wouldn't she? It was the right thing to do. *Unless the terrified kid who had had this child changed her mind. Tortured by guilt at abandoning her baby, needing not censure, but a quiet, calming place to learn how to be a mother.*

And once she *did* call the authorities, what would happen then? The girl who had trusted her, turned to her when she was terrified and lost and alone, could be drowning in legal trouble. Could she even end up in jail?

The possibility chilled Hannah. No. She'd have to think what to do, find some way to keep the baby safe and give the baby's mother at least a little time to reconsider, maybe even change her mind, without facing such grim consequences. . . .

I'm so scared . . . the note had said. Hannah knew just how paralyzing fear could be.

Slowly, she brushed the baby's cheek with her finger, half terrified the little one would vanish if she touched it, the other part of her terrified the baby would still be there, forcing her to take responsibility for deciding what to do next.

A delicate shiver ran down her spine. She'd forgotten how velvety a baby's skin felt, so warm, so impossibly soft. The baby turned her face toward her finger, latched onto Hannah's knuckle with her little mouth, sucking. Dewy, dark-lashed eyes drifted shut. Hannah lifted the baby in her arms, cuddled it close. Ellie melted into her as if Hannah had held her a hundred times. The baby heaved a contented sigh that wrenched at Hannah's heart.

"Hush, now. Hush," she murmured, laying her cheek against the baby's own, breathing in the soft, clean scent of baby soap and powder. Whoever had left the baby here had tried to take care of her as best they could. It comforted Hannah, made her heart ache, imagining the young mother bathing her little one for the first, maybe the only time. Had she cried when she'd put the baby into the basket? Was she watching, even now, to make sure nothing happened to the little one until Hannah found her?

Hannah glanced up, eyes searching the crescent of ravine that bordered her backyard, looking for any shadow, any movement at odds with the familiar quiet of the place.

"Hello?" she called out, keeping her voice gentle. "Are you out there? Let me help you. Help both of you. Don't be afraid."

Don't be afraid? Who was she kidding? The girl must be terrified. Desperate. With good reason. Or she would never have left her newborn behind.

She heard a crackle of leaves and all but jumped out

of her skin. She took a running step toward the sound, feeling for all the world as if someone were watching. But at that instant, a gray squirrel popped out, eyeing her inquisitively. Hannah's heart dropped. No. It wasn't the baby's mother. Even if it had been, she could hardly chase the girl down the steep slope of overgrown ravine with a newborn in her arms.

She cuddled the baby closer, the miracle of the tiny life seeping into her, a sense of purpose warming the cold places, the need to keep this baby safe easing her weariness.

"I have to think what to do," she whispered against Ellie's downy hair.

But in her heart, Hannah already knew.

Sam O'Connell sped down the road, car wheels protesting on turns taken too fast, engine gunning as he grazed through intersections governed by traffic signals that even the most generous judge couldn't call "yellow." But he wouldn't have pulled over if a whole fleet of squad cars had been tailing him, their red lights lit up like Christmas trees.

His shoulders tightened, the knot in his throat all but choking him as Hannah's voice echoed in his head.

Please come home, Sam. Please. I need you.

He'd begged her to tell him what was wrong. Pleaded with her. But she'd only hung up the phone, leaving him to the mercy of his own imagination and the buzzing emptiness of the phone.

I need you.

The words should have made his heart soar. He'd spent most of his life wanting Hannah to need him, waiting for her to ask him for something, anything. But now, he only tasted the metallic tang of his own fear, felt the sinking sensation of his own dread of the unknown, and the fear that somehow he would fail her.

What the hell could be wrong? In twenty-two years of marriage he could never once remember Hannah calling him at work, asking him to come home. Her voice had been so strange, thready, agitated, refusing to tell him what was wrong. He'd left the office/shop building of O'Connell Construction at a run, his employees staring after him, stunned—boss man gone crazy. But then, if he ever *was* going to lose his mind, Sam thought grimly, this would be the time.

The past months had been torture—not knowing what was wrong with Hannah, not being able to help her. Seeing the warm, vibrant woman he'd married the day after they'd graduated from college fading away into a pale ghost of herself before his very eyes. Watching her slip away from him, wisp by wisp until he couldn't reach her anymore, no matter how hard he tried.

And now this—calling him at work, begging him to come home without so much as a hint why? It wasn't her way, hiding things like this. She was always the calm one, the one who called him after stitches had been finished, broken bones set, crises handled. Then he'd hear her voice on the phone, so reassuring. *I didn't want to worry you. Everything's fine now.* She'd describe whatever had happened in detail, somehow managing to find humor in it, softening the blow with tales of how Becca had charmed her doctors and nurses or taken over her little corner of the emergency room. Then he could laugh, bring home a stuffed animal or coloring books, or whatever "dad" thing he could think of. And when he got home, everything would be just like always except for the addition of a bright pink cast on Becca's arm or a glow-in-the-dark bandage decorating her chin.

Yes, everything would be "fine," just like Hannah said. But not this time. Sam's intuition buzzed. This time things definitely weren't "fine."

Was Hannah sick? Had she done too much, done damage to her incision? He'd been begging her to slow down since the day he'd brought her home from the hospital. Unfortunately his pleas for her to take it easy had only fired her determination to prove he was wrong. She was patient, kind, mothering the whole world, but she could also be the most stubborn woman he'd ever known. If she'd hurt herself—who knew what damage she could have done. She still looked so fragile it terrified him.

Sam pulled into the farmhouse drive, shoved the car into park, then jumped out. Everything looked so normal, quiet. That made it even more nerve-wracking somehow.

"Hannah?" he bellowed. "Where are you?"

"In here," came a small voice from the living room. Sam rushed toward it. She was curled up on the couch looking pale, bewildered, her riot of dark hair tangled about her shoulders and a bundle of peach towel tucked tight against her abdomen.

"Are you all right?" Sam asked. "Should I call the doctor?"

"I already have, but . . . but not for me."

"You're not making any sense. I don't understand." He crossed to her, felt her cheek for fever. Her skin was clammy cold. "Hannah, damn it, what's going on?"

She turned wide eyes to him, pleading. "Josie stopped over, helped me hang up some things on the line. Later, when I went to take them down—"

Damn it, she had *torn something,* Sam thought. "The doctor said you weren't supposed to be lifting."

"That doesn't matter right now. Believe me."

"Then what the hell—"

"I'm trying to tell you if you'll let me!" she cried, exasperated. "I went to bring the basket in, and there was . . . I found . . . *this.*" She tipped up the bundle in her arms, drew back the folds of shirt. Sam stared down at a tiny scrunched-up face.

Sam went ashen. "Hannah, that's a baby."

"I know," she said tentatively.

"Well, what are you doing with it? Everybody around here knows you're still not feeling great. I'm not going to let you be taken advantage of right now, end of story. If one of the neighbors dumped this kid on you to baby-sit, I swear I'll strangle them!"

"That's not it. Not exactly." She was hedging. Hannah almost never hedged. She licked her lips, a nervous gesture from way back. Then she ducked her head, the fall of black curls obscuring her face.

"Who does the baby belong to?" Sam demanded.

"Right now, I guess she belongs to . . . me."

Sam's heart thudded. Hard. "To you? That's impossible."

Balancing the baby in one arm, she handed him a rumpled note. Sam's brow furrowed as he tried to make sense of it. "If this is a joke, it's damned well not funny!" But it was no joke. He knew it in his gut even before Hannah shook her head in denial. Knew it from the memory of Hannah's voice on the phone, the bleached white color of her cheeks.

"What kind of person would just . . . just abandon a baby—" he choked out. But then, why should he be surprised. He had firsthand knowledge about what kind of woman abandoned a child. A woman like his own mother.

Hannah waxed even paler. "Someone scared. Too young." Hannah peered down at the baby, touched its cheek. "Sam, the mother didn't throw the baby in a

Dumpster! She left her where she knew I would find her. The baby was warm, clean, there was even formula and a few bottles tucked in at her feet."

"I don't give a damn if there was college tuition stuck in the baby's diaper!" Sam tried to shove away the memories of the boy he'd been, searching through the house, calling his mother's name, finding silence, nothing but silence. "You don't just dump a baby on a stranger's doorstep!"

"I don't think the mother did. She knew me. Knows me. She asked me to take care of the baby." Her voice softened, obviously awed by that trust. Alarm bells jangled in Sam's head.

"No way are you going to take on the responsibility for someone else's baby!" Sam insisted. "You can barely take care of—" He stopped, his cheeks darkening. She looked as if he'd struck her.

"Go ahead. You might as well finish. We both know what you were going to say. I can't even take care of myself."

The last thing he'd wanted to do was hurt her. But someone had to tell her the truth. "Hannah, I'm just being honest. You haven't been yourself since Becca left for school. And since the surgery— Honey, you have to see how it is. There's no way we can keep this baby."

Fierce, almost feral protectiveness sparked in her eyes, her chin bumping up a notch to that angle he knew was damned dangerous. The baby squirmed a little as Hannah's arms drew her even closer. "The mother didn't ask *you* to take care of the baby. Maybe it isn't for you to decide."

He took a deep breath, struggled to calm his voice. "Hannah, think about this! Reasonably. Rationally! You know Dr. Campbell said your hormones would be out of whack for a while, you'd be overly emotional. You need calm, quiet, to get better."

"I've had enough calm and quiet to choke!" she cried. "Maybe that's not what I need at all. Maybe I need a reason to get up in the morning! Someone to take care of. Love."

"I thought you had me," Sam said softly, his mind filling with so many dreams. Hopes he'd had, the two of them spending time together, nothing to pull their focus from healing whatever was wrong between them. Time to fall in love all over again.

She winced, but she didn't back down. "Sam, please. It won't be for very long anyway. The mother obviously cares for the baby. She wouldn't have taken such good care of her—"

"She dumped the baby in our backyard. It hardly qualifies her for "mother of the year." Besides, if what you say is true that's the best argument yet for not keeping the baby. You'll get attached to her and have to let her go—it would break your heart."

"Don't I have the right to decide if I think it's worth the risk?" Hannah insisted. "I know the baby isn't mine. I won't be able to keep her forever. But why can't I keep her for now?"

"It's not that simple and you know it!" Sam said, groping for some way to make her see reason. "There have to be laws about this—proper legal channels you have to go through. You can't just . . . just keep a baby as if it were a stray dog or cat."

Her eyes narrowed, fierce. "Maybe not, but I don't want to do anything that might hurt the baby's mother, either. Have the police carry the baby off to strangers and issue a warrant for the girl's arrest. Leave no chance for her to change her mind, make things right. Sam, this baby could belong to anybody. Any of Becca's friends.

The girls who giggled over boys in our living room, slept over in Snoopy sleeping bags. What if it was Becca who was in so much trouble?"

Sam's gut twisted. "Damn it, Hannah, that's not fair!"

"Wouldn't you want her to have just a few days' grace? Time maybe to get up the courage to tell someone the truth before the police turned up on her doorstep and it was too late?"

"Becca would never do something so terrible!"

"You don't know that for sure, Sam." Pain flared in Hannah's eyes, the same lacerating pain he'd felt at even imagining their little girl in such desperate circumstances. "God knows, I hope she could come to me, tell me . . . but if she couldn't, I hope someone would help her."

"You're not responsible for saving the world, Hannah!" he snapped, smarting because she'd managed to hit him below the belt. Damn it, she wasn't playing fair.

"I'm not asking to save the world, Sam. Just this baby. Just for a little while. A week at most to give Ellie's mother a chance to come back and claim her. Then, I promise I'll call anyone you want. Please. I'm begging you." She sucked in a deep breath, met his gaze so steadily it made his fists knot. "No, I'm not begging you. I'm telling you I know I'm supposed to keep her for now, take care of her. She needs me, Sam. And I need her."

"Aw, Hannah—" Sam grimaced, shaking his head.

"Have I ever really asked you for anything, Sam?"

No, he thought grimly. He'd always wished she would. He would have given her anything—the stars, the moon, a rainbow painted only in the colors she loved best. But a baby? Someone else's baby?

"Sam, it will just be for a little while. For all we know, this whole thing could be over by nightfall. Tomorrow, three days from now. The mother could come back at any moment. The mother even named her Ellie. Eleanor, after my grandmother. She must know me—know me well. Trust me."

Her eyes pleaded with him, soft, luminous, as she lay one hand ever so gently on the sleeping child. Sam's shoulders sagged. He knew when he was beaten. But it still stung like hell.

"So why'd you even bother calling me if you'd already made up your mind?"

"Because I need you to help me. Much as I want to take care of Ellie, I—Sam, part of me is scared, too." She did look scared. The fear was layered in the dark-fringed depths of her eyes. Afraid of what? Hannah was a born mother. She always had been. Perfect. *He* was the one who had been a hell of a lot less than that. But she was asking him for help. *Needing* him. Or at least she thought she did. The sweetness of that squeezed in around his confusion.

"Okay," he agreed at last. "We'll do this your way. Just tell me what you want to do."

A smile dawned over her features, so grateful it made him feel like a selfish heel.

"I've already got an appointment with Becca's old pediatrician. I thought someone should look at Ellie, don't you think? A doctor, I mean. To make sure she's all right?"

Of course she'd already figured that much out. She probably already had the box full of Becca's old baby clothes in the washing machine. But there were other practicalities she might not have thought of. "Yeah. She should see a doctor. But how are you going to explain that a baby just dropped into your lap? You can't tell him the truth and expect him to keep this secret! He could lose his license!"

For an instant she looked crestfallen, then just as suddenly she brightened. "I'll just say I'm taking care of the baby for a friend. It would be true. I just don't know exactly which friend."

"I don't like it, Hannah," Sam grumbled. "Not a damn bit. But if you're dead set on it . . ."

"I am."

Sam winced at the determination sparking in her eyes, a flash of fire, of strength of passion, the first he'd seen in far too long. *It would only be for a little while,* he reassured himself. *Then, maybe—*

Maybe this would help open doors between them, tumble walls.

Maybe, after the baby was gone they'd remember how to talk to each other, touch each other.

Just maybe.

Sam swallowed hard, tried to silence the voice inside him, the one that whispered:

Or maybe this will break Hannah's heart.

2

O FFICE HOURS WERE WINDING DOWN, the last few kids with sore throats and spring colds filtering out of the toy-strewn waiting room. It seemed an eternity since Hannah had been here. It seemed like yesterday. Becca, trying hard to be brave in spite of her phobia of needles. Earaches and camp physicals and stitches under her chin. Checkups when she went into fifth grade and she'd suddenly seemed so tall. Then, later, another batch of shots before high school. Lollipops still glowed in candy colors in the glass jar up high on the counter. Hannah could remember so clearly the day Becca had waved one in her airy hand.

I feel like a dork sitting in there with all those little kids, Mom. I need a real *doctor.*

Hannah could still remember how she'd wanted to plead with Becca, shake her, tell her she could search the rest of her life and never again find as fine a doctor as Ben Meyers.

She wanted to explain how just the sound of Dr. Meyers's voice had calmed her when Becca had spiked a

103-degree fever on Christmas night the year she was six. And how many times he'd made her laugh when she'd been on the brink of tears. How he'd steadied her, given her courage when Becca had been born five weeks early, a lung infection putting her in neonatal intensive care. Hannah had been so scared, so sure she'd done something wrong, was being punished somehow, her baby so tiny, so sick, so frail. She'd been weeping over the incubator, terrified she was going to lose Becca altogether when Dr. Meyers had come up behind her, laid one hand on her shoulder and chuckled.

Don't worry, Mama. This little lady isn't going anywhere. Look at that chin on her. Never seen a more stubborn one on a newborn in thirty years of practice. This young lady has plenty of fight in her. I'm betting she's going to surprise everyone and be just fine.

And somehow, she'd believed him. She hadn't worried in all the years that followed—at least not much. That is, until her daughter switched to a "grown-up" doctor who always had to check the chart more than once during the visit to make sure he remembered Becca's name.

Hannah had felt disloyal, somehow, switching doctors, and had said so during their last visit. Meyers had chuckled, that comforting chuckle that always reminded Hannah of warm apple pie. *Occupational hazard when you're a pediatrician, Hannah*, he'd said, *patients grow up. I admit, it's hard, but not half as hard on me as it is on the parents.*

She hadn't realized how prophetic those words would prove. But somehow, when she remembered the empathetic light in the old doctor's gray-green eyes, she was sure he'd guessed just how hard this time would be for her, letting Becca go, finding herself alone for the first time in nineteen years.

No, not alone. She glanced up to see Sam standing shell-shocked beside her. Then why did it feel that way?

She cuddled Ellie closer, the baby sleeping in her arms.

"Hannah? Hannah O'Connell, is that you?" A pert nurse in a dinosaur print lab coat poked her head out the window that separated office from waiting room. "My God, I haven't seen you for a jillion years!"

"Only four, Maggie."

Hannah stiffened, aware of Sam's discomfort. His broad shoulders and towering height set against the child-size chairs and playhouse in the corner made him look like a giant who'd lost his way.

"How's that beautiful daughter of yours? Lord, she must be . . ." the brunette calculated in her head. "Nineteen—she must be in college by now! I bet she's knocking them dead!"

"She loves it."

"Always knew she would. Remember how she was always trying to sneak into the lab to see what was going on there. Never wanted to miss out on anything, your Miss Rebekah. Loved an adventure."

"She still does."

"Well, at least now she's not as likely to end up with stitches or a broken bone once she finds 'em." Maggie laughed. "I've almost gotten used to seeing your buddy Josie back here again, baby in tow. But you . . . you're a complete surprise. What brings you here? You said you needed to see Doctor—an emergency?"

Hannah's eyes met Maggie's. She swallowed hard. "I . . . I brought a baby in for doctor to—"

"*A baby? You* have a new baby, too? What did you and Josie do? Make some kind of pact so you could be joint room mothers again?"

"No. I mean, yes, I—"

"Congratulations! I always thought it was a shame you didn't have a whole yard full of kids! You're so good with them! A kid magician! But I thought, well, with Becca grown up—"

"The baby's not exactly mine. Not technically, anyway. I'm just taking care of her."

Sam's jaw clenched and he jammed his hands into his pockets. Hannah didn't even want to know what he was thinking.

Maggie looked into Ellie's little face. "She's awful tiny. Is the baby sick?"

"No. I just wanted to be sure she is all right. Her name is Ellie."

"Ellie. What a pretty name."

"Yes." Hannah whispered, her voice catching. "It's perfect."

Maggie rounded the counter to open the door leading from the waiting area to the rooms beyond. "Come on in. I've got some papers for you to fill out. New patient information. You know the drill—insurance, parents' names and work phones, social security numbers and the rest."

Hannah felt the blood drain from her face, panic bubbling under her breastbone. "I don't—couldn't—I mean, wouldn't it be all right if the mother filled this all out uh, when she gets back?"

Maggie's brow puckered. "It's pretty standard information we need."

"I'll get it to you. I promise. As soon as . . . as Ellie's mother calls."

She winced at the soft sound from Sam, a snort of disgust.

"I don't think . . ." Maggie hedged, then looked Hannah so straight in the eye, Hannah was afraid she could see right through her. "Oh, well, what the heck. If it was anybody else, I'd say no way. But you—" She shrugged, smiled. Hannah's stomach churned with guilt. "You always were our favorite mom. Doctor Ben will be there in a minute."

She ushered them into a sunny, small room with a picture of animals contorting their bodies into letters of the alphabet. Hannah sank down into the chair in the corner beside a basket of books. Sam paced the blue carpet as if acting out the charade L is for lion. He was doing a damned fine job of it, too. Hannah felt as if she and Ellie were being stalked.

She cuddled the baby closer, angled herself away from Sam as if somehow trying to hide the little bundle from those fiercely intent eyes. He couldn't wait to get this baby off his hands, she sensed, hurt. He wanted to be rid of Ellie as much as she wanted to hold on. . . .

"It's a damned good thing most of what you were saying was the truth," Sam growled. "You always were rotten at lying."

Hannah winced. Was hedging about the truth any different? She doubted Sam would think so, if he knew. . . .

The soft rap of knuckles on the door that had always preceded the doctor's entry sounded, and Dr. Meyers bustled in, still so much the same that Hannah felt some of the tension melt out of her. Bushy white hair, Santa Claus eyebrows, a hawk beak of a nose two times too large for his face. Still, with his inner glow of warmth and humor Hannah had always thought him beautiful.

"Hannah? I sure didn't expect to see you here! What's it been? Five years! How's our Becca liking college?" he asked.

"She loves it."

"So, Maggie says you've got someone here you'd like me to meet."

Hannah rose, forced herself to show the doctor Ellie's little pixie face. "This is Ellie. Her mother asked me to take care of her for a little while."

"She can't be more than a few days old. That's a lot of work, a lot of responsibility. I thought I'd heard you've had a tough few months yourself."

He knew about her surgery. She could see it in his eyes, soft with empathy. Her cheeks burned. Why did she feel ashamed when anybody knew what had happened to her? As if the hysterectomy hadn't just removed her womb, but whatever other elusive thing that made her a woman.

"It was nothing," she lied.

"Hmmm." Ben gave her a measured glance. "Some women have a real hard time adjusting, you know. Nothing to be ashamed of. It's a big change. A tough one."

Hannah's eyes stung; unaccountably, after all this time she wanted to cry. Not in grief this time or loss, but because this man with his hawkish nose and wise eyes understood what she'd lost. Somebody finally understood, after all.

"It was hard," she admitted. "But I'm better now. And as for Ellie, well, I want to take care of her. More than I've wanted anything in a very long time."

"I see." Gray-green eyes flashed from Sam's face to hers, and Hannah was very much afraid the doctor *did* see. Perfectly. "And how does your husband feel about that?" He didn't know Sam's name, Hannah realized with a start. But then, she couldn't remember Sam ever coming to the doctor's office with her and Becca. He'd always been working during office hours.

Hannah tensed at the way Dr. Meyers was looking at

Sam, the turbulence in Sam's eyes evident even to a stranger. "Sam and I agree on this completely, don't we?" she asked. Bracing the baby against her with one arm, she reached out with the other, grabbing Sam's hand. She gave it a pleading squeeze.

Sam looked down at their joined fingers in surprise, and she realized how long it had been since she'd been the one to touch him. She saw a flash of something, hunger, vulnerability. Sam's voice sounded strained.

"If this is what Hannah wants . . ." He shrugged.

"Well, then." Dr. Meyers didn't sound convinced. "Let's take a look at this little lady." He reached out for the baby.

Hannah's fingers tightened instinctively, a knot of panic in her chest, fear that if she let go of the tiny girl, she might never get to hold her again.

"Hannah, I need to examine her. That's why you brought her to me, isn't it?"

She'd heard him calm countless distraught mothers. Knew how good he was at it. Even so, she almost held out. It was the darkening of concern on his face that made her surrender.

Hannah swallowed hard, loosened her grip on the sleeping baby. Slowly, she held her out to him. "Her name is Ellie."

He smiled. "Well, come on up onto my magic table, Miss Ellie, and let's have a look at you."

He unfolded the blanket she'd wrapped the baby in, took off the little baby romper Ellie had been wearing, the fabric still stiff with sizing, creases still pressed into it where it had been wrapped around a square of cardboard in the store. Hannah could almost see the scared young mother wandering through the aisle of baby things—pink and blue and yellow and green, bibs and tiny dresses, sleepers embroidered with Winnie the

Pooh. She'd selected the little outfit so carefully, dressed the baby so neatly. Tucked her in the basket—with relief? Regret? Or with a quietly breaking heart?

Dr. Meyers's capable hands moved over Ellie, the chubby, creased arms, her kicking little legs, her belly with the dark stump of umbilical cord tied with a piece of thread. Ellie opened eyes so dark blue they almost looked black, her lips smacking as she sucked on her tongue. She tried to wriggle away as the doctor shone a light in her eyes. Hannah laid her hand lightly on her little chest, humming a lullaby to calm her. The wee one settled, stilled, unfocused eyes searching for the source of her comfort.

The doctor finished, retaped the clean diaper back into place. "Well, I would say this young lady is lucky you're taking care of her. Want to tell me about it?"

She almost did. Came so close. But she could still hear Sam's warning: *He could lose his license.* Risking getting into trouble herself was one thing. Dragging Dr. Meyers into it was another.

"Nothing else to talk about," she said with forced brightness.

He didn't press. Somehow, that touched Hannah. "You know, I'm always here," Ben said softly.

"I know," Hannah squeezed the words past the lump in her throat.

"You're a good person, Hannah. One of the best I've met in all my years of practice. Whatever is going on with this baby, I know you'll do the right thing." The doctor's faith in her humbled Hannah. Touched her. She only prayed that she could be half as wise as Ben Meyers believed she was.

She glanced up at Sam, but if she wanted reassurance, she got exactly the opposite. Storms of uncertainty raged in Sam's eyes, his mouth a tight line, every muscle in his body stiff, as if he were bracing himself against a blow. What was it that he was so afraid of? That she would overdo it and have some kind of relapse from her surgery? Or was it something deeper that was tearing at him right now? Memories of his own childhood and the mother who had left him behind? No wonder he was upset with her, Hannah thought. Was it fair for her to bring Ellie into their lives if her presence was going to rake up all those old feelings in Sam? Confusion? Pain? Rejection? A lifetime haunted by wondering why his mom had deserted him?

But weren't those questions always with him anyway? No matter how hard Sam tried to pretend he'd forgotten about the whole thing? The questions had been there before Ellie, and they'd remain long after things with the baby had settled out however they were meant to.

Hannah bit the inside of her lip, her chin dipping down so her fall of hair drifted over her cheek, hiding her face for a moment. Just long enough for her to gather her wits, tuck away what needed to be hidden, brace up walls suddenly crumbling with doubts. Oh, God, what was she doing?

She had to trust Sam wouldn't hate her for forcing his hand. But she didn't have any choice. Not really. Not if she were going to give Ellie's mother a chance to change things, make things right. A chance to gather her baby back into her arms where she belonged . . .

Hannah's heart swelled, hurt so much her eyes burned. She had to wait and see what she was supposed to do. Put Ellie back into the arms of her mother, or—a tiny voice whispered inside her—was fate offering Hannah the chance she'd longed to have for so long? A chance to adopt this little girl? To fill the cradle

Sam hadn't finished for Becca that was gathering dust in the corner of the attic, a chance to fill the empty, aching place in Hannah's heart?

No, she told herself sharply. You're taking care of Ellie for her mother, to make certain they can be together if her mother changes her mind about giving her up.

But if Ellie's mother didn't claim her? Then what? Hannah thought. Might she have a chance to plant another lilac in her Mother's Day garden at last?

3

SAM SWIRLED THE HALF-INCH of Scotch in the bottom of his glass, watching the last of the ice cubes melt in the brownish liquid. He'd needed a drink badly enough to dig a dusty bottle from some long-gone holiday out of the cabinet above the refrigerator. But somehow, instead of helping to settle his jangling nerves, the stuff only made him more edgy, more restless, more certain he'd been out of his mind when he'd caved in and let Hannah have her way.

He paced to the kitchen window that looked out over the night-darkened ravine, saw the ghostly shapes of Hannah's sheets still rippling from the line, forgotten. But Hannah had had more important things to think about today.

She had tried to include him. Tried to draw him into her enthusiastic embracing of this stranger's child. A quick trip to the store to pick up necessities had delighted her. The car seat, receiving blankets and plenty of outfits, diapers and formula proved that, no matter what she said, she hoped that the baby would be staying at the farmhouse longer than a day or two.

When he'd questioned her, she'd smiled up at him—that vulnerable, impossibly sweet smile he'd fallen in love with so long ago—and said that Ellie would need the baby things no matter who she was with. It could be their gift to her—a start.

But his stomach had churned at how natural Hannah looked, how *right*, with the baby cradled in her arms. Every tiny, instinctive movement comforting the baby, the unguarded expression of tenderness on Hannah's face whenever she looked at the downy head pillowed against her breasts stirring in Sam a jealousy so deep it stunned him.

It had been forever since she'd looked at him like that, touched him as though it were a joy. Watching her opened up a hole in his chest, forced him to look square in the face everything he'd been trying for so long to ignore, make excuses for, pretend away. But seeing Hannah like this, he couldn't deny any longer just how much they had both lost.

Sam winced, remembering how that hurt had finally goaded him to say something in the store when Hannah had been eyeing a teddy bear dressed like a ballerina. *I thought babies couldn't even focus their eyes at this age. By the time she can see it, she'll be someplace else.*

He'd regretted the words as soon as he'd seen Hannah's smile fade. But an instant later, she'd shoved the disappointment down deep inside her, and set the bear back on the shelf. He'd relented, tried to stuff the toy back into the shopping cart, but she couldn't be budged. He was right, she'd insisted. There were so many other things the baby needed, and she could rummage a stuffed animal out of Becca's room. It would have been perfect if they still had Koko to stand guard, Hannah had said wistfully.

If there was anything that could have made Sam feel like more of a rotten heel than he already did, it was the mention of Becca's ratty old stuffed gorilla and his memory of Hannah's grief over the thing. A week after what Becca called "The Great Separation," Hannah had slipped into Becca's room and found the decrepit stuffed animal Becca had dragged everywhere as a kid lying sprawled in a corner, forgotten. Sam knew that of all the painful moments Hannah had endured the past few months, that one had been the worst—realizing that Becca had left Koko behind.

He'd tried to soothe Hannah, tell her to let it go. All kids got touchy about being "grown up" when they went to college. But Hannah had been so sure Becca had left Koko behind by mistake. She'd packed up the stuffed animal, sent him to Becca right away. A week later Sam had caught her crying over a scrawled note from their daughter.

> *Mom, Don't you think I'm a little old to be dragging stuffed animals around? Thought you were nuts sending old Koko—like I have room for him up here! Luckily, the police were having a stuffed animal drive, so they'd have some at the station when kids who've been in accidents or stuff like that came in. Gave me something I could donate . . .*

Sam had known why she was crying—mourning the loss of the last vestiges of childhood Becca was so eager to throw away when Hannah wanted more than anything to hold on, tight . . .

His heart squeezed with empathy, but there was no way to make it hurt any less, was there? Becca was out on her own, and Hannah was still mourning the loss of that gorilla as if it had been a member of the family.

Sam shuddered to think how she'd react on that inevitable day when she had to turn that baby over to somebody else. He grimaced at the memory of Hannah's tear-streaked face, and worse still, her valiant efforts at trying to be brave in the weeks after they'd dropped Becca off. He didn't want to see her go through that kind of pain again. Especially now, when she'd been trying so hard to get well.

Damn it, he'd been an idiot to agree to any of this! Even the doctor had reacted as if he sensed something wasn't quite what it seemed. And what was going to happen when other people caught a glimpse of the baby? They wouldn't restrain themselves politely the way the doctor had. The neighbors would have to be curious. They'd ply Hannah with questions. Hannah never had been able to shut people down when they turned up the pressure. One of the drawbacks of being so open, so empathetic. He wanted to protect her. Always had—ever since he'd first seen her at the reference desk in the college library, so shy, so kind, so—so *good.* He'd wanted to make her smile forever, make sure she would never be sad again.

From the time he'd been a kid, he'd tried to keep a tight hold on anything he could control, held disaster back however he had to. It had been a hopeless quest when he'd lived with his father, dragged out of apartments in the middle of the night to duck rent collectors. Sleeping in the back seat of the car for weeks at a time, his small body wedged between cardboard boxes that held everything they owned in the world.

He'd taken money out of his dad's pockets while the old man had been sleeping off another drunk, hid enough to be able to buy boxes of cereal and hot dogs when he got too hungry to stand it.

He'd learned ways to cope, like never going to sleep

without making sure his favorite toys were stacked in the old milk crate by his bed so that if his father woke him up to run, all he had to do was grab the crate and go.

He'd learned how to make friends in a hurry, to blend himself into wherever he was by being the fastest runner, throwing the farthest Hail Mary passes with the football, or charming the most popular girls. And he'd gotten smart, but rarely let anyone know it. He'd been in fourth grade when he'd figured out that even though he couldn't get a library card because his dad didn't want anyone to be able to trace them, he could tuck the books into the big pockets of his coat and sneak out with his contraband. He'd always written down the date they'd be due where the librarian would have stamped it, made sure he'd gotten them back on time. And one thing the old man knew was that before they ditched a town, the books went into the library drop box.

Yeah, he'd controlled what he could and promised himself that once he was out from under his father's thumb, he wouldn't let anything sneak up behind him again. But somehow, he'd lost his grip in the past few months, first with his marriage, and now, this—being responsible even temporarily for a baby that wasn't his.

Even if they only kept the baby for a few days without reporting they'd found her, would a judge or social worker understand why Hannah had done what she'd done? No matter how she rationalized it? Sam had watched far too many times while his father had done the same thing, sliding around on a dark path to more trouble than he'd ever bargained for. But this time, Sam was the one who should be in control of the situation, Sam was the one who had to figure out what to do, how to do the right thing and

somehow keep Hannah's big heart from getting her
into trouble.

Sam took one last swig of Scotch, set the glass on the
table. He climbed the stairs, saw the dim glow of light
in a strip under the closed bedroom door. He paused,
ready to knock softly the way he'd gotten used to
doing. As if he had to be invited into the bedroom he'd
shared with his wife for twenty-two years. But this
time he didn't want to wake the baby. Carefully, he
turned the knob, pushed the door open.

It always hit him in the chest—that first glimpse of
the room with its slanted ceilings, its antique white
iron headboard, the quilt like a broken rainbow on the
bed. He could remember so clearly how the flicker of
candlelight chased shadows into the corners, and
turned Hannah's bare skin the color of honey. The
whole room smelled of her, the faint hint of her perfume, the clean scent of shampoo and soap. But the
places that had been his were painfully stripped clean.
Except for the big chair where he'd always draped his
clothes for the next day so he wouldn't wake Hannah.
Now, the wicker basket was tucked on the broad
upholstered seat, the baby curled in a little bundle on
his side of the bed.

Hannah lay stretched out next to it, her face luminous as she watched the baby sleeping. Sam's groin
tightened at the sight of her in a cotton nightgown so
white and fine her skin showed in rich shadows
beneath it. It was her favorite, so old he couldn't even
remember when she'd first gotten it. But age had worn
it soft, smooth, made it even more delicate and beautiful, the same way the years had made Hannah even
lovelier than before. Sam's fingers itched to find the
endless row of tiny pearl buttons that ran down to the
ruffle brushing the insteps of Hannah's bare feet. His

palms ached to slide up underneath the folds of cloth to find warm, silky skin. But he didn't have that right anymore, the one he had once taken so for granted. Somehow he'd lost it. Even so, he couldn't help wondering what Hannah would do if he crossed to the bed, sat down on the edge of the mattress, reached out to touch her.

She'd force a smile, her eyes pleading for him to understand. She wouldn't move away, but it wouldn't matter. He'd feel her curling into herself, drawing farther and farther away where he couldn't reach her.

But the baby—she was touching the baby without reservations, without sadness, without that wistfulness, that faint hint of pain he'd come to know far too well.

Sam clenched his teeth against the hurt, the confusion. Quietly, he cleared his throat.

Hannah glanced up at him, surprised. She'd been so absorbed in the baby she hadn't even heard him come in. Her face was stripped bare, the emotions in it so honest, Sam's chest hurt.

"I'd forgotten how tiny they are at this age," she confessed. "I keep waking up, checking to make sure she's still breathing."

"Because of Becca when she was little?" Sam said, remembering those endless days in the hospital, Hannah bending over the incubator, willing their struggling baby to breathe while Sam had paced the room, feeling as helpless as he'd ever felt in his life. He could still remember how scared he'd been, looking down at Becca with all those tubes and machines hooked to her. It had been the first time he'd faced up to the truth, that parenthood terrified him, that he couldn't control everything that happened to his little girl. That he just might fail her, maybe in a different way, but fail her, nonetheless, the way his parents had failed him. It was the last thing he wanted to think of now—that hollow sensation of dread that had never completely left him in the past nineteen years.

"The doctor said Ellie was fine," he said, wanting to drive those old ghosts from Hannah's mind as well.

"I know. It's ridiculous. She's full-term and healthy. Nothing like Becca was at first. I just—I guess I don't want to go to sleep. I don't want to miss a moment. Ellie could be gone from our lives as quickly as she came into them." Wistfulness touched the vulnerable curve of Hannah's mouth. Hell, it hadn't even been twenty-four hours, and already she was half in love with the baby. What was she going to be like after two days? A week? What if this stretched out even longer?

"Hannah—" he began.

She held up her hand to stop him, then rolled to a sitting position, her attention focused on him. It scared him how hungry he was for it. It still panicked him sometimes to realize how much he'd come to need her over the years. "Actually, I wanted to talk to you about something," she said. "I've been thinking. About what Dr. Meyers said. He said he was sure that I'd do the right thing where Ellie is concerned."

There was no question in Sam's mind that the doctor had guessed something was wrong. "And?" Sam asked.

"It's just so hard to know what's right. So confusing. I just thought—" She hesitated, glanced down at her hands. "Maybe I could call Josie. Talk to her. She used to work with kids like Ellie. Maybe she could help me—help us—figure out what to do."

Sam stifled a sound of sheer relief. "I'd been thinking of Tom and Josie myself. You and I— Let's face it, Hannah. We're flying blind here. Neither one of us has any idea what the legalities of the situation are, except to know that we've probably broken half a dozen laws since you found Ellie this afternoon."

"It can't be that bad. At least not yet. I guess I resisted calling her at first because I didn't want to hear what she'd probably have to say. Knowing that I couldn't follow the rules and at the same time, give Ellie's mother a chance . . . But now, well, I want to call Josie before we get in over our heads. Do you think Ellie will be all right up here alone?"

Sam managed a smile. "Even I know she's too little to roll off the bed."

"I just thought, since her mother abandoned her— that's ridiculous, isn't it? She's too little to know." She slid off of the bed, padded, barefooted, down the stairs to the kitchen, Sam right behind her. She picked up the phone, dialed, then glanced up at Sam in surprise as he slid a notebook and pencil in front of her on the oak table.

"In case you need to take notes," he said.

Hannah listened as the phone rang, then, she could hear the receiver on the other end getting jostled, a sleepy voice answering. "Hello?"

"Did I wake you up, Josie? I'm sorry! I didn't even realize what time it was."

"Hannah?" Josie said groggily. "No problem. Tommy's been teething, so I'm grabbing sleep whenever I can. What's up?"

"It can wa—" she began, then stopped. "I wish it could wait, but it can't, Josie. It's important. Really."

Hannah could hear the sheets rustle, her friend getting herself into a sitting position. "What's up?" Josie demanded, concerned. "You sound like something is wrong. You didn't hurt yourself by taking down those clothes?"

"For once it has nothing to do with me or my surgery or any of the rest of the stuff I'm so sick of. It's something else. Something . . . I still can't believe."

"So spill it."

"When I went out to take down the clothes, I found something in the laundry basket. Josie, I found a baby."

"A baby?" Josie exclaimed, the last vestiges of sleepiness evaporating from her voice.

"The mother left a note asking me to take care of her. She even named the baby after my grandmother. The mother has to be one of Becca's friends, some scared, desperate kid."

"Got to give the kid credit. If I had to leave Tommy with someone, you'd be my first choice."

"I'm calling because I'm not sure what to do. I didn't notify Children and Family Services because I wanted to give the mother a chance to change her mind, come back for the baby. I don't want to get Ellie's mother in trouble."

"Or yourself in trouble, I hope."

"That's where I was hoping you could come in. Maybe this situation should be plain and simple, just make a call to the police and be done with it. But I'm so confused. What's right, Josie? That poor girl trusted me. I know I can't just keep Ellie without telling any-body, but the courts could take her right out of my arms if I don't go through proper channels. How long can I wait before I report finding her?"

"You can't wait. You have to call now."

"What happens when I do? I guess that's what I need to know."

Josie sighed. "Lots of legal mumbo jumbo. The court will appoint a guardian ad litem—someone who has nothing but Ellie's interests in mind. A lawyer, a social worker, someone to monitor Ellie wherever the court places her, make sure she's getting the best care possible. They'll award temporary custody to the best caretaker they can find for the baby. It depends on what emergency foster care is available. I'd call my favorite foster mom for you, but she has her hands full at the moment. She took three siblings in, along with her brood of four, and is hoping to adopt them. But there are major behavior disorders involved."

Hoping to adopt them? Hannah couldn't stifle a tiny flicker of excitement. What about Ellie? In time would she be eligible for adoption? No, she was getting ahead of herself. She was keeping Ellie safe for the baby's mother. She just needed to make certain the baby was in her keeping for now.

"I want to take care of Ellie, Josie."

Hannah held her breath at the long silence on the other end of the phone. If Josie started in with all the reservations Sam had voiced, Hannah thought she'd scream. "I'll support you a hundred percent, Hannah, as long as you're sure. But I'd be a rotten friend *and* a rotten social worker if I didn't make sure you were going into this with your eyes wide open. It would be great if the court just put the baby in your arms and everybody lived happily ever after, but it's not quite that easy. There's no way of knowing if Ellie's mom took care of herself while she was pregnant. If she was drinking, doing drugs, there could be consequences for the baby."

She wanted to protest, insist that the kids she'd known forever, Becca's friends, would never do drugs. She prayed that was true, but Josie was right. There was no way to be certain. If Ellie was sick— Then Hannah would deal with it, the way she had when Becca was tiny. "I understand there might be problems," she said.

"And those are just the physical possibilities. The

emotional ones can get even messier. Ellie's mother could come back any time, say she changed her mind, and more often than not the courts will side with the mother. Then there's the possibility the birth father might assert his rights. Or a member of either of the parents' extended families."

"I understand that."

"Cerebrally. It's a lot tougher when you're handing over a baby you've started a 'college tuition piggy bank' for to a fifteen-year-old with spiked hair, tattoos and a 'get out of rehab clean card.' Don't get me wrong, Hannah. I think you'd be the best thing that could possibly happen to this little girl, but I don't want you wandering in blindly to a situation that could hurt you."

"I can do this, Josie. I want to, so much."

Something in her tone must have reassured Josie. In spite of miles of streets between them and the telephone line, Hannah knew Josie was smiling. "Well, I'll see what I can do. Call in a few favors. Cutting through red tape used to be my specialty. Of course, it won't be quite as easy anymore, with me and my best ace lawyer buddy, Rick Parrish, retired. Even so, maybe I can pull a few strings. You and Sam will have to go through a series of home evaluations, but the two of you should pass with flying colors. I can't guarantee anything, Hannah, but there's a good chance you'll get to keep Ellie. Of course, the longer you hold onto her in secret, the less that chance will get to be."

"But what if Ellie's mom comes back to the farmhouse tomorrow or the next day? I feel like I'm betraying her."

"I know it's hard," Josie sympathized. "But Ellie's mother is a scared kid. She probably doesn't know half of the legal ramifications of what she's done. I guess the question to ask yourself is this: Exactly what did Ellie's mother ask you to do?"

"Take care of Ellie."

"Then that has to be your first priority. You'll be no good to either Ellie or her mom if Children and Family Services has to take her away from you because you broke the rules."

Hannah hesitated, torn. But Josie, as always, made perfect sense. "I guess you're right," she said. "But I'm scared for Ellie's mother, Josie."

"I wish I could reassure you and tell you that everything will be all right. But real life isn't always that simple. I'll make some calls. You'd better be ready to meet Tom and me at the courthouse whenever I can set something up."

"Josie?"

"What?"

"Ellie's mother trusts me."

"I know," Josie said. "That's why you have to go through the proper legal channels. Take care of that baby the best way you know how."

"But what if it's not good enough? What if they take Ellie away from me and put out a warrant for her mother's arrest? Josie, what if I end up failing both of them?"

"I'm really sorry I don't have a better answer," Josie said. "I'd find Ellie's mother if I could. Help her. But for now, the best I can do is take care of you and that baby."

"Josie, thanks."

"I hope you'll still be thanking me when this is all over," Josie said. "There are no guarantees, Hannah. And the regulations—well, I know they might seem harsh to you right now, but the rules are there to protect babies like Ellie. To make sure the courts do what is best for them."

"I'm what's best for Ellie. I am, Josie. I know it."

"Then we have to make sure the judge thinks so, too. You get some sleep. We could all be in for a bumpy ride."

Hannah hung up the phone, trying to ignore the hard knot of dread in her middle.

"What did Josie say?" Sam asked with a searching glance.

"She says it won't be easy. I have to . . . to go to the courts about Ellie. And once I do, the situation will be out of my control. I can never take it back. Ellie's mother will be in trouble. But if we don't go to court, the minute they find out, the authorities would take the baby away. I can't let that happen, Sam. Ellie's mother begged me to take care of her the best way I could. And that's what I'm going to have to do. Even if it hurts the poor girl who gave birth to her."

"You're doing the right thing," Sam said.

"It's the only choice I have."

"You'd better get some sleep. Morning is going to come early and you're looking a little pale yourself."

"Not used to late-night feedings and so on yet. But I'll get there with practice. I promise you won't have to lift a finger. I know this isn't something you wanted."

Not something he wanted? No. It wasn't something he wanted. Maybe that was why the contentment deep in Hannah's eyes scared him so damned much.

It was almost five in the morning when Sam padded downstairs to get a drink of water, a glimpse of light pooling into the hallway from the kitchen. He'd been sure Hannah would be asleep by now. She should have been exhausted after the day she'd had. Unless something was wrong—

She was probably just heating up a bottle or something. People did have to heat up bottles, didn't they? He mused, feeling a little like an idiot. But what the hell did he know about it? With Becca, Hannah had just tucked up her shirt, cradled her against bare skin so the baby could breast-feed.

He could remember waking up nights, watching the two of them through half-opened eyes, Hannah in the rocking chair by the window, moonlight bathing her in silver, her face luminous with contentment as Becca made tiny suckling noises. They'd looked so beautiful, the two of them there, together, the sight of them had squeezed his heart, made it hurt with love, ache with dread.

Love, because they were everything he'd ever dreamed of. Dread, because he could feel the subtle closing of a circle around them, a place they belonged, fitted so easily, while he could only hover on the edges the way he had when his mother had brought Trisha home from the hospital. The beginning of the slow separation that had torn his childhood world apart, as they squeezed him out of their lives inch by inch until there was no room for anything anymore except a crumpled note on the kitchen table. Not even a last touch, last kiss, last word saying good-bye.

Sam shook himself inwardly, and entered the kitchen. Hannah stood there in her nightgown, the light outlining the shadows of legs still long and willowy as a girl's. Her hair rioted almost to her waist in a cascade of midnight-colored waves. Her eyes seemed almost painfully awake despite the dark circles that smudged the delicate skin beneath them.

She looked so damned young, so alone, there in the kitchen, her features set in a way that tugged at Sam, told him how hard she was trying to be strong. He

wanted more than anything to scoop her up in his
arms, carry her to the couch, tuck her safe on his lap
and let her pour out her troubles. He wanted to make
everything right for her, warm her chilled feet with his
hands, smooth the rough waters of emotion so evident
in her eyes.

"You should be asleep," he growled. "Is something
wrong?"

"No. I'm fine. Everything's fine," she insisted, but he
could almost see the worry nibbling away inside her.

"The baby sleeping?"

"Like an angel."

It took some effort for Sam to force a smile. "I figured you would have been hovering over her like a
miser who'd just discovered a potful of gold."

"I didn't want to wake her up. I just couldn't hold
still." She crossed to the cupboard, took down a mug
she'd made back in college art class—hand-thrown
pottery with a mischievous clay dragon peeking over
the rim of the cup. It was a miracle it had survived all
these years. *Still damned fine work*, Sam thought.
Sometimes it was hard to remember Hannah's art at
all, it was so long since she'd done any. "Want something to drink?"

"No thanks. Just had coffee."

She poured herself a mugful of milk, then drizzled
chocolate syrup into it. She stuck it into the microwave
to warm. Hot chocolate—her panacea for all ills—better than Valium, she'd joked more than once.
Obviously she was as restless as he was. Whatever was
on her mind, it was preying heavily.

The microwave buzzed, and she almost jumped out
of her skin. She dove in to get her hot chocolate,
sloshed the liquid over her hand. She hissed in pain.
Sam grabbed the cup away from her and turned on the

cold water, thrusting her scalded fingers under the stream of water.

He still wasn't used to Hannah spilling anything. For years she'd flown about, so capable, so perfect, not drizzling soda on countertops or scattering crumbs on the floor like lesser mortals. It had just been since she'd started getting sick that he'd caught her like this. A little awkward, a little clumsy. Damned distracted by whatever silent wars were going on in her mind.

"Burn yourself bad?" he asked.

She shook her head. Turning off the water, she grabbed a dish towel and wrapped it around her fingers.

"Want to talk about it?" he prodded.

"Talk about what?"

"Whatever it is that's making you spill cocoa and keeping you up at night?" Sam braced himself. This was the time Hannah would close the vulnerable part of herself away, say there was no problem, somehow turn the attention to whatever was upsetting him. This was the time she'd deftly close him out.

But she surprised him, tracing the rim of her mug with an unburned finger, her mouth soft, not shaped into an expression that hid things away. Sam sucked in a steadying breath, dared to reach out, ghost his knuckles against the soft curve of her cheek. "C'mon, Hannah. Tell me."

"Shouldn't be too hard to figure out. I mean, it's been a crazy day. Everything that happened. I'm nervous about going to court. Scared what might happen. And then, on top of everything, Josie coming over and telling me—" She stopped, looking a little unnerved for an instant.

"Telling you what?"

"Oh, someone I know fell, broke her hip. An old woman I knew a long time ago."

Sam arched a brow in surprise and sympathy. Hannah had had a heck of a day. "I know how that kind of thing upsets you. Especially when you can't go running over there, casserole in hand to help out."

Her cheeks flushed—embarrassment over the things she still had to struggle to do?

"Don't worry, Hannah," he soothed. "I know how much you want to help. But you've got your hands full right now."

"I know. Finding the baby. Knowing you didn't . . . you don't . . ." Her voice cracked. He saw her fight to steady it. "I'm not stupid, Sam. I saw the look in your eyes. The last thing you want right now is a baby dumped in your lap."

Sam steadied himself, choosing his words carefully, trying to be honest, trying not to hurt her. "I won't deny I have plenty of doubts. I think that's only human, considering the circumstances. I made the decision to back you on this, though. I'll keep my word. So if that's what you're worried about—"

"Some, but . . . but that's not all of it." She turned away from him, paced to the window, her face turned out to the night. He could see the wash still on the line, left out for the night, forgotten, for the first time he could ever remember. The graceful shapes rippled in the breeze, the trees edging the ravine seeming to watch them, guarding the house. But Hannah was looking past the sheets, not even seeming to notice them, her gaze searching deeper, probing into the darkness beyond.

"I just keep looking out there," Hannah murmured, "can't stop wondering about . . . about *her.*"

"The baby?"

"No. I know the baby is fine. Ellie's tucked up in the basket, a little blanket tucked around her, her sleeper all soft and new, her tummy full of warm milk. She's sleeping like newborns do, as if they still remember the faces of angels."

Strange, Sam realized with a start, that's how he'd always felt about Hannah, as if there were something purer about her, sweeter, more heaven than earth. If anyone knew children's special angels, it was Hannah.

"If you aren't thinking about the baby, who are you wondering about?"

"Ellie's mother."

Sam grimaced. "Anyone who can abandon their own baby doesn't deserve your sympathy, Hannah. Save your energy to take care of the baby. That's who you should feel sorry for."

She turned away, hugging herself tight. "Is it? I remember when I had Becca, it was so strange. Wonderful. Terrifying."

"Terrifying?" Sam asked, stunned. "You mean you were scared, too? I don't believe it. You seemed so . . . so sure of yourself. Like you'd been born knowing secrets, older than time. You knew everything about taking care of Becca, making her happy."

"I didn't know anything, not really, except that my life had changed forever. Nothing would ever be the same. I loved her so much, wanted to be perfect for her. She deserved perfect."

"I've never seen a better mother. You were . . . perfect." His voice dropped low, drifted to silence, the sudden quiet filling up with his own inadequacies, far too many even to count. "She was damned lucky to have you."

The stiffness in her shoulders eased a little. She turned back to him, her arms still crossed protectively over her middle. "I remember lying in the hospital bed. I'd been through twenty-three hours of labor, toxemia, a Cesarean section."

"An emergency one. You scared the life out of me. When the doctor just swept you out of there to surgery, I felt so helpless. You were holding my hand all the way to the operating room. Then, the nurse made me let go of you. I remember the doors shutting me out. Standing there, staring at them, knowing you and the baby were in trouble and there wasn't a damn thing I could do to help you."

The first of plenty of times he'd felt useless, awkward, hadn't had a clue what he should do. But maybe that time had been the worst. Until then, somehow Hannah had made him feel invincible, like one of those knights in the fairy tales she used to read to Becca before bed.

"I just remember waking up, knowing my baby had been born. She was real. Alive. Part of me. Nothing in my life would ever be the same again. I kept the night nurse in my room, talking for three hours after you'd gone home to sleep. I felt . . . magical, somehow. Sure, I was scared. I knew Becca was early, the doctor had told me about the infection."

"But you always had faith she'd be okay. No matter what they said. And she was."

"It had more to do with Becca's fight than my faith. Do you remember how crowded that wing of the hospital would get? Mom and Dad, Grandma, you and me. Friends would stop. There were baskets full of flowers and balloons, piles of baby gifts to open. I needed all of you so much, needed to talk and laugh and even admit how scary it felt to be a mother, have that tiny, perfect little being depending on me for everything."

Hannah sipped her chocolate, her eyes warm and

dark and filled with sweetness like the liquid in her mug.

"That's why I couldn't sleep," she admitted.

"You're not alone," Sam said, his voice rough with emotion. "No matter what doubts I might have, I'm here, Hannah."

"I know. And I'm so grateful for that." Her lips curled into a smile so rare now it made it hard for Sam to breathe until the smile slowly faded, her mouth vulnerable, sad. "But this isn't about me. I just keep thinking of Ellie's mother. Wonder where she is, what she's thinking, what she's feeling right now. I wonder if she's all alone, hurting from childbirth, her arms empty with no baby to hold. Her body won't know that baby's gone. Her milk will be coming in, her breasts aching. What if she hasn't told anyone at all? That she was pregnant? That she had the baby? What if she's curled up in a bed someplace, her face buried in her pillow, trying not to let anyone know that she's crying?"

Sam recoiled from the picture she'd painted far too clearly, one he didn't want to creep into his own mind. "Hannah, for God's sake—"

"It haunts me, Sam. I want to . . . to find her, to smooth back her hair, hold her while she cries it all out. I want to tell her—I don't even know what. That someday it won't hurt so much. She'll be able to breathe without feeling like her chest is caving in, will be able to see a baby on the street without wanting to run, sobbing, in the opposite direction. I wish I could tell her everything will be all right, but I know it wouldn't be true. Things will get better, but what she feels now will never entirely go away."

"It shouldn't go away. A mother shouldn't be able to abandon her child, go on as if it had never existed." Bitterness edged Sam's voice.

He knew the instant Hannah realized she'd struck a nerve. She reached out, threaded her fingers through his. It had been so long since she'd touched him that way, soft, comforting, that special healing that was Hannah's own warming him where their palms were pressed together.

"I'm sorry, Sam. I didn't mean to stir things up inside you. Remind you—"

Sam almost laughed. If there was one thing nobody needed reminding of, it was the fact that their mother had thrown them out like so much trash.

"You're wasting your time worrying, Hannah," he said. "I promise you, no matter what happens now, even if God Himself came down and took care of that little girl in our bedroom, it wouldn't change the fact that her mother, the one who was supposed to love her, protect her, take care of her, just tossed her away. Nothing can change that."

Hannah turned away, wistful, so sad it wrenched at Sam's heart. "I know that," she said softly. "And wherever Ellie's mother is—I'm scared she knows it, too."

Hannah dumped out the last of the cocoa, filled the dirty glass with water. "I think I'll try to sleep now."

Sam nodded, but as she disappeared into the dining room, the soft sound of her bare feet making their way up the stairway, he couldn't help but doubt her. No, Hannah wouldn't sleep tonight. But then, neither would he.

4

THE DORM WAS QUIET, most of the kids asleep except for the spring rain on the windows and the echoed sounds of some late night partygoers laughing on the floor below. She slipped, barefoot, down the hall, her feet cold on the tile, her mouth tasting of blood as she bit down on her bottom lip to hold back any sound.

No, she couldn't start crying, not here. Couldn't make any noise. Someone might hear her, ask her questions she couldn't answer. Someone might guess—

No, no one could guess. She'd been so careful, so withdrawn, holding everything tight inside her. She could imagine the look on their faces if she'd ever told them—disbelief, maybe laughter, as if it had to be a joke.

It had been so long since she'd laughed at all. She wondered if she'd ever remember how.

The sound of footsteps rang up the steps, the rhythmic *tap tap tap* of heels mounting the stairs, light, bouncy as a child's, with no weight of worries, of guilt, of loss.

Cupping her hands over her middle to support her stomach, she hurried to the bathroom in the center of the hall, ignoring how weak she felt, how much it hurt to run, desperate to reach the door, hide herself behind it before whoever was on the stairs reached the floor.

Breathless, dizzy, she stumbled into the bathroom, leaned on the inside of the door, trying to catch her breath, push down the pain and the wild pounding of her heart. She was bleeding again. She could feel it. But the book she'd read about childbirth said that was natural, didn't it? It had only been two days.

Two days since she'd locked the hotel room door, turned up the television so no one could hear her cry out. Two days since she'd given birth to her baby alone. She'd held her close through the night, exhausted, touching her tiny cheeks, the creases behind her knees, the perfect curves of her ears. When she'd been able to get up the next morning, she'd hidden her in a book bag lined with an old sweater, and taken her to the only place she could think of—the one place she knew for certain Ellie would be safe.

Safe. Her baby deserved to be safe. Have someone to take care of her. Someone who knew how to keep her from crying, how to bake cookies and teach ABCs. Someone who could love Ellie far better than she ever could.

She should be relieved. It was over. Ellie was safe and no one at college had guessed her secret. No one would ever have to know what she'd done, how badly she'd messed up, how she'd failed. . .

Besides, she'd be able to see Ellie sometimes, even hold her, watch her grow up, even if it was from a distance. And as for her own life—everything could go on just the way it was supposed to before she got into so much trouble—

Maybe on the outside, a voice whispered in her head.

But not on the inside. She'd never be the same. Never. It hurt too bad.

She swallowed hard, tried to squeeze back the sobs that had threatened all day, the sobs she'd choked into silence when her roommate had burst into the room, raving about the Chris O'Donnell lookalike who sat behind her in Bio class. But now, with Macey sound asleep after bringing her a sick tray from the caf, she couldn't hold her grief in anymore, felt like the tears would split her open wide, come pouring out and never stop.

She stripped off her robe, the grinning crescent moon and smug-faced stars seeming ludicrous, so innocent and childlike it made her sick to her stomach because she was anything but. She staggered into one of the shower stalls, turned the water on full blast, the racket of it pounding against the tiles so loud it drowned out the desperate sounds rising in her throat.

Hot, the water was hot. So hot it almost burned as she stepped under the stream. She wanted it to hurt, wished it could sear away all the ugliness boiling up inside her, wash her clean of what she'd done.

She shouldn't have any tears left. She'd cried so many. A lifetime's worth in the months since she'd stared down in disbelief at the little plastic stick that told her what she'd been terrified of for so long. That she was pregnant. Everything she'd wanted, everything she'd hoped, dreamed about herself, her future, crumbling away under her feet, leaving her falling, falling until all that was left was guilt, shame, fear.

She'd been scared, so scared. But it was over now, wasn't it? She'd had her baby. She'd survived. The baby was fine.

No.

Not fine.

Beautiful.

Ten tiny fingers. Ten perfect toes. Fingernails impossibly small, pink like the insides of the shells she had gathered in her green plastic bucket at the ocean when she was eight.

And her eyes—they'd been so blue. She'd read in the baby book that all babies' eyes were blue when they were first born. Her hair was just this soft, soft fuzz, gold, the color of a baby duck's down.

She closed her eyes, seeing Ellie's face so clearly—round, red cheeks, a nose that wrinkled up, a little pink mouth sucking on her fist. She wondered if Ellie would find her thumb. She'd sucked her own until she was seven, even though her mother had painted it with some awful tasting goo.

She shook her head, trying to chase the images out of her mind, silence the millions of questions welling up inside her.

She'd promised herself she wouldn't think about things like this once she'd given her baby away, she wouldn't keep wondering what color her eyes would be or whether her hair would be straight or fall in soft curls. She'd promised herself she'd put it behind her, start over. She'd done the best she could for Ellie, the best she could for herself. The only thing she *could* do. Hadn't she?

But it didn't stop the hurting—the stinging between her legs, the burning swelling of her breasts, the terrible stillness where she'd felt Ellie moving inside her just days before.

She leaned back against the wall of the shower stall, her whole body shaking, her knees too weak to hold her up. The sobs tore from her chest as she sank down, down toward the wet tiles. She curled into a little ball on the floor, rocking in an effort to comfort herself as she might never get to rock her baby.

5

SAM SCRAWLED OUT THE LAST of his instructions on a
yellow legal pad, hoping the notes would make sense
to the supervisor on his biggest construction job. Sam
sure wouldn't be around to troubleshoot this morning.
But then, Sam felt pretty useless at the moment anyway. He hadn't been able to clear his head since the
moment he'd seen that baby in Hannah's arms and in
spite of his best efforts, he hadn't even found relief in
his favorite survival tactic—burying himself in the
work he'd always loved. He'd hoped work would help
him get through the hours until he and Hannah had to
troop down to the courthouse for the appointment
Josie had made. But it seemed like the hands on the
clock barely moved while his doubts grew and grew
until the air in his office felt too thick to breathe.

A low pitched buzzer sounded, alerting him that
someone had entered the office. But instead of his secretary showing up, bright-eyed and smart alecky for
work, Tom Wilkes's linebacker body filled the doorway.

"Sounds like you had a big night, Sam," Tom said, his

blues rumpled from a night of patrolling. "I got in from working third shift and Josie had an earful to tell me."

Sam ran his fingers wearily through his hair. "I've had better nights."

"You've had better years. As if you and Hannah don't have enough to handle at the moment, you get an abandoned baby dumped in your laps."

"She wants to keep it."

"Of course she wants to keep it. You've been married to Hannah long enough to know that she would. How do you feel about it?"

"It's crazy, Tom. We've raised Becca. We're through with diapers and bottles and all that stuff. Even if we were younger, it wouldn't matter right now with all the problems Hannah's had. She's still so pale, so fragile, it scares me."

"Josie stopped over at the farmhouse yesterday. Said Hannah was still looking peaked but trying damned hard not to let anyone notice it. Josie almost had to hogtie her to help with the laundry. It was hard as hell for Josie to see her that way. Can't imagine what it's like for you."

"Tough," Sam admitted. "Damned tough."

"Josie says the good news is that Hannah is feeling well enough to argue with her again. So she's got to be on the mend, huh? Just a matter of time."

"Yeah. Just a matter of time." Sam fought to keep the doubt out of his voice. Hannah wasn't healing as fast as the doctor had said she should in spite of the determination with which she started every day.

Sam ran his fingers wearily back through his hair. "I guess I just don't get it, Tom. This whole hysterectomy thing has devastated Hannah in ways I never expected. I mean, it's not as if we were planning to have any more kids. Becca's nineteen and gone. And the diagnosis could have been so much worse. I know the doctor was worried about cancer."

"Scary stuff. If I ever thought I might be losing Josie that way I'd go crazy. It's understandable you were relieved."

"When they told me a simple surgery and everything would be fine I felt like I'd won the lottery. But it's not simple and everything sure as hell isn't fine. It's like Hannah is grieving and I'm not sure why."

Tom chuckled. "I was stupid enough to tell Josie how 'relieved' I was when I heard curing Hannah's problems was going to be 'no big deal.' She almost took my head off. She said 'if snipping around down there is no big deal, why is it that the minute men hear the word vasectomy every guy in the room wants to cup his hands over his crotch?"

"That's not the same," Sam started to argue.

"I tried to make the same point, but Josie said it was *exactly* the same, except that Hannah's losing the place where her baby grew, and a large part of her identity as a woman. 'We men' are fertile forever. At ninety we can still have kids if we're stupid and selfish enough. But women—they have to lose that part of themselves. Face up to the fact that it's too late to change their minds."

"I guess I never thought of it that way," Sam confessed.

"Made me start thinking—would I still feel like a man if some doctor told me I had to get cut when I didn't want to? Suddenly—*bang!*—I couldn't father kids anymore, no matter how much I wanted to? It's easy to say it's no problem. But when I look at it that way, I guess I'm not so sure how I'd feel if it happened to me. Talk to her about it, Sam."

Sam stared down at his desk. Talk to her? It sounded so easy. Yet how could he when she was still shutting him out? But he couldn't say that to Tom. It was too raw. Too personal. Made him feel too much like the failure he'd sworn he'd never be. He shifted the spotlight to something safer. "She sure misses Becca."

"To be expected. That wife of yours is a hell of a mother. Josie's always said she should write a book. But that doesn't mean keeping this baby is the best thing for you to do. Don't rush into anything. It's a hell of a responsibility. If you take on a kid, you both need to be in it, give it a hundred percent or it'll never work."

That was an understatement and a half. But how the hell could Sam give it a hundred percent when the whole thing scared the living hell out of him? Hannah had taken to mothering so easily, so naturally. It hadn't ever been that way for him. He'd struggled, made mistakes, fumbled around. It wasn't like he'd had any great example in his own parents. In the end he'd just done his best to stay out of Hannah's way and been relieved that he hadn't messed Becca up too badly.

"I don't mean to be sticking my nose in," Tom said. "Feel free to tell me to shut up anytime you want to. But I feel like I owe you guys big. If not for you and Hannah, Josie and I would never have had a chance. Josie wouldn't have gone on our first date, let alone married me."

Sam rubbed his eyes, remembering. The Wilkes's wedding day had been magical—he'd been Tom's best man, Hannah Josie's matron of honor. Hannah had been glowing, laughing, and Sam thought it was a miracle that she'd looked even more beautiful than on the day he'd married her so many years ago. He'd never have believed that just three years later, they could feel so lost to each other.

Tom cleared his throat gruffly. "I can't help but see that you're both having a hard time of it right now, even before this whole baby issue came up. I know it's none of my business, but Josie and I—we really care about you."

"Hannah's been having a hard time ever since Becca left home," Sam allowed.

"How about you?"

Tom surprised Sam. How about him? How did he feel about Becca going off to school? He hadn't taken time to think about it, really. Any emotions he was going through seemed so pale next to the loss in Hannah's eyes. There hadn't been any room left for his pain.

Sure, there were times he missed Becca. The sound of her running down the stairs, her quick hugs before she ran out the door, her smile so much like Hannah's, but confident where Hannah's was shy, her eyes bold and flashing with excitement where Hannah's were quiet, soothing. Sometimes looking at his daughter had made him wonder if Hannah had ever had that same sparkle.

He could remember Hannah's tears, her pride when they'd driven away from the college that was to be their daughter's new home. *She's not like me,* she'd whispered. And just for a moment, her eyes had shone.

As if being Hannah was something to be ashamed of, something less than wonderful. As if that impossibly big heart of hers was a burden instead of the most incredible gift Sam had ever been given.

"I guess I've never thought about it much—how I felt about Bec leaving. There just wasn't any room to think about it, what with Hannah getting sick." *And my marriage falling apart.*

"Just wanted to say I'm here for you. I'll be at the courthouse. And after, no matter when. Things will work out for the best. I know they will."

Whose best would they work out for? Sam's or Hannah's? Because whatever happened in the courtroom, one thing was certain. One of them would lose.

Hannah had only been in the old courthouse twice, once when they'd signed the papers to buy the farmhouse from her grandmother, the other when she'd come to lend moral support to Becca during the ordeal of handling her first speeding ticket. They'd waited for their turn forever, sitting in the row of hard, wooden chairs that lined the hallway. To take Becca's mind off of her nervousness, Hannah had pulled a pad of paper out of her purse and started a game of "hangman"— her first word: LEAD FOOT.

She'd been so wrapped up in her daughter that day, calming Becca's nerves, that she hadn't paid much attention to the people milling around the building.

Now, Hannah cuddled Ellie close, as if she could shield the baby from the coldness of the building, the dreary gray of marble floors and walls spattered with portraits of men who'd been pillars of the community and were now long dead. Everything felt grubby to Hannah in spite of the workers diligently buffing the floors and dusting the stair rail. It was as if human misery had left its own kind of silt over everything, layering it with depressing gray.

Divorces were settled here, criminals sentenced, custody given or taken away, cutting children's lives in two. People who still had nightmares faced down their attackers, battered wives refused to press charges against the husbands who had hurt them and drinkers surrendered their driver's licenses in the wake of DUIs.

Lawyers milled around with bulging briefcases, some in expensive suits and Italian leather shoes, others rumpled with a bargain basement style that made

Hannah feel sorry for their clients. What kind of a defense could they put together if they couldn't even bother to have a dirty suit dry-cleaned?

She shivered, cuddling Ellie closer. This was no place for a baby. It was too cold, too hard, too sad. Ellie belonged in places with light, bright colors, wise jolly faces like Dr. Meyers and his nurse.

Court workers looked out onto this world every day. Would they be able to see beyond it? Hannah wondered. To the world Hannah wanted so badly to make for little Ellie? Or would they be so used to seeing the dark side of things they'd take her away, cite broken rules or regulations or bureaucratic red tape to justify sweeping Ellie into the system they built in this gray, cold building. A maze of strangers' faces and unfamiliar houses with no place to really call her own?

Her stomach twisted. She'd already thrown up the breakfast Sam insisted she eat while they were waiting for Tom and Josie to arrive. She was so scared. She kept eyeing the door, more tempted by the moment to run.

But that wouldn't solve anything. Not now. They knew about Ellie. They'd come after her, find her, take her away for sure.

She glanced over to where Sam stood, somber in his dark blue suit and red tie, his white dress shirt crisp against his tanned neck. The outfit made him look every inch the businessman, but somehow, even the best tailored clothes could never quite tame the touch of wildness in him, the outdoorsy breath of wind and air and racing waters that clung about him more certainly than his woodsy cologne.

Tom stood beside him, conversing in low tones, the policeman's whole body intent, a little nervous in spite of his blue uniform. She'd always thought Tom had the most honest eyes she'd ever seen, and she knew he'd do the best he could for all of them. It was hard to face the truth—it might not be enough.

Josie had run down to the social services office, hoping she could find someone to help with the case.

"How you holding up, kiddo?" Tom asked, making Hannah suddenly aware both he and Sam were staring at her.

"Be glad when it's over."

"We all will. Josie's gotten us a bunch of testimonials from neighbors and friends about what a terrific parent you are. They could look clear across the state and not find anyone half as well suited to take care of this baby as you are. Even got a letter from old Miss Ida Beene. She worked in child services for forty years before she retired. She thinks you walk on water as a mother."

The vote of confidence warmed the coldest places in Hannah's chest. "Tom, thank you. Both of you."

"Josie and I are happy to do it, Hannah. You know we are. I just wish we'd drawn a different judge. This one's a stickler for details and regulations. Not to mention irritable as hell because of all the confusion around here lately. Too many cases—not enough people to do the work. And we haven't had as much time to prepare as Josie and I would have liked. But Judge Jones said that if we didn't get on the docket for today, they'd have to place Ellie somewhere else until we were ready."

"Do you think things will turn out okay?"

"I hope so. I'd feel better if Josie could pull a lawyer out of her hat, but I know they're scheduled so tight since Rick Parrish retired, it's going to be all but impossible. I just hope she's watching the time so she gets back here when this whole thing starts. She knows more about this stuff than any of the rest of us do."

"Heads up, everybody," Sam alerted them. "Looks like we're center stage."

The door to courtroom 3 was opening, a thin man in a suit searching the crowd. "O'Connell? Samuel and Hannah?"

Tom cast a glance down the hall, looking for Josie, but there was no flash of red hair anywhere down the length of dingy gray hall. "Don't worry," Tom muttered under his breath as they started toward the courtroom. "Josie will be here."

The chamber was set up just like the ones in courtroom dramas—a tall mahogany desk where the judge would sit, rows of wooden benches gated off from the front of the room by a spindled rail. Tables where lawyers and their clients could sit. It seemed so strange, thinking that a baby was the one who's future was on trial here, and that there was no way Hannah could fix things if the judge's decision went the wrong way.

As if Ellie could sense Hannah's nervousness, she started to fuss. "Not now, baby," Hannah whispered, jiggling her a little to comfort her. "Not now." The last thing she needed was to seem inept at handling the baby in front of the judge.

"Don't hold her so tight," Sam breathed into her ear. And Hannah realized she'd been squeezing the little one close to her, as if holding on could somehow keep Ellie safe in her arms.

Sam slid his arm around her, the feel of it warm, solid, bracing her, the scent of him, so familiar, so warm, soothing her frayed nerves. She tilted her face up to look into his eyes, saw him flash her a strained smile, and she knew he was trying to make her believe he had confidence that everything would turn out all right.

All right for her, she knew instinctively, not all right for him. Her throat felt tight with gratitude, tenderness, regret because even now, when he was touching her, there was distance between them. Distance neither one of them wanted. Distance neither one of them knew how to bridge.

Sam guided her up to one of the front tables, pulled out the chair to help her settle in with Ellie. The baby's blanket slipped. He tucked the edge between Ellie's body and Hannah's own.

Hannah smiled up at him, wanted to say something, to thank him, but at that moment an inner door to the room swung open, a woman in long black robes sweeping in to take her place at her desk.

"There is some sort of confusion about the baby's caseworker. Last minute changes. Not that we have time for this," she said, looking a trifle perturbed.

Hannah prayed the confusion wouldn't make the judge even more hard-nosed about the case. Sam was trying hard not to look nervous. Tom bit a hangnail, the big cop's habit whenever he was on edge.

There was a clatter outside the courtroom door, the sounds of fumbling as the person on the far side of it tried to open it. The door swung open and Josie rushed in, her face flushed, her eyes snapping with nervousness.

"Forgive me, your honor," she said. "With such short notice, it was hard to—I mean, you know that finding legal help is a challenge here at the moment."

"I'm aware of that, Mrs. Wilkes."

"I just thought, in light of the time crunch, if there was someone who could take the case, someone familiar with Mrs. O'Connell, it might, um, make things easier." Josie glanced at Hannah, a strange look of half satisfaction, half apology on her face. "I'm sorry I didn't have time to run back and . . . and clear it with everyone. But what matters most is what happens to the baby the O'Connells want custody of, isn't it?"

Was Josie talking to the judge? Hannah wondered. Then why did it seem as if her friend was talking to *her?* Making excuses? Asking her pardon? For what? Doing everything she could to help Hannah get custody of Ellie? Hannah would move heaven and earth to keep the baby. Do whatever she had to do. Surely, Josie knew that.

More commotion outside the door.

"I'm sure whatever you decided is fine," Hannah said, wanting to reassure Josie.

"I hope so," Josie murmured under her breath as the door swung open again. "It's just that time was running out, and then, there he was, offering to help. I didn't know what else to do."

A man strode into the room, a few inches taller than Sam, pants pressed to a knife-blade crease, shirt expertly starched and buttoned tight all the way to his Adam's apple.

Every inch of him exuded an aura of power, a kind of ruthlessness that came from being able to scent people's weaknesses and exploit them, if necessary, to win. Instinctively, Hannah pushed herself back in her chair, as if she could somehow shield Ellie from the laser beam intensity of the man's gaze.

But a lead wall couldn't have blocked that searing green gaze, or the way it hit Hannah like a rifle shot right in the middle of her chest.

She couldn't breathe, couldn't speak, reeling inside as Josie explained. "Your honor, this lawyer has agreed to serve as Baby Ellie's guardian ad litem until things in social services get more settled."

"The name's Tony Blake, your honor," the man introduced himself, his lips curving into a smile, a smile too familiar, echoing the smile of a boy long ago. "Hello, Hannah," he said, low. "Aren't you going to welcome me home?"

6

Hannah's jaw dropped as she stared into the face of the man looming over her, his sun-blond hair styled to perfection, his smile toothpaste white, a little crooked. Just the way she remembered it from the first day he'd slid into the seat next to her in British Lit class her junior year in high school, breathless, laughing. Charming the teacher into letting his tardiness slide.

Old Toothless Ruthless—the wizened English teacher whose loose-fitting false teeth had once fallen out of her mouth when she was screaming at someone—was the last person anyone had expected to be influenced by twinkling green eyes and a handsome face. But she'd been just as vulnerable to Tony Blake's brand of charm as the horde of giggling girls who had flung themselves at him every chance they got.

But Tony could have cared less about the stir he'd created in the high school where most of the kids had known each other since kindergarten. An army brat, just arrived in Willowton, he couldn't wait to shake the dust of the small Iowa town off his shoes, trade school books for the gleam of a jet pilot's wings. The air force—traveling everywhere, flying, fighting, winning more medals than his old man—those were the only things he'd cared about.

How many times had he described his future to Hannah, his eyes shining, so far away from her she felt lonely even when he was right there by her side. And he'd done exactly as he'd always planned: he'd taken a bus to the Air Force Academy and never once looked back.

Until now.

Hannah prayed no one could see the hundred conflicting emotions roiling inside her. *This* was what Josie had been apologizing for. Bringing Tony Blake into this case.

Josie must have figured Hannah would be happy to deal with a little awkwardness and discomfort with an old boyfriend if it meant she'd have a better chance at keeping Ellie. But Josie couldn't have guessed what kind of Pandora's box she'd just opened.

Tony grinned down at Hannah as if twenty-eight years had never stretched between them. As if he'd just been down the hall at his locker and come to walk her to class.

"I couldn't believe it when I heard you were down here, in need of legal help," Tony said. "I've been camping out around here, using the law library upstairs to keep up with cases back in Chicago while I'm trying to get things settled with my mother. Seems like nursing help is about as hard to find around here as lawyers are at the moment."

"I was trying to recruit one of the lawyers I'd worked with before when he offered to take the case," Josie interrupted, her cheeks so red her freckles disappeared. "I hope it's okay."

"I'm sure it's fine," Tony cut in smoothly, before Hannah could say a word. "There's no reason I shouldn't help just because Mrs. O'Connell and I are old friends, is there, Mr. O'Connell?"

Sam shrugged. "If you can help us, we'll be . . . grateful."

"Considering the tough cases I handle every day, I think I can manage this one. Of course, it will take some effort to concentrate on the case."

"Are you . . . too busy?" Hannah asked.

"I've got plenty of time to help you, Hannah," Tony assured her. "It's just that, well, I'm not sure what I expected once I saw you again, but it sure wasn't this. Didn't anyone tell you we're supposed to be getting old?" he asked, something terrifyingly soft in his eyes. "You don't look any different than you did when you were sixteen."

She tried not to let the compliment matter. But the way he was looking at her made it impossible to doubt his sincerity—that low simmer just beneath the surface of his eyes, the intensity with which he searched her face, as if comparing every curve and hollow with some cherished picture in his mind.

"I've changed a lot in the years since you've been gone, Tony." She hadn't said his name aloud since he'd left town. Almost like the ancient people, afraid to mention the names of the dead, as if they could steal your soul somehow. If she didn't say his name, she wouldn't think of him. If she didn't think of him, she wouldn't miss him. And it didn't matter how much she missed him, it didn't change anything. He was gone and he'd been bluntly honest with her from the first. He was never coming back.

"I suppose plenty has changed," Tony admitted. "But you know how it is—the older you get, the more you like to idealize what it was like when you were young. Guess I've been doing that a lot lately. Something about being here in Willowton again makes you stop and think." He paused, shrugged. As if maybe he'd touched some painful memory, too.

"So, this must be Ellie," he said, reaching for the baby so naturally it startled Hannah. "Mrs. Wilkes told me all about her. Do you mind if I hold her? The two of us should get acquainted, don't you think? Since I'm going to be looking out for her until we get things settled?"

Hannah couldn't keep herself from tightening her hold on Ellie, afraid she might have betrayed her own unease. It was as if Tony read her mind. He smiled, his voice soothing. "I promise to give her back."

Hannah felt like an idiot. She could hardly refuse to let him hold the baby, no matter how badly she wanted to keep Ellie safe in her arms. She offered him the baby. Tony scooped her up so deftly, resting her against one broad shoulder. Hannah tried to hand him the burp cloth to protect his suit, but he waved it away with a chuckle.

"A little princess like this—she wouldn't ruin her knight in shining armor's suit, now would you, Miss Eleanor? You are one lucky little girl, you know. Must not have irritated any bad fairies after all, or you'd never have ended up in Hannah Townsend's backyard."

"O'Connell." Sam corrected. "Her name's O'Connell now." She glanced up at Sam, his brow arched in question. He'd lived with her for twenty-two years, thought he knew everything about her. But Hannah knew she'd never mentioned Tony.

"Yes," Tony said, sparing Sam barely a glance before he turned the full force of his gaze back to Hannah. "I remember. Mom wrote me you'd gotten married." Was there regret in his voice? Or was she just imagining it because she felt strange herself—that odd peeling away of years, protective layers that had hidden memories in the darkest corners of her heart? She'd thought she'd erased them altogether by force of will, but she'd been wrong. They came flooding back, overwhelming, so vivid they cut deep.

Tony patted Ellie's back, that large, masculine hand looking so big, so powerful, astonishing in its gentleness, framed against Ellie's tiny form.

Hannah caught a glimpse of Sam and couldn't help seeing the difference between the two men. Sam hadn't held the baby once since Ellie had been left at the house. He had done everything he could to avoid even touching her. It would have meant so much to Hannah if he had just reached out to Ellie a little bit. But no.

He'd gone shopping because he'd had to, argued with her about what was best to do. He'd paced the doctor's office and come to the courtroom. He'd even capitulated and said Hannah could keep the baby—if they could clear things legally. But he'd never touched Ellie. Never talked to her the way Tony was. He'd never acted glad to see her, glad Hannah had found her, never teased or joked or comforted.

No, he'd just fought back his doubts and bit his tongue. Not that it had mattered, considering how loud he'd been thinking. His silence still roared in Hannah's ears.

Tony pulled back the edge of Ellie's blanket, hooked his finger under her little hand, tiny fingers curled around it, holding tight. He smiled. "You are one lucky little girl, princess, to land in Hannah's arms."

"Mr. Blake?" The judge's voice cut him off. "If

you're ready, perhaps we can begin the proceedings?"

"Forgive me, your honor."

"Will past knowledge of Mrs. O'Connell affect your ability to guard this child's best interests?"

"Not at all. As Mrs. Wilkes suggested, it will make me better able to judge the quality of home Mrs. O'Connell would make for baby Ellie."

The judge seemed satisfied. She glanced down at the papers on her desk. "You are Samuel and Hannah O'Connell of 209 Linden Lane?"

"Yes." Sam and Hannah answered at the same time. She glanced up at him, a sinking feeling in her chest. She could imagine what he was thinking, how he was trying to piece things together, how he must be wondering why in all their years of marriage, she'd never so much as mentioned Tony Blake's name. Sam would have to know it wasn't an oversight.

She'd talked constantly about home, spun out story after story about the farm and Willowton, people she'd known, people she'd cared about. He'd been hungry for every story, as if he could fill up the hollow places where his own childhood should have been, replacing the hurt and emptiness and betrayals with the clean, wholesome, fresh warmth of what it had been like growing up in the small Iowa farm town.

She'd told him so much, told him everything except this—from the day Tony had walked into her world, until the day he'd walked out.

"You've been married twenty-two years," the judge said. "One daughter, Rebekah, aged nineteen, now in college. Is that correct?"

"Yes," Hannah said.

"The baby has been in your custody for approximately twenty-four hours?"

"Yes."

"And during that time you did not call Children and Family Services or the police station to inform them that you had discovered an abandoned child?"

"Your honor? May I?" Tom stepped forward, looking eager and hopeful and incredibly young in spite of his burly frame.

The judge nodded her assent. "Officer Wilkes."

"As for the O'Connells' failing to report finding the child—that is not exactly true. My wife and I have been friends of the O'Connells' for years. They called us for advice."

Oh, God, Hannah thought in alarm. *Don't get yourself in trouble, Tom!* But he continued.

"As you can see in the documents we filed, there are a dozen testimonials, signed by residents of Willowton citing Hannah O'Connell's superior parenting skills. It's highly likely Hannah O'Connell knows Ellie's mother, or at least has met her at some time. She was reluctant to get the girl in legal trouble. Hoped the mother might show up at the house to claim the child. Perhaps Mrs. O'Connell wasn't exactly following procedure, but it was a very understandable mistake to make. One proving Mrs. O'Connell's compassion, which makes her an even better candidate for temporary custody of a minor child."

"In your opinion, officer." The chill in the judge's voice unnerved Hannah. She tried to stop her hands from shaking. What if Sam had been right all along when he'd pressed her to call the police? What if keeping Ellie last night cost her the baby?

Hannah sucked in a deep breath, groped for something, anything to say that might influence the woman looming above them in her dark robes. "Please," she began, but Tony's voice cut her off.

"It is my opinion as well, your honor."

"Mr. Blake? Have you read the testimonials Officer Wilkes has mentioned?"

Tony chuckled, waved one hand in dismissal. "Your honor, nothing in those documents could tell me any more than I already know. Hannah O'Connell is a compassionate, warm, generous woman, who can give baby Ellie a higher quality of love and nurturing than you could find anywhere else in the county. I move that the court accept the O'Connells' application for temporary custody of the child, and that we consider ourselves lucky to have Hannah in Ellie's corner." Hannah's stomach fluttered at the certainty in his voice, gratitude flooding through her. She smiled up at Tony, tears in her eyes.

"If you're willing to allow it, I'll take the responsibility of being the child's guardian ad litem temporarily. By the time I leave Willowton, you should have gotten your staff shortage under control and someone else can be appointed if necessary."

"Unusual, but—under the circumstances, the court accepts your offer. All your questions have been answered to your satisfaction, Mr. Blake?"

"Completely, your honor."

"And to mine. Therefore, I hearby grant temporary custody of the minor child known as Eleanor Doe to Samuel and Hannah O'Connell, said custody to be monitored by the child's guardian ad litem, Anthony Blake, until we fill the vacancies in our staff and a more permanent guardian can be appointed. I will expect Mr. Blake to file a report on his first home visit to the O'Connells no more than one week from today. One more thing, Mrs. O'Connell. You will need to give a statement on record as to whom this child's mother might be. Child abandonment, even in cases that turn out well for the child, must be followed up."

Hannah shook her head, reluctant, not wanting to name anyone, put anyone in the position of being tracked down, especially the girl who was Ellie's mother. "It could be anybody. I don't know for certain—"

"Give it some thought. I'm sure you can at least give the officers a place to begin their search. After all, it would be a show of good faith if you were to help us. A small price to pay in baby Ellie's best interests. Court is dismissed." The judge banged her gavel, swept up her papers and disappeared out the side door in a whirl of black robes.

Hannah stared, stunned, afraid to breathe for fear the judge would charge back in, change her mind. It was over. Ellie was hers. At least for now. And as for helping the authorities find Ellie's mother, she'd do the bare minimum, protect the girl as much as she could, while still seeming to cooperate with the courts. She'd spent every spare minute trying to guess which of Becca's friends might have given birth to the baby who was fast stealing her heart. Yet all she could manage to come up with was a list of girls she was certain weren't involved. She could give the authorities the names of those girls. Girls like Jana and Rachel, who would be taking off for foreign study sometime in the next week or so. Megan Flanders and Katie Long, whom she'd seen a dozen times this year, thin as rails and more giggly than ever. Josie's daughter Andrea was a safe bet, too. Maybe it was a little dishonest to try to protect whoever had given birth to Ellie, but she would have done far worse out of empathy for the girl who had put Ellie in her arms.

It seemed impossible, the whole hearing was over so fast. But she had little doubt as to how that had happened. It had been settled the moment Tony had waved his hand like a magic wand, swept all the judge's reservations out of the way because he still, after twenty-eight years, believed in her.

Tears welled up, trickled down her cheeks as she rose with Ellie cradled in her arms. "Tony," she breathed, letting her heart show in her eyes. "Thank you. Thank you so much. We'll take good care of her."

"I know that. I'm glad for you, Hannah. Truly." Then why was there a touch of wistfulness in his eyes? He cleared his throat, glanced at Sam. "Take good care of them, O'Connell. You're a very lucky man."

"Right." Sam looked confused, a little bit hurt. And yes, a part of her felt a little guilty. Maybe she hadn't ever mentioned Tony, but the bottom line was Tony had been out of her life for years before she'd met Sam. There wasn't some law that she had had to tell Sam everything, was there? Maybe not. But maybe the problem was that she'd let him believe that she had. . . .

Seemingly oblivious, Tony bent over her, kissed her cheek. The kiss of an old friend. A gesture of congratulations. So warm, so easy, his lips touching her skin for just an instant. Long enough for her to feel it to her toes.

Her face burned.

"Take care of our baby, Hannah," Tony winked, flashing her a conspirator's smile. "I can't wait to see your grandma's house again."

"Whenever you want to come. We'll be there."

"O'Connell?" Tony offered his hand to Sam. Sam took it, but his expression said he'd rather not.

Resentment knotted in Hannah's chest. Couldn't he even pretend to be glad she'd gotten to keep Ellie? Couldn't he be just a little bit grateful Tony had made it happen?

Or was it possible that whatever Sam had said about

supporting Hannah in this custody hearing, all along he'd been secretly hoping that the judge would take Ellie away from her?

Josie drew near. "Hannah, I'm so glad it's settled. I hope I did the right thing asking Blake to help out."

"Perfect." Hannah said absolutely. "Thank you."

"Congratulations, Mama," Tom said, giving her a quick hug, the big cop's brow creased with confusion as he glanced from her face to Sam's. "I hope this little one brings you much joy."

But there wasn't much joyful about Sam's face. And hurt at his reaction was gradually killing at least some of Hannah's pleasure.

"You guys want to go out for pizza to celebrate?" Tom asked. "We could pick the kids up at the sitter's."

Sam shook his head. "I've got to work. I've got two days now to catch up on the Main Street project."

He was going back to work already? Hannah realized, stung. She'd wanted things to be different. Hoped they could take a little time, both enjoy Ellie. Share pleasure that they'd won. But obviously he had something else in mind. Hiding out as he had so often down at the office. It seemed some things hadn't changed since Becca was little, after all. Well, she wouldn't let it ruin things, Hannah resolved determinedly. She and Ellie would go home, be just fine.

Then why was it she felt like crying?

Her chest hurt as she walked through the court-house, out into the sunshine. Sam was preoccupied as he opened the car door for her, silent as she fastened Ellie into her infant car seat. Hannah climbed into the passenger's side, resentment stinging in her veins, part anger at him, part guilt because of secrets she'd kept.

She managed not to speak until they were almost home. "Aren't you going to say anything?"

"Strange. We've been married twenty-two years. All that time, you never mentioned this guy."

"I didn't think it was important. Sam, can't I just be glad I get to keep Ellie? I mean, I wouldn't want you to go to any trouble. Work up any enthusiasm or anything."

"Like your—what did he call himself? Your knight in shining armor?"

"He didn't call himself *my* knight in shining armor. He called himself Ellie's knight in shining armor. And as it turned out, he was. I'm just grateful Josie got Tony to help us, or we might have lost Ellie."

"I know that. It's just—maybe I'm out of line, Hannah. But the way Blake looked at you, it made me—" He hesitated, flushed dark red, embarrassed, confused. Hannah could see him search for a way to explain it. "Hell, I don't know." He surrendered at last.

"I think you do. Finish what you have to say."

"It made me edgy."

"Sam, you're my husband." She tried to dismiss his words. For once, Sam wouldn't let her back away from what he was trying to say. He glanced over at her, his face stark, vulnerable.

"We haven't slept together in over five months."

Hannah's cheeks burned, she turned her face away from him. "I've been sick. You know that."

"Yeah, I know. How you draw away when I try to touch you. How busy you get the moment I walk into a room."

She hated the hurt in his voice, the sense of rejection, as if every time she'd turned away from him, she'd taken a piece of his self-confidence with her, leaving him uncertain, questioning himself, trying to figure out what had opened this chasm between them. And yet, hadn't she lost herself as well? Didn't she lie in bed in the dark, crying sometimes, trying to figure out how she'd ended up alone?

"Sam, there's nothing for you to worry about."

"We barely even touch each other. We sleep in different rooms. Now, Ellie will always be there."

Hannah bristled. "Sam, you can't blame any of this on Ellie."

"I don't. But I know you, Hannah," he said, sadly. "I know what kind of mother you are. I want so much to reach you, get close to you. But now—all you'll see is Ellie. All you'll think about is Ellie."

"She's a baby! Abandoned. Helpless. Of course I have to think about her! You said it was all right for me to keep her." She wanted him to get angry. It would have been easier. Instead, pain, loss, months of dread etched deep lines in his face.

"Would it have mattered if I'd said no?" he asked softly. "Whatever barriers there are between us would only have gotten higher, wider. Either way, I lose."

It was true. Hannah stiffened, wishing she couldn't see it so clearly. "I don't want you to . . . don't want to . . ." To what? Upset him? Hurt him? Make him feel left out? From his expression he already felt that and more. Raw, stung, she shifted at least some of the responsibility for the way things were between them back on his shoulders. "Sam, this baby—she means so much to me. If you could just try a little. Hold her. Talk to her."

"Like Tony Blake? Sweep her up as if she were a kitten in a box by the side of the road? Taking a stranger's baby into your home is a little more serious than that, don't you think?"

"It doesn't have to be that complicated. It's just for a little while."

"That's where we disagree. You can't take on a child

'for a little while.' They love you, depend on you. And you can fail them. Ellie doesn't need a baby-sitter, Hannah. She needs a home. And I know what it feels like when a kid is damned sure that's what he's got—a safe place to belong forever—and then has it ripped out from under him."

"Sam—"

"It's serious, Hannah. It will affect this little girl's life forever. We're making a promise to her, by taking her in, and I don't take that promise lightly, even if people like Blake see it as no big deal."

"People who've worked in the court systems have to seek temporary custody for kids all the time. They have to have a different perspective. Tony Blake is just doing his job, that's all," Hannah insisted, and yet she had always had an uncanny ability to put herself in other peoples' places.

What would it feel like if their positions had been reversed? a voice inside her whispered. If a beautiful, successful woman had shown up in Tony's stead? Had laughed with Sam, kissed Sam's cheeks, her eyes full of secrets Hannah didn't know? She felt sick to her stomach, even thinking about the scenario.

She wanted to soothe him, ease the tight lines of worry creasing his face. And yet, wouldn't the real truth only make Sam more tense? Wasn't it even possible that if he knew the truth, he'd change his mind about keeping Ellie? Not want Tony in the house? In her life? Even in an official capacity as the baby's guardian ad litem?

"Sam, you don't have to worry about Tony," she hedged. "He's just a friend from way back in high school."

"Just a friend," Sam echoed, but she knew he wasn't convinced. She'd have told him about a "friend" a long time ago. And her cheeks wouldn't have burned when she did so.

If I told you the truth now it would only hurt you, Hannah wanted to explain. *And I've hurt you so much these past months already. There is just no way I can tell you Tony was my first kiss, my first date, the first boy who'd ever shown the least bit of interest in the painfully shy girl with the dark hair who always sat at the back of the class.*

The words rolled through her, and yet she didn't say them. She couldn't say them. Because there were other things about Tony she didn't dare tell.

The stormy afternoon they'd spent in the abandoned stable behind the home Tony's retired sergeant of a father had rented. A soft old quilt her grandmother had always used for picnics. A basket with sandwiches and pop they'd planned to share at the lake where crowds of other kids would make kisses furtive, touches desperate, hidden behind trees, in the shadows, always fearing they'd be discovered. Safety checks Hannah had known even then were the only thing that kept her and Tony from getting swept away.

She couldn't tell Sam how they'd decided to have their picnic in the old barn. Not wanting to waste what little time was left before Tony would be gone. Off to the Air Force Academy, and everything he'd ever dreamed of.

While Hannah's dreams were so much simpler then, just as they were now. She'd never thought anyone like Tony would ever care for her, someone so fine, so handsome, so full of adventure. Sure, it had saddened her that he'd be leaving, and yet, even from the beginning, she'd known she could never expect to keep him.

There was only now. Only here. She'd tried her best to make that be enough. Maybe she'd gotten hurt, and badly, but she'd walked into that pain with her eyes wide open. In all these years, she'd never blamed Tony for that. Only herself. Wide-eyed innocence. Stuffed full of fairy tales and wanting so much to be loved. If only she'd known then what love really was, maybe it wouldn't have hurt so much, maybe she wouldn't have paid . . .

More than Sam could ever know. More than she'd ever dared tell him.

How could she ever explain why she'd understood Ellie's mother so well? Her pain, her panic, her guilt and desperation? Because long before she'd met Sam she'd held a baby in her arms—a baby with her mouth and hands shaped just like Tony Blake's. She'd held the baby just long enough to imprint the little one's face in her heart forever. And then she'd let her baby go.

7

HANNAH DOVE FOR THE PHONE, praying it wouldn't wake Ellie and start her crying again. Poor baby. The little one had had a long day, the tension of the court-room and Sam and Hannah's conversation afterward seeming to have penetrated deep inside her, leaving her restless, weepy, and determined not to go to sleep. But despite a will almost as formidable as Becca's had been, the baby had finally dozed off, sour faces she was making alerting Hannah like storm warnings that Ellie was still seething underneath that sleepy exterior, ready to go off at the least disturbance.

"Hello?" Hannah whispered breathlessly into the receiver, glancing over her shoulder at the baby cud-dled up in the wicker basket.

"Mom?" Becca's voice, a little wary. "Is that you?"

Pleasure washed through Hannah in spite of the strain she was under. "Hi, sweetheart," she said, stretching the cord around the corner into the kitchen where the sound of talking would be at least a little bit muffled. "Of course it's me. Who were you expecting?"

"I don't know. You sound funny, I guess. Anything wrong?"

"No. No, nothing's wrong." Hannah paused, suddenly off-balance. She hadn't even thought about what she was going to say to Becca about all that had happened in the past few days.

It was so strange. Ever since Becca had gone off to school, Hannah had spent every day holding conversations with her little girl in her head, tallying up what they were going to talk about next time, storing up things to share with her, to laugh over with her. But this whole drama involving Ellie had wiped everything else out of Hannah's head—the baby's vulnerability, the uncertainty as to what might happen to her, the old memories, old guilt, old fear of secrets being revealed hadn't left room for anything else.

She hadn't thought about how Becca would feel. But surely Becca would be pleased about the fact that there was a baby in the house. She'd always adored little ones— been a magnet for all her friends' little sisters. When Jana or Rachel or one of the others had wanted to ditch their siblings, Becca had been the one who convinced the girls to let them tag along. Sometimes, Hannah had watched her daughter walk off with a little one skipping along beside her. And she'd wondered if Becca thought almost as much as she did about the empty places at the kitchen table, the quiet of the spare bedroom where a brother or sister should have been, or the spaces left in the lilac garden that had never been filled. "Mom, I said is anything wrong? You're not talking."

"I . . . it's not that something is wrong, really," Hannah said, feeling almost as if she were about to hand over a much anticipated Christmas present. "It's just that we've had an exciting few days here."

"In Willowton?" Becca scoffed. "Don't tell me! The

ladies' club decided to add gold ribbons to evergreen swags on the Main Street Christmas decorations next year! Gasp!"

Hannah couldn't help but laugh. One of Becca's greatest gifts had always been the way she could surprise Hannah with bursts of wry humor. "Don't say that too loud," Hannah teased. "If Mrs. Middleton heard an idea that revolutionary, I'm afraid she'd have palpitations."

"Not unless she had an audience," Becca quipped. "No, really, Mom. Things have been exciting here, too." Her voice rose, eager. "I'm thinking of—well, how would you feel if . . ."

Becca hesitated in what Hannah used to call her "dramatic pause," the tool used to drum up excitement before a major revelation. Hannah smiled in indulgence, willing to wait to make her own announcement. "If what?" she prodded, knowing it was all part of the game.

"I have an opportunity to go to France," Becca burst out.

Hannah made sure she was excited enough about the opportunity to satisfy even Becca. "That sounds terrific, sweetheart."

"It's a program for kids gifted in language. They only pick one student a year. I'll get to see Notre Dame cathedral and Chartres," Becca rhapsodized at warp speed, "and on weekends I could meet with Jana and Rachel and some other kids from Eastern and bum around Europe. They're over in Vienna studying music. Did you hear Rachel beat out every violinist at the school to win first chair?"

"Did she? That's terrific." Hannah was truly glad for Rachel, prayed the triumph would give the shy girl some confidence. "How did Jana take it?"

"Probably pouted for about five minutes, but when

it came right down to it, she knew she could never keep up with Rachel."

"And Rachel's mother? She must be proud."

"What you're saying is she ought to be. But you know Mrs. Johnson. The only one she pays attention to is Mark and his rocket-scientist brain. Music's a waste of time to her."

Hannah resolved to call Margo Johnson, congratulate her on her daughter's accomplishment, do whatever she could to get the woman to realize what a treasure of a daughter she had. And a card—she'd send a card, maybe a box of homemade cookies to Rachel to congratulate her. Someone should show Rachel they were delighted after all she'd achieved.

"Anyway, Mom, about the trip," Becca said, doing her best to bring focus back to the subject at hand. "It would be so great—the three musketeers seeing the world! They've got youth hostels all over Europe that barely cost anything."

"Sounds wonderful." Hannah tried not to panic at the idea of her baby an ocean away. Becca was a bright, intelligent young woman. *She'd be fine,* Hannah reassured herself. Besides, sometimes Jana could be a little flaky, but Rachel had always been rock solid. The one among Becca's friends who had always kept things from getting out of hand if the other girls got a little drunk on freedom.

Hannah grimaced. Hadn't there been times she had wished she'd had an adventure like this trip the girls were planning when she'd still been young enough to enjoy it, free of responsibilities? Maybe it was a fact that every time she heard Becca's voice on the phone she pictured a pigtailed little waif proudly displaying a missing front tooth. But the truth was that Becca was all grown up. Independent. Ready to fly. And that's what Hannah wanted for her, wasn't it? Besides, maybe she could take the postcards Becca sent and tack them up in Ellie's room. *See, angel, this is where your big sister is—she'll be home soon to tell us all about it. . . .*

"Would you be gone for the summer? Or is it just over break?"

"It would start in June, but here's the coolest thing of all." For the first time Becca sounded a little uneasy. "I would stay on in Paris a whole year."

"All year?" Hannah's stomach plunged, the pleasant pictures of Ellie and Becca loving each other crumbling under the shock.

"Mom, I know you were counting on me being home this summer, and how much you love Christmas, and I feel terrible about not being there for you, but it's such an amazing chance I just can't miss it! My French teacher says she's never had a student with a better natural ear for French. She claims I'm perfect for the program, and this will be my only chance."

Hannah struggled not to let Becca know she felt like she'd just been kicked in the stomach. She forced her voice into its usual steady tones to answer. "Of course you can't miss it."

"I mean, I know you'll miss me. And I'll miss you. I really will. But we can celebrate all the stuff I miss once I get back home. There'll be other Christmases we can be together. But this is the only time I'll ever be able to live in France."

Even with Christmas seven months away, it was a blow. Hannah tried to get her mind around a holiday without her daughter. Christmas without Becca's face lighting up the house far brighter than any twinkling lights or rainbow colored balls glittering on the branches of the freshly-cut pine tree. "Becca, I don't know. I'll have to talk to your dad."

"He'll be okay with it. Christmas has never been his thing. It's you I'm worried about."

The sudden wistfulness in her voice touched Hannah. "Oh, sweetheart. As long as you're happy and healthy and don't completely forget your mom, I'll always be fine."

"I wouldn't even have asked, except I remember when one of your cousins visited when I was little they said something about you being gone during Christmas one year."

But she hadn't been glorying in an elite language program in France or "bumming around Europe" with a bunch of friends. She'd been alone in Aunt Mary's big house in Redmond, Oregon, too shamefully pregnant to travel back home to Iowa with them to share Christmas at the rambling, beloved farmhouse with the rest of the family.

They'd told everyone she was taking special classes at an art school out west during the seven months she was gone and was spending the holidays in Montana with a new friend she'd made. Most people hadn't questioned it. And Hannah's grandmother—Hannah had often wondered if the old woman she'd loved with all her heart had felt hurt when she'd vanished in September. Left without even saying good-bye. Her mother hadn't wanted to risk Hannah spilling her dirty little secret, especially to the grandmother Hannah had always told everything to.

Everything except that she'd gotten pregnant. Everything except that she'd had a baby. By the time her own mother had finished shaming Hannah, she'd been afraid that her grandmother would be as repulsed by her and what she'd done as Mama and Daddy had been. And that was one thing Hannah could never risk. She'd needed the haven of the white farmhouse and the gentle, wise woman there with her snowy white braid coiled around her head and the brown eyes that twinkled and saw Hannah as perfect.

No, that Christmas had been the most miserable one of Hannah's life in some ways. In others, it had been precious—one week out of seven long months when she'd actually had a bit of peace, alone, where she could touch her stomach and talk to her baby without someone glaring at her. Where she could rock in the chair that looked out over the mountains, sing the only lullabies her baby would ever hear in her mama's voice. Off-key, so young and faint and uncertain, those long ago nursery songs, and yet so full of love.

"Mom, I won't stay on in France for the internship if you don't want me to. Really." Becca's voice on the other end of the line startled Hannah, bringing her back to the familiar kitchen with its gingham walls and scarred, scrubbed oak table, the phone with its stretched-out cord in her hand. "I'm sure my teacher could pick someone else."

"I think it would be wonderful for you, baby," Hannah said. "I'm sure Daddy will, too."

"Really?" Becca exclaimed. "Do you really think so? Could you let me know for sure soon? I've got to let Madame du Ville know."

"Gotcha." Hannah refused to sigh. She'd known it wouldn't be long before Becca's summers and holidays filled up with things far away from Willowton. But she'd thought she'd at least have her home this summer, a little more time to cherish.

"Okay," Becca said, "so now that I've dropped my bombshell, how about telling me what's up back home that's supposed to be so exciting. Revolutionizing the Christmas decorations for next year is out, so tell me, what is it? Can't wait to hear what you call excitement back there, Mom."

Hannah hated to admit to herself that at least a little of the glitter had faded when she thought about telling Becca about the baby. Faded along with the pictures she'd been spinning in her head of when Christmas came next year—a new stocking on the mantel along with the three that had hung there for so long—buying toys again and wrapping them with Becca late into the night. Picking out Christmas outfits for both the girls and spending long, wintry days building Ellie's first snowman.

But those were Hannah's dreams, not Becca's. There might be other Christmases with Ellie there—at least, she hoped so. Christmases the baby would remember. Times when Becca and the baby could get to know each other, come to love each other. Times Hannah and Sam and Becca and Ellie could all become a family.

Hannah pushed back her own disappointment, kept her voice bright, cheerful. "Well, actually, I found something in the backyard yesterday."

"Don't tell me! A baby raccoon like that one we raised the summer I was nine? Oh, Lord, it was so cute! Remember how its hands held the bottle just like a baby?"

"Just like a baby. Well, um, what I found—it's too little to hold the bottle on its own yet, but—" Hannah paused, taking a lesson in drama from her daughter. "Becca, when I went out back yesterday, I found a baby in a basket."

"A baby?" Becca echoed, bewildered. "A baby what?"

"*A baby* baby. A little girl."

"One of the neighbor kids ditching their little sister so they could play a quick game of kick the can? Man, will they be in trouble if their mom finds out."

"No, honey. Somebody abandoned the baby back there. Left her for me to find."

Silence. Dead silence. Hannah waited to let what she'd said sink in. Of course it would take Becca a moment to get her bearings, get her mind around what had happened. No matter how well things had turned out, with Ellie coming into their lives to love, there was no way to get around the hard, painful fact that the baby had been deserted there, for whatever small time, left all alone.

"Mom, you . . . you've got to be kidding."

"No. Part of me wishes I was." Maybe that was a little bit of a lie. And yet, there was truth to it, too. She wished Ellie's mother had had the courage to come to her, to confide in her, instead of being so scared she'd left nothing but that painfully written note with her newborn daughter.

"The baby is fine, Becca, fine." Hannah tried to reassure her. "I took her straight to Dr. Meyers, and he checked her over."

"You took her to the doctor? But you don't even know who she belongs to!"

Hannah shook herself—Becca's reaction was nothing like she'd imagined. Hannah hesitated, wondering just how much she should really tell Becca, but knew Becca deserved the whole truth. Even if it wasn't the easiest thing to hear.

"You're right," Hannah admitted. "I don't know exactly who Ellie's mother is. But I do know this. Whoever left baby Ellie, left her at the farmhouse on purpose, because she knew me. Knew us."

"Who . . . who did it?"

Hannah hated the sudden vulnerability in Becca's voice. "I don't know. One of your friends, maybe. The kids who used to hang out here."

"No way," Becca cried, horrified. "None of my friends would do anything so . . . so terrible! I know them, Mom!"

Like she knew her own mother? "Sweetheart, the

baby's mother left a note. She said she'd always wished I was her mother."

"Yeah, her and half of Willowton! All my friends loved you! Every time I had a slumber party, they'd go up and sit on your bed and talk."

Hannah remembered. It had been one of the happiest times she could ever remember, seeing the trust in the kids' faces, hearing their laughter, their hopes, their dreams. Listening to their troubles. They'd trusted her so much. She only wished Ellie's mother had trusted her enough to tell her she was pregnant, let Hannah help her, before the girl felt forced to abandon her child and run. Maybe she could have helped the girl, told her . . . told her she wasn't the only one who had made a mistake, the only one who had paid . . .

"Everyone knows you're a great mom," Becca insisted. "It wouldn't have had to be one of my friends."

Empathy filled Hannah and she berated herself for not realizing how this would affect her daughter—that maybe someone she knew, someone she trusted, someone she believed in had left little Ellie in the basket alone. But it wouldn't help anything to keep things secret in an effort to shield Becca. Becca deserved the whole truth. The sooner she had it, the sooner she could put it to rest and join in the delight Hannah felt whenever she looked down into Ellie's fairy-child face.

"She named the baby after your great-grandmother."

"The granny you loved so much?"

"Yes. Becca, only your friends would know that name, how much your great-grandmother meant to me. Baby Ellie's mother did."

Hannah could hear Becca thinking furiously, trying so hard to sort it all out. "Mom, I don't understand.

How—I mean, if you're pregnant, you can hardly hide it, can you? Besides, all my friends are off at college. Really, I don't think it could be any of them."

Hannah wished she could agree with Becca, dash away the doubts she could hear clinging to her daughter's voice. And yet, there were other issues as well—threats Ellie's mother could be facing all alone. Even if Becca was upset right now, wasn't it likely Ellie's mother was in a far worse position? One far more dangerous health-wise, a far more precarious position legally, not to mention what the girl must be going through emotionally after enduring pregnancy and childbirth all alone and giving her baby away. Hannah had to ask a few questions of her own.

"Becca, if you *can* think of anyone who might have gotten herself backed into a corner, please tell me. Anyone who's been acting strange. Different."

"Nobody, Mom."

"Okay. Just keep your eyes open. I want to help her if I can find out who she is. Make sure she's all right. I'm sure she didn't see a doctor. And . . ." Hannah hesitated. "I think the police are going to be looking for her."

"You mean they're going to arrest her?"

"I don't think so. But they have to try to find her, get her to give up custody so the baby can be adopted by someone who can love her and take care of her, give her a home."

"Oh. Do you think they'll find somebody nice?"

Now came the good news, Hannah thought, praying that it would help to dash away at least some of the gloom that had fallen over her daughter. "I'm as sure as I can be. You see, we get to keep the baby, at least for now—and if we can make it happen, maybe forever—"

"Maybe forever what?"

"Daddy and I are going to keep her."

Hannah didn't know what to expect. Becca had had a shock, it was true. But surely, she'd feel at least a little bit of happiness? For the baby who had found a home? For Hannah, and for Becca herself?

"You and Daddy? Keep it?" Becca stammered.

Hannah tried not to feel hurt. "She has a name. Ellie."

"I don't care if she's named Genghis Khan!" Becca cried. "You can't just—I mean, you're too old!"

"I'm hardly ready for the geriatric ward, honey."

"I know, but you can't take care of a baby! You've been sick! You need rest! Daddy said that the doctors told you that you had to take it easy to get well."

"Don't worry, Becca. Ellie's better than any medicine they can give me. It makes me happy to have a baby around again."

"But new babies are tons of work! You can't just—"

"I can 'just.' I have." Hannah tried to keep disappointment over Becca's reaction out of her voice.

"What does Daddy say?" Becca challenged.

Hannah bristled. Becca was talking as if *Hannah* were the child, reckless, irresponsible, as if she were overreaching boundaries someone else had set.

True, Becca had surprised her by being less than enthusiastic, demanding to know about Sam's reaction to what had happened. Hannah wondered if the girl had any idea she'd hit a sore spot. But then, that was one thing Hannah had learned early about parenting—when it came to "sore spots," most kids had perfect aim.

"Daddy can't be happy about this," Becca insisted. "I mean, he was talking all summer about stuff the two of you were going to be doing together. Stuff you can't do with a baby hanging around."

So Sam had talked to Becca about plans? He hadn't said much to Hannah. "Daddy's okay with it," Hannah hedged. *About as okay as Becca seemed*, she thought. But the two of them were both just off-balance because of the surprise of it all. Given time, they'd get used to things. Come to love Ellie the way that Hannah did. Wouldn't they?

What if you're wrong? a voice inside her whispered. *What if they resent Ellie—and you?* She drove the thought out of her mind, tried to hold tight to her patience.

"Becca, I know this has to seem strange to you," Hannah began in a carefully measured voice, "but nothing is certain. Dad and I have custody of Ellie temporarily. But things could change at any time. Ellie's mother could come and want her back."

"Well, she can't have her back!"

Hannah's heart wrenched at the confusion in her daughter's voice, Becca torn, not wanting the baby to overstress her mother, not wanting to give a helpless baby back to someone Hannah could tell Becca thought was some kind of monster.

"You can't just . . . just have a baby and dump her in somebody's yard and then change your mind like . . . like the baby was a sweater you're not sure fits right!" Becca insisted.

"You know it wouldn't be like that. Whoever Ellie's mother is, she's got feelings, fears, she's hurting and confused right now. Needs compassion from us, not judgment."

"Mom, think that if you want, but I can't," Becca said stiffly. "I don't want to know who did this. I don't want to."

"Why not?"

"Because once I knew, I'd never be able to feel the same way about them again."

Hannah winced at Becca's instinctive recoiling from the girl who had given birth to Ellie. It sickened Becca, disgusted her, frightened her. Horrified her. The whole thing was beyond Becca's comprehension—getting pregnant, trying to hide it, being so desperate you gave your baby away.

Maybe Becca was a little naïve. Maybe she hadn't seen how capricious and unfair life could be, how you could be skipping merrily down a path one moment, and suddenly have the ground fall away underneath your feet, plunging you down to a place you never expected to be.

But one thing Hannah knew for certain. Becca was telling the truth. She would never be able to feel the same way about her friend. She wouldn't see her own mother the same way either if she ever learned the truth. Never be able to look at either one of them without seeing the dark, incomprehensible things they'd done, the impossible choices made. The terrible failure. One mistake. One dangerous choice. One night when they weren't good, weren't careful, weren't perfect. Oh, God, to be innocent enough not to understand how easy it was to slip and fall.

"Do you want me to tell you what the baby looks like?" Hannah asked. "I could send you a picture."

"No, thanks." Something had died in Becca's voice. The elation, the excitement, the anticipation she'd felt when she'd told Hannah about the trip to Europe. "I guess I'll see her soon enough. When I come home for break, she'll be there."

"Probably." Hannah hated the awkward silence falling between them. In all the years she and Becca had been together, there had only rarely been silence—laughter, sometimes arguing, constant chatter. But never this crippling silence.

Hannah searched for a way to fill it, but her mind went blank, her thoughts washed away by a vague sense of hurt and disappointment and confusion. She'd expected Sam's reluctance about keeping Ellie. Hadn't really expected anything different from him. But from Becca—from Becca she'd hoped for so much more.

"Mom?"

Hannah started at the sound of her voice. "What, Becca?"

"I've got to go. I've got a study group in fifteen minutes."

"Okay. Hope it goes well."

"Terrific," Becca said, making an effort to keep her voice light.

But Hannah knew the girl would be lucky if she could spell her own name tonight, let alone stuff her brain full of Hinduism. She could only hope Becca could concentrate.

"Becca, I love you. You know that, don't you?"

"Yeah, Mom." She didn't sound nearly certain enough to make Hannah feel any better.

"I know, once you come home and meet her, you're going to love Ellie, too."

"Yeah. Is Daddy home? Can I talk to him?"

Hannah ached. So much for being in a hurry to get off the phone. Obviously Becca just didn't want to talk to her anymore. Becca so rarely asked for Sam. But this time, Hannah could hear that Becca needed him—the reassurance, the calm. It hurt Hannah to sense her daughter turning away from her for comfort.

"Daddy's working late tonight. He has a bid due tomorrow morning."

"Oh. Tell him—tell him hi."

"I will."

"Could you have him call me? I just—I need to hear his voice."

Hannah agreed, knowing Becca could never guess just how much doing so stung her heart. Always it had been Hannah she reached for. Hannah she needed to listen. Hannah, who had held her and cuddled her and made her feel better, made her feel like she was just as she was—the most marvelous, wonderful, talented, loving girl who had ever been born.

"I've got to run, Mom. I'm going to be late," Becca insisted. Hannah held the phone long minutes after it went dead, second-guessing herself. Had she done the right thing, telling Becca about the baby? She couldn't keep Ellie a secret. Let her come home and then spring Ellie on her.

The way you sprung the baby on Sam?

She hung up the phone, then crept into the room where Ellie slept, quiet at last, peaceful. Ellie sucked on nothing at all, her dark lashes fanned on porcelain doll cheeks. Hannah breathed in the scent of her—baby shampoo and Ivory soap flakes, baby powder and lotion smoothed ever so gently over chubby arms and legs after the sponge bath Hannah had given her on the counter beside the kitchen sink.

Love welled up in her heart until it felt like it would burst. How could she make Becca and Sam understand what Ellie meant to her? That somehow, mothering Ellie made the pain of her hysterectomy bearable again? All her nagging doubts about her femininity quiet? That with Ellie, she knew who she was, what to expect of herself? The scar was still there, a low, red arc against the white of her skin. But with Ellie, she could still be the Hannah she'd been before the doctor had made the incision.

She couldn't ever remember wanting anything except another baby. Had never told anyone, especially Sam or Becca, how her arms had ached, how her heart had yearned, how often she'd dreamed . . .

Hannah touched a fingertip to Ellie's plump cheek, marveling at how soft, how sweet, how perfect she was.

It was true, Hannah thought, she regretted the confusion in Becca's voice, the vague hurt. And Sam—his anger, his pain. She would do anything to wipe it away. Anything except give up the only thing she'd ever wanted, the only thing she'd ever asked for herself.

They'd love Ellie as much as she did, she reassured herself. She just had to give them time.

Time . . .

I know what kind of mother you are, Hannah, she could hear the pain echoing in Sam's voice. *You won't see anything but Ellie. . . .*

The words rang too true not to sting. She remembered all too well times with Becca when she'd caught him watching from the doorway or a place across the room. Just watching. Had he been waiting all those times just for her to invite him in?

Maybe this time she would.

If Sam would give her a chance. He'd been hurt when he'd driven off after they'd left the courthouse. Confused. He'd sensed that something was wrong, known she was holding something back from him. Secrets. She'd always known how much he hated them. Dreaded them. One more legacy of his mother's walking away. Worst of all, she couldn't set things right this time. Tell him the truth . . .

With Tony Blake as Ellie's legal guardian? Tony coming to the house, Tony overseeing Ellie's custody— Hannah's first love, the man who had fathered a child she'd never mentioned to Sam. Tony, who had left her alone to suffer the silent shame of what they'd done.

No. It was too late to tell Sam the truth of all that now. If she did, he'd never tolerate Tony breezing in and out of their lives, and, God help her, Hannah wouldn't be able to blame him.

Maybe it was possible that Sam could learn to love

Ellie given time. Maybe they could work on the problems they'd been having in their marriage. Maybe they could manage to find each other again. But not if Sam ever found out the truth.

But he wouldn't find out, she told herself. Her secret was safe, wasn't it? No one had guessed it in all these years. Because no one in Willowton had known. Her mother had seen to that.

But now there's someone else in Willowton who knows, Hannah realized with a jolt. *Tony . . .*

She wrapped her arms tight around her middle as if to hide—from whom? Tony? Sam? Or herself?

There's nothing to worry about, she tried to soothe herself. Tony would hardly run around announcing they'd had a child together. Especially since he'd left her alone to deal with the consequences of what they'd done. It was hardly something he'd be proud of.

Sure, it would be a little nerve-wracking for a while, but Tony would be in and out of their lives in no time. He had no reason to tell her secret. Truth was, he had more reason to hide it than she did since he'd deserted her. Even as a teenager, Tony had always had a fierce sense of pride.

Besides, he'd probably forgotten anything had happened. Forgotten the letter she'd written him. Forgotten how determined she'd been not to ruin his life. Forgotten how certain she'd once been that she loved him.

She stared down at Ellie and tried to stop her hands from shaking. *It had all been a long time ago,* she told herself again. It couldn't hurt her anymore.

Or had her secret just been lurking in the shadows, waiting to threaten everything she loved?

8

Tony Blake stood at the window, listening to the low wail of the train whistle a few hundred yards from the house. Every night he'd spent in this room during the year he'd lived in Willowton, he'd lain awake, listening to the railway cars roar by, racing off to destinations far away, places he'd never seen, places he hadn't even heard of. Places he couldn't wait to charge off to explore.

Restless—damn, he'd been restless back then. Felt buried alive in the middle of nowhere. He'd resented his father for having the rotten manners to get injured on the job. As if "Saigon Sarge" had dragged the family away from the series of air force bases that had always been home, planning the whole thing on purpose just to ruin Tony's life. Of course Tony knew better now. A few decades of experience and a few mistakes of his own to regret had left him ashamed of his attitude as a kid. Now, he could imagine what it must have been like for his father. The old man had taken a solid whack to the head, and lost his sense of equilibrium forever.

The larger than life hero who had flown more successful missions in 'Nam than any other pilot, hadn't even been able to make it across a room without having to grab the back of a chair or the surface of a table so he wouldn't fall.

The disability wouldn't have been easy for anyone, but for a legend—well, it had been damned hard to come crashing into the truth at such a late date—discover that you weren't invincible after all. Especially when you had a cocky teenaged son who was determined to set the world on fire, and had the talent, the strength and the intelligence to do it.

But there was no excuse for the mess Sarge had left his wife in. A tiny house with a mortgage, no insurance, no savings, and no way to take care of herself once he was gone. If it hadn't been for Tony, she would have been out on the street.

And now, Tony had yet another challenge to face—making sure his mother wasn't alone again, if something else happened. The doctor had made it clear his mother would never fully recover.

He paced to the kitchen table where his mother had laid out the day's mail for him. A half-dozen thick envelopes stamped with the logo of his law firm. Questions about clients he'd handled for years, no doubt. Pleas that he regain his sanity and let someone else make the necessary arrangements for his mother so he could come back where he belonged. The corner office with windows looking out on Lake Michigan. A polished mahogany desk wide enough to play ice hockey on. Bonus checks that could feed a third-world country for a year.

But it wasn't as easy as his partner thought to find nursing help in a town like Willowton, and his mother deserved to live out the rest of her years in this house she loved, after being dragged all over the world most of her life.

Tony crossed to the bookshelf where his mother had saved all his stuff from high school. Sports trophies, yearbooks, the framed picture he'd sent her after basic training. A kid with jet fuel in his blood, just waiting for his chance to get behind the controls of a plane and show everybody what he was made of.

She'd kept it all there during those long years he'd been too busy to come visit.

It had been decades since he'd come to Willowton. Almost as long since he'd thought of Hannah. She'd vanished the minute she was off his radar screen, like every other girl he'd known back then. And yet, now that he'd seen her again he was surprised at how easily he'd put her out of his mind. Truth was, she'd never been much like his usual fare in women. And the difference had been intriguing then and, he was astonished to realize, now.

Tony pulled out his senior yearbook, opened it up to pages stuffed with memorabilia his mother had kept. His graduation announcement, the newspaper clipping that he'd gotten into the Air Force Academy. Big news for a town the size of Willowton. And pictures, a handful of pictures from the senior prom. Hannah, the corsage of daisies he'd gotten her tied around her wrist with a ribbon that matched her dress.

Hannah smiled up at him in the picture as if he already were everything he wanted to be—something fine and strong and brave.

In the years since then, he'd managed to charge to the altar three times. He'd succeeded in saddling himself with paying enough alimony to empty the safe of a small bank. But he could never remember any other woman looking at him the way Hannah had in that photograph. He wouldn't have even believed that kind of adoration was possible if he hadn't had the proof in his hand.

"Anthony?"

His mother's voice, frail, reedy with age, but so full of pleasure at his presence that it gave him a twinge. She'd been so touched when he'd come home. Sometimes her gratitude made him feel like a heel.

"Hi, Mom."

He wished she would go back to sleep, leave him with his memories. He didn't like anyone to see him when he was off-balance. But he heard the sound of her fuzzy slippers shuffling along the hallway toward him.

"Is one of your cases troubling you?" she asked. Tony looked into her wrinkled face, remembering how pretty she'd once been. Before the Sarge's bitterness over the accident had sucked the life out of her, turned her old before her time.

A case *troubling* him? Not exactly.

"As a matter of fact, I ran into someone I used to know today," Tony said as his mother sat down at the table. "Hannah Townsend."

"It's Hannah O' Connell now," his mother corrected.

No one needed to remind him of that, Tony thought. Hannah's husband had made that point perfectly clear.

"Where did you see her?" his mother asked.

"The courthouse."

"Hannah? At the courthouse?" His mother marveled. "What can that poor child have done to land there?"

"She and her husband wanted custody of an abandoned baby."

His mother's shoulders sagged in relief. "Ah, that sounds like something she would do. Hannah always was a nice girl. You should have married her when you had the chance."

He hated to admit it, but maybe his mother was right.

"Oh, well. Too late now." His mother shook her head. "She's got that wonderful husband of hers and a beautiful daughter."

But not *his* daughter, Tony knew. Considering Becca O'Connell's age, the timing was years off. Tony looked at his mother, knew she was seeing a parade of grandchildren in her mind. Children she thought had never existed.

What would she say if he ever told her the truth? That there was a child wandering around out there somewhere with Hannah's eyes and his face?

He'd put it in the back of his mind over the years, had done his best to forget the pregnancy had ever happened. But after seeing Hannah again, he had to admit, he was curious. What had happened to the baby he and Hannah had made together?

Tony closed his eyes, remembering the scene in the courtroom earlier that day. Hannah, her eyes bright and anxious, her hair flowing down her shoulders, her slender body and sweet, soft breasts. Breasts he'd touched when he was too young to appreciate them, eyes that shone with a rare quality he'd been too stupid to understand. A treasure. That was what Hannah had always been. He wondered if her jerk of a husband realized it.

One thing Tony knew for certain was that Sam O'Connell hadn't recognized his name when the judge first announced it in the courtroom. O'Connell had been wary, yes, but not with the rage Hannah's husband would have shown if he'd known the history that lay between Tony and Hannah.

That could only lead to one conclusion.

She hadn't told O'Connell that Tony was the father of the baby she'd had in high school. Tony wondered why. Didn't she trust her husband enough to share that pain? Or was O'Connell the kind of man who would never forgive his wife for sleeping with another man?

Whatever the reason for her silence, it only meant one thing. Hannah—the most honest and transparent person Tony had ever met—was hiding things from her husband. Maybe the O'Connells' marriage wasn't quite so perfect, after all. Tony remembered Sam O'Connell's face—so wary, uncertain, his eyes haunted with the expression of a man who wasn't sure of his wife. Hadn't anyone in this one-horse town warned the man it was dangerous to let someone else smell blood?

Tony chuckled. He'd left Willowton, moved to the big city, become so wealthy and successful half the men in the law practice would have killed to be him. He'd seen the world, learned how it felt to have real power and yet, none of it had satisfied the gnawing of dissatisfaction in his belly. He'd been looking for something ever since he'd left this down-at-the-heels town. Wouldn't it be funny if what he'd been searching for all this time was the girl he'd left behind?

Sam swore at the blueprint spread across his desk, the familiar lines and dimensions as indecipherable to him tonight as a NASA flight plan. He'd given up using his calculator to try to figure the bid on the new high school gym hours ago, resorting to pencil and paper in an effort to try to force himself to focus. But the mound of crumpled papers filling the wastebasket in the corner stood silent witness to the fact that his strategy had failed miserably.

From the time he'd been a kid he'd buried himself in

action to distract himself from things that preyed on his mind. Football, baseball, odd jobs whenever he could find them and making people laugh—he'd immersed himself in anything he could think of to show the world that he was nothing like his old man, to prove that his mother had made a mistake the day that she left him behind.

He'd blocked out all the ugly places inside him, filled them up with accomplishments he could take pride in, point to and say he was more than the poor kid whose father was a drunken failure. More than the kid whose mother threw him away.

But tonight work didn't numb him at all.

Hannah was hiding something from him.

Secrets—they'd always terrified him—that part of him that was still seven years old, standing alone in the kitchen, his mother's farewell note in his hand. He'd told himself then he should have known something was wrong that morning, should have seen it, been able to do something to stop her from abandoning him. He'd sworn to himself he'd never get caught by surprise that way again. He'd tried not to let anyone guess how sensing secrets in people he loved had terrified him ever since. Time bombs ticking underneath the surface of familiar smiles. Familiar words hiding disaster. *Don't forget to brush your teeth, Sammy. Here's your lunch—peanut butter and jelly. Kiss your sister good-bye. . . .*

He just hadn't known it was going to be the last time. He'd never seen Trisha or his mother again. Tried to forget they had ever existed.

And now, Hannah was hiding things, secrets whispering from her eyes. Alarm bells jangled in his gut, that intuition he'd developed over the years that had warned him when his old man was about to fold and run, or come home drunk, or disappear for a few days while he drank up his paycheck.

Something was threatening him, threatening her. Something—or was it some*one*.

He kept seeing Hannah's face when she first saw Anthony Blake. Kept remembering the way she averted her eyes, hid herself away between irritation and defensiveness and insisting whatever lay between her and the big city lawyer didn't matter, wasn't important.

But it damn well *did* matter when another man made that shy color rise in Hannah's cheeks, her face showing embarrassed pleasure at the attention someone was paying her. It had charmed Sam as a young man—that sweet blush, seeing her so flustered, so delighted, her emotions not hidden behind a blasé façade so many other girls showed to the world.

He'd loved the fact that he could rattle her so easily, loved to tease her, touch her, tell her she was beautiful and do everything in his power to make her believe it. But most of all, he'd loved believing he was the first man to realize what a treasure she was. Her blushes, her smiles, her shy laughter belonging only to him.

Sam shoved to his feet, paced to the window that opened out onto the rest of the office. The other desks were empty now, the rest of his staff gone hours ago. Fresh coffee filled the office with its rich smell, the pot brewed by his office manager before she'd left. *A few cups of this will keep you on track, boss*, Sandra Kinnon had said. *Not that you need much help—oh, king of concentration.*

It was going to be a long night, he'd told her. She'd figured it was because he wanted to get the bid in the mail by morning. He knew it was something far different.

He couldn't go home. Couldn't work. Couldn't sort

out the churning uncertainty Tony Blake had stirred in him.

Sam still chafed at the way the man had breezed in, touching Hannah, smiling at her, swooping up the baby and cutting through the legal tangles to give Hannah what she'd wanted most. Blake had won her gratitude. Made her eyes shine the way Sam had wanted to so badly in spite of his doubts about taking Ellie in.

The phone rang, startling Sam. He glanced at the clock—well past midnight. Who would call down here? Hannah. It had to be Hannah. Oh, God, was she calling because something was wrong? Or was she calling to ask him to come home? Wanting to make up? She'd always hated it those rare times they fought.

Sam grabbed the phone, wanting so badly to hear her voice. "Hello?"

"Daddy?"

Sam's fingers tightened on the receiver. "Becca? Is that you?"

"Yeah. Mom said you were working late."

Sam shook his head, confused, worried. "Is something wrong, honey?"

"No. I just wanted to talk to you. Are you busy?"

Just wanted to talk to him? Sam had gotten used to getting his messages from his daughter through Hannah a long time ago. Becca sends you a kiss. Becca got an A on her history exam. Becca's roommate accidentally erased her homework disc.

"I'm never too busy for you, sweetheart." And he never had been. He just wasn't used to her needing him. "So, how's school?"

"I've got a chance to study in France next year if you and Mom say I can."

"That would be great! I'm sure we can work something out. Send us the information. Mom and I will talk it over. But consider this as close to 'yes' as it gets." Sam expected jubilation. He got something far more subdued.

"Great, Dad."

"Something's bothering you, kiddo. What is it? School?"

"School's okay. It's home I'm worried about."

"What's worrying you?"

"Dad—that baby. Mom keeping it."

The baby. Sam should have guessed. He tried hard not to sigh. "Ah, so you've heard the news then?"

"Daddy, you can't let her do it! I mean, she's not well enough! I'm scared she'll make herself sick again."

He hated the worry in Becca's voice. Hated that he didn't know what to say, how to ease her concern, soothe her, make her laugh the way Hannah always did. He was rotten at this, he thought with a twinge. But damn it, Hannah and Becca hadn't given him the chance for much practice. He groped, trying to think of the right thing to say.

"Your mom is pretty determined," he began. "She thinks she can handle it just fine."

"She always thinks she can handle things," Becca cried in disgust. "And she always takes on too much stuff! You know that as well as I do!"

Did he ever. He'd watched Hannah charge year after year through a schedule that would have made most people collapse just to look at it. He'd seen her exhausted, seen her worry, and when everything seemed hopeless, he'd seen her pull things off as if she were a magician. No wonder the world had come to expect her to be superwoman. Hell, most of the time he expected it, too.

"I know your mom tends to bite off more than she can chew," he said slowly. "But I'll be there. I'll keep an eye on her. I promise."

"Daddy, I just—it really scared me when she got sick. I mean, Mom never gets sick. I don't want to lose her."

"I don't want to lose her either," Sam admitted. "It'll be all right, baby. I promise." He hadn't dared to call her "baby" since she'd been six years old. He prayed he'd be able to make good on his promise.

"I wish—" Becca started, then stopped. "It doesn't matter. Just—could you call me? Let me know how she's doing? I'll be worried."

"Sure. I'll keep in touch."

"Don't call from home. I want to be able to talk."

"If that's what you want." Sam couldn't help feeling strange—a little guilty, a little glad. He hadn't known for sure that Becca knew the number to the office. He knew for certain most of the times she'd talked to him on the phone had been pure accident—he'd just happened to be home when she'd called to talk to Hannah.

"Guess I'd better go," Becca said.

"You take care, darlin'. I won't let anything happen to your mom."

Sam meant it. He couldn't imagine Becca's life without Hannah—her anchor, her biggest fan, her safe place to run to. He couldn't imagine his own life without Hannah to come home to.

Or maybe the problem was, he could imagine it too well. Either way, it was time to make good on his promise to Becca.

It was time to go home.

9

SAM CREPT QUIETLY into the house, the kitchen light still left on for him even though Hannah had been mad when he'd taken off hours before. Or was hurt a better way to describe it? Whichever it was, she'd had pretty good reason to be unhappy with him, he had to allow. He'd shut her out when she was bursting with excitement, gone to work when she'd been ready to celebrate winning custody of Ellie. And he'd let her know he had plenty of questions regarding Tony Blake.

But no matter how uneasy Blake made him, there was no denying the bottom line, Sam had to admit to himself. Hannah hadn't done anything wrong. It wasn't against the law for a woman to be acquainted with other men—especially if she'd become acquainted with the man *before* she'd met her husband. It wasn't her fault Sam was feeling so off-balance.

Regret nudged him as he stepped into the light's warm glow. It had always been Hannah's way of welcoming him home, a kind of signal that said she was sorry, that she wanted to smooth things over between them.

At least Sam figured he had pretty good odds that she would be willing to listen to what he had to say. He just wished he could get his apology over with now, while the words were still fresh in his head, before they got stiff and tangled up because he'd had too much time to think about them. But the house was quiet. The rest of the lights all out.

No doubt, she'd gone to bed. She'd assume that once he got into one of his stubborn fits he wouldn't show up until he got good and ready, his usual way of cooling off so she wouldn't have to deal with his darker moods.

Whatever his motives for staying away, he hardly had the right to come charging in now and wake her up because it would make things easier for him. If she could sleep, he should let her, even though he wouldn't be able to get a wink with things such a mess between them.

He started up the stairs by instinct, not bothering to turn on the lights. Moonshine lit the path he'd taken so many times, outlining the bulk of Hannah's breakfront full of antique dishes, his overstuffed chair crouching like a sleeping cat in the corner, the spindles on the stair rail gleaming soft white.

It was probably silly to hope, but he couldn't help wishing he'd find her still awake as he crested the stairs and neared the bedroom. He paused outside the half-closed door, listening for a moment, hoping she might call him in to talk.

But all was quiet except for the softest sounds of someone shifting against the sheets. Had he been wrong about the forgiveness he'd read into Hannah's signal? Was she lying there, silent, awake, shutting him out?

His spirits sank and he started toward the room

where he slept. But he'd barely taken a step when the sounds from the room got more insistent, a discontented humming sound drifting through the darkness.

"Buzzing," Hannah had always called it—that distinctive noise babies made when they were winding up to let out a wail. She'd always claimed you had a tiny window of time to distract them before they got themselves all worked up. Sam peered through the opening in the door.

Moonlight streamed over the bed where Hannah lay curled up in a ball as if trying to protect herself from the distance that had come between them. She looked so young, so vulnerable with her hair tossed across the pillow, but what yanked hardest at Sam's heart was the way her arms hugged the pillow that had once been his against her heart. What was it that had left her so troubled even in sleep? The strain between the two of them these past days? Worrying about the doubts she knew he had about keeping Ellie? Or had her conversation with Becca left her feeling raw and uncertain? Had she realized that their little girl was going to turn to him?

God knew, Hannah had the biggest heart Sam had ever known. Her ability to sweep people into its warmth, its acceptance, its overwhelming sense of healing had always amazed him, amazed anyone who knew her. How could she understand that other hearts weren't able to open so wide, make themselves so vulnerable, embrace everyone around them. How could she ever understand the stark, white-knuckled terror of letting people too close?

Just look at the price one could pay—it was etched deep in the exhaustion and pain that wreathed Hannah's face right now.

Ellie whimpered, but Hannah was so tired, she didn't even stir. Sam remembered how she'd been alert to

Becca's tiniest sound. The barest hint of a nightmare, a whisper of fever, and Hannah would glide out of bed like a homespun angel in her white nightgown, off to comfort or soothe, bring water or comfort or kisses to blow the bad dreams away. Even when Becca grew older and came in from a date, Hannah had always sensed when their daughter needed to talk or be left alone with whatever heartache or delight she'd known.

There had been times he'd started to get out of bed, but Hannah had always stopped him—he'd never been quite sure why. If she'd been worried that he needed sleep with the long hours he worked building the company. If she'd thought he couldn't handle Becca's tender feelings right. Or if she'd just loved being needed by their little girl, mothering Becca the way she wished she'd been mothered herself.

But tonight Hannah wasn't moving, and baby Ellie's patience was wearing thin.

Sam padded silently around the bed to where Ellie's basket sat. He peered down into it, half expecting the baby to let out an ear-splitting wail. The poor thing barely knew him, and when she *had* seen him he'd been withdrawn at best, growly as a bear at worst. Kids always went by gut instinct, Hannah had insisted. Even little tiny kids. And if that was true, Ellie probably saw him as her public enemy number one. He hoped that for once Hannah was wrong. Sam knew too damned well exactly what it felt like to know someone didn't want you. And he knew what it would have meant to him when he felt so lost, so rejected, just to have someone touch him so he wouldn't feel so alone.

Tentatively, he reached down, splayed his hand over the baby's little belly. Ellie kicked her arms and legs as if in acknowledgment, then went still, peering up at him with wide, searching eyes.

Quiet, she went so quiet, as if she'd been waiting all this time for him to come. Sam swallowed hard. He'd only wanted to get her settled so she wouldn't wake Hannah. Nothing more. But as he felt the birdlike flutter of Ellie's heart, the warmth of her little body, he felt fingers reach deep inside him where it hurt, peeling back a layer of something tough and hard over his heart.

Ellie reached up her chubby arms, trying to catch hold of him, and he was astonished to find himself sliding his hands underneath her, lifting her up into his arms. God, she was so tiny, light as the baby dolls Becca used to drag around the house. But she was bursting with life—seeking, nuzzling her body as close to him as she could, melting into him with a sigh of pure contentment that struck right through him. Her little fingers found a fold of his shirt and closed on it with fearsome determination for such a tiny little girl. She was holding on to him, the way Becca had turned to him just an hour ago.

And he didn't want to let her down, just as he hadn't wanted to let Becca down. He just wished he could be sure he knew he wouldn't fail them. Or fail the woman sleeping in the big iron bed.

It had been seventeen years since he'd changed a diaper, and even then he'd never done it often enough to get comfortable with the process. And he'd fixed the occasional bottle of juice once Becca got old enough. But he'd never handled milk bottles in his life. But surely a man who'd made a living building houses for twenty-two years could figure out how to construct something as simple as a baby's bottle. Couldn't he?

With one final glance at Hannah, Sam carried the baby out of the room and headed back downstairs. Reaching the kitchen, he thanked God Hannah was as

dependably organized as ever. Baby bottles and steril-
ized nipples were stacked on a clean kitchen towel on
the counter. Plastic baggie-like things to line them were
in a box right beside the bottles. A cardboard case holding cans of formula stood nearby. He started to lay Ellie
down in the infant seat Hannah had balanced on the
kitchen table, but Ellie wasn't about to be pried off of
him. The sound Ellie let out this time was worlds away
from "buzzing." It was a full-fledged howl.

Sam grabbed her back up, holding her close, jiggling
her gently the way he'd seen Hannah do it a thousand
times. Ellie snuffled the last of her outrage, then qui-
eted again. But it didn't help the guilt Sam felt when he
saw those big baby eyes liquid with tears.

Balancing Ellie, he fumbled with the bottle accou-
trements, assembling the thing one-handed. He was
damned relieved when he stuck the bottle into the
microwave to heat it—just a few seconds, he told himself, and be sure to test it so you don't scorch the kid's
mouth.

He retrieved the bottle the instant the microwave
timer buzzed, and struggled to squeeze out drops of
milk onto the inside of his wrist while still holding
Ellie. He swore as the liquid hit the tender skin, burning it. "Damn, I didn't have it in that long!"

Quickly, he stuck the bottle into the freezer, praying
the liquid would cool off before Ellie's patience wore
out. He grabbed a pacifier Hannah had left by the bottles and brushed it against the baby's lips, praying she'd
take it. A pacifier was one thing he *did* know how to
handle!

"I'm sorry, kid," Sam said aloud, hoping to distract
her with the sound of his voice. "I'm not the greatest at
this bottle thing. My little girl—well, her mama always
fed her, and, well, not that your mama wouldn't feed

you if she were around, but she's not, so . . ." Sam's voice trailed off. "How could she just leave you like that?" he murmured, staring down into Ellie's little face. "Like you were nothing. Your mother is supposed to love you."

"You're not 'nothing,' Sam." Hannah's soft voice startled him. He looked up to see her framed in the doorway, her cheeks tear-damp, voice wobbly with emotion. "Neither is Ellie. I love you both."

Sam's throat constricted, his cheeks burned. He turned his face away, too raw even to let Hannah see. "I overheated the bottle. It's in the freezer."

His shyness, his awkwardness, his obvious wish to please made Hannah's chest ache. She filled her memory up with him—images of those strong hands that could shape buildings now cradling Ellie with an almost defiant tenderness, a reluctant compassion, and a far deeper understanding than anything Hannah could imagine of what the abandoned baby would suffer. She wanted to put him at ease, but she didn't want to startle him—swoop in and take things over. She wanted to savor the miracle of Sam, here in the kitchen, the baby in his arms, a rare, wary softness clinging to his ruggedly handsome face. Hannah reached for some way to make him feel more at ease with this new side of his personality neither of them had ever seen before.

"I practically scalded my wrist off the first time I heated a bottle," she tried to soothe. "Probably a good thing I breast-fed Becca. Those bottles supposedly designed for convenience are a lot more complicated than they look."

She crossed to the counter and started to assemble another bottle. Strange, how awkward her fingers suddenly felt, painfully aware that Sam was watching her.

"Hannah, I—" Sam hesitated, his voice roughened with regret. "I acted like a real jerk today."

"Let's just forget about it," Hannah said, wanting nothing more than to do just that, even though she knew it was impossible. She couldn't "forget" Tony Blake and all that had happened between them, any more than she could forget the shape of her baby's face. The wide-eyed innocence, the softly clinging fingers the nurse had gently unfastened from her hospital gown just before the baby had been swept out of Hannah's arms forever.

"Becca called," she said, trying to change the subject. "She wants to spend the year in France."

"I know," Sam said. "She called down at the shop. I think it would be terrific. A once in a lifetime opportunity. Hope it was okay. I gave her a tentative yes. At least as long as you agree."

"I'll miss her, but you're right. She'll never get a chance like this again, but talking about Becca won't solve any of the strain that's been between us since the court hearing."

"Aren't you the one who's always saying we need to talk about things?" Sam prodded. "Not let them fester?"

Not when the "things" they were talking about danced perilously close to the edge of a chasm she didn't want to fall into—rivers of misunderstandings, half truths, downright lies—that could destroy everything she and Sam had built together. A life he must never know had risen for her, at least, out of the ashes of disaster. "Sam, I know you were edgy. You didn't mean to be."

"Oh, yeah, I did." Sam gave a wry chuckle. "I knew exactly what I was doing—acting that way because of my own insecurities. I know things have been strained between us lately, but there's no reason in the world you shouldn't be able to talk to somebody you knew before you met me. How big a deal could Blake have been, anyway? I still remember the way you blushed every time I even glanced at you when you were sitting at the library desk."

His eyes warmed at the memory. "There's no rule that you have to tell me about every friend you had, every secret crush. God knows, there are girls in my past I'd just as soon you didn't come face to face with, and probably with a hell of a lot more reason than you'd ever have."

He was trying to make her feel better. Instead she felt sick with self-loathing. She couldn't bear his tenderness. Not when she was still lying to him. Not when she didn't have any other choice. "Sam, don't," she pleaded.

His brow furrowed, his eyes so sincere it crushed Hannah's chest. "I just need you to know this," he said, cradling Ellie in one strong arm while he reached with his other hand to skim the backs of his knuckles against Hannah's cheek. "If you ever decide you want to tell me about Blake, I'll be here to listen. But if you don't, hey, that's all right with me. You just said everything I needed to know. That you love me."

Hannah stifled the sob rising in her throat. Love him? Had she ever loved him more than she did at this moment? Here with the counters littered from his clumsy efforts at making a bottle, and his arms cradling Ellie as the baby sucked contentedly on her pacifier?

For five months now Hannah had stiffened when he touched her, been afraid she'd never be able to let him get close to her again. Close enough to see how scared she was, how flawed, how fragile. And the longer she'd slept alone in the room they'd once shared, the wider the gap between them seemed to grow, the harder it became to imagine asking him to come back to the iron bed, back into her arms.

It wasn't fair, a voice inside her wailed. It wasn't fair—the *wanting* that filled her up inside as she peered at him across the kitchen. So many things she'd forgotten somehow these long, barren months. The way he smelled, like soap and shampoo and wood shavings. The way his cheeks would flush, dark, his eyes on fire with wanting her. The way his hands knew every inch of her body, could draw from her gasps and sighs and ragged cries of release. The way he could make her feel beautiful instead of awkward, whole instead of broken, alive instead of just going through the motions the way she had for so long after she'd returned from Oregon.

Why did those feelings have to come flooding back to her now, when Sam seemed so far out of her reach? Lost, across a sea of truths she had never told him, flaws she'd hidden so deep she'd believed no one else would ever find them, lies about who she was, what she'd done, where she'd come from. Secrets that would change everything Sam had ever believed about Hannah, everything Becca had been so certain of.

With so much separating them, how could Hannah live with herself if she drew Sam back to their bed now? Tony, not only reappearing in her life, but coming to the farmhouse as Ellie's guardian, sipping coffee at their kitchen table, prying into their private lives as he'd have to to protect Ellie's interests. It would be hard enough for Sam having someone nosing around even for the sake of Ellie's custody. Sam had always been a fiercely private person. But if Sam ever knew about the relationship Hannah and Tony had shared, discovered she'd kept it a secret, he'd never forgive her.

Hannah looked down at baby Ellie, her chubby

cheeks, her toothless smile, oblivious to anything evil or selfish or dangerous. How Hannah envied her. God, Hannah thought, she'd give anything to take just one breath without being weighed down with guilt and regret.

"Hannah?"

Sam's voice startled her, jerking her back to the warm kitchen. Her cheeks flushed guiltily, and she did her best to hide it. But Sam seemed too preoccupied with his own thoughts to notice.

"Remember that cradle I started building for Becca before she was born? The one I never finished?"

"You got the contract for that housing development east of town. Your first big break." Hannah had always known how much that contract had meant to Sam—how exhilarated he'd been, and underneath it, how terrified. Make or break, win or lose, do or die. There hadn't been any middle ground. He'd had to prove he could succeed—not only to everyone in Willowton, but more importantly, he'd had to prove it to himself. He'd thrown himself into the job with single-minded fury, so tunnel-visioned for a while it had chafed at Hannah, left her lonely.

She'd dreamed things would be so different back then, when they'd brought their baby home. She'd imagined long evenings together, marveling at Becca's baby tricks. Imagined Sam adoring their daughter every bit as much as she did. She'd painted a perfect picture in her heart of what it would be like to be a family, hopes made even more precious because they were built on the broken dreams she'd left behind in Oregon years ago.

The cradle had been part of that never-to-be "perfect" world. And when it had languished in the corner of the attic, gathering dust long after Becca had outgrown it anyway, the knowledge that it was still there, as incomplete as Hannah's dreams, had weighed on Hannah, made her feel wistful over what she had lost.

"I don't think I ever told you how damned scared I was when I got that contract. I mean, it wasn't just you and me anymore—we couldn't scrape by. The first minute I looked down into Becca's face, it hit me—she depended on me. Everything she needed—braces and bicycles, college and clothes the other kids wouldn't laugh at—I had to provide all of that for her. And more."

His voice dropped low, more fierce than Hannah had ever heard it. "I wanted her to have everything she wanted, too. Like a princess. Like those kids I used to be so jealous of in school, the ones who always showed up with the new secret decoder ring or the shiniest shoes or a Rin Tin Tin lunchbox. The kids who brought friends back to their house for cookies and milk and to watch television, while I kept wandering around in circles trying to make sure no one was following me, ditch anyone who might see the kind of dump I lived in. My old man stinking drunk in the corner and nothing in the refrigerator because he'd ended up spending his check at the bar instead of the grocery store across the street."

Hannah wanted to close her eyes, but it wouldn't help to block out the image of the lost, hurting boy Sam had been. He'd etched his pain too clearly in her own heart.

"I wanted everything to be perfect for my little girl," he said. "Wanted to make sure she never had to be ashamed of where she lived, what she wore."

Hannah's heart twisted. Why hadn't Sam ever told her any of this before? Strange, so strange to realize that he'd been trying to make things perfect for Becca, too, in his own way. While Hannah had wanted to lavish time and attention and unconditional love on their daughter, all the things Hannah had needed and rarely gotten as a child, Sam had been struggling to uproot ghosts from his own childhood. See to simpler, more basic needs, practical needs that no one had bothered to meet for him. A full stomach, a decent home, a Christmas tree full of every toy Becca could imagine. Money enough to make sure she never did without things like new shoes, school supplies, clothes that didn't come from the Goodwill.

"I was so scared I wouldn't be able to provide for her any better than my old man had provided for me," he admitted, eyes downcast.

"You never told me you were scared."

"How could I tell you? You were so happy. You just glowed. All lit up inside. I was scared enough for both of us. Couldn't stand the idea of failing Becca, failing you. But I didn't, did I?" He looked up, a little hopeful, a little defiant, heartbreakingly vulnerable. "At least I didn't fail you the way I was so scared I would. You and Becca had everything you needed. Never had to worry about money."

No, Hannah thought, grieving for Sam, grieving for herself. She'd never had to worry about money, and neither had Becca. Time with Sam was the thing they'd lost. Cradles finished and sitting in the sunbeams next to their bed. Building snowforts, the three of them together, hanging wet mittens by the heat register and sinking marshmallows in rich cocoa until they melted into delicious white foam.

Would it have made a difference if Hannah had known Sam's self doubts earlier? Would it have soothed away the sense of loss she'd felt? Being left behind? Would it have helped to know that the reason he was fighting so hard to make the business a success wasn't because he wanted the glory, the money to show everyone in town he was worthwhile? When the truth was, he was only trying to take care of his little girl the only way he knew how?

Maybe, just maybe, he hadn't always wanted to be in the office or poring over blueprints, charting up job profits and trying to get the best deal possible on materials. Maybe there were times he'd worked so late in the night that he'd been wishing as much as Hannah had that he could be sitting on the other side of the big stuffed couch, trying to sink "popcorn free-throws" into Becca's wide-open mouth.

Hannah's eyes burned, and she tried to hide it by finishing putting the fresh bottle together for Ellie, heating it to the exact right temperature she'd found by trial and error. Sam sat, quiet, too. No doubt raw from telling her the truth after so long. Letting her see the cracks in his armor. His courage in doing so humbled Hannah. Made her wish she had the grit to do the same. Tell him—

That she'd lost her virginity to Tony Blake? Gotten pregnant? That she'd given away her own child? Left her baby daughter behind and went off to live her own life, just the way Sam's mother had left him so many years ago? That she'd been scared, too? But instead of facing up to that fear the way Sam had, instead of fighting until she conquered it, she'd run away, tried to pretend it all away—her baby, her mistakes, her cowardice?

She wasn't sure how long they both stayed silent, each alone with their own ghosts. She started at the sound of the microwave buzzer and removed the bottle, testing. Instead of taking Ellie out of Sam's arms, she held out the bottle. He smiled, oddly shy, grateful, then popped the pacifier out of the baby's mouth. Ellie scrunched up her face in displeasure, but Sam only made a low, soothing sound deep in his throat.

"Easy, now." He rubbed the nipple gently against Ellie's upper lip. "I know you're hungry."

Ellie latched onto the bottle, sucked on it with determination. Her eyes drifted closed, blissful in the certainty that someone would be there when she cried, someone would feed her when she was hungry, hold her when she was lonely. "Anyway, about the cradle," Sam said quietly, peering intently into little Ellie's face. "I thought I might finish it, you know? It wouldn't take much. A laundry basket's no place for a baby to sleep."

Love. He was showing love the only way he could. Why was it that, much as it touched her, it hurt as well? The cradle he hadn't finished for Becca. Hannah had always imagined the polished wood gleaming in their bedroom, a keepsake, a treasure to be passed to other babies—her own that had never been and someday Becca's babies. How many times had Hannah imagined in those early days that sometime off in the future she'd be able to give the cradle to Becca, when she was awaiting her first child.

This is the cradle your daddy made for you. I tucked you into it so many nights, watched you sleeping. Now you'll tuck your own baby into it and know how much your daddy and I loved you.

Sam's offer to give the cradle to Ellie helped, but it didn't fully erase Hannah's memories of what might have been. She wondered if she'd ever see the cradle without feeling a sense of loss.

"Do you mind, Hannah?" Sam asked. "About the cradle, I mean. We could buy anything you wanted."

"No," Hannah said hastily. "I think it's . . . wonderful you want to do this for Ellie."

It was what she'd wanted, wasn't it? For Sam to bond with the baby? To have a second chance as parents, to get the balance between her and Sam right this time? From the moment she'd seen Ellie in the basket with the shadows from the drying clothes rippling across the baby's face, she'd thought Ellie was a miracle, dropped from heaven into her arms though she had no idea how long she'd get to keep her. But she'd just never realized the painful feelings the baby would open inside her, along with the joy. The insecurities, the disappointments, the failures Ellie would remind her of. She had never imagined Tony Blake charging back into her life, unleashing all the memories, resurrecting secrets that could destroy her.

Hannah stared down at Sam, tenderly feeding Ellie, opening himself to the pain of loving, the fear of it. Emotions he'd dared to confess to Hannah for the first time. But she couldn't help but wonder how his face would change, his eyes harden with anguish and betrayal if he ever found out the truth about her.

That she'd let him believe she was perfect, her heart open wide, when part of her was closed off more tightly than he had ever been. That she'd lied to him about everything she was. And most ominous of all, she'd committed the one sin Sam O'Connell could never forgive.

Leaving a child behind and acting as if it never was.

10

THE CRADLE GLEAMED UNDER the lights in Sam's work-shop in the garage, every speck of dust left from the attic swept from its surface, each tiny spindle in place now, finally filling in the gaps that had been left there for the past nineteen years. Sam, so earnest and eager, putting on the finishing touches. He'd dragged Hannah and Ellie out of the house to see, his eyes shining Christmas bright, full of surprises.

"I need Ellie's help," he'd insisted, disrupting nap schedules, dinner preparations, with impunity. But as Hannah watched him maneuvering around the cradle, she still couldn't figure out what he had in mind.

The cradle was beautiful. She'd done her best to remember that, and to be grateful Sam wanted so much to give it to Ellie.

She looked down at Sam's dark head, his hands so deft as he squeezed paints onto several paper plates, still guarding his "surprise" with delight. As if he were grabbing on tight to this chance he had to get things right.

A new beginning. A second chance for them to

share all the joys of parenting, without paying the price they had the first time, losing touch with each other. Wasn't that what she'd wanted this time with Ellie to be? Then wasn't it only fair that she let go of things Sam could never change? Hurts she hadn't realized until lately that she'd been holding on to? Shouldn't she be even more understanding now, considering the fact that her own past mistakes had reared up in the courtroom to haunt her? A solid reminder that she had regrets of her own, had made choices she could never change, no matter how much she might want to.

Hannah shivered, reliving the jolt of surprise, the disturbing mixture of pleasure and dismay that had shot through her when she'd first seen Tony striding toward her, his smile still dazzling, his face tanned, his eyes intense and so astonishingly familiar.

Hannah bit her lower lip, unable to stifle the unease that rippled through her when she remembered the expression in Tony's eyes. Something disturbing, something that set her off-balance, that made her feel raw, exposed. Nothing surprising in those sensations, she told herself wryly as she tucked Ellie's blanket up around the baby's chin to keep out the spring chill. She was experiencing pure, unadulterated guilt because of everything that had happened between her and Tony so long ago. The furtive lovemaking, the shame of a teenage pregnancy, the surrender of the baby they'd made together. And maybe most unnerving of all, the secrets she'd kept from Sam all these years, telling herself it had all happened a long time ago, that it didn't matter. Now, with Tony Blake swaggering back into her life, she had to admit that it did.

Hannah's stomach churned, and she struggled to quell the knot of panic tightening beneath her sternum. She had to work hard to keep it from her eyes as Sam turned around with great satisfaction.

"All ready," he said, plopping down plates full of bright colored paints. One large one with a puddle of bright blue, another with smears of other shades—orange and yellow, black and white.

"Time to get dirty, Eleanor Rose," he said.

"You don't mean . . . she's not—"

"Finger painting?" Sam swept the baby into his arms. "Absolutely. I can't finish this project without her." He took one of his old white tee shirts and slipped it over the tiny baby, covering her outfit with white cotton from just under her chin to her toes.

"Shouldn't there be some minimum age requirement for finger painting?" Hannah asked warily as Sam ever so carefully flattened Ellie's tiny hand in blue paint, the baby's comical faces driving darker shadows from Hannah's mind.

"Don't worry, Ellie and I can handle this just fine."

"But is the paint nontoxic? I just don't think—"

Sam chuckled. "Don't you remember in the hospital how they make ink prints of babies' hands and feet? I hardly think they'd do it if it posed some sort of danger. Now, Miss Elli-pants and I have two bluebirds to make on this cradle, and if you keep blowing our concentration, they're going to be deformed. You want that kind of responsibility? Deforming bluebirds on an heirloom cradle? There's got to be some sort of major penalty for that. Like maybe, getting your nose painted blue."

Hannah grinned, watching as Sam gently spread Ellie's tiny fingers and made a perfect print of her hand on the wood on the inside of the cradle. Another hand-print faced it, making it look as if the two little thumbs were almost kissing.

"But you put it on the inside of the cradle. It'll be harder to see."

"Not for the only one who matters," Sam assured her. "Miss Ellie will be able to see them just fine."

Sam dipped Ellie's hands into a pail of warm water, laughing as she tried to splash, her round baby eyes wide with astonishment when water sprayed up around her.

Sam dried off her hands, and Hannah started to reach for Ellie, but Sam swept the baby out of her reach. "Not so fast, Mom. Your turn."

"What?"

"Well, we have our Ellie bird and Becca bird. Now its time to make mama bird right up here." He pointed to an empty space on the wood.

"Oh, Sam, I don't think—"

"No arguments." Sam set Ellie in her baby seat, then took Hannah's hand in his. Strong, callused, his fingers against her skin sent tingles running up her arm. She knew he felt it, too, saw his eyes darken in response, but he kept his tone light. "This piece is a work of art. You don't want to interfere in my creative process, do you?"

He flattened her palm in the gooey paint, positioned her hand just so, and pressed it to the wood close to Ellie's prints.

"But now it looks lopsided." Hannah complained, eyeing it.

"Still the artist," Sam said, shaking his head. "Trust me. See?" He repeated the process with his own hand, leaving a bluebird shape far larger than the other three.

He cleaned his hands, then handed Hannah a small brush and the other plate with its dabs of color. "Here you go, Rembrandt. Turn them into bluebirds. You know, just like the ones you and Becca used to put up on the windows every spring."

Hannah cocked her head, surprised. "I didn't know you even noticed them," she said.

"Of course I did. I loved it when I'd drive up and see them there. They always looked so happy. They reminded me of you."

"Is that why you want them on the cradle?" Hannah asked. "Because of the memories?"

Sam sobered, shook his head. "No. Well, sort of. I just . . . When Ellie's going to sleep, I just want her to be able see us there, standing by her. Know that she's not alone."

Hannah blinked hard, so touched by Sam's words she had to fight to keep her hand steady as she painted on eyes and beaks and spindly bird legs, outlining wings on the handprints to turn them into the birds Sam asked her to. But when she came to Sam's hand-print, she didn't whisk the wings back toward the fanned finger-tail as she had on the others. She painted one of his wings in a swooping shelter over Ellie's tiny birds, as if he were protecting her.

Sam looked up and Hannah knew he understood without words.

"There," she said gently. "Now she never has to be alone again."

Hannah tucked Ellie into the cradle Sam had brought inside three days ago, triumphant as he settled it into the dormer garret in the bedroom, the place Hannah had pictured it when Becca was a baby. It fit even more perfectly than she'd imagined it would. The surface shone glassy smooth, gleaming, a cozy, sheltered place to dream. An army of stuffed animals and bright flower arrangements filled Ellie's garret, boxes filled with baby clothes and bursting with best wishes from friends and neighbors who had been flocking to see the "new addition." Josie had even thrown a surprise baby shower, and Hannah still got teary-eyed when she remembered the joy in the faces of her neighbors and friends. Astonishing to realize that, alone as Hannah had felt during those months when everything had been shadowed with sadness, they had been thinking of her, praying for her, wishing there was something they could do to help.

You've always been there for anyone who needed you, with a smile, a plate of cookies, a bunch of flowers to make people feel better. I'm so happy I could finally do something for you. The phrasing had been different, the meaning all the same as they'd come up, one by one, to admire the baby and congratulate Hannah.

Old Miss Ida Beene had given her a pink crocheted baby blanket she must've stayed up three days to make, complete with Ellie's name embroidered in blue thread. Becca's friend Jana's mom had brought an herb pillow she'd made herself—her secret hippie recipe to soothe babies who couldn't sleep. It filled the room with the scent of lavender, and must work, Hannah figured, since every time she smelled it she wanted to take a nap.

Even Becca's friends sent little packages through the mail, filled with congratulations. Pint-size teddy bears Ellie could actually handle, booties that looked like fuzzy ducklings, bubblebath for Hannah so she could relax after midnight feedings.

Maybe everything would work out fine after all, she tried to soothe herself. It wasn't her imagination—Sam really *was* warming to the baby. Becca would be home soon, and in spite of an unexpected bout of teenage sulks, Hannah was sure her daughter would fall in love with Ellie at first sight. Best of all, even after all her unease about the expression on Tony's face, he hadn't shown up at the house yet. He hadn't even contacted them on the phone to ask how things were going with the baby.

Those two factors alone should have made Hannah feel better. Instead, Tony's silence scraped at her nerves, made her edgy. She couldn't make up her mind what she wanted—Sam to be there when Tony came, a solid reminder to everyone involved that choices had been made, decisions reached. That this was *now*, not twenty-seven years ago.

Or was it too dangerous to have Sam hovering close by? Hannah wondered. What if he noticed . . . noticed that *something* between Hannah and Tony he had sensed the first time he had seen them together. What if Sam's suspicions, or instincts, whatever one might call them, got stirred up in that place in his gut where he knew she was keeping secrets?

What if the truth tumbled out and destroyed her marriage just when things were finally starting to get better?

It took every ounce of her will to shove her fears back into the dark corner where they belonged. No, she reassured herself, everything would turn out all right. Tony had as much reason as she did for wanting to keep the fact that they had had a child together a secret.

Any way you sliced it, the situation made him look bad. There was no way to soften the fact that he'd fathered her baby, then left her alone to deal with the consequences. There was no way to excuse what he'd done, no matter how young he'd been, how scared, how determined to make his own dreams come true. When it was held up to the light, his desertion was ugly. Selfish. Even though he may have thought it was the only thing that he could do.

Hannah shook herself inwardly and gave Ellie a kiss, then crept from the room. For heaven's sake, she thought as she padded down the stairs, she was getting so good at being overly dramatic, it was a performance worthy of Becca!

Tony was hardly going to charge in like the villain in a movie and blurt out her secret. What possible reason could he have to do so?

The man had been her first love, but that had all been over long ago. He'd cared about her in his own egocentric, teenage boy way, but he'd never wanted anything permanent. He'd made that clear. Just the fleeting sweetness, a taste of romance before he dashed off into the world. And there was no reason to think he'd ever regretted leaving her behind. Whatever else had happened in the time since they'd been apart, he'd become a successful lawyer, built a life that she knew nothing about. One that he was perfectly happy with, no doubt.

As for the baby he'd fathered, he'd never even bothered to answer the letter she'd written him about their daughter's birth. So she hadn't shared with him her ultimate decision to give their child away. Hannah figured he'd put the whole incident behind him, forgotten all about it until he and Hannah had come face to face in the courtroom. Even if Tony *did* ask about their child sometime in the future, it would probably be more a question of politeness than anything deeper.

So if their meeting again was no big deal to Tony, why hadn't he come to the farmhouse? The question echoed for the hundredth time in Hannah's head. Hadn't the judge ordered him to make home visits? And if there was one familiar thing still evident in Tony Blake's face, it was that determination to do a job well. Was it possible that he'd figured his presence would make Hannah uncomfortable? Or had he already managed to hand Ellie's case off to somebody else?

Hannah snorted in self disgust. Wouldn't that be perfect? She'd have turned the art of worrying into an Olympic-level sport for nothing!

She trudged down to the main floor, considering lacing her morning coffee with a shot of whatever was in the liquor cupboard when suddenly she heard a knock on the door. A jolt of panic shot through her—that edginess that had her thinking every car that drove down the lane, every ring of the phone, every knock on the door might be Tony Blake. Brushing a stray hair from her forehead, she went to the back door. She was so relieved it wasn't Tony, she grinned a wide welcome at the woman on the other side of the windows. Margo Johnson peered back at her in surprise.

Hannah's cheeks stung with the knowledge she'd never greeted the woman with so much enthusiasm before. Their acquaintance had begun as one of convenience when they each drove a leg of the neighborhood carpool that went to and from kindergarten at the Willowton Elementary School. But it was love for Margo's shy, solemn, musically gifted daughter Rachel that had kept the relationship going, impelled Hannah to see more of Margo than either of the women had expected. The differences between them had little to do with any stress over the "stay at home vs. working mom" issue. Hannah had plenty of friends who did a fabulous job with their chosen profession and their children— Josie Wilkes, for example. It was the distance Margo kept between herself and her daughter that saddened Hannah, made her want to try to help.

Over the years, the women's relationship had developed over cups of coffee in the farmhouse kitchen, Hannah doing her best to serve as a buffer between a mother and daughter who didn't understand each other at all. Rachel had summed up the relationship with an insight that had astonished Hannah with its clarity when she'd confided "I know my mother loves me. She just doesn't *like* me very much."

Hannah had tried to smooth things over yet again, but in her heart she knew it was the truth.

In spite of crisply ironed khakis and a white button-down shirt, Margo looked more harried than usual today. In bad need of a cup of tea and a place to drink it where she wasn't feeling the compulsion to wipe off counters that were spotless or chase imaginary spiders' webs from corners sterile enough to perform surgery in. Somehow, Hannah had always felt sorry for Margo, mainly because the woman had no idea how to relax and take joy in the treasure of a daughter she had.

"This is a surprise," Hannah said, swinging open the door.

Margo fidgeted with a button on her shirt, the white cotton so starched Hannah figured it could probably stand on its own. "I just got back from a two-week business trip and the whole neighborhood was buzzing. Saying that you've taken in a baby and that Josie Wilkes even gave you a baby shower. Have you completely lost your mind?"

Hannah laughed. "I'm afraid it's true. About the baby, that is. My mind is just fine. Thank you very much."

"You took in a baby?" Margo reiterated in horror. "One someone just dumped in your backyard? You don't even know where it's come from! It might have some—some disease or birth defect. It might be the child of a serial killer!"

If anyone else had maligned Ellie that way, Hannah would have bristled. But Margo had a habit of seeing rabid wolves in every golden retriever puppy that toddled past her front door.

Hannah laughed. "I took her to the pediatrician, so I'm pretty sure she doesn't have any communicable diseases. And she can't reach the matches, so she hasn't burned down the house yet."

Margo paled and brushed past her into the kitchen. She sagged down in her usual place—the one nearest the cookie jar. She didn't believe in baking, and was piously against eating unhealthy food. But somehow, every time she left the O'Connell table there were noticeably fewer cookies in the jar.

"Hannah, it's not funny," Margo insisted. "I know we don't always see eye to eye on things, especially where raising kids is concerned. But I really am worried about you. You haven't been yourself for months. You've just gone through surgery. The last thing you need is an upset like this!"

"Ellie's a baby, Margo. Not indigestion." Hannah tried to keep it light. But Margo wasn't about to be dissuaded.

"It's not a joke! Just think, Hannah. You know absolutely nothing about what kind of people this child's parents are. They could be drug addicts or criminals or God knows what. And they could show up on your doorstep at any moment." Margo shuddered, reminding Hannah of the time one of her sons had sneaked a stray kitten into the house. Margo had bombed the place with enough anti-flea stuff to wipe out the entire pest population in the state. Much as Margo loathed animals of any kind, she'd been almost as wary around kids—bewildering, germ-infested dirt factories that they were. She'd always seemed a little afraid of her own children and bemused by anyone who was relaxed around kids.

"I appreciate your concern." Hannah turned to put the kettle on, and to give Margo a chance to snitch her first handful of the shortbread Hannah had baked as a thank you to Sam for the cradle. "But I'm pretty sure Ellie's mother, at least, isn't any of those things. She's just young and scared and alone. I can't stop thinking about her. Hoping she's all right."

Hannah wished she didn't already know the answer to that question. Her smile faded, her heart ached. Ellie's mom wasn't all right. In some ways she never would be.

"That girl deserves to be arrested, whoever she is! I hope they find her and make her pay for what she's done!"

"Let's not go there," Hannah insisted firmly as she spooned loose tea into her grandmother's "Blue Willow" teapot. "We'll just agree to disagree." It was the only way they had managed to maintain their relationship as long as they had. Don't talk about things that matter, don't tell how you really feel, don't question things no matter how much they drive you crazy. Jana's mother, Erika, unconventional, new-age woman that she was, had always shaken her head, saying she didn't know why Hannah made all that effort.

It wouldn't have been worth it to Hannah, either, if it hadn't been for Margo's daughter, Rachel. She could see the girl in her mind far too clearly. Soft brown hair that fell in waves like a Pre-Raphaelite painting, big blue eyes far too tender for the world and a wide, sensitive mouth that smiled too seldom. Except when she was bending over her violin, the gleam of the instrument matching her hair, the sounds she coaxed out of it making her smile as if she could see angels dancing. She wondered what Rachel was doing now. Hannah seized on the subject—a perfect one to distract

Margo from criticizing Ellie's mother, at least for now.

"Becca called," Hannah said. "She told me that both Jana and Rachel are doing great with their music. Rachel got first chair in the college orchestra touring and studying overseas."

"She did. In fact, she should have landed in Austria a few hours ago." Hannah smiled at the image of Rachel stepping off the plane into the world she'd dreamed of, her violin clutched tenderly in one thin hand.

"You must be so proud," Hannah prodded, hoping she could get Margo to at least consider taking some pleasure in Rachel's accomplishment. Instead, Margo frowned.

"We are. Proud, I mean. I just hope it doesn't confuse her."

"Confuse her?" Hannah echoed. "She's loved music since she was tiny. It's all she ever wanted. How could it be anything but wonderful?"

"It's just—well, you can't make a living with music. She'll have to support herself."

"If she's already good enough to be first chair at one of the finest music schools in the Midwest, and beat out every other kid in the touring orchestra for the top spot don't you think she ought to do just fine? At least she should give it a chance."

Margo stared down at her clenched fingers, her newly reset engagement ring pressing a red mark into her skin. "Maybe we should have done what her father wanted. Gotten rid of the violin a long time ago. When she first started getting so obsessed with it."

"You might as well have told Rachel to quit breathing!" Hannah protested. "Margo, you can't really believe you should have taken music away from Rachel. Rachel has a special gift."

"Hank says it can't be too special." Margo said and Hannah stiffened.

She could get along with almost anyone, but Hank Johnson made her brain bleed. He would've been a prime candidate for dictator of the month. Hannah often wondered what Margo and Rachel's relationship would have been like without Hank's constant criticism or if Margo had ever got up the courage to take Rachel's side instead of her autocratic husband's.

"Jana is every bit as good as Rachel is," Margo continued. "Well, at least almost. And that girl is the most scatterbrained child I've ever met! I mean, it's no wonder, what with her parents! Nobody bothered to tell them that the sixties are over! Raising her like some—some hippie flower child! You know, they didn't even have a television in their house!"

Maybe that should qualify them for parents of the month, Hannah thought to herself. Instead of television, Jana and her brothers and sisters had read books, built rocket ships out of cereal boxes, experimented with chemistry sets. She'd always figured one of them would be a great artist or find a cure for cancer, they were so creative and bright. Even if they didn't fit Margo Johnson's cookie-cutter-kid mold.

But Hannah didn't even bother to bristle in Jana's defense. The girl didn't need protection. She'd always been able to laugh off Rachel's mother's disapproval, made a game out of pulling the woman's chain by wearing peace signs around her neck and tee shirts she'd tie-dyed herself. But then, flighty as Jana might be and unconventional as her parents were, their daughter had a gift Rachel never would have. Jana knew they adored her. That was all that mattered.

"Jana is a terrific violinist, but she and Rachel are different. Jana plays for fun. Rachel plays with everything inside her. I'm glad the two of them are going to spend time together in Vienna. Maybe Jana will be able to get Rachel out of the practice room to see the city and enjoy herself."

Rachel's seriousness would no doubt propel the girl to the top of the music world, but the one thing Hannah wished most of all for the young girl was that she would learn how to laugh.

"Hank and I have been so worried about what kind of influence Jana was having on Rachel. Three times when I called Rachel's room in the past few weeks, her roommate said Rachel was at a party."

"Good for her!" Hannah gave a heartfelt laugh.

"Are you insane?" Margo demanded in horror. "Do you have any idea what kind of things go on at college parties?"

"Can't say I do." Hannah swept the whistling kettle off the stove and filled the teapot with steaming water. "I'm one of the few college graduates who actually managed to get through four years of grinding study without going to a single party. I've always wished I had tried it, at least once."

"Hannah, it's not funny! This is my daughter we're talking about!"

Hannah sucked in a steadying breath, reminding herself to be patient. "Come on, Margo. Take it easy on Rachel. Be honest. I may not know what goes on at college parties, but I can't believe you don't. You and Hank still have fraternity paddles and sorority pledge books hanging in your rec room. I'm betting you didn't spend all your time learning the sorority motto."

Margo didn't even have the grace to blush. She rushed on, obviously feeling vindicated by Hannah's words. "That's just my point! If Rachel had joined a sorority like I begged her to, she would have been invited to the right kind of parties. With people of a certain standard. I wouldn't have been worried sick about what kind of people she's consorting with."

Consorting? Maybe Margo had been a duchess in a former life. Hannah struggled not to laugh out loud. At least now she didn't have to check the "build your vocabulary" word for today in the newspaper. "Margo, Rachel's got a good head on her shoulders. No danger of her turning into a party animal." Hannah had always been more afraid the girl would become a hermit, lock herself in a room somewhere with stacks of music and her violin and never come out, just tap Morse code on the door so someone could slide a new string under the door when she broke one.

"Rachel's got a good head on her shoulders," Hannah reassured. "She'll be just fine. You'll see."

"I won't stop worrying until she isn't hanging around with Jana so much. I'd hoped—well, don't scowl at me like that! I know you think Jana's just wonderful. And she's a nice enough girl. It's just that she's not going in the direction I want my daughter to go."

No, Jana wasn't headed for a nervous breakdown because her parents were putting her under enough pressure to split an atom, let alone a fragile teenage girl's spirit, Hannah wished she could say. But she bit her tongue trying to resist the impulse to stuff Margo's mouth with the shortbread to shut the woman up. Weren't carbohydrates supposed to mellow people out? Next time she'd have to lace a few with Valium.

"Margo, Rachel is a wonderful girl. I wish—" Hannah stopped, but the words rolled on in her mind. *I wish you could open up your eyes and see that.*

Margo sighed, dabbing stray crumbs from the corner of her mouth. "I know you care about Rachel." She almost seemed confused by that fact. "But I am her mother. It's hard. She just left for Austria last night, but already she seems so . . . so far away."

That, at least was something Hannah could identify with. The ache of missing your daughter. Getting used to silence where there used to be laughter, tabletops clean where there used to be clutter, the ledges in the bathroom bare instead of hosting a drugstore full of bubble bath and hair conditioners and scented lotions. Hannah reached out and squeezed Margo's hand in empathy. "Vienna is a long way away. But I'm sure she's going to have the time of her life."

"I don't mean 'far away' like that," Margo said, gesturing helplessly. "I mean, she didn't even come home before she left, just sent the things she didn't need home with Jana's parents."

"But haven't you been gone the last two weeks? Even if she had come home, you wouldn't have been there."

"I know, and yet, I can't help feeling like she doesn't talk to me. Doesn't tell me things. It's almost like she's hiding . . ."

From the constant criticism aimed at "improving" her? Hannah thought. *Who could blame the girl for avoiding the phone?* Hannah wondered if Rachel had ever gotten a compliment that wasn't edged with a suggestion as to how she could do even better next time.

Margo made a wry face. "I'm sure you have no idea what I mean. Becca probably calls you ten times a day and tells you everything."

Hannah busied herself straining tea into cups. The dark liquid almost spilled over the rim. "I don't hear from Becca as often as I used to," she admitted, the ominous silence of the phone another twinge of pain in her heart. "But they're growing up, Margo. Starting their own lives. It's the way it should be, whether we like it or not."

"Rachel seems to be doing her best to avoid me altogether."

Hannah winced at the sudden wistfulness in Margo's voice. No matter what Hannah's opinion of Margo's parenting was, it was obvious the woman was hurting, too, over her daughter's leaving home. How much worse would it be, Hannah wondered, if you'd missed most of your daughter's childhood? Running to meetings and hostessing cocktail parties, going on cruises alone with your husband instead of getting drenched in water rides with your kids at Disneyland? At least Hannah didn't have regrets that she hadn't spent enough time with Becca. She just wished Sam had been with them when they'd gone on the rides.

"I don't know," Margo admitted. "Rachel just sounds so different. Strange. And you should see the way she looks—sloppy tee shirts and not a lick of makeup."

Hannah could only be thrilled. Rachel's parents had always pressured her to dress as if she'd just come from a polo match, a style that had seemed to make the girl feel uncomfortable and out of place in their small Iowa town. Let the kid experiment and make her own fashion statement at last. She hoped Rachel was having a fantastic time. It was about time Rachel got to shine.

The cordless phone rang and Hannah dove for it, hoping Ellie wouldn't wake up, but it was too late. She could hear the baby break into ear-piercing wails upstairs. Hannah thought for a second about sending Margo up to get Ellie, then changed her mind. She covered one ear with her palm, and pressed the receiver tight against her other ear in an effort to hear. "O'Connells'. This is Hannah speaking."

She could barely make out the sound of a voice on the phone—something strange, foreign. Amid a burst of static, a thickly accented voice said, "This is—"

"Can you hold just a minute?" Hannah cut the person off, taking the stairs at a rush. "The baby is crying. Wait just a moment while I pick her up." Hannah figured whoever was on the other end of the line was sorry they called, the way Ellie was shaking the rafters. Bending over the cradle, Hannah scooped Ellie up in one arm, cuddling her close. The baby let out a few more outraged snuffles, then hiccuped quietly against Hannah's breast.

"There," Hannah crooned, kissing Ellie on the forehead. "All better now." She turned her attention back to the person on the other end of the phone. "I'm sorry. Now, I think Miss Ellie will actually let me hear you. What can I do for you?"

"This is a call from Austria—" The operator uttered an exclamation of surprise in some strange language as a horrific clattering sounded on the other end of the phone, someone obviously dropping the receiver.

"Madam?" the operator prompted. "Madam, are you still there?"

"Hello?" Hannah called. "Who is this?" The phone buzzed, an odd, droning sound far away.

"Forgive me, Madam," the operator said after a moment. "The party has disconnected."

Hannah frowned, then slowly pressed the off button on the phone. Bemused, she pocketed the phone, then retrieved Ellie's pacifier and trudged down the stairs.

The call had sounded so odd, the connection static riddled. Could the call have been for Sam? He sometimes special ordered materials for clients who wanted a taste of the international in their homes. But his suppliers would have called the shop, wouldn't they? Or maybe it was just a wrong number. She certainly didn't know anyone in Austria—except for Rachel, that is. Suspicion tugged at her.

Rachel? No. She was being ridiculous. If Rachel had called, why would she hang up? More likely it was just a mistake.

Margo was dabbing the last of some crumbs that looked suspiciously like shortbread from the corners of her mouth as Hannah entered the kitchen.

"Something wrong, Hannah?" Margo asked, glancing from Hannah to Ellie as if the baby might explode at any moment.

"No," she comforted herself more than Margo.

"Who was it?" Margo asked. "You look . . . strange."

Hannah smoothed out the wrinkles in Ellie's blanket, wishing she could smooth out the confusion she felt as easily. "It was a wrong number," she reassured Margo. "Just a mistake."

"Humph!" Margo made a sound of disapproval deep in her throat. "If you ask me, that baby you're holding is the mistake, Hannah! Mark my words, the kind of people that child comes from are people you wouldn't even let in your front door." Then she made a face. "Well, you'd probably let them in, but no one in their right mind would."

"Look at her, Margo," Hannah said, drawing down a fold of blanket to better show Ellie's face, pink from crying, her lashes still spangled with tears that shone like diamonds. "Just look at her. How can anything this tiny, this innocent, frighten you so much?"

Margo bristled. "I'm not afraid of the baby. It's her parents. It's—well, you don't know what kind of people she might drag into your life. What if they show up on your doorstep?"

"Then I'll offer them some shortbread," Hannah said with a forced smile. "That is, if there's any left."

Margo huffed and puffed, made her excuses. Hannah had never been so glad to see the screen door slam behind her.

"Say hello to Rachel if you talk to her," Hannah called after Margo.

Obviously still irate, Margo said, "I doubt Rachel will telephone. After all, she only just arrived in Austria this morning. Besides, she'd be more likely to want to talk to you than she would me."

Irritated as Hannah was with Margo, she felt the undercurrent of hurt in the woman's voice, felt a brief sense of kinship she'd never experienced before. Before Becca had reached out to Sam for comforting instead of turning to Hannah.

She carried Ellie back into the quiet house, peered into those tiny baby features, trying one more time to picture Becca's friends, guess who Ellie might look like.

Rachel? No, Rachel Johnson was the least likely of all Becca's friends to turn up pregnant. Rachel's eyes had shone, wistful for as long as Hannah could remember. Even as a shy eight-year-old, Rachel had confided to Hannah the dream she longed for with all her heart. A world full of music, as far away from her judgmental parents as she could get. Rachel deserved to realize that dream and more.

"Someday I hope you'll get to meet her, Ellie," Hannah crooned. "Maybe she'll get us front row seats when she plays at Carnegie Hall."

Hannah looked out the window to the play fort where Rachel had come sometimes to be alone and practice where no one would bother her. "Sometimes,

I'd open the window, let the music drift in," Hannah confessed. "I wonder if Rachel ever guessed I was listening? You'd like her, Ellie. So much. I wonder what she's doing now."

Hannah smiled, imagining the delights Rachel would find in Vienna. She did her best to forget about the strange voice on the phone and the nagging questions it had left inside her.

Rachel Johnson fumbled with the receiver, banging it into the cradle of the pay phone with a sickening metallic *thud!* Her heart pounded so hard it should've cracked her ribs, her palms sweating as if she'd almost gotten caught robbing a bank. Oh, God, what had she been thinking? Calling the O'Connells? It had seemed like such a good idea—pretending she was just phoning to chat, hoping desperately that Hannah might mention something about the baby someone had left in her laundry basket.

But then Rachel had heard the baby—wailing at first, the sound fading into little hiccuping cries as Hannah obviously picked her up. And then quiet. It was just what she'd wanted, wasn't it? Rachel thought. Hannah mothering Ellie? Then why did it cut so deep, picturing her baby girl snuggling into someone else's arms, feeling safe, comforted? She'd have to get used to it, wouldn't she? Someone else would always be drying her little girl's tears.

Rachel's eyes had burned, her throat so swollen she'd been sure that if she spoke one word she'd break out in tears. And then, Hannah would know that the "somebody" who had deserted her baby was Rachel.

Rachel had hung up the phone, her knees quaking as she imagined the look on Hannah's face, the disgust, the loathing, the betrayal the instant she realized

Rachel was Ellie's mother. Those eyes that had always looked at Rachel so kindly, as if she really mattered, changing forever. Because if Rachel had said just one word, Hannah would discover the truth she'd tried so hard to hide.

Hannah O'Connell had always had an uncanny ability to sense trouble in the kids who'd drifted in and out of the farmhouse, not only attracted by friendship with Becca, nice as she was. But rather, drawn to the quiet calm of Becca's mother, the safe feeling you always got at Hannah's kitchen table, the way she'd meet your eyes, as if she really wanted to hear what you were saying. Not like Rachel's own mom, who always looked as if she were checking her shopping list in her head whenever Rachel tried to talk to her.

Sick to her stomach, shaking because of the mistake she'd almost made, Rachel stumbled out of the phone booth, grateful for at least one thing. She'd heard Ellie crying. Ellie was there, in the cozy farmhouse, being loved, taken care of. A part of the home Rachel had always wished could be hers.

It's going to be all right, she thought, her chest squeezing. At least, it would unless one of the kids from the music school was among the crowd of people who kept staring at her as they passed. She glanced around nervously. How would she explain what she'd been doing if one of the students had seen her? No one who actually knew her would believe she was homesick and calling her mother. Especially not Jana. And it would be just like Jana to come back and try one more time to convince Rachel to come with the crowd of kids who were going off to see the city.

"You can't still be airsick!" Jana had pleaded until Rachel thought she would scream. *"We've been on the ground for hours! It'll be good for you to get some fresh air with the rest*

of us. C'mon, Rache, we've waited forever to get here!"

A lifetime, Rachel thought with a twinge. She'd dreamed of this day from the first moment she'd realized there was a world beyond Iowa, far away from critical eyes and snickers half-hidden behind other kids' hands. She'd studied herself into pop bottle-thick glasses in an effort to make her escape happen, practiced with her nails bitten so short they bled, and permanent lines streaked through the calluses on her fingers from the strings of her violin.

Not that Rachel had cared—at least not *too much*—about what the other kids thought of her, not as long as she saw everything she'd always wanted dance closer, tantalizingly closer, until at last she could grab it with both hands.

She'd just never imagined the terrible choice she'd have to make to get here. She'd never dreamed what she would have to leave behind.

She tugged the voluminous folds of one of the oversized shirts she'd used to hide her pregnancy, thinking of how lucky she'd been that so many college kids wore the same style. No one but Jana had ever said a word, or seemed to notice the change in her figure at all. Jana had just told her not to worry. The freshman fifteen weight gain was notorious. It would come off once summer came and Rachel could be more active. Jana would probably be saying, 'I told you so' before the month was out, attributing Rachel's shrinking figure to walking all over Vienna. She'd never know Rachel had been hiding a baby that she could never claim as her own.

Rachel stumbled down one of Vienna's streets, in the opposite direction Jana and the rest had set out a half an hour before, wanting to find a shadowy corner to hide. Somewhere far away from prying eyes and

Jana's worried face. Somewhere she could sort through the sadness and the pain, the guilt and confusion she'd been lost in ever since the moment she'd stared down at the white stick of the pregnancy test and seen it turn color.

She should have been relieved. The nightmare was over, for her and for her baby. No one knew their secret. No one ever would, unless she told them. And Rachel would never, ever tell anyone what she'd done. What a terrible person she'd been. How she'd deserted her baby. Left her—

With Hannah, Rachel thought fiercely. *The best mother in the whole world.* Didn't her baby deserve that instead of a clumsy, awkward, brainless girl so stupid she'd actually thought a guy loved her? Would listen when she said "no"?

She shuddered, cold in spite of the warm breeze that drifted through the streets.

"Dear, are you quite all right?" A concerned voice laced with a heavy Irish brogue startled her, and Rachel looked down into the face of a rosy-cheeked old woman who looked like the good witch in one of the fairy tales she'd always loved. "You look a wee bit pale and lost. May I help?"

Help? No one could help, Rachel thought hopelessly as she looked into those kind eyes. She wondered how quickly they would change if she actually told the old woman what was wrong. What she'd done. How fast would the concern turn to disgust? Horror? How quickly would the old woman hurry away from the American girl who had dumped her baby in a basket?

"I'm . . . I'm not lost," Rachel lied. She'd never been more lost in her life. "I'm at the music school. I can still see the tower over there."

The Irishwoman glanced to where Rachel was

pointing. "Well then, are you feeling a wee bit lonely? Been missing my own babies, I have—grown up, the lot of them, and sending Mum off on a holiday for a treat." The old woman chuckled. "They don't know I'd rather be at me own fireside with the lot of them racketing around me than be anywhere else on earth. Maybe we could sit and have a cuppa, cheer each other up a bit. 'Tis like a film scene here, it is. Have you ever seen such hats an' people really wearing them? Feathers an' all, I'll be blessed! We could sit awhile and watch them sail by. They've pastries in this shop that make you think you're eating with the angels."

Rachel's throat ached at the woman's unexpected kindness. It hurt to know she didn't deserve it. "Thank you, but I . . . I can't." She turned and fled, not caring where she was going. But it didn't matter which way she turned. Vienna was still heart-stoppingly beautiful.

She shoved away the nerve-wracking jolt of hearing Hannah O'Connell's voice. Trying to forget how close she'd come to betraying her secret, Rachel focused on the sights and sounds of the city. The Irishwoman was right. Vienna did look like a scene from one of the old movies she'd adored, magical and elegant as Sabrina's Paris, women dressed like something out of *Vogue* magazine with ostrich feathers in their hats. Classical beauties sailing into shops for pastries ornate as wedding cakes and coffees sipped from paper-thin porcelain cups. Sculptures climbed up corners of buildings like ivy as she walked the streets, the beautiful art of generations decorating walls with lions and mythic heroes and clusters of marble flowers so real it seemed you could smell their fragrance.

It was everything she'd ever imagined, Rachel thought, her heart twisting at the memory of the girl she had been, peering out her window over Iowa farm fields she'd never belonged in and imagining places far away that fit her perfectly as Cinderella's glass slipper.

She'd been five when she'd first heard Mozart, seven when she'd picked out the first few notes of "Eine Kline Nacht" on her violin. And she'd been ten when she'd fled in tears from a music class full of kids sneering over a film of Amadeus, a musical version of Mozart's life that made her idol far too human—vulgar and disgusting and ridiculous instead of the musical god she'd worshiped in her heart.

She'd wanted Vienna even before she'd known it existed. A place where she could be on her own, where what mattered was how hard you worked, how much you practiced, how deeply you felt the music in your heart. A place where other people understood that music wasn't a "nice" hobby she would grow out of when she became an orthodontist or a communications major.

Coming here should feel like a fountain of water when you'd been thirsty forever. The music was laughter and tears and the blood in her veins. Her first night in the city should have been perfect, she thought, peering out across rivers of streetlights setting Vienna aglow. But every carved cherub's face reminded her of another rosebud mouth, chubby cheeks, wide, wonder-filled eyes. Every cherub's tiny hand seemed to reach out in her imagination, warm and soft, so innocent and perfect, plucking sad melodies deep in her heart.

Yes, this night should have been perfect. It would have been if she hadn't been forced to make a terrible choice—stay trapped in a life she hated forever, or leave her baby behind.

It will get easier, she'd told herself over and over

again. *Just give yourself time. You did what was best for Ellie and what was best for you. What kind of life could you have given a baby? You don't even know how to take care of yourself.*

And it wasn't as if there was anyone out there who'd be willing to show her how. Help her sort through things. She could see her father's veins popping out on his head, his face fire-engine red, as he yelled.

"This is what comes of running around with musicians!" he would have raged, as if orchestra students were no different than kids in spiked dog collars and chains, banging heads at a heavy-metal concert. *"I should have thrown that violin in the trash years ago, but no! I had to be soft with you! And now look at the mess you've made!"*

"How could you do this to us, Rachel?" Her mother's wail sounded so real, Rachel wanted to slap her hands over her ears to block it out, but there was no way to block words harder than blows this time, not when they were coming from inside her own head. *"How could you humiliate your father and me this way? What did we ever do to deserve this from you?"* She ranted, as if Rachel had plotted out getting pregnant on purpose just to spite her. *"What am I supposed to tell my friends?"*

Rachel shuddered, the scene as vivid in her mind as if it had really taken place. And it had. Over and over and over again as she'd imagined different ways of confessing to her parents that she was pregnant. But no matter how she presented it, no matter what she'd said, the end was always the same.

She'd ruined their perfect lives, embarrassed them in front of their friends. How could she have done this to them—never mind the fact that she was the one who was throwing up every morning, whose body was changing so fast it terrified her. Never mind that she felt stupid and naïve, used and thrown away. Worthless. Or that she was sorry.

So sorry for what she'd done. To herself. To her parents. But most of all to the baby girl she'd brought into the world and hidden like a dirty secret. Ellie should have been welcomed with tears of joy and family all around her, flowers and stuffed animals and a mother who could give her everything she deserved. Tell her she was beautiful and special and wonderful even when the rest of the world told her she was not.

A prickly lump of tears lodged in Rachel's throat. She forced it down, swiping at her burning eyes. No matter how many other mistakes she had made, at least she had done one thing right, Rachel thought fiercely. She'd given her baby to Hannah.

She winced at the sound of Hannah's voice on the phone—just a few words, and yet they had told Rachel so much. Hannah had sounded so happy—and so warm—comforting Ellie as she cried.

Rachel could picture Ellie curled up in Hannah's arms, hear Hannah hushing her with one of the little songs she was always singing while she did the dishes or hung out clothes to dry. Rachel could see it all so clearly. What she wanted for her baby. Ellie safe, loved, cherished by the mother Rachel had never had.

Gratitude and pain shoved hard at Rachel's heart. It was everything she'd wanted for her baby, wasn't it? A home in the sprawling farmhouse, Hannah's smiles that came so freely. The patience Hannah had showered on everyone who'd ever come through the farmhouse door. Rachel grimaced. Hannah had even managed not to let Rachel's mother get under her skin, and no one could grate on people the way she could.

Hannah O'Connell could give Ellie everything, be everything Ellie needed, Rachel told herself sternly.

Hannah—a perfect mom, the exact opposite of Rachel.

Tears burned her eyes and she blinked them back. There was no point crying anymore. She'd done the only thing she could. Taken care of her baby the best way she knew how. Hadn't she? She should feel relieved. At peace. She was here in Vienna and Ellie had the best home in all Willowton. The whole nightmare was over at last for Ellie and for her.

Why hadn't it seemed like a nightmare during those brief hours she'd gotten to hold her little girl? Rachel wondered. Why had Ellie seemed to fit so perfectly in her arms? And why did she feel so empty? Even Vienna's bright lights and childhood dreams fulfilled couldn't warm the cold, lonely places in her heart.

Rachel wandered down the streets, alone. But the sights and sounds of the city she'd imagined for so long faded away, until all she could see was Ellie's face, all she could hear were the funny gurgling noises Ellie made when she sucked on her fist.

Her baby.

No, not hers. Not anymore. Ellie belonged to Hannah now.

She was glad.

Truly.

She was.

If she gave herself long enough, maybe someday she'd believe it.

11

HANNAH TURNED THE OVEN down to warm, eyeing the casserole through the tiny glass window. She sighed. It would keep. She'd gotten good over the years at making meals that could be saved or heated up whenever Sam got home. He'd called to excuse himself from dinner plenty of times in the past, just as he had tonight.

She'd always figured there was some kind of jinx at work. She and Becca had made up stories about little gremlins who hid in boxes of nails or in forests of drill bits watching their tiny wristwatches until the hands hit five. Then, the instant quitting time came, the crew of mischief makers would start blowing up pipes, splitting two-by-fours, or adding in too much water so the concrete wouldn't set up. Yes, if Sam was going to face a disaster any time during the day, it would always come at dinnertime.

She supposed she really couldn't complain. Since the night after Ellie's hearing, Sam *had* been making an effort to get home early. Almost as if he were trying to make up for all the meals he'd eaten alone at the kitchen table while Hannah was putting Becca to bed. It was warm, wonderful to sit across the kitchen table from him, watching him devour bread slathered with jam she'd made from last summer's raspberries, lamplight turning his hair mahogany while she waited to see him smile.

She'd wanted the freedom to reach out and touch him, hold his hand, stroke back the strand of hair that always fell across his forehead. But she hadn't been able to do it. Every time she looked at him, she thought about how much it would hurt him if he ever discovered what had gone on between her and Tony Blake a lifetime ago.

She swallowed hard. It wouldn't be fair to Sam to try to bridge the gap between them until she'd had the chance to settle things that had remained unresolved for so long. And then . . . ?

If only she knew the answer to that. Could she really ignore all this? She'd already kept secret from Sam the fact that she'd had another man's baby. But she'd been barely seventeen then, scared and ashamed and so certain no one could ever forgive her for what she'd done. Her mother hadn't forgiven her, or her father. More than that, she'd never forgiven herself.

But if she kept it secret this time, wouldn't it be different? Did Sam deserve the truth? Or did it matter? It had happened so long ago. And finding out about what she'd done would hurt Sam so deeply. There was nothing anyone could do to change it.

But now, she had even more to lose. What if Sam turned and walked away?

The phone jangled, and she nearly jumped out of her skin. She grabbed the phone, not sure whether she hoped it was Sam saying he'd cleared up whatever snag had come up and he was coming home, or whether she needed more time to sort things out herself.

But the voice on the phone gave her a jolt.

"Hannah? It's Tony."

As if she hadn't known the moment he'd drawled "hello." Her heart gave an uncomfortable leap in her chest—dread, she assured herself, only dread. She'd pictured disaster riding into the farmhouse on Tony's heels so often in the past days, it was as if she'd lived it a dozen times. But she could hardly blame Tony for showing up in Willowton, and the fact that she hadn't told Sam the truth about the baby she'd had so long ago—that wasn't Tony's fault either. It was nobody's fault but her own.

Meeting him again was just one of fate's little practical jokes, and they'd just have to sort it out as best they could.

"Hannah?" Tony said again.

"Tony. Hi. I've been waiting—" she choked on the words, terrified he'd take them the wrong way. "I mean, um, Sam and I expected to hear from you days ago. About Ellie. You know, because the judge said you should check up on her."

Her cheeks stung at the sound of his low chuckle. "I know what you mean. No need to get all flustered, Hannah. The last thing I want to do is make you uncomfortable."

Of course he didn't want to make her uncomfortable. He doubtless didn't want anything to do with her at all except where his guardianship of Ellie was concerned. She was overreacting. Big time.

"I . . . ah, I'm not uncomfortable. Really."

"Don't even try to fool me. I've gotten damn good at reading other people's emotions. Part of the job description when you're a lawyer."

But as she recalled, he'd been good at figuring people out long before law school had ever crossed his mind. He'd read people so perfectly that he'd fit in from the first moment he swaggered into Willowton High. No small feat, since most of the kids had been together since kindergarten. New students were usually outsiders, regarded with mild suspicion. Tony Blake had immediately taken a top spot in the "popular crowd," as if there could never be any question that was where he belonged.

She'd envied him his ease with people, his self-confidence and the keen intelligence that made class so easy for him. But then, everything had always seemed to come easy to Tony. She wondered if it still did.

"I was wondering," Tony said, "would you mind if I stop over on my way home from work? I could talk to you and Sam—"

"Sam's not here. He got called in at the last minute to figure some plans on a new senior center they're hoping to build downtown."

"Really?" Was it her imagination, or didn't Tony sound very surprised. "Well, we could postpone it, I suppose, but the judge called for the report tomorrow morning. Oh, well. I'll just tell her I screwed up. Hey, it's my own fault. I was working overtime on an adoption case I took pro bono for a couple in Twin Oaks. Breaks your heart. They tried for ten years to have a baby of their own, then, out of the blue, they're chosen to adopt a perfect baby boy. Before the adoption is finalized, the dad is diagnosed with inoperable cancer and the birth mother changes her mind. I tried to get the courts to let the adoptive mother keep the boy. But it just didn't work out. Just like that, the woman goes from having the family she always wanted to being alone."

Hannah's stomach clenched as she imagined that woman—the silence of a house that had been filled with a baby's laughter, the emptiness on the side of the bed where her husband had slept. Maybe Becca was grown up, but Hannah had a heart full of memories and a future full of adventures just waiting for her daughter to experience them. She had a baby drowsing in a cradle upstairs, an unexpected gift so precious it still awed her. She and Sam might be struggling right now, but she could still reach out her hand to touch his, feel the warm pulsing of life through his veins.

"I'm sorry for your client. And for you," she said to Tony, imagining all too vividly what it would be like if she lost Ellie after a whole year of loving her, mothering her. "It must be . . . difficult, seeing people's pain all the time."

"Lawyers don't get called in on many happy occasions, that's for sure," Tony said. "But those times when you can do some good, right some wrong, win justice for someone who wouldn't have gotten it without your help—that makes it all worthwhile."

He sounded tired. *Harmless*, Hannah thought. And he was only trying to do his job and check on Ellie. Any threat only existed in her overactive guilt complex.

"There's no reason you can't stop over, I mean, as long as Sam doesn't have to be here." Even as she said the words, they made her a little uncomfortable. If the situation was reversed, she knew she wouldn't be thrilled to have Sam's old high school flame rendezvousing with him at the kitchen table. It seemed vaguely wrong, somehow. But surely it couldn't be right to get Tony in trouble after all he'd done to help them, either. Maybe Sam would get home before Tony even got there.

"I don't really need to see Sam. I just need to check on Ellie, see how she's doing. I bet she's growing like crazy."

Hannah's mouth twitched in a reluctant smile. "It's amazing. You can almost see it, they change so fast."

"Terrific. I'll be over in a little bit."

"Do you remember how to get here? I mean, it's been years since you've been in Willowton." Somehow trying to explain why she'd asked made it worse.

"I could find my way there blindfolded," Tony said,

his voice making her stomach give a quiver. "Though I think your grandma was always hoping I'd forget."

Strange, Hannah thought, Tony had been one of the few who hadn't found cherry pie and peace in her grandma's kitchen. He'd never been able to settle down, as if the frayed edges on the cushions had been needle sharp, and Grandma's voice had been off-key. Grandma had always been unfailingly polite to him. That was what had disturbed Hannah. Not once had she ordered Tony around, clucked over him like the hens she kept in the yard. Not once had she welcomed him with the warm hug everyone else seemed to get at her door.

"I'll see you soon, then," she said, unsettled by the memory. How many times had Hannah tried to convince her grandmother just how wonderful Tony was, recounting all the places he'd traveled to as an air force brat? How he was smarter than any other boy in class? Grandma had only told her that there were many kinds of education. Studying books was grand, but she'd far rather a person had "learning of the heart." And nothing Hannah could say would convince her that Tony had much of that.

Sam, her grandmother had loved at once, always trying to feed him, sending home baskets bursting with cherry pies and crocks of soup to warm on the stove, the homemade jam he loved so much and tomatoes still warm from the garden.

When Hannah had gotten embarrassed and said she was treating Sam like he was starving, Grandma's eyes had grown warm, soft and a little sad. *He's hungry, that boy. I'm filling him up the only way I can.*

After that, she'd started to notice that whenever he took her out he said he wasn't hungry. He'd just had pizza with friends, grabbed a bite at one of the three jobs he was working to put himself through school. He'd always gotten her whatever she wanted. Insisted she have a sundae or milkshake, or the biggest size popcorn at the movies, but he'd never treated himself to so much as a soda.

But even more, she'd begun to see that he wasn't just hungry in his stomach. *Look in his eyes, Hannah-baby*, her grandmother said. *It's home he's hungry for.*

Hannah had believed her. But obviously she and her grandma had been wrong about both men. Her greatest hurt in her marriage had always been that Sam was away from home far more than he was there. While Tony had been so kind and compassionate with Ellie, maybe he'd learned whatever it was her grandma had insisted he was missing.

Confused, Hannah went to the hall mirror, started to straighten her hair. Not because she cared what Tony thought, she assured herself. She just needed to make a good impression on the lawyer who was Ellie's guardian. She should at least do him the courtesy of having her hair brushed, shouldn't she?

She stopped, her hand midair, a few wayward tendrils clinging to her fingers. This was going to be more complicated than she thought, with Sam gone. Or maybe this was a gift from God, a chance to talk to Tony alone, lay her cards on the table. Tell him—tell him what? A voice jeered in her head. That you're a married woman? He already knows that—Sam being in the courtroom was a dead giveaway. Or maybe you want to make him feel guilty about deserting you? Tell him what it was like for you out in Oregon, after he'd left you pregnant with his baby?

No, she denied sharply. She'd never intended to tell him anything about the hellish months she'd spent there. How lonely she'd been. How ashamed and scared. How young and foolish—hoping against hope that he'd read the letter she mailed him about the birth of his daughter, and that would change everything. He'd ride up on a white charger and rescue her, tell her he loved her and the baby, that he'd been wrong to leave them. That he was going to make everything all right.

Hannah winced, aching for the girl she had been, remembering the scores of other letters she had written him in her head, those letters she'd never sent. The way she'd cried and pleaded with him in her heart. The times she'd imagined, just imagined what it would be like to unload all the suffering, all the anger, all the confusion she'd felt because he'd betrayed her.

But he hadn't really betrayed her. She'd always known that deep down. He'd told her the truth from the beginning. He'd been no more than a kid himself, trying hard to prove he was a man. What had happened between them was sad. It was tragic. It might even still be dangerous. But it had all happened a long time ago. They were different people, now. With different lives.

The only things they shared were old, painful memories and the baby who lay kicking in her swing. Hannah crossed to where Ellie was trying to get her fist into her mouth and unfastened the narrow safety belt that held her into the padded plastic seat.

"You're the one Tony is coming to see, aren't you, Miss Moo? Let's change you into something you haven't decorated with your last bottle of milk, huh?" She scooped Ellie up and snuggled her close, laid her cheek against the baby's downy hair.

Hannah closed her eyes for a moment, letting Ellie's warmth seep deep inside her, to soothe her, calm her, gentle the confusion stirred up inside her. For a moment, just a moment, it wasn't Ellie in her arms. It was another baby girl nuzzling close, never guessing that the footsteps approaching in the hospital hall belonged to the nurse who was coming to take her away.

* * *

The old farmhouse was just boards and bricks, paint peeling a little bit here and there. But as Tony turned his car down the lane, he couldn't keep himself from pressing on the brakes, pausing to take it all in after a lifetime away.

It seemed frozen in time—the only changes to the building, paint a little more crisp and fresh than he recalled, a cherry-shaped birdhouse hanging from the gnarled crabapple tree and a basketball hoop fastened to the peak of the garage. The once-purple net had faded to lavender from the sun, its backboard smudged and battered where Hannah's daughter must have tried to sink shots as a little girl.

Flowers still rioted in a tangle, too undisciplined for his taste. His father had never had much time for gardens, but whatever plants the Blake family had come in contact with over the years had been whipped into shape with military precision, just like everything else in the army of houses they'd lived in.

Tony could remember offering to cut back some of the rose vines clambering up the south farmhouse wall. It had been one of the first times he had heard Hannah laugh. She'd tipped back one of the branches so show him tight clusters of deep red buds hidden under the glossy foliage.

Think of all the flowers we'd miss if you cut them away, she'd said.

He'd shrugged, glancing up at the branches as wild and overrun as Jack's beanstalk must have been, trying to climb their way to the clouds. *What would it matter if we lost a few? Look at them all! There would still be mountains of flowers left.*

She'd touched the buds as tenderly as if they could hear every word. *Don't you know that every one is different? Special? Every bud has the right to bloom.*

How many times had he thought of that moment in the miserable weeks after he'd gotten the letter telling him she was pregnant. He'd wanted to leave the air force base long enough to talk some sense into her. Tell her not to make things so damn hard for herself. Have an abortion and no one would ever have to know . . .

Maybe he hadn't bothered because he'd figured that a girl who couldn't bring herself to trim back roses would never be willing to cut off the life of a child, no matter how tiny. Or had he realized that in spite of his determination to charge forward with his future, he'd cared about Hannah. So much so that a part of him liked the idea of Hannah having his baby. That way, even if she met another man, married him, a part of Hannah would always be Tony's.

If you'd asked him months ago, he would have told you he barely remembered Hannah. And yet, had she been quietly luring him back to this small town for longer than he could remember? Luring him with flashes of a long ago innocence impossibly sweet.

It wasn't hard to convince himself that this Sam O'Connell would always be second-best in her heart. After all, O'Connell couldn't be such a great husband. The whole town of Willowton was littered with buildings constructed by O'Connell, but the man hadn't so much as changed the shutters on this place.

But most telling of all had been the shadows in Hannah's eyes, the touch of sadness, cheeks a little too thin, a little too pale. That spring before he'd left Willowton, she'd been blooming like one of her roses. Maybe he didn't know why, but she wasn't blooming now.

Easing off the brake, Tony pulled into the driveway and parked. This would give him the chance he needed to find out exactly where things stood with her marriage. If there might be a chance for him.

She'd never been able to hide anything from him.

He winced with guilt as a thought came, unbidden. When he hadn't wanted to see what lay in her expressive eyes he'd just made sure he turned away.

Not the thought he wanted on his mind when he walked into Hannah's kitchen. He struggled to lock the unwanted emotions up until he didn't feel them at all, a skill he'd learned in the air force and perfected in years of litigation.

Glancing in the rearview mirror, he smoothed his hand through his hair. Man, if only his old law partner could see him now. No ice in his veins here.

He climbed out of the car and mounted the back stairs, then knocked on the door.

She appeared in the window so fast, he felt a jab of embarrassment. Had she been watching him the whole time, seen him stop in the driveway, check his hair? The key here was to act casual. Hannah had always been the most loyal and honorable person he'd ever met. If she had any idea he might want more of a connection with her than their shared interest in Ellie, she'd slip out of his grasp forever. But then, years practicing law had taught him subtlety if nothing else.

She opened the door, smiling uncertainly, Ellie nestled contentedly in her arms. He wondered what it would have felt like to see mother and child like this if Ellie had had his eyes, the shape of his mouth, if she'd been something the two of them had made together. "Looks like you remembered your way here after all," Hannah said, sweeping her hair back with her other hand in a nervous gesture he remembered all too well. He drew in a whiff of the fragrance that was all Hannah's own—lilies and lilacs and sunshine.

"I told you I'd find you." He held her gaze for one long moment, then before she could be certain what he meant he looked down at Ellie, flashing the baby a grin.

"Hello there, princess," he said as the baby stared up at him with unfocused blue eyes. "How are things going at the castle?"

"Would you like to see? I mean, where she sleeps? Where she plays? She takes a bottle every four hours and—"

"I'm sure you're giving her everything she needs and more. But if you'd like to show me it would give me something to write in my report. First, though, let's just sit down and you can tell me how you're both doing. Mind if I hold Her Majesty while we talk? It's not often I get the chance to hold a little one."

Hannah handed Ellie over, and he felt good at the look of approval she gave him at the way he supported her head, techniques learned from the women he'd dated. When you got into your late thirties and early forties, almost all of them had kids.

"You're so good at holding babies," Hannah said. "Most men look like you've just handed them a bomb." She led him into the sun porch with its white wicker swing and rocker. She gestured toward the rocker and he sank into it. Hannah sat in the porch swing, but in spite of its cushions she seemed uncomfortable. "Do you have any kids of your own?" she asked.

Tony didn't know why the question chafed. She didn't seem to have bothered to keep track of him at all. It hurt somehow. Hell, the tiniest question and his mom would've been thrilled to rattle on about him for ages. Hannah must've seen her at the store.

He shook his head in answer to Hannah's question. "Always hoped I would, but no. Sometimes things just don't turn out the way you want them to."

Her lashes dipped over her eyes. What was she hiding? The fact that she felt the same way, too? "Married?" she asked.

He gave a cynical laugh and Ellie's blue eyes stared up at him, startled. Her lower lip trembled. He set the rocker in motion to settle her down. "Liked getting married so much I couldn't seem to do it often enough. Heard somewhere that the third time was supposed to be the charm. It turned out to be the worst one of all."

Hannah's cheeks turned red as the cherries he remembered in her grandmother's pies. "I'm sorry. I didn't know." She looked appalled, terrified she'd hurt him by bringing up painful memories. There was no way she'd be able to understand that the divorces were only vaguely embarrassing memories now. The end of relationships that should have been right for him, perfect corporate wives, brilliant hostesses, polished beauties his colleagues would envy. Women who turned out to be absolutely wrong.

He smiled, shifting his arm more comfortably under Ellie's chubby legs. "Don't worry about it. Hurt my pride more than anything else."

He surprised a question out of her. "Didn't you . . ." The words trailed off, unspoken. If her cheeks got any redder, he figured they'd catch on fire.

"Love them?" He finished for her.

"It's none of my business," she said hastily. "I don't even know why I asked."

"What's a few questions between two old friends? We've got to catch up, don't we?"

"It *has* been a long time."

Longer than she could ever imagine.

"I thought I loved them at the time, but as it turns out, I'm a rotten judge of what love is. When I think it's the real thing, it's phony as a three dollar bill. But the one time I had heaven in my hands, I'm not smart enough to hold on. How about you? Your daughter's all grown up and gone. You and Sam must have been together a long time."

"Since college."

Why did the information hurt? He'd wanted her to wait for him longer than that. He'd imagined her thinking of him, measuring every man she met against him and finding them lacking. Even more than that, he'd been dead sure that she'd keep their baby. It never even occurred to him that she'd give it away. But Becca O'Connell was an only child. And she'd been born years after he'd been long gone.

What had happened to the child he and Hannah had made? He'd been too much of a coward to write and ask at the time.

"What was it about Sam?" *That made you forget me*, he added silently. *What was that strategic advice everyone was always giving? Know your enemy?*

"He made me laugh. And when I was with him, I forgot to be shy."

A fierce kind of possessiveness reared up in Tony. *He* had been the one who first got her to laugh. *He'd* teased her out of her shyness. O'Connell had just come after him.

But before he could take much pleasure in it, Hannah's voice softened. "Most of all, Sam made me feel safe."

Tony winced. He glanced down at Ellie in an effort to hide it. He'd given Hannah a taste of excitement. But he hadn't made her feel "safe." You couldn't feel "safe" with someone who told you right up front he was going to leave you. Leave you no matter what—even if his baby was growing inside you.

"You must have needed that," Tony admitted. "To feel safe after. . . after everything you'd gone through."

It cost him more than she could ever know to give O'Connell credit.

"That was all a long time ago. It doesn't matter anymore."

"Maybe some people could just put it in the past and forget about it. But somehow, I don't think you're one of them."

Ellie snuffled, drifting off to sleep. Hannah bent over to a basket full of baby things and retrieved a receiving blanket with Pooh Bear on it. She handed it to him to tuck around the baby. Had he hit a nerve? he wondered. Or was she merely being Hannah—considering so carefully what she was going to say.

"People make mistakes," she said. "No matter how much you regret it, you have to go on."

"How did you? Go on?" He asked. "If you don't want to talk about it, just tell me and I'll shut up, but I can't help wondering how you got through it. God, you must have hated me."

"It would have been easier if I could have. But you never lied to me. You never promised me anything more than that single springtime."

"You didn't ask to get pregnant. It wasn't exactly what you'd planned for your life, either. But I got to walk away, pretend like nothing had happened. While you . . . ."

He'd felt like enough of a heel for ditching her when he'd been eighteen. Now, as a man, facing what he'd done made him sick to his stomach. What could a raw kid have known about the kind of mess she'd had to face alone?

What had it been like for Hannah here, in this tiny town? When old biddies walked past did they still whisper behind their hands about how Hannah had been "in trouble"? The image made his gut knot.

"How did you ever get through it?" he asked, half-scared she might tell him and that once she did, he'd never be able to get it out of his mind again.

"My parents sent me to my aunt in Oregon so nobody would ever know. I couldn't even tell Grandma. I was so sure she'd be disappointed in me."

He could imagine what the old lady would have had to say. He'd tried so hard to win her over, but she'd never thawed the way most people did when he turned on the charm. She'd always seen deeper than that, and the knowledge had made him squirm.

Tony looked away. Damn it, it would have been so much easier for her if she'd just gone to the clinic in Iowa City, a half-hour procedure and she could have walked straight out of their office back into the life she'd always known. No one would ever have guessed.

But he'd been the one to take the easy way out. For all her shyness, Hannah had been too strong for that. Maybe she was better off with O'Connell, after all. O'Connell had looked the situation straight in the eye. It would have made Tony crazy with jealousy, knowing Hannah had borne another man's child. But obviously Sam O'Connell was above that. Whether he knew it was Tony Blake's or not didn't matter. Hannah would have told him about the baby. O'Connell had accepted it, taken her just the way she was.

"What . . . what was it?" Tony asked, the question grating in his throat. "The baby?"

"A girl. She was beautiful." She glanced down at Ellie, but he knew it was another baby she saw there. Hannah's face glowed, soft, sad, like the madonnas he'd seen in church as a kid, a mother still grieving even after eternity.

"Did she look like you?"

"More like you. She had your eyes and your hands. But she had my smile."

"What did you name her?"

"I didn't." She looked as if that still hurt her. Not even being able to give her baby a name. "The people from the adoption agency said it would only have made it harder to give her up."

"I figured you'd keep her. I couldn't picture you ever letting your own baby go to strangers."

She winced and he could have kicked himself, the words sounded so hard. "I'm sorry, Hannah. Who the hell am I to judge you? First I asked you to get rid of the baby. Then I walked away."

"Mom and Dad convinced me it was the only thing I could do. I didn't have a job, didn't have any skills. And if I'd kept the baby, I wouldn't have had anyplace to live. So I did the only thing I could."

"I know it couldn't have been easy for you to let her go."

"It was the hardest thing I've ever done. And the one I regret the most."

Tony had had regrets of his own, but he hadn't let them get in his way. He'd made his decision the way his father had taught him—with his own best interests in mind. And he'd never given himself a chance to reconsider. Decision made. It was done. Beating yourself up wouldn't change anything. And just because you had doubts didn't mean you made the wrong choice. It just meant that sometimes you might wonder.

"Did they tell you anything about her? What happened to her? Is she still in Oregon?"

"No. I went back, tried to find her. I don't even know what I intended to do. Try to get her back or just make sure she'd be safe, taken care of. Loved. But when I got there it was too late." Hannah looked up at him, anguished. "My baby was dead."

12

"WHAT?" Tony felt like she'd kicked him square in the stomach. Ellie whimpered in sleepy protest, and Tony realized he was holding her too tight. He loosened his grip. All these nights he'd tried to piece together a picture of their child's life, wondered what it looked like, whether he played football or she could play piano. He'd imagined high school graduation and birthday parties and the whole time he'd been imagining what the son or daughter he'd never seen was doing, it had been lying in a little box in Oregon. Dead. What kind of people had Hannah given their daughter to? People who had let her die? "When . . . how?" he asked.

"I found out five months after she was born. She just stopped breathing. Sudden infant death syndrome, they called it. They told me where she was buried. I went there once and left a flower. It was so quiet and green, the mountains in the background. I could tell you—tell you where she is if you ever wanted to see her."

See nothing but a headstone? What the hell was the point? He knew it wasn't fair, but he felt like Hannah had cheated him out of something. She could have let him know, damn it!

But why would she? A cooler voice of reason demanded. He'd made it clear he didn't want anything to do with their baby alive, why would she think he'd care if it died? Hell, she might have even been afraid he'd be glad. He'd always been plenty glad to escape whenever things got too hard.

Even the Air Force Academy he'd wanted so badly hadn't been able to keep him on track. He'd dropped out during his second year, hated the reality of discipline and flight as much as he'd thought he would love it. His father had had a hell of a fit of rage over that. *It's too hard?* the Sarge had yelled. *Who the hell cares about that? Life is hard! Stick to something for once in your life, boy!*

He'd blown the old man off. Like his father had any right to be handing out advice. The old man had hung onto his military career like a pit bull, no matter how miserable it had made him, no matter how downright humiliating it got.

But somewhere, in the back of his mind, Tony had assured himself he could take all the time he wanted, having things his own way. That he'd be able to find his child, tell her he was her father if he ever chose to.

But even if he and Hannah had lost the daughter conceived when they were kids, he'd made it up to her, hadn't he? He'd made it possible for Hannah to have another child. He looked down at Ellie lying there in his arms. If he hadn't stepped forward, the courts might never have let Ellie be part of her life.

Was that supposed to be atonement for his long ago sins?

Or was there another one he was about to commit

that was even more reprehensible? The ugly truth was he wanted to see if he could break up the woman's marriage, for God's sake!

But if he *could* do it, would it really be his fault? He tried to excuse himself. There would have to be something wrong with it in the first place. That *something* he'd seen in the shadows beneath Hannah's eyes, that sadness that haunted her mouth, that left her looking lost in a house she'd lived in and loved her whole life.

You should just walk away, Blake, he told himself. *You've done enough damage, left enough scars.*

He might have been able to do it except for the solid core inside him he couldn't ever change. Never in his life had he learned how to give up what he wanted. And he wanted Hannah. It surprised him just how much. She was everything his other wives hadn't been. He could trust her. Wouldn't have to worry about her spending too much or finding more excitement in other men's beds. Even if, at their age, it was too late to have kids of their own, they could adopt half a dozen like Ellie. Hannah would be happy to raise children instead of balking at how it would impact her career.

"Tony?" she asked. "Are you all right?"

Yeah, I'm just terrific, he wanted to snap. He'd just found out their child was dead. And every minute he spent in the same room with Hannah deepened his resolve to break up her marriage. "All right" was the last way he'd try to describe the way he was feeling right now.

"Can I ask you something, Hannah?"

"Sure."

"In the courtroom, I couldn't help wondering. I mean, your husband didn't act like he'd ever heard my name. Does he know I fathered your baby?"

Her cheeks flamed. Her stricken gaze dropped to fingers suddenly trembling. She hesitated, her voice whisper soft when she finally spoke. "Sam doesn't know who—who you are because . . . I never told him about the baby."

Tony stared at the crown of her bent head, stunned. Disbelief and triumph jolted through him. She hadn't told O'Connell she'd had another man's child? He'd never have believed she'd keep that secret from the man she'd been married to for twenty-two years! Hadn't she trusted him to understand? Had she been afraid he'd walk out on their relationship?

Maybe O'Connell wouldn't have been able to take the truth, after all. Ever since their meeting in the courtroom, Tony had been wondering just what Sam O'Connell was made of. Fearing he was some strong, noble hero who had ridden into Hannah's life and driven out any memory of the relationship she and Tony had shared. He'd dreaded the thought that O'Connell had been the one to keep the bitterness from Hannah's eyes, who'd helped her forgive herself for what had happened. That he'd been her knight in shining armor when Tony had left her, alone and shattered and scared. But she hadn't told him about the baby—hadn't trusted him enough.

Or had she just been too ashamed of what had happened to tell O'Connell? He liked that possibility a whole lot less than the others. But whatever her reason, Hannah had kept secrets from her husband. And that fact alone gave Tony hope, a place to start.

Suddenly, he was aware he was smiling, and Hannah had raised her gaze to his face, her eyes suddenly clouded, confused.

Ever so carefully, Tony transformed his expression into one of compassion and concern.

"Your secret is safe with me. I'm sure you had your

reasons for deciding not to tell O'Connell. If you ever want to talk—well," he shrugged.

"Talk? I'm not sure what you mean. I think I've told you everything that matters."

"I don't think so. There's something in your face, Hannah, something in your eyes that makes me wonder."

"Wonder what?"

Wonder what you would do if I held you, wonder if you'd catch fire under my lips, wonder if you'd let me . . . Tony reined his thoughts in savagely. He was good at hiding his emotions, but Hannah had seen him aroused before. He couldn't risk the chance she might know the smoldering in his eyes for exactly what it was. She'd send him packing before he'd even had a chance to kiss her.

"If maybe you could use a friend," he said, reaching for her hand. She looked startled for a moment, but he kept the touch light, simple, as if he were telling the truth, being a friend instead of a man who had every intention of getting her back into his bed.

"Have you ever talked to anyone about what happened?" he asked gently. "Your baby died. *Our* baby died. Maybe Sam doesn't know. Maybe no one else on earth does except you and me. But that doesn't make the loss any easier, does it? In some ways, it has to make it even more difficult."

She swallowed hard, stood up from the swing. Her fingers pulled away from his. She pressed one hand against the window as if she were checking to make sure the barrier were still there—the barrier years had placed between the two of them, the barrier secrecy had placed between her grief for their child. Grief, Tony was certain, must be haunting her at least a little since Ellie had come into her life, bringing with her memories Hannah must have fought so hard to suppress.

"I don't mean to push," Tony said hastily. "I just thought—we could talk about what she looked like, what she sounded like when she cried. You could tell me what day her birthday was and how you felt when it came, year after year, and there was no one else who knew why you were sad. I know I was a real bastard when I walked away from you, Hannah, and there's nothing I can ever do to fix that, but I'm here, now. There must be a reason we were thrown together again, don't you think?"

"Your coming back here had nothing to do with me or our baby. You came back to town to take care of your mother and I just happen to live here. Our paths crossed by pure chance."

"You're right about chance," he said carefully, sensing she was teetering on the edge. She didn't feel right talking to him like this in the house she shared with her husband. She felt guilty as hell about keeping secrets from O'Connell and was terrified the truth would slip out somehow, so many years after she must've thought she was safe.

"Maybe what we've both been given is a chance to find some sort of peace at last. Finally sort out what happened, grieve about it, forgive ourselves and each other and, God willing, let it go at last. We made a child together, Hannah. We lost her. And we both hid it away, locked up our feelings, stopped up our tears because there was no one we could tell, no one we dared talk to. But silence only made it all worse, didn't it? I know I need to talk about our little girl, and I think you—"

Hannah all but jumped out of her skin as a noise came from the direction of the kitchen, keys rattling in the lock, the door swinging on its hinges.

She blanched, her face so guilt-stricken Tony's stomach clenched. "Please," she breathed, "don't—"

"Not a word," Tony promised solemnly. He wouldn't have to say a word. He had the grace to feel empathy for the woman before him. O'Connell would find out the truth all in good time—when his nagging suspicions could no longer be subdued or when Hannah's guilt got too heavy for her to carry. No, Tony wouldn't have to say anything at all.

"Hannah?" O'Connell's voice rang through the house. "Somebody's blocking the drive."

Tony could hear O'Connell's footsteps approaching. The look on Hannah's face ought to be enough to set O'Connell's nerves on edge.

If Tony were going to come out on top in this situation, he'd have to make damn sure O'Connell was the one who looked like the bastard.

Tony cradled Ellie expertly in his arms and stood as close to Hannah as he dared. "Welcome home, Sam," he said heartily. "Hannah and I were just catching up on old times."

O'Connell eyed him warily.

"Tony came to see Ellie," Hannah explained a little breathlessly. "Remember, the judge ordered him to. I was going to show him where Ellie sleeps, and—I'm so glad you got home. You can go with us."

"Don't even know why you have to check the place since you know Hannah," Sam said.

"Just a formality. Besides, I haven't seen this place in years." Tony let just the hint of a smirk show around his lips. "I admit to being curious."

Something unexpected flashed into O'Connell's eyes for an instant. A vulnerability so raw Tony scented blood.

What had he said that dug so deep under O'Connell's

skin? It was no secret Tony had been in the farmhouse before, or that he hadn't seen it in years. Then what . . . the word *curious*, Tony realized with a jolt. That was what had unsettled O'Connell. What did O'Connell have to hide?

"You go ahead," Sam said, trying to mask his unease with action. "I've got work to do."

Tony sensed it was an excuse the man had used plenty of times before. But there was something layered underneath it. O'Connell looked as if *he* were the one who'd almost gotten caught with a guilty secret, instead of the other way around.

Hannah obviously noticed his discomfort, too. She gave O'Connell a nervous smile, paused to brush a kiss on his cheek before she hurried past him. Tony started to follow, bemused at how awkward that kiss had seemed, not the easy intimacy one would expect in a marriage of twenty-odd years. At least, he thought hopefully, not a *happy* marriage.

"I'll take Ellie," O'Connell startled Tony, and held out his arms to take the baby. Maybe O'Connell had good instincts after all. If only the man had guessed he should have grabbed for his wife as well. "It will be easier for you to take notes or whatever you have to do for your report if you're not trying to carry a baby at the same time," Sam explained.

Tony handed Ellie over, then followed Hannah up the stairs. As he walked into the master bedroom, he barely glanced at the glossy cradle with its bright quilt. Instead, he took in the rest of the room.

Hell, couldn't O'Connell even buy his wife a decent bedroom set? One that matched instead of this mishmash of old junk? One of the rails on the white iron bed wasn't straight anymore. Just the tiniest wave was visible in its length, as if some kid a hundred years ago had stuck his head between the bars and they'd had to bend them to set him free.

The bed was flanked on one side by an antique commode with a rack for towels and space where a pitcher and washbowl would once have stood, while on the other side of the bed stood a piecrust table.

A tall armoire carved with flowers was made of oak. A chest, long and low, was mahogany, the frame of the mirror above it the same wood, carved with sea shells.

But there was something else strange here, something that didn't make sense.

Wait! Tony realized, his instincts sharpening. *It made perfect sense!*

No wonder O'Connell was acting like the soles of his shoes were on fire!

No masculine clothes draped over chairs. No pocket change lay forgotten on the dresser. And he couldn't see even one bottle of men's cologne on any surface waiting to be used. In fact, there wasn't a single thing that showed Hannah shared this big sunny bedroom with anyone at all.

Was it possible . . . ?

It had to be! God knew, Tony was familiar with the signs. He'd gone through the process of moving from the master to the guest bedroom himself often enough—three times, to be exact, with three different women. But how to find out for sure if he was right this time?

Tony gave a disarming laugh to hide the fact he was probing. "If I'd been as neat as your husband, maybe my ex-wives wouldn't have divorced me."

"Sam is—he's always kept things—in order." Hannah stammered, her cheeks so red Tony expected them to catch fire.

Tony smiled as if he believed her. But the instant he

wandered into the second bedroom under the pretext of seeing how much the farmhouse had changed, he knew his suspicions were right.

Men's toiletries squeezed between a bunch of stuffed animals on what was obviously Rebekah O'Connell's dresser, size eleven men's shoes tucked under the ruffle of a flowered bedspread.

So *that* was how things really stood, Tony mused with fierce satisfaction. It looked like coming between the O'Connells should be a lot easier than he'd expected. First visit to the house and he'd already figured out the man's humiliating secret.

No matter how pretty the O'Connells might try to make their marriage look on the outside, all wasn't perfect in the old white farmhouse.

Hannah and Sam O'Connell weren't sharing a bed.

Tony could barely contain himself until they got back downstairs. He asked Hannah for one more glass of lemonade, buying time alone so he could hunt O'Connell down under the pretext of saying good-bye.

O'Connell sat in a worn leather chair near the old brick fireplace in what looked to be a study, but he hadn't even bothered to unroll the stack of blueprints that littered the rolltop desk. Tony sensed the only "work" O'Connell had been doing since they'd left him at the bottom of the stairs was listening to the movements on the floor above him, wondering if Tony had unearthed his little secret.

"Good to see you again, O'Connell," Blake said with flawless manners designed to irritate the hell out of him. "Everything about Ellie's living arrangements seems to be in order."

"Did you expect to find it any other way? Hannah would sleep on the floor if she had to so that baby would have a bed."

"She would, wouldn't she?" Blake gave a perfect country club chuckle, listening to the clink of ice from the kitchen, the shutting of the freezer door. "But then, Hannah always has given away everything she has—food, clothes—never taking anything for herself. Easy to take advantage of, God bless her."

"Not while I'm around."

"Of course not. I can see just how much help you've been." More rattling around from the kitchen. He still had plenty of time.

"I do what I can."

That's not much by the looks of things around here, Blake thought.

He let his lips curl in an innocent smile. "Yeah, those nighttime feedings are hell, aren't they? Every three or four hours, the baby waking up screaming. Bottles to warm up, diapers to change. It can be damned exhausting."

"Have any kids of your own?"

"No. Well, one. But I've never . . . seen her."

"An expert on fatherhood, then. Picking up a baby who's sick and screaming is a whole lot different than just grabbing one for a photo op."

Touché, Tony thought. Maybe O'Connell wasn't as easy a mark as Tony had believed. But there was no way Sam O'Connell could win any contest between them. All the weapons that mattered were in Tony's hands. Tony could hear ice clinking against glass, the sound of Hannah's footsteps approaching.

He satisfied himself for the time being with imagining what O'Connell would look like when he finally found out the truth. How Tony had made love to O'Connell's wife in the tumbledown stable, in the woods behind the old schoolhouse, down by the river on a strip of sand he'd found. He imagined telling

O'Connell just how much Hannah had liked it. He'd been a little fast on the draw like all teenaged boys, but he'd made sure Hannah enjoyed it enough to want it again, even when he'd "forgotten" the protection that cut down on his sensation when he wanted to feel her, all of her, closed around him.

"Tony?" she asked glancing nervously from him to her husband. "Here's the drink you asked for."

I haven't even begun to ask you for what I really want, Tony thought, flashing her his best smile.

It should be easy to make things turn out the way he wanted them to, Tony thought. He just had to get past Hannah's oversize conscience. Get her talking about the baby they'd lost. Show her how much better her life could be. That he could give her everything O'Connell never could.

No question, breaking through her scruples would be a challenge. But it wasn't as if it couldn't be done. After all, he'd managed to get past them when they'd made love in the stable. This time—uncomfortable as it might be for her at first, it would be for her own good.

He was doing her a favor. She'd be better off without O'Connell.

And that was something Tony could arrange.

It was all a matter of doing what he was best at—getting exactly what he wanted.

Hannah would thank him in time.

13

SAM STRETCHED OUT in Becca's canopy bed, but in spite of the deep, soft mattress beneath him and mounds of pillows at his back he might as well be trying to sleep on broken glass. Becca's room still felt frozen in a happier, sweeter time, worlds away from the tension that had marked the hours since Tony Blake had climbed into his Porsche and sped away, the smirk on the lawyer's face leaving Sam edgy and Hannah pale with strain. Blake's visit seeming to dash away the warmth, the healing Sam had been trying so hard to nurture between Hannah and himself. His work on the cradle, and his efforts to spend evenings sprawled with the baby on the floor, playing, his way of trying to show Hannah he wanted to be close to her again.

He'd even thought things were getting better. But tonight, he'd lost major ground. She felt farther away from him than ever, and nothing he said would make her share whatever was shadowing her eyes with trouble, her mouth with sadness.

Had Blake said something? Done something to upset her? Or had something reminded her of whatever was causing the distance between them? Reminded her of old hurts or his past failures, in spite of how hard he was trying to please her?

He glanced around the room he'd slept in for so many months, feeling isolated. Confused. Every shadow and corner and shelf accenting how wrong things were, that he couldn't figure out how to break down the walls, find his way back to the bed where he belonged.

Reminders of Becca's growing-up years filled the room. Award plaques she'd won for making All State in choir. A framed picture from senior prom with Becca and all her girlfriends clowning around with black top hats they'd worn as a joke. The papier mâché mask that had transformed her into the Cowardly Lion in the junior class play dangled from a loop of yarn mane from shelves he'd run all around the top of her room. Perched on the ledge, rag-tag dolls still stood at attention, like an army whose general had gone missing.

Most nights, Sam made sure he was so exhausted when he finally trudged up here to bed, that he could barely keep his eyes open long enough to turn back the coverlets. His one defense against remembering how things used to be, with Becca bouncing in and out of the house and the certainty that when night came, he'd be able to fit Hannah gently into the curve of his body, smell the fragrance of her shampoo. Her skin, fresh scrubbed and glowing soft under his hands as the petals of the flowers she loved so much.

But things weren't the way they had been for so long. Not for any of them. He felt more shy about touching Hannah now than he had the first time he'd taken her hand on the college green.

And as for Becca . . . she had sounded so lost the last

time he'd talked to her. Confused and resentful, as if she could feel the foundations of everything she'd ever taken for granted being shaken beneath her feet, her childhood at home over, her relationship with Hannah strained.

If only Becca knew just how off-balance things had gotten at home. How would she feel if she found out how things really stood between Sam and Hannah? Discovered that her father was sleeping in her room, alone? Or would they scurry around to hide it? Move his things back into the master bedroom and pretend he kept falling asleep on the couch watching TV? But even that wouldn't work for long.

Becca was plenty old enough to figure out what the change in bedroom arrangements meant.

And she wasn't the only one it was obvious to. Sam winced inwardly. Troops of stuffed animals seemed to stare at him with shoe-button eyes, and laugh behind a rainbow of plush paws.

Do you think Blake suspects? a stuffed tiger leered. *Wonder if he can guess how long it's been since you slept in your own bed, touched your wife, let alone made love to her?*

Sam threw back the last of the covers, a fine sheen of sweat dampening the back of his neck and prickling his brow. Humiliation burned inside him, the unshakable sensation that during his visit to the farmhouse, Tony Blake had scented blood.

Sam had seen the glint in Blake's eyes, feared he'd guessed the truth—that Sam missed Hannah so much it ate him up inside. That Sam had agreed to take Ellie in at least partly in hopes that the baby could help Hannah heal? And maybe, in bringing her joy, help fix what was wrong between the two of them?

Sam swore under his breath. One of the clearest lessons he had ever learned had come in the days after his mother had walked out on him. He'd learned to hide his hurts, not let anyone see them. People would only use them against you. While teachers and some of the kids had been kind, plenty of others jeered at him, saying he was so worthless even his mother didn't want him. The truth in the words made the hurt cut far deeper.

He'd been so careful, ever since. Even with Hannah, much as he loved her. Sworn he'd be damned before he ever made the same mistake again and handed someone the sharpest weapon they could use against him. Let someone see the naked place in his soul. But he'd tipped his hand this time. He'd seen it register in Blake's eyes. That sharp pleasure of discovering something another person wanted to hide. Knowing that at least a part of their peace of mind was in your control. You could shatter it at your will.

Sam's gut clenched at the thought of Blake having any hold at all over him. Sam's fists knotted. But much as Blake chafed Sam's nerves, the lawyer couldn't even touch the deeper pain he felt. How the hell had he lost touch with Hannah? How the hell had they come to this? A room away, a million miles apart?

So close, she was so close he could hear the soft rustling sounds of her moving around in bed. So familiar, he could imagine the way her hair rippled in waves across the pillow even though a wall stood between them. He'd wondered if she'd kicked the covers off. If she'd remembered to put a glass of water on the bed-side table so she could take the pain medication the doctor had prescribed if she needed it in the middle of the night. He'd wondered if, while lost in dreams, she ever reached out to him, even though he wasn't there.

Sam leaned over to the window beside the bed and shoved it open wider, letting the night breeze drift over his fevered skin. Hot as he was, he wouldn't strip out of his pajama bottoms. Somehow it didn't feel right to sleep that way in his little girl's bed, even with Becca three hours away.

But with Hannah—he'd slept naked every night until the coldest part of winter hit and Hannah bullied him into pajamas, her laughter silvery sweet and rare when he told her he'd take his chances with pneumonia. It was more than worth enduring a little chill for the indescribable luxury of feeling her with every inch of his body.

She'd always thought he'd hated winter because it was brutal working outside then, but he couldn't have given a damn how cold it got when he was at his job. It was the loss of that delicious intimacy with her that was the real reason he hated Iowa blizzards and temperatures plunging to twenty below zero. And while Hannah waited eagerly for spring's flowers, he'd waited just as impatiently for the day when he could draw her nightgown up over her breasts, draw her tight against his body with not so much as a wisp of cotton between them.

He'd even had fantasies that once Becca was away at school, he might be able to coax Hannah into shedding her thin nightgowns before they climbed into bed. He'd imagined waking up to feel the pillowy weight of her bare breast against his arm, the brush of a pearled nipple. He'd imagined being able to bend over her sleeping body in the moonlight, and ever so gently taking her nipple into his mouth, suckling until she came awake, drowsy and flushed and moaning softly in pleasure.

Sam's groin tightened, swelling until it ached. It had been so long, so goddamned long since he had felt Hannah arching underneath him, felt her climax pulsing around his shaft as he surrendered himself to a release so total it seemed as if he'd poured out his very soul.

He'd known the first time she'd opened her body to him what a gift it was, a miracle to have someone give themselves to you so completely. After twenty-four years, had some of the awe he'd felt melted away? Had he been fool enough to start taking the way they shared their bodies for granted? But then he'd believed that he would always be welcomed into the big white iron bed, that he would always find Hannah waiting for him there, her skin gleaming, flawless as it had been when she was a young girl, her eyes shining.

She was his wife, his lover, his best friend. The one person above all others he'd cherished. And yet, somehow, when he hadn't been paying attention, she'd slipped through his fingers.

Oh, she'd still been here these past months, tending the house, sitting across the table, pouring his coffee and telling him about her day. But it was as if her essence had drifted away until only the ghost of the woman he loved was left.

He'd cursed himself a thousand times for not knowing how to stop it. He was supposed to be the man who could fix anything. And now, he couldn't fix the only thing that mattered.

Had Tony Blake guessed that when he prowled around the upstairs? Did the man have any idea how hard Sam was fighting? How damn scared he was? How hurt? Confused?

The possibility that Blake had seen the places where Sam was raw and bleeding sickened him. One thing Sam had known for certain, though, was that the polished lawyer suspected that something in the O'Connell house wasn't as it should be. Sam had seen it in the other man's eyes, a "knowing" that had turned Sam's stomach, and worse still, a satisfaction that raised every hair on the back of Sam's neck in warning.

Why the devil should Blake take such obvious pleasure in seeing the cracks in their marriage unless the lawyer wanted it to fall apart? And why would Blake want their marriage to fall apart, unless Blake wanted Hannah himself and wasn't going to let something as paltry as marriage vows hold him back?

Sam cursed, low, hating the sudden tremor in his hands. He had no proof. And Hannah would think he was crazy if he ever confessed how he felt. Maybe things weren't perfect between them right now, but hadn't they both been trying hard to set things right since they'd gotten custody of Ellie? Hannah had never been anything but honest with Sam. Honest and fair and loyal to a fault. For a kid who'd been dumped by his mother and never been able to count on his father, it had been almost terrifying how completely he trusted her.

Maybe he should try to remember that now.

He climbed out of bed, dragged one hand through his hair. Maybe Blake *had* been looking at Hannah as if he wanted to swallow her whole. But no matter how sly and superior Blake acted, no matter how often he sneered at Sam's work-callused hands and windburned skin, no matter how many diplomas Blake could pull off the wall of his office to prove he was a better man— it didn't matter a damn.

Hannah was Sam's wife.

Sam had to remember it wasn't Hannah's fault even if Blake *was* attracted to her. He trusted her. And he wasn't about to question that trust, especially for a snake like Tony Blake.

But trusting Hannah didn't mean giving Blake free rein. No, Sam resolved. He'd watch every move Blake made. There was plenty in the lawyer's eyes he didn't like. An arrogance, a kind of mockery, as if he had some kind of advantage, some wild card up his sleeve and he wanted Sam to know it.

Yeah, Sam had sensed it from the moment Blake

had swaggered into the courtroom. There was one main reason Blake had gone into law. The bastard liked to make other people sweat. Damned if Sam wanted to give Blake the pleasure of knowing just how much the man was rattling him.

And yet, he hadn't given a damn what Blake had thought that instant their eyes had locked over Ellie's little head. He'd wanted to snatch the baby away from Blake, hadn't been able to breathe until he'd had Ellie safe in his arms.

Why the hell had he reacted from the gut that way? He'd felt plenty protective of Becca. Other kids, too, in a general kind of way. But this—this had reminded him all too clearly of the time when Becca was three and he'd grabbed her just as she started to chase a ball in the path of a speeding truck.

Heart-pounding, pure instinct, adrenaline rushing emotion. He'd acted on it without thinking. Why?

Because he hadn't been able to stand seeing the baby in the arms of a user, a lawyer used to seeing people as tools to win cases, advance his career? Or, a voice whispered in Sam's head, win the gratitude of a woman obviously desperate, scared, wanting to keep Ellie with all her heart? Or was it something more? Had Sam snatched Ellie away for Ellie's own sake, because he cared? . . .

Sam winced. It had been terrifying enough to love Becca the way he had. Terrifying to know how he could fail her. And he had seen all his shortcomings far too clearly. He still wasn't sure he wanted to take the risks again. Doubted he would have had the courage if he hadn't been trying to mend things with Hannah. Was *he* the one who was being a bastard now? Accusing Blake of using an abandoned child to his own ends?

Or were his own insecurities making the man seem more dangerous than he was? Was Sam feeling so uncertain about where he stood with Hannah that he was looking for an excuse to hate any man who came near her?

In one way, it was easy to understand why anyone would admire Hannah. After all, a man would have to be blind not to see how special she was, whether he knew she was married or not.

But realizing Hannah's worth was one thing. Letting her husband see that you would be willing to take her if you could was another thing altogether.

And Blake had let him know that, with a dozen small gestures, the undisguised glint in his eyes when he looked at her. The smug curve to his mouth as if to say she may be your wife, but she's so far above you, let's see just how long you can hold her.

The unspoken challenge burned in Sam's gut. He paced the room, unable to hold still. Thinking like that was only going to make him crazy. He had to keep focused on what really mattered so Blake couldn't blindside him.

What the hell was Blake taunting him with? A knowledge of something, some history between Blake and Hannah, that made Sam feel like the man was sliding something sharp, cold, dangerous, down Sam's spine. Something that could turn agonizing with just the slightest twitch of Blake's hand. But that wasn't the most terrifying thing of all. Far worse was the look in Hannah's eyes—wariness, dread, and, God, was it possible? Guilt? As if she knew whatever Blake did. Feared it. Instinctively, Sam padded through the shadows, out Becca's bedroom door, silently, and made his way into the room where Hannah lay sleeping. It had always comforted him to see her in slumber. She usually slept so soundly, no nightmares haunting her in the darkness.

But tonight, the covers were tangled where she'd

tossed and turned, her limbs restless, and instead of the angelic peace that had comforted Sam on many sleepless nights, her face was tight with worry, dread . . . guilt? he wondered, with a sharp sting of nervousness.

Bad dreams. She'd had plenty in the early days of their marriage, but slowly, they'd gone away. Sam had held her, whispered to her, soothed her until she'd melted against him, sleeping again in his arms. He'd lie there, unwilling to disturb her even when his arm fell asleep, when it burned and tingled and ached. He hadn't wanted to move, stir up whatever demons had been haunting her.

She'd sigh, and he'd understood. She knew he'd keep her safe. But how could he keep her safe now, when he wasn't lying beside her? When he could barely touch her, let alone hold her tight?

He would have given everything he possessed if he could have touched her now. Even in sleep, the usually soft curves of her face clenched tight, lines etched in her brow. Dark shadows bruised the delicate skin beneath her eyes, as if she'd been beaten by some enemy only she could see. She mouthed words he couldn't understand, her face twitching, head tossing in distress.

She rolled to her side, one hand reaching out, groping at the emptiness on his side of the bed. A soft moan of loss breached her lips as her fingers closed on nothing but a fold of the sheets. Oh, God, Sam wondered. Was she reaching for him? Begging him to make the nightmare stop?

Sam couldn't stand it. He crossed to the bed, touched her face lightly with the tips of his fingers. She was dewy with sweat, her face ash pale.

"Hannah?" he said softly.

She cried out, came awake with a start, her eyes

wide. Even in the faint ribbon of moonlight streaming through the window he could see them fill with fear.

"Don't let them . . . don't let them take her . . ."

Sam's heart squeezed in alarm. He'd never heard her this way. "No. I won't let them take her. I promise. Hannah, listen to me!"

She was fighting him, frantic.

"Hannah!" Gripping her by the arms, he shook her, hard this time. He could almost taste her terror, feel the sobs wrenching through her.

Her eyes flashed open, wide, so desperate Sam couldn't breathe. "It's a dream, love. It's only a dream. I'm here."

Recognition flashed into her eyes. She stopped struggling, her whole body trembling. "S—Sam?"

"She's right here in the cradle. See?"

Hannah struggled upright, one hand clutching him, hanging on as if he were the only solid thing in a world lost in storms. With the other hand she dashed the waves of black hair from her face, eyes searching the alcove. He knew the moment she saw Ellie. A ragged sob burst from Hannah, and she scooped the sleeping baby into her arms, holding on as if she expected Ellie to be snatched away from her in a heartbeat.

Sam's throat closed, his own eyes burning. Had she been this terrified from the beginning? If that was so, his reluctance must have fed her worst fears.

Ellie snuffled her objections at being so rudely dragged from her sleep. Her little fists waved in protest as she let out a wail that should've shattered glass.

Hannah rocked her whole body, holding Ellie too tight, as if trying to protect the baby from things she alone could see. Ever so gently, Sam eased his arms around Hannah. "I'm here, Hannah. No one is going to hurt either one of you. Not while I'm here."

Slowly, so slowly, he could feel a little of the tension ease from her body. She curled against him, breathing in soft, shuddering sobs. "S—Sam. I was so . . . I thought—"

"Ellie's here, angel. A little ticked off since you interrupted her beauty sleep, but I figure she'll forgive you. She's beautiful enough as it is."

He sensed when Hannah came to herself. Part of him hated it, even though he was more grateful than he could believe that she'd stopped fighting, that the wild light in her eyes had faded. Replaced by . . . what? Not embarrassment for overreacting. Not dismay because he'd seen her so vulnerable, or that he'd charged across that invisible physical barrier they'd let grow up between them and held her through the worst of her nightmare.

No. It was grief in her eyes, raw, terrible grief he'd never known his Hannah had inside her. How the hell could he have lived with her for so long, loved her for so long but never seen it?

"Ellie," she whispered. "It's Ellie." Something raw edged her voice. Something that mystified him.

"Was your nightmare about Becca?" he asked. Strange, he'd forgotten how many times she'd had nightmares when Becca was little. She'd dreamed Becca had fallen off a cliff, dreamed they were lost in a flood and she lost hold of Becca's hand. She'd wake up, damp with sweat and shaking, murmuring over and over "I lost her. She's gone . . ."

He reached over to switch on the reading lamp at the side of the bed; the low light made Hannah blink, and the baby rub at its teary eyes.

"Becca?" Hannah repeated, shaking her head as if she hadn't even thought of her. "No."

"Then what was it about? You want to talk about it?" Sam struggled to draw in a steadying breath, but it was as if Hannah's fear had sucked all the air out of the room. Her face ice white, her eyes huge and dark, she looked like she'd seen a ghost. But the ghost wasn't gone, Sam sensed. Somehow, even with Hannah awake, it had stayed in the room. "Whatever the dream was about, Hannah, just tell me. Let me take some of the hurting away."

"No. I . . . I don't want to . . . to talk about it." She eyed him warily, as if she'd just come back to herself, remembered that he wasn't supposed to be holding her and she wasn't supposed to want him to. Back to playing according to whatever crazy rules they'd managed to think up in the months that had distanced them.

"Hannah, I just want to help." He tried to hold onto her, but she pulled away, climbing out of bed, Ellie cradled in her arms.

"You can't help. It's too late to help."

"I don't understand! Hannah, damn it—"

She turned to him, her lips curved into a wobbly smile. "It was just a nightmare, Sam. Even you can't . . . can't fight off dragons while I'm sleeping."

"I did when Becca was little. Remember? When I held you the nightmares wouldn't come back. Sometimes I stayed up all night, watching your face to make sure . . ."

Sam hesitated, felt his cheeks burn. He'd never told her that. How he'd keep vigil. If her face had started to tighten, lines deepening in her brow, if she'd started to get restless, he'd wake her with kisses, hide what he was doing by arousing her, making love to her until she was so sated no dreams would come.

She remembered, too. He could see it in her eyes. A memory both had forgotten. One so tender it hurt to touch it, to remember how close they'd been then. Her knight in shining armor—he'd held off her dragons with a kiss instead of a sword.

He'd never felt more like a man than those nights he'd watched over her. He couldn't protect himself from terrors in the night. But that was because the monsters in his closet were real. His mother had thrown him away like yesterday's garbage. The smells, the feelings, the sounds he remembered from the day she deserted him were real. But Hannah's were only shadows that had never been. Hannah he could keep safe.

But she didn't look "safe" now. She looked as if she'd just wandered in from a battlefield, shell-shocked and bleeding. She surprised him with a wan smile. "I'd wake up sometimes. See you . . . see you looking at me."

"I have to admit it wasn't always to make sure you weren't dreaming. Sometimes it was just because . . ." His voice caught, roughened. "Because you were so beautiful. I couldn't believe you were real. That you'd married me. I kept thinking you might disappear."

"But I never did."

Not in body, Sam thought sadly. *But somehow, your spirit, your joy, everything that makes you amazing slipped right through my fingers. I know how hard you're trying now. But sometimes when I look at you, it's like part of you is already gone. I'm scared someday I'll wake up and I won't see any you at all.*

He couldn't say it, not now when her skin was still damp from fear, her body still trembling, vulnerable. Couldn't tell her how afraid he was that he'd never again find the Hannah he'd fallen in love with.

Sam swallowed hard. He cupped one hand over her pale cheek, told the only truth he could. "I miss you, Hannah."

Her mouth wobbled, tears welling in her eyes. "I'm

sorry. Sometimes, I don't understand why . . . what . . . what's wrong with me."

She lay the baby back in the crib. Ellie wriggled to make herself a little nest, then sighed, her eyes fluttering closed. Hannah straightened, stood in a shaft of moonlight, still as a stone. "I just . . . you always think I . . . I'm perfect. But I'm not. Every person has . . . has ugly places, Sam. I have one here."

She spread her hand low on her stomach, as if to hide it from him. Her scar? Sam realized with a jolt. She was covering the scar from her surgery. Could she possibly think he'd find that ugly?

Yes. Whatever he thought, he saw in her eyes what she felt. That something hideous lay underneath her hand, something repulsive. How could he tell her? Explain to her that there was no part of her he didn't find beautiful. That nothing as trivial as a scar would ever make him see her as less than what she was. His Hannah. The woman who had made him dare to trust more than he'd ever believed possible. The woman who had given him the courage to risk—

No, he couldn't tell her. But then, words were never enough. He'd have to make her believe—

Swallowing hard, he mustered all the courage he could, tried to drive back the terror he'd be turned away. He'd tried before to touch her—at least wanted to, started to—but he'd never pushed it all the way, always made sure he could retreat, maintain some sort of pride, keep the cut of rejection from driving too deep.

"Hannah, you can never make me believe you are anything but my angel. So beautiful. With a heart so . . . so big it takes in everyone around it. This baby, with no mother to love it. The kids in the neighborhood. Becca. And . . . me."

"Sam, don't—"

"You think a scar will make me . . . what? Turn away? Be revolted? Because you think it makes you less than perfect?"

"Oh, God, if only—" She stopped, with a ragged laugh.

"If only what?"

"If only things were simple. If only we'd found some way to stop it when we started losing hold of each other. If only I could have told you—" Her face contorted, and the agony in it cut him to the bone.

"Told you that you needed me when I was gone too much after Becca went away to school? Told me how much you missed her? That you didn't know what to do with all the time, all the love you'd spent on her for nineteen years? How could you tell me any of what you were going through when I wouldn't even admit that the pain was real? I pretended nothing had changed— just kept on marching off to work, pretending she was still asleep in her room, like she was every morning of her life. And when I got home, I imagined she was at Jana's or play practice or barricaded in her room talking to some boy on the phone. I got really good at not admitting what was real, Hannah. It was too hot to touch, hurt too much to hold on to the truth: that my little girl was grown up. And somehow, somehow I had missed it."

"Sam—"

"It's true, Hannah. Isn't it? I kept my distance, kept everything nice and safe. If I admitted to myself how badly you were hurting when you'd spent every minute you could with her, when you hadn't wasted a moment of her childhood, then I'd have to face the fact that she was grown and gone—and it was too late." Sam's voice broke. "Too late for me."

Hannah peered up at him through eyes filled with his pain.

"I haven't wanted to look at anything ugly for so long, it's no wonder you didn't feel like you could trust me. With your hurt about Becca's leaving. And, with your scar." He hesitated, his hands curling into fists, tight, trying to muster the courage he needed. "Hannah, trust me now."

Her gaze pierced through him, so deep it was as if she could read his soul—all the ugliness his own mother must have seen. The ugliness he'd tried so hard to hide from her.

She didn't say anything. He didn't want any more ghosts between them—imaginary monsters she'd created in her own head, reactions she'd probably pictured a hundred times since she'd first looked under the dressing in the hospital, seen what the doctor had left behind, a mark that would never go away.

Sam untied the satin bow that held her nightgown closed, it parted to reveal a wedge of satiny skin. Ever so gently, he skimmed the fabric from her shoulders, letting the gown slide down her body in a waterfall of white.

He took her hand, led her to the floor-length mirror on their closet door so she could see his face as he first saw the scar. Sam knelt, his eyes devouring every curve he remembered so clearly, every shadowed dip and scented hollow that was Hannah. The swell of breasts, tipped in roses, her waist, the delicate cup of her navel. The slight curve of hips that had risen up to meet him when he'd come inside her.

His gaze skimmed to the feathery curls in the hollow between her thighs. His place. The place he'd touched, kissed, loved for twenty-two years. The place where he'd watched in amazement as she struggled to bring new life into the world in the long hours of labor before they'd had to take her off to have the Caesarean section that had given them Becca.

Soft—the curls were even more soft, lustrous than

he remembered, her skin pale as marble, but warm, so warm it was as if that secret place of loving had the power to melt all the pain around Sam's heart.

So familiar, her body was, and yet, as his gaze swept across her, he saw it—dark red, a line of proud flesh, like a grin carved from side to side beneath a soft layering of curls.

God, how much had that hurt her? How would it feel to have that part of your body cut into? Marred forever? How would he have felt if he'd been the one the surgeons had cut? True, she'd had a scar from the Caesarean nineteen years ago. But she'd been so overjoyed with Becca, she'd barely noticed. And over time the scar had faded to a thin, white line. But that wound had come from giving life. The scar so angry red now stood for a death of sorts. The death of Hannah's hopes and dreams of another child.

Sam searched for the right words, but he didn't know what to say. Couldn't fail her. His eyes filled with tears, his throat so tight he couldn't speak. He did the only thing he could. With a soft groan, he pressed his lips against the scar. Kissed it more tenderly than he'd ever kissed before. Then he laid his cheek against it, his arms tight around her hips.

Fingers threaded through his hair, so gently at first he thought he'd imagined it. Hannah touching him the way she used to. Sam raised his face to look up at her, hope burning in his chest.

Let it be over—God, let this nightmare between us be over! Please, let me touch you . . .

For an instant he saw an answering desperation in Hannah's eyes, a wild reaching out of something far deeper than bodies. Something that made his heart soar. It was over. It was going to be all right! She wanted him—

He kissed his way up her body—the hollow of her hip, the soft swell of her stomach, the underside of her breast. Standing, he cupped her cheeks in both hands, wanting to make this good, wanting their lovemaking to be perfect. It had been so damned long.

"Hannah—" he ground out, trying to find the words to tell her what this meant to him, tell her how scared he was. He didn't want to screw up. Wanted it to be perfect—what she deserved.

But before he could form the words, something dark darted into her eyes, something that tightened the knot of dread in his gut.

"Hannah, don't pull away! What is it? What's wrong?"

"I can't . . . I just . . ."

Quick as a flash of moonlight, she drew away from him, pulled the nightgown back over her head. She stood, her arms wrapped tight around her middle, shivering, as if she were cold.

Sam's heart plunged, something breaking inside him. Had he repulsed her that much? Had he fooled himself about the wanting in her eyes? She wasn't ready to let him touch her. Maybe she never would be.

He shoved the thought away, unable to bear it.

"I'm sorry. I just hoped that—it's so hard, Hannah. Not being able to touch you. Don't you understand? I don't give a damn about your scar. Whatever you might think. I just—" His voice broke. "I wish I knew why . . . what I did . . . why you don't . . . want me anymore."

Her face twisted in anguish. She knew just how much her rejection had hurt him. "It's not you, Sam. It's me."

"What is it? Let me help fix it, Hannah. At least let me try." He almost hoped. Saw indecision clash in her eyes. She turned her face away, hiding behind the waves of her hair.

"I . . . can't explain."

He wanted to argue with her, wanted to plead. But he knew her well enough to be certain she meant what she'd said. He could almost hear the doors closing between them again, the rasp of keys turning in all the feelings they'd locked away.

Shoulders sagging, Sam turned, walked to the window. He tried to breathe past the knot of pain in his chest.

After a long moment, he said softly. "Go to bed, Hannah."

"Wh—what?"

"Go to sleep. I'll stay here. Make sure that your nightmare doesn't come back."

"No, you don't have to—"

"I know that. I want to. At least it's one way I can still be here for you." He sank down in the rocker, dragged one hand wearily through his hair. "Go on. Lie down. I'll turn out the light."

She stood there, uncertainly, fretting the bit of lace on her nightgown's cuff. It reminded him all too poignantly of their wedding night. He'd gone downstairs for champagne, but really, he'd wanted to give her time to change.

They had made love before, but he'd known this time was special. When he'd returned to the room, she'd been waiting for him, her nightgown like a butterfly wing, soft peach, gossamer, her glossy mane of hair a black river over her shoulders, her fingers toying nervously with a bit of lace.

But her eyes had been so different then—shy and yet sexy, wide with wanting—wanting him to make love to her. Wanting to know if he found her beautiful.

He'd always found her lovely—exquisite, warm, deliciously touchable. Even then, he'd known he would never change his mind. He'd told her that, over and over again as they'd made love. She was his angel. His chance. He wanted her to teach him everything love meant. This was forever, the magic between them. No matter what, he'd always love her.

But back then, she'd believed him.

Sam forced the memories from his mind, not wanting her to guess what he was thinking, not wanting her to feel the same sharp sense of loss.

He looked up at her, smiled. She'd never guess just how much it cost him.

"It's all right, Hannah," he soothed. "I won't try to touch you. I just . . . just don't want you to be afraid of . . . of whatever scared you when you were dreaming."

She sank down onto the bed, pulled the quilt up around her. Sam reached over, switched out the light.

But even with only the dim light creeping from beneath the curtains, Hannah could still see him.

She stared at him, his dark hair gleaming in the moonlight, the line of his jaw so strong, his eyes filled with hurt she'd put there.

She hadn't trusted him. And it had cut him, deep.

Oh, Sam, she cried silently. *I'm sorry—I'm so sorry I can't tell you—but how can I tell you something that will hurt you so badly? You trusted me, and I lied from the beginning. But if I tell you, what if you* leave *me? How could you ever forgive what I did? You'd think I was like your mother. Nothing could change that. I had a baby and I gave her away.*

I'm so scared, Sam, she thought, fighting back tears. *Scared you'll hate me. Despise me. Turn and walk away. I'm so scared you'll leave me.*

No, Hannah thought, turning her face to the pillow to hide the tears leaking from the corners of her eyes. She couldn't tell Sam the truth, no matter how much she wanted to.

She could never ever tell him that the baby she'd cried out for in her nightmare wasn't sleeping in the cradle.

She was lying in a tiny white coffin on a rain-swept Oregon hill.

14

Hannah climbed out of the car, unloading the stroller and snapping its braces into place, praying that her latest attempt to distract herself would prove more successful than the last dozen or so ideas she'd tried. The days since she'd awakened to find Sam bending over her in bed had left her restless and edgy. Made her feel as if her feet were on fire and she couldn't bear to sit down for more than a moment before images started pouring into her mind, yearnings clamoring for her attention, guilt searing her conscience.

She'd figured things couldn't get worse in the days after she'd first had her hysterectomy. She'd assured herself that it would get easier to adjust once she got used to Becca being off to school. She'd been certain all she needed to be happy was for Sam to accept Ellie into the family.

But she couldn't fool herself anymore. Even with Sam letting Ellie into his heart and the prospect of Becca's visit home to look forward to, Hannah had little hope that she'd finally be able to calm her nerves, silence her doubts, trust that everything would be all right in the end.

The problem wasn't Becca or Sam or even Tony Blake, in spite of the fact that she seemed to stumble across the man with a frequency that made her want to curse small towns for the first time in her life. The trouble was inside *her*. Maybe that was why she couldn't seem to settle down. Whenever she tried to dodge her uneasiness, she carried it with her. Working in her Mother's Day garden in the backyard, visiting Josie Wilkes's house for lunch, or taking a quick trip to the post office to mail yet another care package full of cookies and fun pens and new CDs to Becca. A venture, by the way, in which she'd almost tripped over a breathless, windblown Tony Blake on her way out.

Considering her track record, she doubted she'd have much better luck getting things off her mind here in the park. But she'd been too restless not to at least give it a try.

She'd phoned Josie, inviting her and Tommy along on the outing, but Tommy had been wailing in the background. Probably just teething, Josie had explained, but he'd been fussy all night and was running a temperature. There was no sense in taking chances. She didn't want Ellie catching something if Tommy was contagious.

Hannah had been disappointed, but knew they were only putting the outing off until another day. One of the sweetest changes having Ellie around had made was the fun of spending time with Josie and Tommy. Running to the park and the zoo and having picnics in the backyard had become a delightful part of the week. The babies lying on the quilt Hannah spread on the grass, Ellie gazing out at the world with unfocused eyes while Tommy busied himself by trying to catch ants or grab a single blade of grass.

Hannah had rarely had company when Becca was tiny. She and Margo Johnson had attempted a few trips to the zoo together, but they'd always ended with strained nerves and none of the sense of connection Hannah had so craved. Margo had been so jittery with Rachel, constantly hovering, worrying about dirt, tiny bumps on swing sets, anything she could find to obsess over.

Finally, Hannah had started slipping out of the farmhouse alone so Margo couldn't make the precious time stressful. Afternoons with Josie were glorious, and Hannah caught herself imagining the two of them taking Tommy and Ellie trick or treating together, getting their pictures taken on Santa's knee. Dropping them off for the first day of school, both she and Josie trying not to cry.

Don't get your hopes up, Hannah warned herself. But she couldn't help it. If Ellie's mother really wanted to give up her baby, it couldn't be wrong for Hannah to want to keep Ellie, could it?

Hannah ducked into the back seat to haul Ellie out of her car seat. Tucking the baby into the stroller, she adjusted the brim of Ellie's white eyelet sunbonnet to keep the glare out of the baby's eyes.

"Becca always liked the monkey bars best," she told the baby. "When it was time to leave, once, she got up on the highest rungs and refused to come down. When I chased her, she'd just shinny out of my reach. It was a game I'd just as soon you don't learn."

Truth was, at this point, Hannah would be thrilled if Becca had been willing to teach the baby how to swing from the gazebo's flagpole—any sign of interest at all from Becca would have been an improvement. But there would be time for that when they went to pick her up at school. Surely, Becca would be reasonable then.

Hannah gave a low whistle, and Reckless lumbered out of the car, trailing his red leash. He thumped his tail in approval, but seemed to be looking around for his girl. What point was there in coming to the park without one's girl to throw Frisbees for you?

"Give Ellie a chance, old boy. She'll grow into it," Hannah soothed, looping the leash around her wrist and settling the diaper bag full of goodies into the rack under the stroller.

"Grow into what?" The sound of a familiar voice made Hannah's breath catch. She froze, not certain whether it was dread or anticipation that suddenly made her hand tremble.

"Tony," she greeted him as he strode toward her, his hair windswept, his teeth gleaming in a wide, white grin. "I was just telling Reckless Ellie would be big enough to throw Frisbees for him before he knew it. Sometimes I think the poor old fellow misses Becca almost as much as I do. And he doesn't even know where she's disappeared to. At least I can talk to Bec on the phone."

"I bet you're one of those people who holds the receiver up to the dog's ear and tries to get him to talk."

Hannah blushed. Okay, so she might've tried it once or twice, but Becca had thought it was hilarious.

"So, decide to come out for a picnic?" Tony asked.

"Thought it would be nice to get out. What about you? Have they decided to move the law library into the gazebo in honor of summer?"

"Nope. Our court system isn't that civilized, unfortunately."

"Then why—" Hannah's cheeks burned. She hardly had a right to give him the third degree.

"Why what?"

"Never mind. It's none of my business."

"C'mon Hannah. What's a question between friends as old as we are?"

We're not friends, she thought. *We never were.*

"I don't know, I just always seem to be running into you. At the post office, the grocery store."

Far from taking offense, Tony threw back his head and laughed. "Simple enough explanation. I needed stamps, so I stopped at the post office. Groceries—well, in spite of popular belief, lawyers need food like everyone else. We can't just exist on the blood we suck from our clients."

"And the park?"

Tony's smile faded. He looked toward the courthouse that stood on the other side of Main Street overlooking the small businesses clustered around it like a mindful mother hen. "I've always loved kids. Remember the year I was here? I helped coach Bitty Basketball. Worked with one of the sixth graders on his curve ball?"

"I remember." Little Jerry Phillips, the sixth-grade pitching ace, had been almost as heartbroken as Hannah when Tony had left Willowton for good.

"You ask why I come to the park? It's simple. I come here to remind myself what I'm fighting *for* in the courtroom. To see that there are some things, some *people* who are innocent and pure." He paused, his gaze warming Hannah's face.

"I'd gotten real jaded, working in the city. Seen things so terrible, the whole world looked ugly. I'd forgotten people could be good and honest and kind until I saw you again."

Hannah squirmed inwardly at the tone of Tony's voice, almost worshipful, as if she were something special.

"Maybe you've been right all along, loving this one-horse town the way you do. Since I've come back to take care of my mother, it's like I've been able to wash all the legal grime off my hands. Breathe again without choking. Be able to look at myself in the mirror and not see criminals I'd helped get back on the street, corporations I'd helped cheat their workers. Marriages I'd split down the middle as if they didn't involve people's hearts at all, only assets and alimony and custody of kids whose worlds had just fallen apart."

His voice dropped, low. "I guess I needed to see things that were beautiful again. Things like a woman loving an abandoned child, opening her heart even though her husband wanted to turn the baby away."

Hannah pushed the stroller, walking, not knowing what to say. She'd brought on this confession of his with her question, but it made her even more edgy. Made her feel sorry for him. Somehow, she'd imagined him as Mr. Success, living dreams and ambitions far too grand for her. To hear Tony mourning the loss of innocence hurt her somehow. Maybe because she wasn't sure he'd ever had "innocence" at all—even when he was a cocky teenaged boy dazzling everyone in Willowton.

"You're awfully quiet all of a sudden," Tony said. "You asked. I told you the truth."

She sucked in a deep breath. "Tony, maybe you can convince yourself that there was something special between us, but I was there. I remember. Maybe to me it was wildly romantic, but to you, well, lets be honest. I was nothing more than a distraction to you. Something to keep you from getting bored to death before you went off to the Air Force Academy. I was your distraction, and you were . . . were my one chance to taste something wild, something completely outside my world, before I settled down in my grandmother's house, with my flowers and my front row seat at the school Christmas play."

Tony's face clouded, and Hannah winced to see the shadow of hurt in his eyes. "Is that how you really see our time together?"

"You were my first love. But we never—we didn't fit together right."

"Maybe because I was a fool."

Hannah started at his growled words. She caught her lower lip between her teeth, felt Tony watching her. But when she dared to glance up at him again, the dark intensity on his features had vanished. Maybe it had never been there at all.

"Hannah, you know why I came back here. My mother fell, broke her hip. She needed someone to take care of her. There wasn't anybody but me to come back here, arrange things."

"I'm sure your mother is glad to have you close by."

"Yeah. You know, when I told her about Ellie, and seeing you in court and everything, you should have seen her light up. She asked if maybe you could stop by sometime, show her the baby."

Mrs. Blake was one person she hadn't kept in touch with. It had been too painful. Felt too dangerous.

"Mom doesn't know about my getting you pregnant, if that's what you're worried about. It wasn't exactly something I was proud of—knocking up the sweetest girl in town and then leaving her flat. I just thought, well, Mom's had a hard time of it since she fell. Thought it might cheer her up to see you, talk about old times. At least the good part."

Hannah wanted to refuse, but all she could see was Mrs. Blake's face—so wistful, so gentle. Hannah had always felt sorry for her. Some people adored traveling to new places, seeing the world along with their military husband. Mrs. Blake had always seemed to envy the perfect gardens bordering properties generations old. Houses full of family heirlooms, and streets full of friends you'd known forever.

"I suppose it couldn't hurt anything to stop for just a

minute," Hannah allowed, but she didn't feel right about it. Sam wouldn't have any objection to her visiting a lonely old woman, but somehow, Hannah doubted he'd be thrilled by anything that drew her any deeper into Tony Blake's life. And Sam didn't even know the half of it!

"Mom will be thrilled! That night we talked about you, she dragged out my old high school yearbook, pulled out the things I'd stuffed in it. My letter in track. A picture of you and me going to the prom. She'd even pressed the boutonniere you got me."

Hannah knew she had the same picture buried somewhere in the bottom of a box. Somehow, she hadn't been able to bring herself to throw it away. "I couldn't find all that stuff if someone paid me a million dollars," she lied.

"Funny," Tony said with a quizzical expression. "I figured you'd keep it all pressed and dusted somewhere, maybe take the yearbook out once in a while and leaf through it. You were always sentimental about things. Remember how you pressed the flowers I gave you?"

"You don't have much time to be sentimental when you're raising a baby," Hannah brushed it off. "Guess I lost my taste for pressing things in books when I missed most of my senior year."

She wished the words back the instant she said them. Tony flinched. "I hadn't thought about that. Guess once I walked out of your life, your memories of high school couldn't have been that good."

"By the time I got back from Oregon, I hardly even recognized the girl in all those pictures anymore. I was somebody else."

"You haven't changed that much, Hannah. You still care when other people don't. You still try to make the best of things. You still ask for nothing but simple pleasures out of life and are damned grateful when you get them. And you're still willing to forgive people who have hurt you. The way you've forgiven me."

"I'm no saint, Tony. It was just a long time ago. I'm sure it was hard for you, too. We were young, foolish and so sure we knew everything. When we got caught, well, who could blame you for panicking?"

"You can panic and not disappear for twenty-seven years. I could have stopped to see you, found out how you were doing. Asked after the baby. I could have made sure you were okay."

"It might have made you feel better about yourself, but it wouldn't have changed anything that happened. Would have just dredged everything up. I didn't want to think about it. Didn't want to be reminded."

"Then you must not have been too happy when Josie dragged me into the courtroom to help you."

"I wasn't thinking about the past. The one thing I cared about was keeping Ellie in the future."

"How did you feel when you first realized it was me?"

The question stunned Hannah, made her stammer. "You were the last person I expected."

"That was obvious from the look on your face. But how did you *feel* when you knew I'd come back?"

"Wh—what?" Hannah tripped over an uneven place in the sidewalk. Tony gripped her elbow to steady her. The contact jolted through Hannah so sharply she wanted to yank away, but it would have made her look even more ridiculous.

"Are *you* glad to have me close by?"

She glanced up at him, saw her alarm register in his eyes. "Tony, I—"

He smiled. "Don't panic, Hannah. I just wondered— well, it might not be the greatest news to you, finding out that I'd come back even temporarily. I mean, seems like you've worked real hard to put the past behind you. It would only be natural not to want it to come rearing up again just when you least expected it. And let's be honest, it wasn't as if I left you under the best of terms. Walking out on you and the baby the way I did. You'd have every right to hate my guts, plain and simple."

"It was all a long time ago. It's hard to hold onto such fierce emotions for so many years. I've always found hate takes way too much effort."

"I'm glad. I didn't want you to hate me."

"So, now you know. Nothing more to say. We can both go on with our lives in peace."

"Can we?" he eyed her sharply. "You don't look like someone at peace to me. You look unhappy. Hurt. You look as if you've been lost."

Hannah stiffened her shoulders, tipped up her chin. It was one thing to feel so vulnerable, it was another to have someone talk about it. Someone acting as if they knew you better than they really did. There were enough dark places in Hannah's heart Tony knew about. Secrets and grief that they shared. But this new sadness in Hannah's world—the troubles with Sam, her missing Becca, her struggle to figure out what to do with the rest of her life—those dark places were hers alone. She didn't want anyone prying around in them.

Sam's face flashed into her memory, the planes and angles etched with pain, vulnerability, fear. Shadowed with doubts. No matter how raw she felt, she wasn't going to expose his uncertainty to anyone, especially not to Tony.

"Tony, I'm just fine. But even if I wasn't, I wouldn't . . . wouldn't share it with you. It wouldn't be right. It wouldn't be fair."

Tony ducked his head, then nodded. "I respect that. I'm not trying to pry, Hannah, but I'm not blind. Can't pretend I didn't see. I know something's wrong, big time. Maybe it's not my place to say, but I'm worried about you as a friend. When we were upstairs, looking over your arrangements for Ellie, I couldn't help noticing that, uh, you and Sam, well, your sleeping arrangements aren't . . . what one might expect."

Hannah felt like a cold stone had slammed hard into the pit of her stomach. "How . . . ?"

"How did I know?" Tony looked uncomfortable, but earnest, his eyes dark with concern. "His clothes were in your daughter's room. It wasn't hard to figure out."

"Our sleeping arrangements aren't anyone else's business," she bit out, defensive.

"You're right," Tony admitted, chagrined, yet pale with dogged determination. "But I just . . . just wanted you to know that whatever the problem is, it's not because of you. Not because you aren't . . . aren't beautiful, desirable. Forgive me if I'm being too honest, Hannah, but I have to tell you the truth. If you were my wife, an army couldn't keep me from holding you at night. Making love to you."

Hannah shivered, stung by his tone. "Well, I'm not your wife. And you made it clear a long time ago you never wanted me to be."

Tony gave a raw laugh, fell silent. She wanted him to leave. Wished she'd never stuck her head out of the house. Wished the park would crumble away under her feet.

"You know, I think it's a little too cool out here for Ellie," she said, turning back toward the car. "Maybe we should wait for another day when things warm up a bit."

"Hannah, I know what you're afraid of. And I don't blame you. But I swear, if Sam should ever find out the truth about our baby . . ."

Blood drained from Hannah's face. She glared at Tony, trying to quell a sting of panic. "Why would Sam ever find out? Are you planning to tell him?"

"God, no!" Tony exclaimed. "I guess it just seems like secrets have a way of coming out. Critical mass, is my theory. It just builds and builds, little bits falling into the fire until finally it blows up in a puff of smoke."

"It's not going to blow up. Sam is never going to know."

"I hope you're right. But if it ever should happen, I just want you to know this." He caught her hand, held it, tight, his eyes burning with emotion. "I'll be here for you, Hannah, no matter what."

She started to argue, started to bluster—say she wouldn't need him. Everything would turn out fine. But Tony was already striding across the green. He paused when he reached the street. Waved one hand. Hannah's fingers were too numb to wave back.

She stood there, her stomach churning, her fingers still aware of the place where he'd touched her hand.

It's a theory of critical mass. Secrets have a way of coming out whether we want them to or not. . . . Tony's words haunted her.

I'll be here for you. . . . if Sam ever finds out . . .

It wouldn't matter who else was "there" for her if the secret came out, Hannah thought hopelessly. Because Sam would be gone.

It had always been one of Hannah's grandmother's favorite bits of advice: If you're troubled or sad or feeling sorry for yourself, do something for someone else. Hannah had always found it the most helpful cure for a bout of the blues, taking gifts of cookies or flowers or cuttings from her plants on a mission to make someone else smile. If her grandmother had known the whole situation, Hannah wondered what she'd have to say about her destination today.

Soft, soaking rain sprinkled the grass with diamond drops of water that glistened in the patches of sun peeping here and there from among the clouds. Hannah shifted the baby in one arm, and tried to knock at the door, the basket she held in her other hand thudding against the door. She glanced down at the red and white checkered cloth covering the basket's contents, but no telltale dampness oozed through the cloth. The pies she'd made seemed to have survived the jostling intact.

But this small house jostled loose things more nerve-wracking than piecrust. How could this place still feel so familiar? The house at the end of Peachtree Lane was down at the heels, a little more worn than she remembered, and yet, it still had a feeling of loneliness about it far deeper than any Hannah had recalled.

Any attempt to fill the flower beds Mrs. Blake had once longed for had been abandoned years ago, no effort made to disguise the patches of dirt so empty and forlorn.

The porch that had once been filled with cozy chairs for sitting of an evening was bare now, as if the woman inside the house knew she would never come outside to sit again. But then, Hannah thought sadly, Mrs. Blake would have little reason to do so. She'd wager the quiet old woman seldom had anyone to talk to.

Mrs. Blake had always kept mostly to herself. And yet, Hannah hadn't noticed how lonely Mrs. Blake had become over the years. In fact, Hannah had tried to pretend the old woman wasn't here at all. But Hannah resolved to do better in the future. It would take so little to please Mrs. Blake. A loaf of pumpkin bread in the fall, some fresh tomatoes and green beans from the garden. A bouquet of sunflowers to brighten up the kitchen table when she ate her solitary meals. Maybe Hannah could put a cluster of daffodil bulbs in the neglected gardens before next spring so Mrs. Blake would have a reason to step outside and enjoy the fresh spring air.

The door opened, and Mrs. Blake peeked out with the wariness of someone who rarely had visitors. But the instant the woman recognized Hannah, she beamed with delight.

"Bless you, Hannah! You haven't changed a bit in all these years. Tony said you promised to stop by to see me."

"I should have come a long time ago."

Mrs. Blake gave an airy wave of her hand. "Young people get busy. It's just wonderful to see you now. Come in, come in and let me see this little baby I've been hearing so much about. That son of mine is crazy as can be about her."

Hannah maneuvered Ellie and the basket of pies through the door and into the crowded little kitchen. She settled the basket on the small kitchen table, then turned to smile at Mrs. Blake. "I brought you some pies. Apple was your favorite, if I remember right."

"I can't believe you remember that at all. But then, you were always the most thoughtful girl."

Hannah's cheeks burned. If she'd really been "thoughtful," she might have noticed how isolated Mrs. Blake had grown.

The older woman bustled over and lifted the edge of Ellie's blanket to get a look at the baby. "She's beautiful," Mrs. Blake breathed, awed. "What a perfect little angel. I love babies. Is there anything more precious?"

Hannah had to agree with her. "No, there isn't."

"I always hoped for a lapful of grandchildren. But it doesn't seem likely anymore. Three marriages, and not one baby has Tony had."

He had one baby, Hannah thought. *A beautiful baby girl*. She couldn't help but wonder what this woman's reaction would have been to the birth of the grand-daughter that had so horrified Hannah's own mother. Would Tony's mother have delighted over the little girl? Fussed over her? Cherished her? That was, if she'd ever been given the chance?

"You know, I always hoped Tony would marry you," Mrs. Blake confessed. "The two of you would have made such lovely children."

Hannah tried to hide her discomfort. "I don't think that's what Tony had in mind when we were dating. He never wanted anything but the Air Force Academy."

"Humph. He wanted it so badly that he dropped out first chance he got. No. That boy of mine needed an anchor, someone to give his life purpose. He's always been so restless. He never realized all he really needed was a sweet girl like you to settle down with."

Hannah didn't correct Mrs. Blake, tell her that an "anchor" was the last thing her son wanted. But then, Tony's mother hadn't said "want," she'd said "need." Maybe in the end, she was right. That restlessness was still in Tony's face. What if Hannah and Tony *had* married? Would they have been miserable? Or might Tony have discovered a peace, a sense of purpose that had eluded him for so long?

"Trying to marry me off to Hannah again, Ma?"

Hannah started at the sound of Tony's voice. She hadn't seen his car when she'd driven up to the house or she wouldn't have stopped. It was one thing to visit Mrs. Blake, another entirely to do so with Tony filling up the house's small rooms with his broad shoulders and cocky grin.

"Tony," Hannah choked out. "I figured you'd be at the courthouse."

She could tell he knew she'd been doing her best to avoid him.

"Just catching up on some stuff at home. That case I told you about, the one where the adoptive mother lost custody? I'm going to give another loophole a try, see if we can appeal."

Hannah felt a surge of admiration, of hope, of kinship with the woman she'd never even met. How could a cold courtroom, a detached judge, a troubled fifteen-year-old girl understand how easy it was to give a baby your whole heart, even if that baby didn't come from your body? How could they understand the bond that curled into every cell in your body until it could never be ripped free, not even if the baby was swept out of your life forever. How could they understand the gaping hole it would leave in that adoptive mother's heart? A hole that nothing would ever fill?

"Hannah?" Tony looked into her eyes, concerned. "You look as if something's wrong."

Hannah forced a laugh, her thoughts and fears about the other woman and her child too frightening to share. She groped for something to say. "I was just puzzling over where your car is. It isn't in the drive."

"Ah, it's in the shop at the moment. Guess I should be grateful for the broken muffler. Without it, I doubt we'd be having the pleasure of your company."

Hannah couldn't deny it.

He crossed to Hannah, took Ellie deftly out of her arms. He looked so natural with the baby, it gave Hannah a jolt. What would it be like to have a family with a man who was so at ease with children? A man who knew just how to comfort a fussy little one, how to banish monsters from closets or calm first day of school jitters? What would it be like if it was Daddy a nightmare stricken toddler called for when it woke up in darkness? She felt a twinge of guilt at her disloyalty to Sam, and yet, she couldn't help being a little bit wistful. She'd wanted so much for him to feel so easy with Becca. But he'd always been just a little stiff, just a little awkward, just a little unsure.

"I should have listened to your advice, Ma, and married this girl on the spot," Tony said. "Hannah and I could have had a half dozen of these little monsters by now. A big house, with a jungle gym in the yard. And a tree house out back. But, then, guess I blew my chance." He smiled. "Of course, people are starting families a lot later than they used to. There are plenty of first-time parents in their forties. Maybe it's not too late, after all."

He was just teasing his mother. He couldn't really mean it. His eyes flashed mischief, and yet, there was something in his face that unnerved Hannah. A touch of longing, a scrap of daring, as if he were willing her to imagine what it might be like to start all over, have a flock of babies with him.

Would he look at her the same way if he knew about the vivid red scar that arced across her abdomen? The fact that even if she wanted a yardful of babies, she could never have even just one. Or would that matter at all to Tony Blake? He'd always been so used to getting his own way. Would he merely rake up adoption candidates, and make the family he alluded to appear out of thin air?

Hannah didn't want to feel the surprising glow of admiration for him. Didn't want to be disloyal enough to imagine, even just for a moment, what it might be like to be married to a man who was as eager to parent as she'd always been. A man who wanted to begin at the beginning with a little one like Ellie, not slam the door on parenting as if he'd just survived a marathon and never wanted to take another step in his life.

He shot her a grin over the tiny bundle he cradled so

naturally in his arms. "Why is it kids are always so determined not to listen to their mothers?" he asked, making a face. "You spend your life doing exactly the opposite of what she tells you just to show your independence, and twenty some years later, you realize she was right all the time."

"You don't believe that," Hannah said.

"Don't I?" Tony brushed one strong thumb over the downy hair at Ellie's temple.

Hannah swallowed hard, felt like a coward. But she'd done what she came for—said hello to Mrs. Blake and delivered the apple pies. It wasn't good to keep her up on her sore hip.

And it wasn't good to keep raking fingernails over Hannah's own raw memories. "Well, I'd better go," Hannah said, avoiding Tony's eyes. "Becca is coming home from college soon, and I want to make certain everything is perfect."

"Wouldn't it be wonderful if life really worked out that way," Tony said, undercurrents in his voice making Hannah feel unsteady on her feet. "Perfect."

Perfect. Was it possible things might have worked out that way if she'd kept the baby he'd fathered? If his mother had known about their little daughter? What if Mrs. Blake had come to love the granddaughter she'd never known existed, and swept the child into Tony's world, where he couldn't pretend anymore, couldn't ignore Hannah or the baby she bore him?

What if . . . ? Hannah had never given herself the chance to wonder. But tonight, she knew the questions would come. . . .

Hannah paced around the kitchen, looking for something to keep her hands busy, a pastime that was getting all too familiar. But the baby's bag was packed, the basket of treats for the trip to Becca's college was stuffed to overflowing, and she'd already taken the bottle warmer Josie had loaned her out to the car to test it three times to make sure it worked when plugged into the car lighter's socket.

She'd even changed Ellie's outfit half a dozen times, trying to guess which one was likely to charm Becca most. In the end, Hannah had settled on the outfit Josie had given her at the baby shower—a pair of soft pink balloon overalls with Peter Rabbit embroidered on the bib. Trust Josie to remember the stories Hannah had told her about Becca as a baby—those tender stories mothers liked to tell again and again, until most people get bored to tears. Josie had sensed from the beginning how much Hannah needed to share those memories from Becca's babyhood, especially as years went by and no little sister or brother came along to spin stories of their own. It was as if Hannah were running her fingers over a string of pearls, precious, rare, reliving every memory again and again because she sensed . . . feared . . . that this was the only chance she'd ever have.

How many times had Josie heard the story of how enchanted Becca had been with Peter Rabbit. How she'd wandered around for weeks quoting the book in her piping little voice. *He had a blue coat with brass buttons, quite new.*

It had always been one of Becca's favorite stories about her childhood, too. Maybe that memory would soften Becca up a little. It had brought Hannah to the brink of tears. But then, she felt as if she'd been teetering on the edge of them for two whole weeks, her nerves strained until everyone who knew her watched her uneasily—as if their pet kitten were dancing around on the edge of a cliff.

Not that she'd yelled or lost her temper or even *tried* to explain what was eating her up inside. But she didn't need to say a word for Josie or Tom or Sam or even her usual clerk at the grocery store to notice that Hannah O'Connell—the "human tranquilizer," who could walk into a room and turn down the stress level with nothing but a smile—was acting like her feet were on fire.

In fact, if just one more person asked if she were all right, Hannah feared she might give them the shock of their life and tell them exactly how she felt. Crazed. Scared. Excited. Desperate. So far from her usual calm "zen queen" behavior, she could barely recognize herself in the mirror.

But the problem wasn't the one Margo kept suggesting—a newborn baby causing too much strain. It wasn't Hannah's health, the thing that was worrying Josie. There was so much more at stake than Hannah could tell even her best friend.

Her marriage.

Her relationship with Becca.

A future Hannah had always taken for granted as hers—she and Sam growing old in the farmhouse, like her own grandparents had done. Becca staying close, no matter how far from Iowa her own life carried her. Sam's trust—rock solid, never questioned. A trust never more precious than it was now, when she admitted she didn't deserve it, when she feared he'd find out the truth about her secret and never, ever, be able to forgive her.

Hannah shivered, in spite of the warm spring weather. Why hadn't she ever thought about any of this before she'd taken Ellie in? Why hadn't she considered how dangerous it might be?

There was no way to avoid ripping open old secrets

with Tony Blake in town. No way to keep from reminding fate of debts she hadn't paid now that she'd taken in a baby some other terrified girl had abandoned. It was as if her surgery had unleashed some kind of psychic avalanche—the fact that she could never have another child destroying her confidence in herself as a woman. Reminding her of the child she had given away, the secret she'd kept from her husband, Tony Blake returning to Willowton, his mere presence in the town showing her how fragile her life here really was. How easy it would be for her fears, her self-doubt, her guilty secrets to fall down around her ears, threatening everything else she cherished. Not once had she stopped to weigh what she was doing when she insisted on taking Ellie into her life. Never had she stopped to consider how much it might cost her.

"Stop it," she muttered aloud. "Even if you had been able to predict any of this, what would you have done? Turned Ellie over to the authorities? Pretend like you hadn't found her? Take the easy way out, the way everyone else would have approved of, the way you did when you surrendered your own baby girl to strangers in Oregon?"

No. In spite of everything—her past rising to haunt her, her fear of losing Sam, her painful feeling of distance from Becca—Hannah knew she'd done the only thing she could the day she'd found Ellie in the wicker basket.

She had to see this through. Had to keep believing that it would all work out in the end. Or would it? What if she lost Sam as some kind of punishment for letting go of her first child, giving her to people who let her baby die.

Whatever happens in the future, I'll be there for you, she remembered Tony's promise, his eyes warm with a tenderness that alarmed her and in a way she could scarce admit, reassured her. As if he knew her world was crumbling under her feet, and intended to be there if it fell away, offer a hand to pull her back up onto solid ground. It was crazy to feel any comfort at all, to count on Tony even a little. And yet, it steadied her somehow, to see no turmoil in his face, no recriminations, none of the confused emotions she saw so often in Sam's.

It was insane—part of her almost wanted to call Tony just to diffuse some of the tension coiling inside her. Tell him about Ellie's latest trick, finding her mouth with her fist, and how she'd made a funny face at the taste of her own fingers. Was it just wishful thinking that Tony would find it as charming as she had?

"Things aren't bad enough? You want to make them worse?" She scolded herself aloud. "Tony is Ellie's guardian. He's not a friend. The last thing you should do is encourage him."

Encourage him to what? Smile that charming smile? Look at her as if she were young and pretty instead of fragile and faded? He might show concern about Ellie, but he seemed to have unending confidence in Hannah herself, always looked at her as if he thought she could handle any situation. It was refreshing. Different. She couldn't help but like it. And yet, it made her feel guilty somehow, as if even appreciating Tony's confidence in her was wrong.

She shoved the troubling thoughts to the back of her mind, turning her attention to the baby.

Ellie snuffled in her little swing, and Hannah crept over quietly, repositioning the baby's pacifier so Ellie wouldn't wake up all the way. Ellie smacked her lips, sucked ferociously for a moment, then slowly drifted off to sleep. Hannah wished she could just pick Ellie up, hold the baby in a warm and comforting little bundle against her heart. But Ellie had been restless enough this morning, picking up on Hannah's bad case of nerves. Let the poor little thing sleep in peace a little bit longer if she could. Sam should be home in another two hours, and then—

Then they'd throw everything into the car, all buckle in and be on their way up to the college. For a little while, at least, Hannah could pretend that nothing had changed between her and Sam, that Becca was waiting eagerly for them to arrive, and that the instant Becca saw Ellie's winsome smile, she'd be as enchanted with the baby as she had been sullen about Ellie before.

Hannah grabbed a mug from the cupboard, filled it with water and microwaved it long enough to brew a cup of chamomile tea, desperately needing her grandmother's foolproof cure for "fits of nerves."

Picking Becca up from college—Hannah had been imagining how it would be ever since the day she and Sam had driven away and left Becca standing outside the dorms. It would be so perfect, like old times. Becca would show them her dorm room, how she'd made it her own with the mishmash of posters and photographs and trinkets she hadn't been able to leave at home. They'd see the desk where she crammed for tests and meet the friends she split pizzas with on Friday nights. Becca wouldn't be able to chatter fast enough to tell Hannah everything she wanted to as they wandered past waving students and professors intent on where they were going.

Even if Becca decided to be stubborn and keep quiet for a while, Hannah knew her daughter. Becca would never be able to stay silent for three whole hours in the car. Once, when she'd gotten a sore throat on a weekend trip for speech team, her coach had forbidden her to say a single word in order to save her voice for the upcoming competition. Becca had written a three-page letter home, claiming that she'd felt like her head was going to explode by the time the trip was over.

No, Becca would have to start talking before they got back to Willowton. And once she did, everything would smooth out between them. Not a minute of her break would be wasted with this miserable distance between them. They could stay up late at night talking, go shopping the way she'd planned, eat lunch at Becca's favorite café and heal the sore places they had caused in each other's hearts.

Hannah heard the crunch of car tires coming up the driveway. Her heart jumped. Tony? The possibility unnerved her. But then, it was too early for Sam to be home, and Tony's penchant for turning up when she least expected it hadn't changed since the disturbing day she'd run into him at the park.

Hannah peered out the window, saw the mail truck at the box at the end of the drive. She gulped a mouthful of tea, searing her throat. She coughed, choked, her cheeks burning as she leaned over the sink, her hands shaking, Tony's voice echoing in her head.

If Sam ever did find out about the baby, I'd be here for you—

She'd been so stunned by his sudden, impassioned words, she hadn't been able to think. Hadn't been able to remind him that he didn't have a lot of credibility since he'd vanished once before when she was scared and pregnant and had nowhere else to turn. Maybe Sam had moved into Becca's room. But he'd still been close enough to call if she'd wanted to, close enough to hear her when the nightmares came. Tony had left Willowton and hadn't even glanced back.

Hannah closed her eyes, her hands trembling at the memory of waking under Sam's hands the night of her nightmare, his earnest, worried features so close to hers she could feel the warmth of his breath. His hands, so steady, so strong, holding onto her, not letting her fall deeper into terrors that weren't real, that had vanished years ago.

She'd wanted to fling herself against the hard wall of his chest, hold him so tight no fear could squeeze in between them. Feel his heart pounding against hers, his fingers in her hair, his lips on her cheek kissing her, driving away shadows of things that had been, filling her whole body instead with possibilities of magic they could conjure up together.

She'd wanted to feel him all over—hot and fierce, loving her without room for doubt or dread or the ugliness of the scar on her abdomen. When he'd seen it— the scar that had sickened her, made her feel mutilated, ugly, no longer whole—he'd kissed it, laid his cheek against it. He'd turned his eyes up to hers so she could finally see the reaction she'd been avoiding for so long.

But it hadn't been revulsion. It hadn't been horror. His eyes had filled with tenderness, worship, love. She'd seen him grieve for her pain, but also knew the scar hadn't changed how he saw her. That she was still beautiful in his eyes—as beautiful as she'd been at twenty. As if time and illness and pain could never touch her.

Her whole body had ached to open to him, give him the gift he'd earned with his tenderness. She'd closed her eyes, drowning in his touch, could almost feel it— the magic of him covering her body with his own, the fearsome yearning in both of them as his shaft slid deep, home after so very long.

It would have been over. All the distance, all the

loneliness, all the fear and uncertainty. It could have been over. Except for the secret she kept from him. Except for Tony drifting in and out of their lives. Except for the fact that she knew the situation would explode—maybe not now, maybe not next week. But it wouldn't stay hidden forever.

How could she go to Sam, make him believe everything was healed between them when she knew the truth. That something ugly lay underneath all her smiles, all her touches. That the mouth that kissed him was still lying after all these years.

No. She couldn't make him hope that everything was right between them when she knew that everything was wrong. But how could she make things right between them? How could she ever make things right?

One day at a time, she told herself. Let things happen naturally. Pick up Becca, enjoy each other's company. Mend things between you. Then you can figure out what to do about Sam.

But he'll be in your room tonight, he'll be in your bed. So Becca will never suspect how things have really been since she's been gone.

It was one thing to hold herself apart from Sam with a wall between them. But to be able to hold onto that distance with him lying inches away from her, to keep from touching him when she could smell the woodsy-sweet sawdust smell of him and feel his warmth close enough to touch—that was something far more difficult.

Especially since she'd have to face the pain in his eyes from her rejection, see the yearning for her in the sensitive curve of his mouth. Especially since she'd have to lie there, sure of the doubts that would be running through his mind: Why didn't she want him anymore? How had he hurt her? Failed her?

"You didn't fail me," Hannah breathed aloud. "I'm the one who failed you, Sam. I'm sorry. So—"

The creak of the screen door startled Hannah. She spun around to glimpse Sam's dark, flyaway hair. But as he pushed open the door, Hannah froze. His tanned features were pale, stiff, grave.

Oh, God! Hannah thought in panic. Did he know the truth? Had he found out about the baby she'd given away? What else could possibly affect him so deeply?

She felt as if she'd swallowed a golf ball. Her hands were shaking. She thrust them behind her. "Sam," she managed to choke out. "I didn't think we were supposed to leave for another hour and a half. But I've got everything packed and ready."

He crossed to the table, peering down into the basket of goodies so solemnly it scared Hannah to death.

"Of course you're ready," he said thickly. "You've been packing and unpacking and baking all Becca's favorites for days."

"I want everything to be perfect. I know we've picked her up from school before, and we'll do it lots of other times as well, but this is the first time she gets to meet Ellie. There won't ever be another one quite as precious as this."

Sam turned away, his face contorting as if she'd hit him. Her heart sank to her toes. "Sam, what—what's wrong?"

"Becca called from school."

A different, deeper dread shot through Hannah. Becca? Something was wrong with Becca? "What is it? What's wrong?"

"Nothing. It's just that she's riding home with some other kids from school. She doesn't want us to—"

"Pick her up?" Hannah said numbly.

"She said she wanted to save us the trouble."

Trouble? Becca had to know it wouldn't be any trouble. She had to know how much Hannah had been looking forward to it. No. It had nothing to do with convenience. Becca knew Hannah would use the time in the car to try to work on the problems between them. Becca was determined not to give her the chance.

"You said it was all right?" Hannah asked, hurt that Sam hadn't even called her to check, see how *she* felt about it before giving Becca the go-ahead.

Sam sagged down into a chair, dragged his hand back through his hair. "I tried to talk her out of it, but you know how she digs her heels in. She'd made up her mind before she'd even picked up the phone. In the end, I figured it was better to let her have it her way. If we'd made a big deal about it, it would only have made things worse."

That was true enough. Once Becca made up her mind about something, all the king's horses and all the king's men couldn't budge her. Some people would've shaken their heads in disappointment over her "stubbornness." Hannah had rejoiced in her strong will, knowing it would give her the strength and determination to get wherever it was she wanted to go in life. She needed to remember that now, when the trait was wrenching at her heart.

"Hannah, I'm sorry. I know how much you were looking forward to this trip. It's a damned shame it worked out this way, but I don't know what else we could do. The minute you try to force Becca's hand, you've got nothing but trouble. You're the one who taught me that it's better to be patient with her. She's got a good heart. Trust her to sort it out."

Yes, Hannah thought, but that was when the parent Becca was resisting was *you*. She'd never guessed how much harder it would be to be the one facing that stubborn jut of Becca's chin, the sullen, fierce determination in her eyes. She'd never realized how it would hurt to do nothing, say nothing, be patient when what you really wanted to do was grab her by the shoulders and shake her until she saw how much you loved her.

"I wish there was something I could do," Sam said quietly, "to make this easier for you. I just don't know what. . . . Maybe we could still take the day. Cruise upriver to look through those antiques shops you used to love. It would be better than sitting around here, wouldn't it?"

Hannah wanted to curl up in the middle of the bed, have a good cry. She wanted to shove everyone away, so she could hurt in peace. Think what to do now. But Sam's eyes pleaded with her, his face so worried she couldn't bear it.

"All right," she said. Maybe it was time she quit hiding whenever she was hurt.

He started in surprise, smiled at her. "Great! I'll load everything up. We'll be back long before Becca gets here."

Not that Hannah figured it would matter much. She sighed. If Becca was determined to avoid her, it wouldn't be hard with so many of her friends back on break.

Don't worry, Hannah reassured herself. *We've got a whole week. She'll have to talk to me sometime.*

She just hoped that this time she was right.

15

SHE'D BEEN A REAL TROOPER, Sam thought as they pulled back into the driveway. But then, Hannah had always been one to tough things out. She'd managed to smile, carry on conversations, even laugh once or twice as they wound their way through dusty antiques shops, looking for treasures. He'd found some old prints from 1930's children's books with little girls and fairies, and he'd gotten them, insisting they'd be perfect for the room they were going to fix up for Ellie.

The notion of that had brightened Hannah's mood a little bit. He'd helped find an antique baby buggy he promised to fix up so it could hold stuffed animals. She'd looked so touched, her eyes misty, but it hadn't covered the hurt Becca had left behind, her refusal to let them come pick her up at school. Showing in no uncertain terms her reluctance to accept Ellie into their family. Much as she tried to hide it, that subtle sadness shadowed them from shop to shop, filled the empty seat at the table they shared in the quaint little diner they found along the Mississippi River. Sam could hear its echo in the silences that grew longer and longer the closer they got to home.

"When did Becca think she'd get here?" Hannah asked as he pulled the car to a stop.

"About six-thirty." He could see the wheels whirring in Hannah's head as she figured it out. About forty-five minutes, and Becca should be walking in the door. Forty-five more minutes for Hannah's imagination to run away with her. Unless he could find a way to keep her busy.

"I'm starved after pawing through all that dust today. Don't suppose you could whip us up some of that vegetable soup Becca and I both love?"

The soup had been Becca's favorite ever since she'd been tiny. Sam couldn't count how many times he'd come home from work to find the two of them busy at the wooden cutting board, Hannah chopping mounds of potatoes and turnips while Becca carefully skinned the long, orange carrots, a miniature apron tied under her arms. *You haf to be tareful, Daddy. Make long strings like me. But no nife-es for little girls. It could cut you.*

Seemed like he'd barely finished chuckling at her chatter, bent down to give her a kiss, and next moment she was thirteen, chopping carrots with a practiced hand while she jabbered about one of her girlfriend's latest crushes.

Hell, it was almost scary how much he was thinking like Hannah—what time and patience wouldn't heal surely vegetable soup would take care of.

Hannah saw right through him, but she smiled, nodded. "No problem. Just let me get the baby inside."

"I'll put Ellie to bed. Then let me help you."

She gave him a strange look. He'd only rarely offered to help in the kitchen. It was Hannah's domain. But tonight, he knew she needed company, something to take her mind off of the deafening ticking of the clock.

The kettle was bubbling in no time at all, rich, delicious scents filling the house as Hannah fussed and seasoned the soup. She set three places at the table, and Sam's heart squeezed at the soft smile that touched her lips.

"It never seemed right without her place set," she admitted softly. "I just couldn't get used to it. Can't tell you how many times I started to pull out an extra plate, her favorite glass. When she first went off to college, I'd go to the grocery store and buy bubblegum ice cream because it was her favorite. It would sit there, in the freezer, week after week, until I forgot and bought another carton, and another one. Who in their right mind eats that stuff besides Becca?"

Sam started to speak, stopped, both he and Hannah freezing where they stood. Even above the soft bubbling sound of the soup, they could hear the sound of gravel spraying, a car skidding to a stop.

Hannah pressed her hand to her throat, and for an instant, her emotions were raw on her face. Fear, elation, hope, hurt. Expectations so high there was no way she could help but be disappointed. Sam wanted to find a way to scoop her into his arms, shield her until he had a chance to see what kind of mood Becca was in. He wanted a minute alone with Becca, long enough to tell her how much her mother missed her, how hurt Hannah had been when she hadn't been allowed to pick her up at school. He wanted to beg Becca to think about all the times Hannah had soothed her hurts, forgiven her blunders, supported her even when she'd been damned near impossible to deal with in some sort of teenage fit.

But before he could move, Hannah streaked past

him, out the door. Sam sucked in a deep breath, hurting for both of them. Hell, he'd give anything if only *he* could be the one on the outside looking in, the way it had always been before.

Hannah stared at the young woman swinging her long legs out of the door of the beat up old Mustang. Soft folds of ice blue sweater caught the sunlight, her glossy honey-gold hair twisted up in a style worlds more sophisticated than the ponytail she'd worn her senior year. Hannah's throat clenched at the sound of her laughter at something a gawky boy with a Vikings jersey was saying.

Hannah wanted to run to her, scoop her up into a hug the way she had every other time Becca had come home. She wanted so much to feel her baby in her arms, smell the wildflower scent of her hair, know that she was home and safe and still loved her in spite of all the strain.

But Hannah only stiffened, her hands closing tight in the folds of her butter yellow shirt, using all her willpower in an effort to give Becca the space she needed, no matter how awkward it felt, no matter how desperately she wanted to bridge the distance between them.

Grabbing her duffel bag, Becca tossed her hair in a way that made her driver stare, goggle-eyed. "Thanks, Pete. See you next Sunday."

Sunday? Hannah thought in disappointment. So Becca wasn't going to let them drive her back up to school either. *Maybe she's trying to be thoughtful, wanting to save you the trip. Six hours is a long time in a car.* But much as Hannah wished it to be true, she knew it wasn't so. Every time she'd talked to Becca before Ellie had come on the scene, Becca had been chattering about her plans to show Hannah everything—her dorm room, the music building, the concert hall where her favorite band was supposed to play the week before school got out. Becca knew just how much Hannah had been looking forward to getting the "grand tour," and Becca had been dying to play guide. No, the message was painfully clear. Impossible to excuse it all away.

"Will" said something Hannah didn't even hear, then climbed into his car and sped away in an impressive rooster tail of gravel and teenaged machismo as Becca waved good-bye.

Hannah stared at her daughter's back. Shoulders square, stiff. Chin at an angle Sam had always called her fighting pose. God, she looked so grown-up, and yet, somehow, as she turned around, she grew suddenly, terribly young, hurt and defiance brimming in her eyes, the only thing sadder, how hard she was struggling to hide them behind a veil of teenage carelessness.

"Hi, Mom." She breezed up, brushed an emotionless kiss on Hannah's cheek. Hannah's heart staggered under the blow, worlds away from the warm hugs and eager chatter she'd dreamed of.

"Did you—have a good trip home?"

"Yeah. Will's pretty funny when he's not around grown-ups."

"Maybe sometime I can meet him." The words slipped out before Hannah thought. Impatience flashed in Becca's eyes.

"Mom, I'm in college now. You don't have to give every kid I speak to the third degree!"

Maybe not the ones Becca spoke to, but surely a teenage boy who was behind the wheel of a car Becca was riding in for three long hours merited a "hello?" She wanted to argue, but she'd already blundered into making things worse. Will, who was "funny" when he wasn't around grown-ups, surely wasn't worth escalating things when Becca was obviously just itching for a fight. Hannah steadied herself, dared to try again.

"Oh, Becca, it's so . . . so good to see you. You look wonderful. College must agree with you."

"It's great being on my own. Guess you never realize how much your parents treat you like a baby until you get out of the house."

The words stung, but Hannah comforted herself that Becca didn't completely hate her. The instant her daughter saw pain in her face, she relented at least a little.

"I guess I didn't mean that in a bad way." Becca shrugged. "I just—you always wanted me to be independent. Now I can see why. It's awesome not to have to answer to anyone but yourself."

"Daddy and I've been busy cooking up a surprise. We thought you should have something special on your first night home. Vegetable soup. Daddy helped chop the vegetables, though, so there's no predicting how it will taste."

Hannah watched for a reaction, hoping. But instead of showing even a hint of pleasure, Becca looked down, shifting her feet uncomfortably. "Wish you would have warned me. See, I already made plans to go out with Annie tonight. She e-mailed me just before I left, said she's got some hot gossip about the girls in Vienna, something I won't believe. I figured, with the new baby around, you'd be tired."

"Too tired to spend time with you after three months?" Hannah couldn't hide her hurt. "I could never be that tired, and you know it."

"Mom, don't make a big deal out of it. It's just one night. We've got my whole break to talk and stuff."

"But tonight is your first night home. I want you to meet Ellie."

"What's the big deal? Bet she looks like every other

baby I've ever seen. And she's too little to do anything interesting. All newborns do is sleep. What does she care if I stick around for dinner or not?"

"I care. Becca—"

"Mom, don't. Not on my first night home." Becca's voice broke. "I just got done with a bunch of tests. I haven't slept for three days, and I haven't seen my friends forever. I just can't— Just give me a break tonight, please."

Hannah heard footsteps behind her, Sam coming out of the house. "Hey, there, Becca! Welcome home! Wait until you see what we've got waiting for you."

"Hi, Daddy."

Hannah tried not to cry as Becca brushed past her, giving Sam a real hug. Sam's arms closed automatically around her, but he was looking at Hannah over Becca's shoulder, guilt and empathy filling his eyes.

"She isn't staying for supper," Hannah said woodenly. "She's going out with Annie."

"She can go out with Annie later," Sam said, scowling. "Dinner's all ready. It'll only take fifteen minutes."

"I promised I'd run over to her house the minute I got home. We've got a whole week."

A whole week? Hannah thought numbly. A whole week for Becca to avoid her, to close her out. A whole week in which she could let Hannah know in no uncertain terms just how much things had changed between them. And then a long, empty summer, autumn, winter, when Becca would be an ocean away in France. The way she was reacting at the moment, she might as well be there now.

Becca shifted her bag to Sam, and he took it, his mouth setting with the same stubbornness as his daughter's. "I think you should stay home. Your mother's been waiting to see you."

"She's seeing me right now, and she'll see me as soon as I get back tonight."

"At least take a look at the baby."

Hannah wanted to argue, warn Sam to let Becca off the hook. Nothing good came of forcing the girl when she had an attitude. But it was too late. They faced off, Becca's jaw clenched in mutiny, Sam's face implacable as stone.

"Okay, where is she?" Becca surrendered after a moment.

"In our room."

Becca trudged into the house, pausing to greet Reckless with more enthusiasm than either of her parents had gotten. Hannah sensed Becca would've kept kneeling there forever, petting the black moose of a dog if she could have, avoiding everything—seeing Ellie, talking to her mother.

But after a minute, Becca straightened and marched up the stairs with all the enthusiasm of a convict facing a firing squad. Sam followed after her as if he were bent on cutting off any retreat. Hannah brought up the rear.

Was it possible that Ellie would charm her? Once Becca saw the baby that she'd understand? How helpless Ellie was? How very alone? How much the baby needed a family to love her? Strong-willed as Becca was, reluctant to admit she was wrong, Becca still had a warm, generous heart. Maybe once she saw how tiny Ellie was, she'd melt.

Hannah followed the two of them into the bedroom, trying not to hope for too much, not able to stop herself. Becca hesitated, faltered, as she peered into the garret. The sun streamed down on the warm wood of the cradle, Ellie tucked in soft blankets like a drowsing fairy. Delicate lashes fanned across rosy cheeks, her pink bud of a mouth sucking at nothing at all.

Hope welling inside her, Hannah slipped past Sam and Becca, leaned over to pick Ellie up. "This is Becca, Eleanor Rose," she said, looking down into Ellie's face, scared to let Becca see how desperate she felt as she prayed with all of her heart. *Please, God, let it be all right.* "You're so lucky to have a girl like Becca to help you grow. She's the most wonderful daughter anyone ever—"

Hannah glanced up, but Becca's face was turned away. She was still staring at the empty cradle.

"What's this?" she demanded in a brittle voice, shoving it gently to set it rocking.

"The cradle. Daddy got it down and finished it."

"I thought it was supposed to be mine."

"It *is* yours. Ellie's just borrowing it for now."

Becca's gaze flashed from Sam's face to Hannah's, her eyes hot with hurt. "She—she can keep it. Daddy couldn't even bother to finish it for me."

"Becca," Hannah began. "He always meant to. He was working so hard then, he—"

"Didn't have time?" Becca supplied. "But he had plenty of time to finish it for *her.*"

"Becca, don't get mad at the baby. Or at your mom. I'm the one who screwed up, who didn't get it done when you needed it. If you want, I'll build a different cradle for Ellie. We can put this one in your room or back up in the garage rafters. Whatever you say."

"Whatever *I* say?" Becca gave a ragged laugh. "That's a joke! I don't have any say at all in any of this, do I? I'm just supposed to come home and smile and be all happy that somebody dumped a baby in our back-yard and you moved her in here so she can take over my mom, my dad, my whole *life.*"

"Don't you think you're exaggerating a little? Nothing could ever take your place, Becca."

"Could've fooled me. She's sleeping in the cradle—that was supposed to be mine, wasn't it? And those stuffed animals downstairs—those were mine, weren't they?"

"Becca, you gave Koko away when I sent her up to you. You said you were too old for stuffed animals."

"That's not the point! They're mine to give away if I want to. And I don't. At least not right now."

Becca's eyes sparkled with tears. Hannah could see how furious they made her. "Okay, I saw the baby. Now, can I leave?"

"Becca," Sam struggled to keep his voice gentle. "Don't you think we should talk?"

But Hannah knew there was no point. They could talk until their voices went hoarse. Becca was way past the point of listening.

"Let her go, Sam," she said, trying to hide the tears roughening her own voice.

"But, Hannah, we—"

"Maybe we've all said enough for one night."

Becca blinked hard, bright drops glistening on her lashes.

"Can I go, then?"

Hannah nodded, her heart breaking as Becca pushed past her. She held her breath until she heard the screen door slam. What had she expected? Hoped? That at the last minute, Becca might change her mind? Turn around? The old Becca would have—haunted by Hannah's tears, wanting to fix things since she'd already made her point.

Hannah looked out the window, saw Becca running down the lane like she had a thousand times before. She watched, hoping against hope, until Becca turned the corner and disappeared from view.

This time, Becca didn't even glance back.

* * *

Hannah curled up in a corner of the couch, listening to the ticking of the clock on the mantel. Midnight. Becca's curfew. But no telling if she'd hold to it tonight. She expected the phone to ring any time, Becca saying she was staying overnight at Annie's. Heck, she'd probably prefer to sleep on a park bench after the scene earlier that evening.

It had been even worse than Hannah had imagined. It was hard enough to feel your daughter withdraw from you, to try to guess if she was angry or hurting or just preoccupied with school, pulling away naturally, the way she was supposed to. Part of growing up. It was hard to sort out the hope and dread, trying to guess what she was thinking, what she was feeling, how she would react.

But it was far harder to actually look into your little girl's face and see the pain you'd put there. See stark betrayal and fear and hurt and not even be able to reach out and hold her and make the hurting go away.

And, hurt and confused as Becca was, she didn't know the half of it. What would Becca feel if she knew one of the reasons her mother had taken Ellie in? Because of a choice she'd made twenty-seven years ago? Just knowing what Hannah had done would change everything—everything Becca believed about her mother, everything Sam was so sure of in his wife. In an instant, Hannah would be a stranger.

The possibility terrified Hannah, sickened her.

Hannah heard the sound of a car door slamming, glanced out the window to see headlights burning in the driveway. Annie's car. One that had been parked at the farmhouse almost as often as it had been in Annie's own driveway. The petite redhead had been one of the kids who had practically lived at the O'Connells'. She'd always been looking for an excuse to raid the cookie jar, eat homemade jam, and spend all night talking to "the coolest mom in Willowton."

Tonight, it didn't even look as if she were going to stop in to say "hi." Hannah's shoulders sagged. Annie must've believed Becca when she heard about the transformation from cool mom to the Wicked Witch of the West.

Hannah caught her lip between her teeth, trying to remember the speeches she'd been practicing in her mind in the hours since Sam had finally surrendered and gone to bed. So much she needed to say to Becca. And yet, she couldn't muck it up like she had before.

Becca closed the back door quietly, but Hannah knew her daughter didn't have any illusions that she'd be waking her mother up.

Still, she was less defiant, more subdued than Hannah had imagined.

"I figured you'd be waiting up," Becca said, shrugging off her sweater and draping it over a chair. Hannah loved the return of Becca's clutter. Bits and scraps that reminded her this was Becca's home.

"It feels good to wait up for you again."

"Yeah, well. Annie asked me to stay overnight, but I guess we might as well get this over with. Besides, I wanted to tell you about what Annie told me."

Hannah's instincts stirred. Becca's troubled gaze had less than she'd thought to do with the argument they'd had earlier. Was it possible Becca had heard something about one of her friends? Ellie's mother? From the first, Hannah had figured the baby belonged to one of Becca's schoolmates. "What is it? Something wrong?"

"Yeah. I mean, no one died or anything. But it's so weird, it's hard to believe it's true."

"What's true?"

"You know that French internship I talked to you about? How I was going to weekend in Vienna?"

"You were going to hook up with Rachel and Jana."

"Yeah, well, looks like I won't be hooking up with Rachel, after all."

"I don't understand. She wanted to stay in Europe forever. Keep studying—"

"Forever turned out to be a lot shorter time than she thought. Annie says Rachel called her mom yesterday and begged to come home."

"But she's only been there a few weeks." Hannah gasped, disbelieving. "Maybe it was just a bit of homesickness. It's to be expected, I suppose. Surely, Margo wouldn't let her give up this chance—"

"The Johnsons have been looking for an excuse to get her to give up the violin forever. They're probably thrilled she's coming home. Bet her father's already fitting her out with a brand new set of dentist's instruments."

"But why? It's so strange—" Hannah stopped, remembering the odd phone call she'd gotten two weeks before. She'd wondered even then if it was Rachel. But the caller had hung up. She'd figured it was a mistake. Oh, Lord, was it possible that Rachel *had* been on the other end of the phone? If Hannah had just gotten her to talk, could she have sorted all this out? Helped Rachel put her homesickness into perspective before she gave up the biggest opportunity of her life? Maybe there was still time.

"Do you have Rachel's number overseas? Maybe I could talk to her."

"It's too late." Becca forgot to be angry with Hannah in her confusion. "Annie says Rachel's mom and dad are driving up to Iowa City to pick her up tomorrow."

Hannah stared, stunned, helpless. How had everything turned into such a mess? "I don't believe it," she said.

Becca sank down into the chair across from her. In spite of her need to talk, it seemed she was still maintaining space between them. She looked so small in the chair, suddenly so lost. "It's so strange. You go away to school and you think you know just how it's all going to be. All Rachel ever wanted was to play violin in Vienna and now, she doesn't want to anymore. And I was so sure that nothing would ever change with you and me."

"Oh, sweetheart. I'm so sorry. I never meant for this to hurt you."

"What did you expect? Did you think I'd be thrilled that I'd barely left home and you'd stuck another baby in my place?"

"That's not how it is at all, Becca."

"Yeah, you *found* the baby 'cause someone I know left it in a basket in the backyard. One of my friends got pregnant and kept it secret. And then she just threw her baby away."

"She put it where I would find it. She knew I'd take care of it."

"Mom, it's like, every time I look at my friends now, I keep wondering if they were the one. If they left that poor baby outside where anything could have happened to it. If they turned away and didn't even care."

"I'm sure Ellie's mother cared, sweetheart. She did the best she could."

"It wasn't good enough! It makes me sick inside, to think I could ever have been friends with someone so . . . so terrible. If I ever find out who did it, I swear, I'll never speak to them again as long as I live."

Hannah tried to suck in a breath. Her lungs burned. "Never is a long time, Becca. Ellie's mother, whoever she is, will need you more than ever."

"Too bad. I could never, *never* be around someone who could do something like that."

Hannah's throat burned. She should have been glad Becca was at least talking. But the words she was saying seared Hannah like acid. What would Becca think if she ever knew . . .

But then, it was so easy when you were a teenager—everything in black and white, with no unsettling shades of gray. That indescribable arrogance of being certain that you knew exactly what you'd do in any situation—that you would always play the hero, never the scared little mouse cowering from things that were too ugly, too painful, cost far too much.

Hannah could remember feeling that way, too. One of the greatest shames of her life was the fact that the year before she'd met Tony, one of the girls in her class had turned up pregnant. One of the "cool" girls, defiant, her face painted with makeup, her sweaters too tight. She'd acted so hard, so brittle, like she didn't give a damn her belly was exploding, that everyone in school was making fun of her. That whatever dreams she'd had—Hannah thought she remembered something about wanting her own beauty shop—had to be put on hold, maybe forever. Hannah had always wished she could go back to the beginning of junior year, wished she could go up to the girl, talk to her, ask her about her baby. Tony had claimed she was "kind" in high school. But she hadn't been very kind to that girl. Part of her had even taken a sick righteous kind of satisfaction in the fact that she was in trouble.

Of course, that was long before Hannah had ever dreamed that the next girl to fall might be her.

"Becca—" she began. "I know this has to be difficult for you. Really confusing. I wish there was something I could do to make it easier, but I don't know how.

Sometimes life gets . . . gets complex. Things get . . . tangled up. People feel trapped into doing things they wouldn't if they could find any other way. Can you understand that?"

"Yeah. I've been feeling trapped ever since you called and told me you'd found that baby."

"Oh, sweetheart." Hannah ached at the vulnerable light in Becca's eyes.

"I don't have any say in this at all, do I? I mean, whether or not you're going to keep this baby?"

The comment startled Hannah. Opened a window into the emotions Becca must be feeling. It hurt Hannah, made her doubt. She sucked in a deep breath, struggled to explain. "I'd hoped you'd be—" Happy? The word sounded ludicrous now. Hannah winced. She just hadn't thought it would bother Becca. She'd been so sure at least Becca would understand how much this chance to have another baby would mean to her. A chance to recapture at least some of the magic they had shared. Hannah had wanted to share the joy with her, include her in welcoming Ellie into the family. She'd wanted things to be so much different. She could only hope that they would be given time.

"I'm sorry if you're upset, sweet pea," Hannah apologized, and meant it.

"I'll get over it," Becca said, and Hannah knew her daughter was trying to hide an underlying layer of hurt.

"I just want—" Want everything to be wonderful, want everyone to be joyful. See Ellie the way Hannah did—a miracle, a precious, unexpected gift.

"Maybe I went about things the wrong way, but I do want to know what you're thinking, how you're feeling. If you could bring yourself to tell me."

Becca peered up at her, impossibly young, suddenly fragile.

"What is it, honey? Come on. Tell me."

"But you're *my* mom."

Hannah's heart twisted. "Nothing will ever change that, angel. You'll always be my baby."

"Yeah, but I always *liked* having you all to myself, not having to share you," Becca admitted.

"I liked having you all to myself, too."

"I know what you're trying to say. What you mean is—you have to share me, too, now that I'm away at college."

"Right. We just need to find new ways to be happy."

For a moment she saw disbelief brim in Becca's eyes. Hannah could almost hear the words reeling around in Becca's mind.

Had her mother gone crazy? What did she have to be happy about? Happy that a giggly baby had replaced her? Happy that one of her friends had done something she thought was so terrible? Happy that her mother would be rocking someone else, singing to someone else? Loving someone else?

Hannah's heart squeezed. Even though she was in college, Becca just needed some reassurance that her place would still be there for her when she got home.

"Becca, no baby on earth could ever change anything between you and me. You know that, don't you? I love you more than anything in the world!"

"But the baby will change everything. She'll be in my house. And I won't." Strange, so strange, the girl who had bounced off to college, acting as if she never particularly cared if she came home again. That girl sounded almost homesick, uncertain, wistful— Maybe she'd missed home more than she'd been willing to say. When Hannah told her about the baby, it was as if she'd said home would never be the same. The way Becca remembered it. That everything would change—not just Becca herself growing up. No wonder her little girl had been hurting, Hannah thought, sadly.

She stood up, crossed to where Becca sat. Hannah knelt down, just the way she had when Becca was a little girl, so she could talk to her, eye to eye. "This is your home, Becca. It was yours long before Ellie came here. And I'm your mom—I will be forever. We don't have to give up any of that. We just have to open up our hearts a little wider, to give Ellie someplace to grow."

Tears filled Becca's eyes as Hannah took both of her hands in her own.

"Rachel and Jana always hated being big sisters."

"Ah, but they had to live with their sisters, fight over toys and the phone. All you have to do is sweep in on break, spoil her rotten, then dump her in my lap and run when she starts screaming her head off."

Becca gave a watery chuckle.

"I hated giving up dolls. Maybe she would give me an excuse to play with them sometimes."

"No one would ever be the wiser. But Ellie is going to have to wait for a play date with her big sister. You see, I've got something planned for tomorrow."

"What?"

Becca wasn't exactly gritting her teeth. She just looked resigned to whatever kiddie entertainment Hannah might mention.

"I called Josie. She's going to baby-sit so you and I can have the day alone together."

Becca brightened, looked stunned. "But you almost never left me with sitters. I guess I just thought—" She stopped, but her meaning was crystal clear. Poor girl! She'd been imagining that she'd never get any time alone with her mother—when that time was one of the most precious things in either one of their lives.

"Ellie will be fine. Who knows, maybe we'll bring her something home from our shopping trip."

"We're going shopping?" Becca brightened.

"And then, I thought we'd stop by Antonio's for lunch, have a buttercrunch sundae." It took effort to add, "That is, unless you and Annie had something planned."

"I'll call her and tell her we've got something going. She couldn't figure out why I wasn't doing stuff with you, anyway. Everyone always figured I had the most fun when I was with you."

Hannah laughed, feeling as if a rock had rolled off her chest. It would take time, but she was patient. She and Becca would work things out. She didn't even try to stop the tears when Becca opened her arms and hugged her.

She just buried her face in her daughter's hair and held on tight.

"Mom," Becca said softly.

"What, angel girl?"

"About the baby. I know you want me to—to meet her and everything. And I want to. Honest. It's just, I was wondering—"

"What, sweetheart?"

"Could I do it tomorrow? I want it just to be you and me tonight. One last time." Becca pulled away, looked into Hannah's eyes, troubled. "Does that make me selfish?"

"If it does, I'm selfish, too. I want you all to myself for just a little while. I've missed you, Becca."

More than she could ever say.

16

⬧

FOUR IN THE MORNING. Sam squinted at the glowing numbers on the digital alarm clock, eased himself upright in bed trying to get his bearings. Where was he? It felt so right, but strange, the way the bed conformed to his body, the shadowy shapes of furniture peering down on him like old friends.

He blinked hard, the moonlight picking out the oval shape of the picture of Becca and Hannah they'd given him for Father's Day the year she was six. A grinning little doll with a mop of curls and her mama's smile.

Sam caught his breath, almost scared to move, scared to wake up and find that he was dreaming, that he was still in Becca's room, exiled from the bed he'd shared with Hannah for so long.

Fearful, he let his fingers creep across the tousled sheets to where Hannah should lie, drowsing. But his fingers didn't find her warmth, her softness, the silky river of her hair. Only sheets too cool and smooth to have been slept on.

Sam's hopes sank. Had she slept on the couch all

night? He hadn't expected some miracle—that she'd fling herself into his arms, beg him to make love to her after so long. Although, he had to admit, if she had, he'd have thought he'd died and gone to heaven. No, tonight his dreams had been small ones, but incredibly precious. Just to lie down beside her, hear the rhythm of her breathing, sense the beat of her heart. To drown in the luxury of knowing he could reach out whenever he wanted to, touch her to reassure himself that she was there.

She doesn't want you to touch her. Isn't that the point? A voice that sounded a hell of a lot like Tony Blake's mocked him. *Make things look nice for your daughter, pretend everything is just fine when underneath it all, nothing has changed.*

But it *has* changed, Sam wanted to yell. *I could feel it the night she had a bad dream. She wanted me to touch her then. I could feel it.*

Because it was true? Or because you wanted to believe it so badly?

God, he'd tried to be patient. Give Hannah the time she needed. He'd done everything he could to mend things between them. But he needed so much to hold her. He couldn't take much more of this. Living like some sort of ghost in the house, unable to live the life that was supposed to be his.

Yeah, you're suffering like hell, aren't you? he upbraided himself. *What about Hannah? What about what she's going through? Did you see her face when Becca left?*

Sam shuddered inwardly at the stark image branded in his mind. Anguish, confusion, helplessness—no different than if someone had torn Becca out of her arms. He knew that no matter how much he wanted to, he'd never forget Hannah's expression.

A tiny whimper broke through his thoughts. Ellie.

She must be starving. He'd heard Hannah creep in to give her a bottle just before midnight. Sam sighed. Maybe there wasn't much he could do about the situation here. He couldn't fix things with Hannah, couldn't chase the hurt away from her. He'd never been good at comforting Becca—Hannah had always done that. But at least he could manage to fix Ellie something to eat so neither of them would have to wake up.

Sam flicked on the small bedside light so the glare wouldn't blind Ellie. Then, scooping her up, he changed her diaper. She peered up at him with huge blue eyes, so trusting. Recognizing him even after just two weeks. His heart twisted when she gave him a damp, toothless smile. She reached up for him, chubby little fists grabbing nothing but air.

"I'm not the one you should be reaching for," he warned her, throat thick as he lifted her back into his arms. "Ask Becca. And Hannah, for that matter. See that cradle I gave you? It was supposed to be Becca's. But I never finished it. I thought I had more important things to do. Build a business, prove to everybody in Willowton that Hannah hadn't made a mistake marrying the kid of a worthless drunk. I thought it mattered—what other people thought of me. I didn't realize that the problem was what I thought of myself."

Ellie rooted at his neck, searching for something to suck on as they left the room. He glanced to the right, to Becca's room. The bed was empty, her duffel unopened where he'd put it hours before. Heart sinking, he tiptoed down the hall, his voice whisper low, not turning on the light because he was determined not to wake anybody.

"I'm not going to make that mistake with you, Ellie. I just wish I could go back, be everything Becca wanted. Built swing sets instead of condominiums, had tea parties instead of business meetings. Guess I never learned how to—to play with my baby before. Maybe you can help me do better this time."

He almost stumbled on the first step. Blinked in surprise. He might as well have saved himself the trouble of groping his way down the hall. Downstairs, the lights were all blazing, but he didn't hear a sound.

Had Hannah been waiting up for Becca and fallen asleep? Had Becca even bothered to call and let her know she wasn't coming home? It was just the kind of angry stunt most other teenagers would pull. But he never would have thought it possible that Becca would. If she had, they'd have to have a talk, and the last thing he wanted was a confrontation with his hurt, confused little girl.

He flicked on the hall light, padded down the stairs, dreading what he was going to find. The instant his gaze landed on the couch, he could barely stifle a cry of relief. His eyes burned with tears and he wouldn't have given a damn if every construction worker in Willowton had seen them.

Hannah was tucked in the corner of the couch, dozing with such a look of peace on her face it broke Sam's heart, while Becca was snuggled in the crook of her arm. Sam didn't have to guess what they'd been doing—talking, thank God, talking, while Hannah played with the strands of Becca's hair.

Sam's throat closed with gratitude too great to hold. It was all right between them, he thought. It was all healed. He ignored a twinge in the region of his heart, quelled the soft whisper: *But she'll be turning to Hannah now, instead of you. You've lost her again.*

That's how it should be, Sam murmured to himself. *Hannah worked a lifetime to earn Becca's trust.*

What about you? He had to fight a stab of pain.

I'll have to do my best to earn it for myself, but I'd never take it at any cost to Hannah. I couldn't.

"Daddy?"

He started, his eyes flashing to Becca's face. Her eyes were wide open, her mouth curving in a sleepy smile.

"Hi, honey."

"Mom and I, we talked everything out. It's okay now. At least it will be. I just—just have to get used to things being different."

Ellie started to snuffle.

Sam winced. "C'mon into the kitchen before her siren goes off," he said. "Your mom needs her sleep."

Carefully, Becca disentangled herself from Hannah's arms. Twice Hannah's eyelids fluttered, but exhaustion won out. Becca was still dressed, her clothes all crumpled, her hair a mess. She'd shrunk somehow in the hours since she'd climbed out of the college kid's Mustang. Sam warmed to see it.

He busied himself one-handed with bottle-making while Becca sat down at her usual spot at the kitchen table. Suddenly it struck Sam just how empty that place had been.

"Can I fix you something, my lady?" Sam asked. "I was thinking more on the lines of hot chocolate. This vintage of formula leaves something to be desired."

"Yeah. That'd be great." She rubbed at her eyes. Hard as she was trying not to show it, Sam could still sense a wariness in her whenever she looked at the baby.

He hated to think how strange it must've seemed to her, coming home to find Ellie. Not just in her house, but in the cradle she'd never gotten to sleep in.

Retrieving the heated bottle, he tested it on his wrist, then popped it into Ellie's mouth. He'd gotten adept enough at balancing that he managed to get out a mug and fill it with milk. He stuck it into the microwave to warm and rummaged the chocolate syrup out of the fridge.

"Becca, I'm sorry things got so messed up. I just wasn't thinking when I got down the cradle and finished it. I wasn't particularly thrilled when your mom wanted to keep Ellie."

"Kinda reacted like me, huh?"

"Oh, yeah. Worse. Then I thought about it, and, well, I figured if it would make her happy, I owed it to your mom to give this baby thing a chance. I gave her the cradle to sort of make up, you know?"

"A peace offering, huh?"

"Exactly. I can't remember her ever asking for something she really wanted just for herself. Can you?"

"That's what made it so hard. Knowing that she wanted another little girl."

"But not to replace you, Becca. I don't believe it was that. Just—she loved your growing-up years so much. I've never seen any mother who loved it more—taking you to the library, cheering at your plays, kissing your little hurts, and then, when you got older, your bigger ones. I was jealous of Ellie at first, too. Heck," he admitted. "There was a time when you first came I was jealous of you! I thought your mom couldn't love me as much, since she loved you with all her heart. But then, I realized that your mother's heart is different from mine. Most of us only have so much room, and to squeeze in another, it has to take space away from someone else. Your mom's heart isn't like that. The more people she squeezes in, the more love she has to give to every one of us."

It was the greatest miracle Sam had found in living with Hannah for so many years.

"Remember when you were a little girl, having

trouble in math?" he tried to explain. "Well, your mom's heart doesn't understand 'take aways.' "

Becca smiled, her eyes teary. "That's exactly how she is. I guess I just get scared sometimes that things will change. I didn't want it to change. Not here at home."

Sam's smile faded, echoes of hurt rippling inside him from a lifetime ago. "I remember just how that is," he said. "It's funny, isn't it? You go away to school, gulping down change as fast as you can, wanting to drink it all in, become someone wonderful and exciting and new. But you expect everyone else back home to stay frozen in time, somehow. It's only later you realize that you can't ever really come back to things the way they were. Because they've changed as much as you have in the time you've been gone."

"I know," Becca said in a small voice. "That sucks."

"Yeah. It does." He wanted to leave it at that. Didn't want to probe into places that could only hurt him. But his daughter deserved better of him. Whatever comfort he could offer her. "You remember how we talked about your grandfather, sometimes? My dad?"

"He changed a lot. Mom said so. He quit drinking too much."

"Made me mad as hell when he did. Stopped cold when I was away at school. Wouldn't touch a sip of wine at communion. See, I thought I had everything figured out. Settled. I was supposed to get to keep hating him forever. When he got married, straightened his act out, I took it as a personal insult. I kept thinking: Why couldn't he have done it for me when I was growing up? When I needed him."

"I'm sorry, Daddy. Mom said it was . . . was really bad when you were a little boy. She said that was why you had to work so hard. Because you had to sleep on garage floors and move around all the time and you never had a home before this one." Becca flushed, looked down. And Sam could imagine just how often Hannah had tried to explain why he wasn't there for birthday parties or dance recitals. Trying to soothe Becca's hurts at his neglect. Trying to let him off the hook. But, in the end, it hadn't mattered what his old man had done to him. No matter how hard he'd tried to be different, he'd done the same to his own little girl. Maybe he hadn't left her alone for the bottle, but he hadn't been there when she needed him. A child didn't care why.

The microwave buzzed and Sam balanced Ellie gingerly in one arm, careful not to splash hot milk on her as he withdrew the mug. He fumbled with the syrup, trying to squeeze the plastic bottle.

It slipped from his fingers, and tumbled to the counter with a dull, sticky thud. Becca laughed, stood up to come to his rescue. "Let me hold Ellie," she offered.

Sam didn't want to push her. "You could just make the chocolate if you want to—"

"It tastes better when you make it for me. Tastes like home."

Sam swallowed hard, touched. Hannah had made scores of treats for Becca, gingerbread and birthday cakes and fresh-picked apples dipped in melted caramel. He hadn't ever messed around in the kitchen much. The fact that she remembered the times he'd made her hot chocolate made him stop, wonder. If she remembered that, wasn't it possible she'd remember other things, too? Things he hadn't thought mattered at the time. Things that might have shown her what he'd been so scared she didn't know? That he'd loved her his whole life. Maybe not as well as Hannah did. But the only way he knew how.

"Ah, a master's touch," Sam said, his voice breaking as he gently drifted Ellie into Becca's arms.

Becca peered down into the baby's face, her brow creased, intent. "She's so tiny. I can't believe—"

"Believe what?'

"That one of my friends may have had Ellie inside her. Growing for nine whole months. That she never told anybody. She just stuck Ellie out in the yard and hoped mom would find her."

"It must seem strange." Sam squeezed out a stream of chocolate, stirred it in a rich, dark swirl in the cup.

"Mom says I should feel sorry for her—whoever Ellie's mom is. She says people make mistakes and . . . and sometimes they need to start over. But it doesn't seem right when the mistake is a little baby."

Sam's mouth set, grim. "No. It's doesn't seem right to throw away a baby."

"Hey, Mom!" Becca's exclamation made Sam look up, see Hannah framed in the door.

Hannah should have been smiling. Wasn't this what she'd wanted so badly? Becca home, happy. Taking Ellie into her heart. But it wasn't joy in Hannah's eyes, not even contentment. Sam stared at her, puzzled.

She looked sad, lost. Even when she smiled. "Welcome to the family, little one," she said, touching Ellie's cheek. She leaned over, kissing Becca on the crown of her head. "Now we can all live happily ever after."

The words were perfect, Sam mused, his nerves tightening, an ending to Hannah's fairy tale. So why did she look like she was still lost in the woods, with the wolves circling around her?

17

"MOM, IS SOMETHING WRONG?" Becca licked the last bit of hot fudge from the corner of her mouth, then peered worriedly across the speckled linoleum-covered tabletop littered with the remains of the feast they'd just finished—Café Antonio's finest, topped off with the pièce de résistance—the sundae that was his specialty.

Hannah shook herself inwardly, forcing a smile. "Of course nothing's wrong. What could be? I'm out shopping with you, aren't I? We've run up enough on the credit card to satisfy us, and not give your dad heart failure. And I got extra crunchy toffee stuff on my sundae. Life doesn't get any better than this."

Becca looked unconvinced. "Yeah, well, you've been real quiet all afternoon. Oh, you're trying to hide it, I know. But you don't even laugh at my jokes until I remind you it's supposed to be funny."

"I always love your jokes!" Hannah exclaimed, stung by the crestfallen look in her daughter's eyes.

"Sure you do. When you really hear 'em. But today

you just keep staring into space looking all worried, like your nerves are all on edge. You even broke your glass, and you *never* drop stuff."

Hannah chuckled. "It was the way that waiter kept looking at you. Like you were a living buttercrunch sundae and he'd been starving for a week. Takes a little getting used to—having my baby girl turn into a 'hottie.' "

Becca flushed with pleasure, but she wasn't so easily distracted. "You're trying to change the subject, Mom. When we dropped the baby off at Josie's you repeated the same instructions three times, like Josie hadn't ever changed a diaper in her life. She looked at you real funny. Worried. And Josie never gets all worried. Not like you do. She's like—a free spirit."

"It gets tougher to be a free spirit with a five-month-old baby keeping you up all night," Hannah tried to tease. "I'm going to owe her big time for adding Ellie to her daily craziness."

"Don't try to joke. I really need to know what's bothering you. I know I've been a real brat for the past couple of weeks and I guess I deserve it if you're still mad at me. I just thought once I said I was sorry, everything would be okay again. It wouldn't be weird between us anymore."

"Oh, Becca! Of course I'm not mad."

"Then what's wrong? You *are* acting weird. You know you are."

Guilt bit deep. Hannah grimaced. She figured she'd been doing pretty well at first, hiding the stress eating away at her. She'd managed to ignore the worries that kept clamoring inside her until Becca had darted into an elegant lingerie shop. She had touched silk and wisps of satin, spritzed cologne on her wrists and held them up for Hannah to sniff, Becca as always taking delight in everything feminine.

Hannah had been laughing and joking and teasing her in delight until the moment Becca paused at a rack of delicate nightgowns. She'd pulled out a gown of sky blue satin, its deep-cut bodice appliquéd with lace, a slit running up the side of the skirt.

Hey, we should get Dad a present! Becca teased. *He'd think you were gorgeous in this!*

Trouble was, Hannah had been tempted to buy the confection of satin and lace. She could imagine the heat in Sam's eyes when he saw her in the gown, so far from the prim, white cotton ones she'd always preferred. And she might even manage to feel pretty in something so delicate and luxurious, in spite of her scar.

With Becca getting home so late last night and the two of them talking until they fell asleep on the couch, Hannah and Sam had managed to avoid the touchy question of sleeping in the same bed. But tonight she wouldn't get off so easy. Tonight, there would be no avoiding it—changing into her nightgown, turning back the covers, sliding into bed next to Sam.

She'd be able to feel the warmth of him, smell the woodsy scent that was his alone. When her eyes got used to the dark, she'd be able to see his head upon the pillow, the dark waves of his hair rich and tousled. The suntanned planes of his face, chiseled with such hard masculinity, a stark contrast to the white down pillow, its edging of crocheted lace only serving to make Sam look even sexier.

Hannah had been on edge ever since she'd left the shop with its satin gown. Of course, Becca had sensed it. Hannah knew she couldn't pretend the strain she was feeling didn't exist. Becca wasn't a little girl anymore. Hannah couldn't fool her. Better not to try.

"It's not your fault that I'm edgy, honey. It has

absolutely nothing to do with you. I'm just a little pre-occupied."

"A *little* preoccupied?" Becca rolled her eyes. "I think you could get run over by a truck and not notice the tread marks until you looked in the mirror tomorrow morning."

"That bad, huh?"

"Oh, yeah. You always tell me I'll feel better if I talk about stuff that bothers me and after I do, well, you've always been right. That was the hardest part about being mad at you for so long. I couldn't talk to you about how much you were ticking me off. Especially since my strategy was to give you the silent treatment." She made a funny face. "Remind me not to try that one again."

Hannah chuckled for real this time. "It's a deal."

"Anyway, what I'm trying to say is that you've always listened to me when I was having problems. I want to do the same thing for you if I can." Her eyes glowed, so earnest it tugged at Hannah's heart. "I know I've been acting like a baby, Mom. But I'm not one. Really."

"I know that, sweetheart. You're an amazing young woman and I'm so grateful you're in my life. No stupid little fight could ever change that. Not even the dreaded silent treatment."

"Then tell me, Mom. What's wrong? When I'd call from school, I just figured you were mad at me because of the stuff with the baby. But that's not the only thing that's bugging you, is it? Daddy isn't acting like himself, either. He's spending lots more time at home, doing stuff around the house he never did before. He's trying to pretend everything's just great, but he looks at you, all sad, when he thinks no one's watching."

Hannah looked away, swallowed hard. She'd seen it, too, the expression Becca was describing. The raw places in Sam's heart showed through more every day.

"Daddy said the reason he gave you my cradle was because you guys were fighting. He wanted to show you he was sorry."

Sorry for what? Hannah thought sadly. He hadn't done anything wrong. Even when they'd disagreed about Ellie, he tried to be reasonable. Rational like any other person would have been. He'd wanted time to consider carefully whether or not they should take Ellie in, because with Sam, once he *did* bring her into his home, into his heart, there could be no changing his mind. He'd never do to another child what his mother had done to him.

Besides, troubling as the discord between them over Ellie had been, the problems between Hannah and Sam had started long before she'd found the baby in the basket. And before Tony Blake had returned to Willowton with, what the high school cheerleaders had called his "bedroom eyes."

Hannah sucked in a steadying breath, searching for the right words to say. She could hardly tell Becca the truth about what was on her mind. About the man from Hannah's past who had come back to town, troubling her thoughts more than she'd ever have believed possible. Or that tonight would be the first time in months she and Sam would share the same bed.

She couldn't tell Becca how scared she was. That the instant she and Sam slipped under the colorful wedding ring quilt, she would be trapped. The night could only end in one of two ways. Hannah could brace herself, hang onto what she knew was right and keep her distance from Sam, even though it would hurt him more deeply. Knowing that she couldn't even explain her behavior to him—tell him she was trying to be fair to him, not make love when there were so many dan-gers threatening, so much of a chance that things between them would fall apart, could never be put back together again.

Or she could make love to him. Make him believe that everything was healed between them, resolved forever. It would have been perfect, a dream come true, except that she didn't deserve Sam's trust. She hadn't been honest. And that love, without trust, wasn't love at all.

So tell him the truth, her conscience prodded.

But how could she? She couldn't tell him the truth. He'd never forgive her. And yet, how could she keep living with herself if she held onto Sam's love with a lie?

She struggled for a way to ease Becca's worry while still protecting her from the insidious shadows clouding the marriage. *Poor, poor little girl,* Hannah thought. People pretended divorce was easier for kids once they reached a certain age. Hannah had never believed it. Whether you were twelve or twenty, it still shattered your world, pitted people you loved against each other, showed you that nothing was forever, not to trust in that for yourself. Hannah would do everything she could to spare her daughter that loss.

"It's true that Daddy and I have been having a rough time of it lately. But every marriage has bumps, sweetheart. You just work them out."

"What's making it rough? Is it having Ellie around?"

"Things were strained even before Ellie arrived. I guess the two of us hadn't been paying enough attention to each other, to us as a couple. We'd used the fact that we were busy as an excuse. But any way you look at it, it was a terrible mistake."

"Was it because you were paying too much attention to me?" Becca asked softly.

"This isn't your fault, Becca. Understand that, plain and simple. Sure, it was important to spend time with you, focus on you the past couple of years especially. Dad and I both knew we were on borrowed time. That you'd be spreading your wings, flying off to college and into your own life. There was nothing more precious to either one of us than the time we spent with you. And now that you've left home it's only natural that our relationship needs some adjusting, getting used to each other again. Everybody has to renegotiate things at this time of their life. Daddy was looking forward to doing things we couldn't do when you were home. Traveling more, spending time together. Then I dragged Ellie into the mix."

"Daddy adores her. You should see the way he looks at her. All gooey. It's really cute. And I even caught him talking baby talk to her."

Hannah tried not to let the wistfulness she felt show in her smile. Sam *was* "gooey" with Ellie. So fiercely protective of her now. The day he'd come home to find Tony holding the baby he'd all but snatched Ellie out of the man's hands. She'd overheard Sam talking to the baby herself, and his words had wounded her, humbled her.

I've got you now, Ellie. Doesn't matter if your mom left you behind. That's her loss. You're my little girl now and I'll never let you go.

Hannah rubbed her temple with her fingertips. "I couldn't ask more of your dad," she said. "He's trying so hard. And it's not easy for him to open himself up to loving someone so much. He's been hurt so badly before."

"When he was a little boy," Becca said. "I know. His mom dumped him, too, but he wasn't lucky enough to be a baby and not remember it like Ellie. Maybe she won't ever even have to know about what happened with her mom. But Dad remembers it all, doesn't he? His mom taking his little sister and not even bothering to tell him good-bye."

Hannah nodded. She'd told Becca the story when she was old enough to understand, old enough to be hurt and confused sometimes when Sam grew withdrawn. Hannah's heart swelled with pride at the depth of empathy in her daughter's face.

"I can't imagine how that would feel," Becca said. "Your mom is supposed to love you no matter what. She's supposed to fight grizzly bears and walk through fire to get to her kid. A mother's supposed to be like you, Mom."

A knife twisted in Hannah's middle. *Fraud! Liar! Cheat!* a voice shrilled inside her. She'd walked away from her child and she'd never even had the guts to face up to what she'd done, let people know the truth. See her for who she really was. No, everyone believed she was perfect. The perfect wife, the perfect mother. And she'd let them believe it. Tried to believe it herself.

"Becca, nobody is perfect. Our hearts play tricks on us. Make us believe what we want to believe about people we love, people who love us. I'm not half the person you and your dad think I am."

Becca rolled her eyes. "Yeah, right. You're disgustingly modest on top of being perfect. Daddy worships you, and you know that I do, too. We're so lucky to have you, Mom, and we're both going to try harder to show you that we know it. Dad and I were talking before he left for work, and we thought that while I'm on break the three of us could paint the spare room for Ellie. Fix it all up for her. I've already called Pete and told him I won't be riding back up to school with him. He was a crummy driver, anyway. It's a miracle he didn't get a speeding ticket. And when he went around the barriers to try to beat that train—"

"He did *what?*" Hannah's heart stopped.

"Oh, it turned out fine. Plenty of time. But it was still a stupid thing to do." Becca waved her hand. "Anyway, what matters is that you and Dad and Ellie can take me back up to school, and I'll show you everything on campus. My room and the college union, our little coffee shop and the library. I'll even make sure you get to meet some of my friends if you'll just . . . just really smile instead of trying to fake it."

Hannah's throat prickled with emotion. She reached across the table, held Becca's hand. "I promise I'll do better," Hannah promised. "I don't want to waste a minute of your break."

"My psych professor says that worrying is completely useless. You spend tons of time in your mind, living through things that may never happen."

"He's right." Most things Hannah had worried about had never happened. But this time—this time felt different. What was it Tony had said? That secrets came out when they hit critical mass? It didn't get much more "critical" than this.

"Listen, Mom, I have the greatest idea!" Becca exclaimed. "Yes, it's true. I *am* a genius!"

"Okay, genius. Let's hear it. I'm waiting to be amazed."

"You admit you and Dad have been having trouble, right? He wanted to do more stuff with you alone?"

"Yes," Hannah admitted warily.

"How about if you and Dad go on a date tonight? I'll watch Ellie, make all the reservations. You won't have to do a thing except look gorgeous and have fun."

"No way, Becca! It's a sweet idea, but you just got home. I want to spend time with you."

"We will. Bunches of it. But you know, I *do* have to spend *some* time with my friends. I'll have 'em all over to our house so they can meet Ellie. I had to put up with their siblings often enough. And Ellie's still little enough to be cute."

"That's really thoughtful, Becca," Hannah said, "but I don't know."

"Why not? Don't you trust me with the kid? I promise I won't drop her. And if we watch a scary movie, I'll cover her eyes at the gross parts."

It was hard not to get caught up in Becca's enthusiasm. "I guess I just—well, have you considered how odd it might feel? If one of those girls is—"

"Ellie's mom." Obviously it hadn't occurred to her. She nibbled at her bottom lip, contemplating what Hannah had said. "Well, if one of them is Ellie's mom, she's Ellie's mom. Having the girls over to the house now or waiting until later won't change that, will it?"

"I guess not."

"Besides, everybody at Annie's last night was stunned about the baby. Nobody was acting sad or weird or anything. They were all just the same as they've always been. I'm pretty sure none of them had anything to do with Ellie. Please, Mom. Let me do this for you and Dad. I want to!" Suddenly Becca's expression changed. She frowned, perplexed. "Hey, Mom," she said sotto voce. "That guy over there at the candy counter keeps staring at you. And whoa, is he a babe!"

Blood rushed to Hannah's face. She angled a glance over her shoulder, but she already knew who Becca was talking about.

Tony Blake ambled toward them, a white paper bag of homemade chocolate in his hand. "Well, hello, ladies," he drawled. "What a nice surprise to see you here! Enjoying your break, Rebekah?"

Becca's brow furrowed. "Have I met you before? I'm sorry. I know almost everybody in Willowton, and I don't remember you."

Tony laughed warmly. "I've never met you in the flesh, but I feel like I've known you forever. Your mom can't say enough about you. But from the sound of things, she's got plenty of reason to brag." Tony turned the full force of his electric grin on Becca. "Your mom and I were in high school together, back in the dark ages."

"Oh. That's nice."

"We were just friends," Hannah said more sharply than she intended. "A long time ago. Tony was only in Willowton for a year."

"It was long enough for my mom to fall in love with the place. I think she always kinda hoped after I got out of the air force I'd come back here and marry your mom. Turned out your dad was a whole lot smarter than I was. He grabbed her first. Guess he knew what he was doing. He got to have a daughter like you." Tony let his gaze trail over Becca. He grinned. "Just look at you. You're as pretty as your mama was at your age."

Becca squirmed a little, just as charmed as most women were when Tony waylaid them with his smile. "Thanks."

"My name is Tony. Tony Blake. Did your mom mention me?"

"No-o-o." Becca said.

"Why would I?" Hannah asked.

"Oh." He looked a little disappointed. "Well, I'm the guy the court put in charge of keeping tabs on Ellie. You know, making sure everything's going right, that she's getting the best care."

"We're painting her room this week," Becca offered

eagerly. "My dad made a really cool cradle for her and everybody in town will tell you my mom and dad are the greatest parents in the world."

"I believe it. Just took one look at the fine daughter they've already raised."

Becca grinned.

"It's great to see how close you are to your mom. I didn't mean to spy, but I couldn't help noticing it when I came in to get my daily supply of chocolate. I work a lot with kids who aren't as lucky as you are. It always does me good to see a kid who is happy. Loved. It's the hardest job in the world—being a good parent. You end up owing your folks a lot." Tony sighed. "You know, I came back to Willowton because my mom fell and hurt herself. It's pretty miserable when you get older. Not much company and hurting all the time. Your mom stopped by a while back. Made my mother's day. Maybe you could help me twist her arm a little to stop by again once you head back to school?"

"Sure." Becca had been raised with her great grandmother's teachings just as Hannah had. When people were sick and lonely, you did what you could—brought treats and flowers, a pot of soup and a bit of laughter to make them feel better.

"I work from seven in the morning until way past dark most nights, by the time I prepare the next day's cases," Tony said, and Hannah knew he was trying to ease any fears she might have of running into him. "If your mom would stop by, it would sure break up my mom's day."

"Mom's always doing stuff like that, aren't you, Mom?"

"Sometime next week then," Hannah succumbed to the inevitable. Tony *had* said he'd be at work. There was nothing objectionable about it at all. Then why did she feel so uneasy? Was it the fact that she now knew Mrs. Blake had wanted her for a daughter-in-law? Was it the fact that Tony had admitted his mother might have been right in choosing Hannah for his wife? Or was it the fact that—even for a moment—Hannah herself had wondered what a marriage between them might have been like?

He smiled. "Well, I'd better go. Off to fight for justice and the American way."

Before Becca could move, he scooped up her hand with all the polish of a foreign diplomat and brushed a kiss across it. "A pleasure to meet you!" He turned to Hannah with a flourish. She meant to bury her hands behind her back, but the arm of the heavy wooden booth got in the way. With a laugh, Tony captured her hand and pressed his lips to it, sending a jolt of guilt and irritation through Hannah. She tried to hide it, not wanting Becca to see. The last thing she needed was to stir up the girl's keenly honed teenage sense of suspicion.

"Have a wonderful break, you two," he said before turning and striding from the shop. Hannah couldn't see him leave, but Becca obviously watched the whole time. When the old-fashioned bell above the door tinkled, Hannah stifled a sigh of relief.

"Wow," Becca said, curiosity obviously piqued. "I thought I knew everybody you went to high school with. You never told me about *him.*"

Hannah shrugged. "He wasn't around that long. Guess I forgot."

"About a guy that looked like that? Maybe Grandma should've taken you to get your eyes checked! Hey, let's dig out your old yearbooks! See if we can find his picture!"

Hannah's heart thudded against her ribs, alarm zinging through her. Dig out the yearbook? What a disaster that would be! There were pictures of the two of them together—something about the biggest surprise of the year—that the shiest girl in the junior class hooked the cutest transfer student ever to come to Willowton High. Knowing Becca, the girl would be so amused by the whole thing she would run straight to Sam with the story, thinking it would be great fun for the two of them to tease her about it. Hannah knew one thing for certain. Sam sure as heck wouldn't be laughing.

Where were the blasted yearbooks, anyway? Hannah thought desperately. Surely she'd had the sense to bury them somewhere deep in the junk in the basement. With luck they were being guarded by really fat spiders.

"It's all ancient history," Hannah brushed Becca off. "I want to concentrate on *now*. You and Daddy and Ellie. That's what matters."

"Then will you go out on that date? C'mon, Mom! Do it!"

"Okay," she agreed. "We'll head home. You can drop me off and then run out to the store, pick up whatever snacks you want for tonight."

"Why don't we just stop on the way?"

"No way," Hannah hedged. "If I'm going to go on a date, I plan to look gorgeous. I've got a hot bubble bath waiting for me and I want to steam my red dress."

"You go girl!" Becca laughed, so pleased with herself her eyes sparkled.

Go girl? Hannah thought. Oh, she'd be *going* all right. She'd be going like a maniac in the time Becca was at the store. But her red dress would have nothing to do with it.

She'd be rooting around in the basement so she could find her old yearbooks, hide them someplace Becca would never lay her hands on them.

Hide them? It would be better just to throw the things away. Sentimental junk measured against imminent calamity was no contest. It wasn't worth the risk to keep the stupid book around. She couldn't imagine why she'd kept the thing in the first place. All she'd ever wanted to do was to forget that disastrous year had ever happened.

She couldn't afford to have the past rear its ugly head now—any more than it already had, she amended. She'd seen that wicked glint in her little girl's eyes before, knew how determined Becca could be once she got her mind set on something. Hannah grimaced. She'd bury the book in the garbage can, under the grossest garbage she could find. Then she'd count the hours till trash day and wait for Becca to forget all about it.

It *could* happen. It was possible that Becca would let the notion die in peace.

If only because she had to go back to school on Sunday!

"So what do you feel like tonight? You know, so I can make reservations." Becca asked. "Chinese food? Italian?"

A stiff drink of Scotch, Hannah retorted in her head. Too bad she hadn't had a drink since the wine she and Tony had shared in the stable, just before she made the biggest mistake of her life.

18

A SOFT BREEZE DRIFTED over the top of the hill from the river, rippling the waves and dropping the temperature a few notches. It would have been a perfect night, except for the fact that even though Ellie had cooperated and napped like an angel the whole time, the only thing Hannah had come up with in the basement that afternoon was a broken nail and itchy eyes from the clouds of dust she'd stirred up.

Hannah's one consolation as she dashed up the stairs and jumped into the tepid bubble bath she'd drawn to assuage Becca's suspicions before she'd gone to search downstairs was that Becca was going to have the baby to watch and a houseful of kids to distract her tonight. Even if she wanted to, she'd have to abandon the search for the yearbook for now.

No, it made no sense to let worrying about that ruin tonight. She had plenty of other things to make her crazy. The image of Sam's delight when he'd heard about the plans Becca had made for them. The heart-wrenching care he'd taken in getting himself ready—

his tousled, windblown waves of hair wrestled into some semblance of submission, his broad shoulders encased in the shirt Hannah loved best. He'd even rooted his sport coat from the back of the closet and tortured himself with a necktie.

He'd been so attentive, so tender, it broke Hannah's heart, reminded her of a million reasons she had fallen in love with him, dared to trust him in spite of how badly she'd been burned.

She drew the folds of her shawl around her shoulders, the jewel-toned pattern warming more than just her body. Every time she'd worn the lush square of cashmere Sam had given her for Christmas two years ago, she'd felt as if she were wearing a hug. She could hide in the flowing garment when she needed to, and yet still feel pretty. And she needed to hide tonight— hide the raw places in her heart, the vulnerable part of her that needed him more than she could ever tell him.

Sam curved his hand under her elbow to steady her as they made their way down the landing that provided access for restaurant patrons to come by water rather than road. Benches at the end of the long T-shaped dock offered a place to sit, to sip cocktails or coffee or maybe steal a kiss after a romantic dinner for two. Like the one they'd finished ten minutes ago.

"How long has it been since the two of us went out on a date?" Sam asked, turning his face into the wind.

"Too long." Obviously, Hannah thought, since Sam had stared at her as if she'd suggested a ménage à trois when he'd gotten home earlier that evening instead of a simple dinner out.

Music wafted from open windows where Hannah could still see couples dancing. Twice, Sam had asked if she wanted a turn on the floor. The second time she'd asked to go for a walk instead. It was already hard enough—not touching him. And to melt into his arms, even just for the length of a song, would only make it harder for both of them tonight when they got home.

"It's already done you good, you know, having Becca home," Sam said. "I'm so damned glad you two got things straightened out." Just the tiniest hint of wistfulness shone in his smile and Hannah knew he was thinking of the unexpected closeness he and Becca had shared during their estrangement. A part of him couldn't help but mourn the loss.

"I'm glad things are better, too. I just wish—" Hannah stopped, looked away. Lights from the Illinois side of the Mississippi twinkled against the dark purple curtain of night, their reflection trapped under the rippling layer of water—like stars some wayward angel had hidden at the bottom of the sea.

"Wish what?" Sam urged.

She almost made something up, something that wouldn't be too bright, too hot, too painful. Something that wouldn't break the mood of the night. But whether she told him the truth now or not, they'd still have to face the disrepair their relationship had fallen into. It would be staring them both right in the face the moment they walked into their bedroom and shut the door behind them only to find they were both still alone.

"I wish that I could make things right between you and me."

"I know. I do, too. But things are getting better, aren't they, Hannah? I mean, we've still got plenty to settle between us. I know that. But it seems like—like we're both trying. That we both *want* this to work." His voice fell, his gaze shifting to the far horizon. His mouth curving, sensitive, sad. "I have to admit, for a while there, I wasn't so sure."

Alarm jolted Hannah. Had Sam sensed her fleeting

interest in Tony? Or was Sam's admission making real her greatest fear. "You weren't so sure that you still wanted to be with me?"

Sam laughed out loud, shook his head in astonishment. "Are you crazy? Of course not. I can't imagine my life without you. Never could. Not from the first moment I realized I could actually trust you. Believe you when you said you loved me. Do you remember that night, Hannah?"

She could close her eyes and make the scene appear like magic. See the moonlight running its fingers through his hair, smell the after shave he'd used back then, see his eyes, fierce with tenderness and dread and delight so deep she could tell he could hardly believe it was real. *I feel like I can tell you anything,* he'd admitted, his face so young and handsome, his eyes so old. *That has to be what love is, isn't it? To be able to tell the truth and not be afraid . . .*

Oh, yes, Hannah thought miserably. She remembered the night—her one golden opportunity to tell him about the anguished months she'd spent in Oregon, her grief, her regrets, the guilt that clung to her with cold, gray hands.

She'd almost confessed everything. But she'd been too afraid. Afraid of losing him. Afraid of hurting him, of shattering the awe that lit his face whenever he looked at her. Didn't he deserve to be happy? She'd conned herself. Telling him what she'd done could only hurt him. Break the tenuous thread that had cut through years of cynicism, years of not trusting himself, his instincts because he had kissed his mother good-bye, grinned at her and dashed off to school without realizing she had bus tickets in her purse, suitcases packed and hidden away. And that the moment he rounded the corner she'd scooped up his little sister's hand and raced away from the small yellow house on Redding Street and never looked back.

Hannah had convinced herself it would be cruel to ruin the peace he'd found in her arms—ruin it for what? Something that had happened long before she'd met him. A sin she'd tried to go back and make right, only to find it was too late.

The decision to keep silent had made perfect sense then. Because she was so young she hadn't stopped for an instant to consider what it would be like if Sam found out years later.

Like now.

"Hannah? Do you remember the night I told you I loved you?" Sam asked again.

"I remember," she said raggedly, wishing she could turn back the time to that long ago night, tell him everything, and wipe this cloud of lies and secrets and fear from between them.

Maybe he wouldn't have hated you, a voice mocked her. *Maybe he would have forgiven you. And then, all these years would have been real—no secrets, no deception. He would have loved you for who you really were—not who you pretended to be.*

"The way I felt about you, then—well, I thought I'd finally figured it out—knew everything there was to know about love. But I was wrong. In these past twenty-four years since we first met I've watched you, you taught me so much. Made me want to try harder. Give more. Love better. A minute ago you sounded as if you actually thought I might leave you." He shook his head, dumbfounded. "Hannah, nothing in the world could make me stop loving you. Don't you know that?"

Tears seared her eyes. She looked out over the water to hide them. "You just—you don't know—"

"Then *tell* me. What am I doing wrong, Hannah?

How can I love you better? The way you need me to? What have I done that made you . . . not want me to touch you?"

"Oh, Sam!" she choked out his name, hating the anguish in his voice, the confusion.

"I can fix it, Hannah. Whatever's wrong. I can be whatever kind of lover you need me to be. Or have I ruined things too much already? God, I never thought my wife—never thought you would shrink back whenever I tried to make love to you."

She'd pushed him away for months, kept emotions bottled up inside her. Hadn't wanted to hurt him, hadn't wanted to face things herself. Maybe she couldn't tell him everything. But wasn't it time he at least had part of the truth?

"It's not you. It's me," she admitted. "My scar . . . so ugly and . . . I don't feel like I—"

"Like you what?"

"I was sick for such a long time, even before the surgery. Was hopeful, scared. Scared that if I really were pregnant, like I hoped, you wouldn't share my happiness. It was easier to close you out. And then, once I knew the truth, part of me blamed you. Thought you'd be relieved."

"Oh, Hannah."

"I never gave you a chance to react yourself. I had the whole scenario played out in my mind for you. It wasn't fair. I know it wasn't fair. Then, once I had the surgery—it made me feel as if—"

"As if what, love?"

"I feel like when the doctor cut me open, he ripped out everything that made me a woman. I'm damaged goods. Why should you even want me anymore?"

"My God, Hannah! Do you really believe that?"

"Every time we'd make love I'd think 'maybe this

time.' Maybe this time there'll be a miracle and a baby will start to grow inside me. Maybe this time— But that won't happen now. It can't ever happen now. I feel like I've failed you."

"But we have Becca. And Ellie. And each other. How could you possibly have failed me? You were the one who wanted a big family. I was amazed enough that I had you."

"I'm not that great of a prize, Sam."

"Let me be the judge of that." He drew her toward him, cupped her face in his hands. "You're everything a woman should be, Hannah. More than I'd ever dreamed of. I love you. Nothing could ever change that. Not a scar. Not surgery. Not a cradle the two of us couldn't fill on our own. I feel so blessed to have Becca and Ellie in my life. And I'll spend forever trying to show them how much I love them. But I would have been happy even without them. As long as I had you."

He meant it, Hannah thought in wonder. He meant that she was enough. Babies were wonderful—a gift, a joy. But she was the most precious of all. And all these years, while he'd loved her this way, how had he felt, knowing that she wanted *more* than they had together? More than he could give her? Hannah turned her cheek against his palm, kissed him there and tasted the salt of her own tears. "I'm sorry, Sam. So sorry I've hurt you."

"We'll figure this out, Hannah. You taught me how to be patient, wait for flowers to open. I can wait for your heart to open again, too. I want you to know this. That I love you, want to take you to bed, show you just how much—make you cry out my name when I take you over the edge. I want to kiss every inch of your skin. Taste your lips, your throat, your breast. But I can wait, Hannah. Until you want me. Even if it takes forever." The corner of his mouth tipped up, so tender, so teasing. "'Course, I'm hoping like hell it doesn't take quite that long."

She laughed, leaned against him, burying her face against his chest. "I'm scared, Sam," she whispered. "I'm scared."

"I am, too. I don't want to lose you, Hannah. I've been so damned scared for so long now. Scared I might say the wrong thing, do the wrong thing. Screw things up worse than they already are. So I've just kept quiet, gone through the motions, only doing and saying what I knew was safe. But I can't keep doing that forever. Neither can you."

Something in his eyes sparked, a flash of humor that hadn't been there before.

"What's so funny?"

"A memory just popped into my head. Remember when Becca was six and we took her to Dan Smith's farm to see the baby chicks hatch? When we weren't looking she climbed way up into the rafters after a kitten."

"How could I ever forget! Becca scared ten years off my life that day! But what does it have to do with us? Now?"

"I was just remembering her up in those rafters, so little, so damned scared. We couldn't get her to move backward, toward the hayloft, or forward to the ladder Dan put up.

"Finally we took a wagon filled with loose hay and put it underneath her. Told her to close her eyes and—"

"Jump," Hannah finished, remembering a blur of denim overalls and bright pink tee shirt, braids flying and the crunch of the hay as Becca landed in its softness. Then laughter as Becca emerged from the wagon, asking if she could do it again, please.

"Maybe that's what we need to keep in mind, Hannah. Sometimes you have to choose, no matter how scared you are. You have to close your eyes and jump."

The words raced through Hannah's head. Sam was right. She couldn't just stay up in the air, clinging to the rafters, not daring to move up or down, backward or forward. Not daring to move into the future because she was so torn up inside over the past. No, she couldn't hold on, frozen forever. She had to make a choice.

She looked up into Sam's face, so strong, so tender, so vulnerable. Love naked in his eyes. He'd risked everything, saying what he'd said tonight. Risked her rejecting him again, shoving him away. Abandoning him in her heart, even though they still lived in the same house and tonight would sleep in the same bed. Courage, he'd shown—and compassion. And a sensitivity so precious and rare. Her heart seemed to swell in her chest, fighting against the constrictions that had held it captive for so long—guilt and fear and wishing for the moon instead of seeing the beauty held right in the palm of her hand.

Close your eyes and jump. . . . Sam's words taunted her, dared her.

She let go of terror, in spite of knowing she might fall.

For the first time in months, she threaded her fingers through Sam's hair, drew his lips down to hers. Sensation sparked through her—silky strands, the heat of his passion-flushed cheek, the subtle roughness where he'd scraped away his whiskers so carefully before they'd left. And his lips—warm and moist and seeking. His breath hot, ragged, his arms eager as they wrapped around her, pulling her body-long into his embrace.

He groaned as his mouth melted into hers, hungry, so hungry, the hard planes and angles of his body melding to hers. A thrill rippled down her spine as she felt a nudge against her belly, the hardening bulge of his need for her.

"I love you, Hannah," he moaned, kissing a path to her ear. "I love you."

Hannah held on tight—and jumped.

It took forever to get home—the drive seeming to drag on endlessly, the need reawakened in Hannah's body raging after being ignored for so long. This was crazy, she thought, holding Sam's hand as he drove, curling her body as close to his side as she could. She had to be touching him, had to feel the heat of his body, the rough callused tips of his fingers. She had to breathe in the scent of him, and drown in the desire seething in his blue eyes.

If they broke contact for a moment, she was terrified the spell would be broken, and they'd be swept apart again, the confessions they'd made, the resolve in her heart, the courage he'd helped to give her vanishing, leaving them both lost again, alone.

She couldn't bear that. Couldn't bear how cold the world would be again without him.

"Oh, no, Sam," Hannah groaned. "I just thought of something. Becca has a whole flock of kids waiting for us back at the house."

"We'll make sure they turn up the television and we'll be real quiet." Sam arched his brow wickedly. "Although, *quiet* isn't exactly what I had in mind." He glanced over at her, sobered. "Maybe we should wait. Or we could stop at a nice hotel."

"No," Hannah said so quickly, Sam flinched. She could sense the dread in him, the sudden wariness. He was terrified she was going to change her mind. Maybe feared that she already had and was trying to make up excuses.

"Hannah, if you decide this . . . this isn't the night . . ." He left the sentence hanging, but she knew what he meant. He wouldn't push it. Would let her draw the boundaries where she needed to. Even though every atom in his body must need to claim her, charge through the barriers between them, before he lost his chance. His generosity astonished her.

"No, Sam," she reassured him. "I want you tonight. Need you tonight. But not in some strange, cold bed in a sterile hotel room, no matter how expensive and lovely. I want you in our bed, the bed where we made Becca, under the wedding ring quilt with the moonlight filtering from the window. I want to reach for you, on your side of the bed and not find it empty. I've been lonely in there so long. I won't believe that the pain is over until I'm not alone there anymore."

Sam angled a quick glance at her as he kept guiding the car down the road. His heart shone in his eyes. "We'll make it happen somehow, then. In our room. In our bed. And I swear to you, Hannah, you'll never be lonely in there again."

He turned down the lane, streetlights throwing golden pools across the road. Hannah frowned, confused. When they'd left earlier that evening there had been half a dozen cars in various stages of dilapidation squeezed into the limited space for parking on their street, college decals displayed proudly in their back windows. But now, the lane was empty, only one light burning in the house—and that in the kitchen.

Concerned, Hannah murmured. "What in the world? Where did everybody go? You don't think there was some kind of accident."

"No way. I'm sure everything's fine," Sam soothed, but she noticed that as soon as he'd parked the car, he was in a big hurry to get to the house himself.

He unlocked the door, went in first—an oddity, since he'd always had an old-fashioned streak of chivalry in him, always opening doors and letting her enter places before he did. "Becca?" he called out. Silence. "Becca?" he yelled more stridently.

Hannah started toward the living room, then stopped when she glimpsed a scrawl of green marker on the message board mounted to the kitchen wall.

Mom,
    Don't panic, nobody died. The girls and I decided to go over to Annie's and spend the night. We're taking Ellie with us. Yes, I took the car seat out of your car. Don't obsess. I've packed everything she needs and I promise I'll keep the formula in the fridge until I heat it up for her. Figured I'd start out this "big sister" gig right—take her on her first girls' night out. Hope you and Daddy had a great time on your date. By the way, I left a surprise for you upstairs.

                                        Love you!
                                            me

Hannah stared at the message in astonishment. "Sam?" she called to him. "Read this. It's from Becca."

Sam stalked over with a worried frown. He scanned the message. "She's gone?" he said in disbelief. "I don't understand."

"I think I do." Hannah pressed her hand to her heart, touched by Becca's thoughtfulness. "She knows things haven't been perfect between us. She planned the date, made the reservations. I think she was hoping to give us a little time alone. She's not a little girl anymore. I think she is hoping we'll . . . fix things. And she's done her best to give us a little shove in the right direction."

"It was a sweet idea," Sam said. "But maybe we should call her, have her bring Ellie home. I know how you are about babies. You were a nervous wreck any time Becca was out of your sight."

It was true. She'd hidden the full extent of it from Sam—panic attacks when she couldn't breathe, nightmares that held her hostage in her sleep, terror that God would realize he'd made a mistake in giving her Becca. That he'd punish her, snatch Becca away from her because she'd given up her first little daughter.

She could still remember how bewildered Sam had been at her fierce reaction. Confused, maybe a little hurt, feeling left out of the magic circle she and the baby now shared. But he'd been proud, too. Admired Hannah for her devotion to the little girl their love had made. A mysterious bond he'd never experienced with his own mother. A twinge of guilt bit into Hannah's joy. Yes, he'd been awed by the bond, marveled at it. But then, he'd never known the darker reasons that lay behind it.

"Really, Hannah. I don't mind," he said. "We can run over and pick up the baby—"

Hannah fought back the bubble of panic at the back of her throat. Fear that just by thinking about the past, how little she deserved Ellie and this fresh chance, that somehow she'd arouse avenging angels that might sweep the little one away.

You can't be terrified forever, she told herself sharply. *Don't make the same mistakes this time, let your fear take control. Becca will take care of her. You take care of Sam.*

Didn't he deserve her full attention? The chance to make this night unforgettable?

"Go get Ellie?" she mocked horror. "How crazy do you think I am? You couldn't pay me to break up Ellie's first 'girls' night out'! She'd never forgive me. And neither would Becca."

Sam gazed down at her uncertainly. But amidst the

confusion, Hannah caught a glowing ember of hope. "You mean it?"

"This is *our* night, Sam. Becca was thoughtful enough and wise enough to offer it to us. The least we can do is accept the gift, make it as wonderful as we can."

Sam's eyes glistened for a moment. He blinked hard, but Hannah knew he'd been close to tears. "I feel so . . . so strange," he admitted. "Not sure what to do. I want tonight to be perfect, and yet, I feel like a raw kid again, needing you so much, so scared, shy and awkward."

"You were never shy and awkward. *I* was the one whose hands wouldn't stop shaking. Who came close to chickening out."

"No wonder. I wanted to swallow you whole. I know you could see it in my eyes. And how could you know what to expect since you'd never been with anyone else before?"

Hannah winced inwardly. Her heart tore. She'd let him believe that. She could hardly tell him the real reason she was so skittish—she'd told herself she'd never take such a risk again. Never sleep with any man again, ever. She knew what could happen during one brief night of sex—your whole life could spin off its axis. You could get up from the bed or the blanket or the hay and find everything you'd planned for yourself shattered. Everything you'd believed about yourself destroyed. And the most frightening discovery of them all—that, no matter how desperately you wanted it, no matter how hard you tried, you could never, ever go back to the person you were before.

She'd been terrified, yes. Stunned at either her daring or her stupidity. She wasn't sure which. But after their lovemaking was over, and she lay, cuddled close to Sam's body, her cheek resting on his chest, listening to the beat of his heart—she'd been glad, so glad she'd taken that chance one more time.

He grasped her hand, tight, drew her up the stairs to their bedroom and flicked on the light. Hannah gasped. Spread across the bed lay a river of blue satin, the lace on the nightgown's bodice lustrous in the glow of the overhead lamp.

Sam gave a low whistle of appreciation. "Whoa! Where did that come from?" he said. "I don't remember that being there when we left. And believe me, if it had been, I would've noticed."

"Becca." Hannah's throat constricted. Her eyes burned. She opened a small envelope that lay on the gown.

It bore one word, written in Becca's handwriting.
Surprise!

Surprise? Hannah thought, wonderingly. This whole night had been one surprise after another. She gloried in each one. Felt the last bits of hurt, resentment, that lingered after her estrangement with Becca melt away in the light of her thoughtfulness. Felt hope for her and for Sam, hope she hadn't dared allow herself to feel for so long.

Sam scooped up a fold of the blue satin with one tanned, strong hand. He ran the fabric through his fingers.

"Put in on, Hannah," Sam growled, low in his throat. "I want to see you in this tonight. Call me when . . . when you're ready."

He left the room. Hannah could hardly unfasten her buttons, her fingers were trembling so hard. She tossed her clothes on a chair as she shed them, not bothering to fold even the shawl she loved so much. She took up the gown, slid it over her head. Slipping one hand under the weight of her hair at the nape of her neck, she freed the mane of dark locks and let it ripple down her back, free.

She stepped for a moment in front of the full-length mirror, astonished at the reflection peering back at her. The woman wasn't a stranger. No, Hannah had seen her looking back at her before. Huge, eager eyes, lips bee-stung and soft, rosy color staining her cheekbones. The blue satin skimmed along her body like a blanket of raindrops, clinging to the soft swells of her breasts, nipping in at her waist, rippling down over full hips before cascading in a wave of delicate blue to skim her pale, bare feet.

The lustrous blue set her skin aglow, creamy pale, so smooth, as if it belonged to the young girl she'd once been. Was it the gown that had gently peeled back layers of time? Driven the dark shadows from beneath her eyes? Smoothed the fine wrinkles in her face? Or did the magical transformation have a far simpler explanation? That in mere moments, Sam would come to her, pull her into his arms, into his bed.

She'd felt so brittle without him, so parched and withered inside. In a few short hours, now, she felt as if she'd run through the rain, drunk it up until it filled her, softened her, coaxed her to open the way a hard, dry bud swelled in a rain-kissed garden.

She licked her lips to moisten them, combed her fingers through her hair. Drawing in a quick breath, she crossed to the bed, drew back the quilt to reveal sweet-scented sheets beneath.

"Sam?" she called his name, softly, timidly, her heart pounding erratically beneath the layer of lace.

She heard the tread of his footsteps in the hall. He'd shed his own clothes in the bathroom, taking his robe from the hook behind the closet door. Hannah had given it to him two years ago—an unrelenting blend of masculinity and elegance and comfort. Bronze, gold and rich, chocolate brown stripes ran in thin rows from his broad shoulders to where the robe ended just below his knees. A rich piping edged the cuffs and collar. The tie belt was knotted loosely at his waist, the garment above it gapping open in a wide vee to expose Sam's chest, broad, and thickly muscled, tanned and lightly dusted with dark whorls of hair.

His throat rose in a muscular column, his hair framing a face so beautiful in its strength, in its sensitivity, Hannah could hardly breathe.

Nervous, she smoothed palms suddenly damp across the satin at her hips. Her gaze darted away from him, fastened on the tips of her toes for just a moment as a wisp of shyness struck.

Are you doing the right thing? A voice whispered inside her. The jab of doubt jarred her so much, she dashed it away, tossed back her hair, her chin tipping up. She wasn't hiding anymore.

Her eyes met Sam's and she saw his catch fire.

"You're so beautiful, Hannah," he breathed, curving his hands around her waist. "I swear, I'll never take this for granted again. Being able to touch you. See how much you want me."

He smoothed his hands up over her rib-cage, the edge of his thumbs skimming the underside of her breasts, then gliding, ever so lightly, over nipples pearled and aching. He watched intently, watched his hands touching her, his breath ragged, his face dark with passion. Hannah cried out, as he filled his hands with the fullness of her breasts. He kissed her, kissed her temple, her brow, her eyelids as he learned the shape of her body again in hungry, worshipful touches.

His mouth opened over hers, and she moaned as he kissed her, soft, slow, moist kisses that seemed to draw out her very soul. His hands slid back down to cup her bottom, draw her tighter against the hard bulge at his groin, his hands gathering bunches of satin upward, upward, until his callused fingers found what he was searching for. Hannah gasped at the heat of his touch, the sensual, so tender abrasion of his workman's hands as they caressed her bare skin. Hannah groaned, felt herself melting into his touch, wanting more, wanting everything, wanting him to explore her everywhere, relearn the map of her most sensitive places, secret dips and hollows and folds that burned and ached and throbbed with impatience, answering a pagan call she could never fully understand.

His tongue came seeking, tracing the crease of her lips, toying with her, coaxing her, his fingers exploring her buttocks, her hips, the delicate chain of her spine. She parted her lips, invited him inside, and his tongue began the most tender of invasions.

He tasted of coffee, rich and hot, his muscles iron bands, rigid with need. A burning started in her most private places, and she squeezed her thighs together, trying to keep her knees from buckling underneath her.

A flutter of satin, a whisper of cloth against skin as Sam stripped the exquisite nightgown over her head. She stood in a pool of lamp glow, naked except for the veil of her hair. The chill of the night air nipped at her, but she barely noticed. How could she be cold when her whole body was on fire?

"You're so beautiful," Sam ground out, skimming the backs of his knuckles over the elegant line of her jaw, the hollow of her throat, the cleft between her breasts.

Hannah answered the only way she could—she fumbled with the tie of his robe, unfastening it, shoving the cloth from his shoulders. It fell away in a liquid ripple of jewel tones, baring the rugged planes and angles of Sam's body. A landscape so familiar, tears burned Hannah's eyes. She flattened her hands against his chest, reveled in the texture of hot skin, silky hair, hammering heartbeat, ragged breath, the scent of him, musky, masculine, hungry for her.

His erection strained toward her, more swollen than she could ever remember, his shaft more sensitive and responsive because they hadn't made love in so long.

Hannah trailed her fingertips through the band of hair across his chest, ran her touch downward across the flat plane of his stomach, found the steely length of his erection in its pillow of coarse dark hair. Sam's breath hissed between his teeth as she curled her fingers around him, delicately closing him in her small hand.

"You feel so good, Sam. So hard. Strong. It's been such a long time. I want you inside me, Sam. Now. Forever." A sudden desperation surged through her. "Promise—"

Promise you won't hate me. Promise you won't leave me! Promise that no matter what, you'll never let me go.

"Anything, Hannah. Everything." Sam scooped her up, laid her across the bed, naked and needing and new.

"I love you." She pulled him down, down until he lay full length on top of her body, a weight so precious, she wished she could keep him there forever.

"I love you, too. Forever. Nothing is ever going to come between us again, Hannah. Do you believe me? Nothing!"

She gave a shuddering moan as he reached between their bodies, found the place between her thighs that was damp, eager, needing him to claim it. He stroked her, teased her, barely touched her and she was arching, crying out.

"Inside me—" she gasped, arching under his hand. "I want you—you inside me—when I come."

Sam hooked his hands under her knees, opened her wide. He sank into the cradle of her thighs, his penis nudging her tender opening, testing it, so gentle tears sprang to her eyes. She knew how long he had waited. How his body must be raging to claim her. And yet, still he was thinking of her, trying to be careful.

"I don't want to hurt you," he ground out. "I mean, we haven't—made love since your surgery. I don't know if this will hurt you."

Hannah arched her hips up, driving him into her an inch, wanting even more. "Please, it's all right. I need you, Sam. Need you now."

With a groan, he bracketed her hips in his big hands, glided into her inch by careful inch, his gaze locked on her face, searching, she knew, for the tiniest sign that she might be in pain. But she didn't want him to be cautious, didn't want him to treat her as if she were so fragile and delicate a mere touch might bruise her.

She wanted him wild, all control lost. Wanted him to feel the way she did—hurtling out of control. She arched up against him, buried him inside her to the hilt.

Sam held himself still for a moment, breath rasping in his throat. "Are you—okay, Hannah? Is it—"

"Wonderful. It's been so . . . so long. I can't wait, Sam, not any longer. Can't go careful, go slow, or I . . . I think I'll lose my mind! Please, Sam. Please—I need to feel you move."

He clenched his teeth, his face a mask of arousal, her words driving him hard past caution and into a passion so raw Hannah's heart leapt at the power in it. She gasped, strained against him as he moved in sensual rhythm, almost withdrawing so entirely she felt like sobbing at the loss, then surging against her, filling her up to bursting again and again and again.

It was building—the force inside him. She could feel it, see it in his passion-flushed face, hard, contorted, his hands devouring her, his mouth kissing whatever wisp of naked skin he could reach. He arched his back, so that he could capture her nipple between his lips, suckle it with such fierce tenderness he wrung a ragged cry from her lips.

"You taste like heaven, Hannah. Feel like heaven. Please, never close me out again!"

His hips drove deep, once, twice, three times. Hannah cried out his name, again and again as her body writhed beneath his, climax crashing over her in waves of pleasure so intense it was agony, ecstasy.

She shuddered, wept, her hands all over Sam's sweat-sheened back as he drove into her one last time. He cried out as he spilled himself inside her. Pouring out his pain, his need, all his dreams for perfect tomorrows.

Hannah's heart ached as he collapsed against her, his shoulders quavering under her hands. She felt the dampness in the crook of her neck, Sam's face buried against her skin.

She stroked his hair with a tenderness both feral and soul-deep. Her heart breaking because he didn't know what she did.

That he might despise her someday, loathe her for opening her arms to him again.

But he might never find out the truth at all, she cried deep inside. He deserves to be happy! Just let him be happy!

She could almost hear fate's laughter.

He might never find out at all. . . .

Or he could discover your secret tomorrow . . . that's the price that you're going to pay for loving him, keeping secrets from him.

Everything could fall apart tomorrow and you're the only one who knows.

Sam lay still, Hannah cradled in his arms, a drowsy dark-haired angel who had smuggled him back through heaven's gates. He couldn't let himself sleep, didn't dare. He wanted this night to last forever. Feared if he closed his eyes, even for a moment, she might vanish from his arms, and he might wake up to find this night had been just one more dream, torturing him with shadows of what he'd lost.

But this was real, Sam assured himself, trailing his fingers across the spun silk waves of her hair that spilled in a sensual river across his chest. Hannah was here. In his arms. Her body dewy and sated from their lovemaking, so familiar and yet, so astonishingly new.

Feeling as if the weight of a dozen mountains had rolled from his back, Sam breathed in the scent of her—lilacs and lilies—everything that was warm and good and true in a world too often cold. Even in sleep, she held onto him, her fingers curled sweetly against his chest, one long, slender leg thrown over both of his, her head pillowed where it had always seemed to belong, in the cozy hollow of his shoulder.

She'd given herself to him so completely, so eagerly, with the generosity Hannah had always brought to every facet of her life. But this time had been different from all the other times they'd made love in this bed. This time, there had been something more, something fiercer inside her, more desperate. Something Sam couldn't name.

Even now, she was restless, thin lines around her

mouth and in her brow, her leg shifting against him, as if even in sleep she was trying to draw him closer, wanted to draw him inside her very soul.

How could she not know he was there already? Whatever was worrying her had no power over them now that they were lovers again, husband and wife not only in name, but in their hearts, in the very center of their beings. Surely she had to know that he'd never let anything hurt her, that he'd never let anything tear them apart now that they'd broken through the walls that had separated them for so long.

Trust me, Hannah, Sam pleaded silently with the woman in his arms. *Believe in the love I have for you. Whatever is troubling you, let me share it, carry the burden for you, ease the pain. There is no dragon I wouldn't slay for you.*

But whatever it was, Sam comforted himself, Hannah would confide it to him, and soon. The woman had never been able to keep a secret in her life.

Until she *did* show him her dragon, he'd do the only thing he could. Love her until she was wild with it. Make her laugh until her sides ached. Work at the thing that would please her most.

The nursery, Sam thought with satisfaction. That would be the perfect place to start. They'd make it a perfect place for a little girl to dream, a haven for a little princess. One that would remind her mother day after day how much he loved them both.

And there was one more possibility that flashed into his mind. Yes, when the nursery was finished, there was one more thing they needed to do. Something that would fill Hannah's heart to bursting. Soothe old pain. Banish sadness he knew she'd tried to hide for so long.

Bring on your dragons, Hannah, Sam dared her, gently kissing the crown of her head. *Nothing in the world can come between us ever again.*

19

Hannah cradled Ellie in her arms, the precious weight of the baby's little body nuzzling close swelling Hannah's heart with awe, gratitude, joy too great to hold as she wandered for the dozenth time into the nursery of her dreams. Maybe they were jumping the gun, rushing into making this nursery before they were sure whether they could adopt Ellie or not. And yet, Hannah felt touched by the sweet promise in the room. It was Sam's age-old philosophy coming into play—if you want something to come true, act as if it already has. The room was perfect, a labor of love. A gift from the whole family to their newest member.

All three of them had poured their hearts into it, spinning off ideas from the antique children's illustrations she and Sam had bought that stress-filled day Becca had traveled home from school. It was as if the pictures carried their own brand of magic, and with a wave of a star-tipped wand, had transformed the spare bedroom into a child's version of wonderland.

A thick, hooked rug spattered with bluebells and

lilies of the valley, violets and pink foxglove, blanketed the floor in blossoms. The walls glowed with the sweet lavender of twilight. Sam and Becca were still teasing each other about the paint specks on their arms and legs from the day they'd rolled the walls with color. Glow-in-the-dark stars spangled the ceiling, and they'd turned the overhead light into a fat silvery moon with twinkling eyes and a merry grin.

While Becca and Sam had worked and laughed, turning painting into play, Hannah had resurrected a box of art supplies from the attic, where she'd tucked them away soon after she first held Becca in her arms.

It hadn't been until she'd run down to the art shop to get fresh paints and begun to design the magical mural of fairies at their revels in an old-fashioned garden that she'd wondered why she hadn't drawn in so long. Had some part of her offered her art up as a kind of sacrifice to appease a vengeful God? Had she believed that if she gave up her one selfish dream, if she was the best mother she possibly could be to her little girl, maybe some part of her could hope to win absolution? Forgiveness for what she'd done long ago?

But even if that were so, surely God would forgive her just this one time for dabbling in what she had once loved so much. The dancing fairies with their gossamer wings and wispy flower petal dresses weren't going to grace the pages of the children's books she'd once dreamt of illustrating. They were only for Ellie to dream upon.

Hannah crossed to the corner where Sam's cradle stood, framed now by three fairy babes dozing in walnut shells, while field mice nannies in aprons and mobcaps tucked leaf quilts beneath their chins. Other fairies piloted boats made of lily pads across a sparkling stream that ran the length of one wall while fireflies lit their way. And at the garden gate, peering in at the magic land, stood two little girls in flowing white dresses. One wore Becca's face, dreamy and sweet as a Gainsborough portrait as she held baby Ellie up to see the wonder beyond.

It was perfect, with white lace curtains at the windows, garlands of flowers draping them with ivy and roses. A rocking chair that had been Josie and Tom's offering sat beneath a little reading lamp, the table beside it loaded down with books from Becca's childhood, a gift from Ellie's new big sister. Hannah knew if she lived forever she would never forget these past nights when she'd crept near the nursery door, stood there, silent, listening to Becca read to the baby. Her dignified teenaged daughter doing the funny voices Hannah had made up to entertain Becca when she was little.

Hannah lay Ellie in the cradle for a moment, then went to rummage in the chest of drawers whose top Sam had surrounded with a miniature white picket fence and filled with framed pictures of each of them holding Ellie. Even old Reckless, gently sniffing Ellie's cheek, as if he were whispering in the baby's ear, promising he'd stand guard over her the way he had watched over Becca years before.

They were a family, Hannah marveled. All four of them, now. She and Sam and Becca and Ellie. And the days that had passed since the night she and Sam had made love had been so warm and wonderful, she could almost believe the fates were satisfied. That somehow, everything was going to be all right.

Only two more days until Becca went back to school, but they'd made the most out of the time they'd had. And there would be so many more in the future. Easter egg hunts and Halloween costumes.

Stockings to fill and birthday candles to blow out. First days of school and bunches of crocuses for the teacher.

Hannah's eyes filled with tears, her heart so full she could hardly bear it.

"So what do you think, Miss Ellie?" she murmured to the baby. "We'd better change your outfit before your daddy and sister get back. You don't want to greet your adoring throng with spit-up all down your front, after all. Besides, we'd best be prepared for anything. They were acting awfully mysterious when they left, don't you think?"

Ellie gurgled from her spot in the cradle, kicking her little feet in the air. Hannah laughed. She knew the baby was too little to understand her, but Ellie looked for all the world as if she were offering her personal opinion of spit-up, big sisters and surprises. Hannah made quick work of stripping off the soiled outfit, changing her into fresh diapers, and slipping on her newest outfit—a green and white sleeper Becca had picked up on her last trip to the mall.

Hannah snapped it up the front, pausing to tickle Ellie's plump little tummy and reading aloud the crayon colored letters embroidered across the outfit's chest. "I love Daddy," Hannah said. "Well, I know one thing for sure. Your daddy sure loves you. Sometimes, when I see him looking at you, I feel so . . . so lucky . . ."

She stopped, listened, thinking she might have heard something downstairs. She would have dismissed it as just one of those odd sounds old houses made if it weren't for a raucous bark from Reckless. The old Lab as ever, unfailing in his job, announcing visitors, airplanes flying overhead or too many birds making a racket on the redbud tree outside his favorite window.

"Why are they knocking, your daddy and big sister?" Hannah said. "Either they forgot their keys or their arms are so full of packages for some little baby I know they can't open the door. I'm betting on that one. You wait here for a minute and I'll go let them in."

Hannah wound up Ellie's mobile to coos of delight, then hurried downstairs. She could easily have brought Ellie with her, but she was not only looking forward to Becca's "surprises," but even more so, Sam's greeting kiss. She wanted to be able to put both her arms around him, drown in the knee-melting warmth of his mouth on hers, a sensation she would never take for granted again.

But as she rounded the corner she slowed, frowning just a little. It looked like a girl, but it wasn't Becca. She wasn't wearing the bright blue tee shirt Becca had put on that morning. Hannah grimaced. For once, she didn't want company, much as she adored Becca's friends. This time with her family was too precious, too fleeting with Becca soon going back to school. She didn't want to share a moment of it with anyone else.

Still, she could hardly go hide. She was the one who'd always told the kids they were welcome at the farmhouse anytime. She just hoped it wasn't Annie so soon after the last adventure. Annie had magnanimously turned up on the doorstep with a half dozen rag dolls she said her sister had outgrown. Unfortunately, the irate ten-year-old hadn't agreed and had turned up with her much-chagrined mother to reclaim them.

Hannah put on a smile as she approached the door, the girl beyond it suddenly turning so that Hannah could see her face. For a moment, Hannah barely recognized her—lifeless brown hair framing a face even paler than usual, so thin and forlorn it broke Hannah's heart. Rachel. Poor kid. How much had she suffered coming so close to her dream? Only to fail and have to come home a month later to parents who were glad things hadn't worked out? She looked so haunted, so lost, standing outside the door. But then, Rachel had always reminded Hannah of a woebegone fairy, locked out of the kind of beautiful garden they'd painted in Ellie's room.

She'd paint one more fairy on the wall after Rachel left, Hannah resolved. One rosy cheeked and smiling as she bent over the gleaming wood of her violin. Hannah's smile warmed with tenderness for the girl who stood on the porch. Some welcome home Rachel must have gotten! If she could find a little peace here at the farmhouse, far be it from Hannah to deny it to her.

Hannah opened the door. "Rachel, sweetheart, come on in." She hugged the girl warmly, but Rachel's shoulders were stiff. Strange, Hannah mused, since Rachel had always been hungry for Hannah's hugs in the past, more so than any of the other kids who came to see her. But then, the girl had obviously been through hell in the past few weeks. Hannah knew just what it felt like when you were eighteen and your world crashed down around your head. You didn't realize that the sun would still come up tomorrow. Somehow, some way, you'd still keep breathing.

"Hi, um, Mom." Rachel had called Hannah that ever since Jana had decided that Hannah was Rachel's "karmic mom." Hannah couldn't count the number of times she had wished she could tuck Rachel up in the little room that was now Ellie's nursery, put up a canopy bed and a window seat for dreaming and a music stand where she could practice and fill herself with joy.

But being someone's karmic mom didn't give you

anything but worrying rights, and the right to sweep in with comforting hugs whenever you got the chance. Like now.

Hannah wrapped her arms around the girl, alarmed at how thin she was. But this time Rachel didn't melt into her the way she usually did, as if for that one moment, she'd found someplace safe to rest. Hannah stroked her hair once, then let her go. There would be plenty of other hugs waiting when Rachel was ready for them. Obviously the poor girl was just too raw right now. Hannah understood all too well the sensation. Holding on by a thread, fighting tears she didn't want to cry, afraid any show of kindness would break through the shaky hold she had on her emotions.

"Becca said you were coming home soon," Hannah said warmly. "She's out right now, but I'd love a chance to talk to you. Can I get you something to drink? Lemonade? Chocolate milk? I've got gingerbread in the cookie jar."

Rachel almost smiled. "Cut out in little teddy bears with cinnamon hearts."

"Of course!" How many times had Rachel stood in the farmhouse kitchen, earnestly arranging the bits of red candy on the bear's spicy brown chests? For an instant, she looked about twelve, with smears of flour on her cheek and bits of raw cookie dough at the corners of her lips. "You used to be able to eat half a dozen at a time. Do you remember?"

"Yeah. But none right now, thanks. I'm not very hungry lately."

Was she developing some sort of eating disorder? Anorexia or something? Hannah worried. She had seen pictures of famine victims with more meat on their bones. Rachel's cheeks were hollow, colorless. And she'd never seen sadder eyes.

She had to try to reach Rachel, let the girl know she wasn't alone. Hannah took Rachel's hand in her own. "I'm so sorry about the way things turned out, honey. I know how much you wanted Vienna. How hard you worked to get there. I'm so sorry it didn't turn out to be just as wonderful for you as you deserved."

Rachel looked past her shoulder, as if she couldn't bear to meet Hannah's eyes. *Shame did that to you,* Hannah thought. *Made you afraid if anyone saw your face, they'd be able to see the mistakes you'd made, the failures that burned inside you. Give it time, angel,* she wanted to say to the girl. *Someday it won't hurt this bad. It will just be a hollow ache that never quite goes away.*

Until something happens to remind you . . . , a voice inside Hannah whispered. *For me, a baby left in my laundry basket, a man I'd never expected to see again returning to town, a surgery that ended my hopes forever of filling the empty place in my heart that belonged to the baby I gave away so many years ago. Whatever fate can conjure to drag it all up again.*

"Nothing is the way I thought it would be," Rachel confessed, her voice quavering. "I had it all planned. I was so sure what I wanted."

"Sometimes that's just the way things happen. Life just doesn't fall into the shapes and patterns you hoped for. But hard as it is to believe, in the end, things usually work out the way they're supposed to. You can find plenty of music here, sweetheart. Just because Vienna wasn't right for you doesn't mean you won't find the perfect place to belong. I have faith in you, Rachel. You know I always have."

"I know. That's what . . . what makes it so hard. I've made such a mess of things."

"Nothing you can't fix up, sweetheart."

"You don't understand. You don't—"

A tiny gurgle sounded from upstairs, Ellie obviously tired of being excluded from the conversation.

Hannah smiled in apology. "Things around here have changed a little, too. I don't know if your mom told you about what happened. She figures I've finally lost my mind. But I've never been happier. Wait until I introduce you."

She turned and led her up the stairs, to the nursery. Ellie's forget-me-not blue eyes focused on Hannah's face and she smiled, reaching up her little arms, sure of being gathered up, held close and safe. Hannah's heart twisted and she wished she could offer the same comfort to the girl who had followed behind her.

"This is my new little angel," Hannah said, gathering up the baby. "Ellie has decided to keep me company since the rest of you deserted me this year."

She straightened, turned toward Rachel. An icy fist slammed into Hannah's chest.

Oh, God! Rachel's eyes. Hungry. Agonized. Hopeless. As if her heart had been torn from her chest. Tears brimmed at the girl's lashes. "She's so . . . so *big*." Rachel breathed in awe.

Big? Compared to what? Ellie was still tiny—unless the last time you'd seen her was a month ago when she was brand new.

Panic shot through Hannah. She wanted to clutch Ellie to her and run. Oh, God, why had she ever opened the door? But no mere wooden door could close out the image of what she'd just seen. Closing her eyes would never erase the agony in Rachel's face. Pretending wouldn't change anything at all.

Hannah tried to stop the screaming in her head. *Be cold to her. Let her know what she did was unforgivable. Then she won't take your baby away.*

But she couldn't follow through. How could she

when looking at Rachel was like looking at her own face in a mirror twenty-seven years ago? Besides, the girl hadn't said a word about taking Ellie back. Most likely, she just wanted to see her daughter, make sure Ellie was safe, cared for. Hannah could give her that feeling of peace. Tell her just how much Ellie had added to her life, how much joy she'd brought into the farmhouse.

"Oh, Rachel," Hannah breathed, her own eyes welling with tears. "Why didn't you tell me?"

"Tell you what?" For an instant panic widened Rachel's eyes.

"It was you. You're Ellie's mama."

Rachel stared in surprise, then her shoulders sagged in resignation. "Of course you'd figure it out. I should have guessed. How long have you known?"

"I started wondering when I got the call from Austria, but I wasn't sure until I saw your face when you looked at Ellie. Ellie is your baby."

"Not anymore. I gave her up. I can't just . . . just change my mind, can I?"

No, Hannah wanted to say. *I already love her. . . .*

"I just needed to make sure she was okay. See for myself that she—" Rachel's voice broke. She pressed one hand to her face. "Oh, God, how could I be so terrible. Just leave her?"

Hannah curved one arm around her shoulder, guided her to the rocker. "Sit down, Rachel."

"You must hate me! I hate myself! My baby—my poor little baby."

"Your baby is just fine. I took her straight to Dr. Meyers the day you left her. She checked out in perfect health."

"Thank God! I was so scared . . . if there was something wrong—"

"So was I," Hannah admitted. "I was scared to death, not just for Ellie, but for you. So many things can go wrong in childbirth. I kept thinking about what Ellie's mother must have gone through, was scared you'd have internal bleeding, pick up some kind of infection. You're so thin, sweetheart. Have you seen a doctor since Ellie was born?"

"No. How could I without my mom and dad finding out?"

"Now that you're home, I'll take you in myself, to my gynecologist, just to make sure everything is okay. How did you do it, Rachel? Give birth? Please tell me someone was with you, that you weren't alone."

Rachel shook her head, looked down. "I couldn't tell anyone. Trust anyone. I was so scared if someone found out they'd tell a friend, slip up or . . . first chair orchestra is plenty competitive. If the director had found out I was pregnant—had a baby right before we left—he wouldn't have risked taking me overseas, especially without parental permission. And if he'd called Mom and Dad and told them about the baby—" Her face crumpled, miserable.

"What about Ellie's father?" Hannah prodded gently. "Did he help you at least?"

Rachel gave a bitter laugh. "I doubt he even remembers my name. He was working at Smith's farm while I was selling stuff at their roadside stand, earning money for school. No boy had ever paid attention to me, you know? I just wanted to know what it was like. To flirt, to laugh, to be kissed, like all the other girls I know. He made me feel pretty, made me feel daring. It was stupid, I know, but I felt like it wasn't real. Like I'd stepped into some kind of movie—all fantasy. Nothing to do with what was real. But it got real in a hurry when my period was late. And even more real when he dumped me. I was fun, he said, but he didn't have room in his life for a serious girlfriend. He was premed and getting into Harvard medical school was the only thing that mattered to him. But I had plans, too. I didn't have time to have a baby. But she was there, in my stomach. She was real."

Hannah ached for her, imagined all too vividly the thrill of this boy paying attention to Rachel, the wondrous sensation of being like the other girls around her for just a little while, the temptation, the excitement, the fear. The thrill of doing something dangerous for just once in her life. And then the horror and disillusionment when she crashed back to earth. It was a ride Hannah was all too familiar with. She still bore the scars. "I'm so sorry, Rachel."

"I was, too. I didn't want my baby. When I first found out I was pregnant, I hated her. But then, I felt her move. I know this sounds strange, but when I played music, I could tell she liked it. Felt this peace inside. I'd touch my stomach when no one could see, talked to her when no one else was listening. I knew I couldn't keep her, but I wanted her to know I loved her."

Hannah ached, remembering her own teenage pregnancy, the baby she wasn't supposed to "get attached to" because she was going to give her away. And yet how do you keep from loving a baby that grows under your heart? Whose first flutters of life you feel inside you, new life, endless possibilities.

"When I went into labor I went to a hotel. Bit down on towels to keep from screaming. There was so much . . . much blood and I was so scared. I didn't know what to do."

"You should have called a doctor."

"He'd have to report the birth. To the college and to

my parents. If he did, there'd be no Vienna and you know my parents. They would have disowned me in a heartbeat. They'd never have paid for the doctor's bills. And I didn't have any money. When things got bad I guess I just thought that, well, if I died, I probably deserved it for being stupid enough to get in this situation."

"It's not stupid. It's painful and scary. But lots of girls get into trouble. Good kids, just like you."

"I sure don't know anyone else who got themselves into this kind of mess. I was so ashamed. I didn't want anyone to guess. And then . . . then I thought if I could just keep her a secret, if nobody knew and I gave her away right after she was born, maybe someday I would even start believing that she'd never existed at all."

"I know," Hannah choked out.

Rachel gave a bitter laugh. "You don't know anything about it! You'd never do what I did! Never! That's why I thought—if you were Ellie's mother—she'd be better. Safer. Happier. I don't know anything about babies."

"Oh, Rachel. Honey, you can come here and see her whenever you want to." Hannah knew it was a risk, but it was one she was willing to take. "You can be her favorite aunt. Hold her and rock her and I'll send you pictures as she grows. You know Sam and I will take care of her. But it's so much more than that. I want you to know what you've given me, through your courage and your generosity, bringing this baby into our lives."

Hannah looked down at Ellie, still awed, praying she could find the words to tell this young girl how much Ellie meant to her, how Ellie had changed her life. "You know how much I love kids."

"Everybody in Willowton does."

"But I don't know if you knew I've wanted another baby forever. I couldn't have one of my own. And then, this summer I had to have surgery. A hysterectomy. That meant no more babies—not ever. I was heartbroken, felt this empty hole inside of me. One that would never be filled. It hurt so much, sometimes it was hard to breathe."

"It's not fair. You should have had more kids. I always thought you should've. Sometimes I was so jealous of Becca I almost hated her. She didn't know how lucky she was to have you because you'd always been there for her. She didn't know what it was like to know your parents didn't want you around."

"Sometimes parents aren't good at showing how much they love you, but that doesn't mean they don't, deep down. Someday, I hope they'll be able to show it. In the meantime, this has always been your second home. Now, I hope you'll come here more than ever. Be a part of Ellie's life. Unless . . ." Hannah hesitated. "Unless you think it would be too painful, too hard. You need to do whatever is best for you."

"You're so . . . so kind. I love you all so much. I wish—" She stopped, turned her gaze to her trembling fingers.

"Wish what?" Hannah asked.

"Wish I'd known what it would feel like to leave Ellie behind. But I didn't know it would hurt so much. I didn't know I'd wake up in the middle of the night hearing her cry. That I'd turn on the light and look for her and she wouldn't be there and that every time that happened it would hurt just as much as the first night I let her go."

Rachel's thin fists clenched so hard the knuckles were white. Hannah knew Rachel was fighting, fighting not to reach out for the baby, not to take her in her arms. Because if she did, she might never be able to let Ellie go.

Hannah held Ellie close, felt her squirm, a tiny miracle in her arms. "I know it's hard, Rachel. But giving up Ellie—it was brave and unselfish, no matter how guilty other people might try to make you feel. You wanted her to have a home, two parents to love her. I can be home with her every day and play with her in the backyard as she grows up. There's nothing shameful in wanting those things for your baby. And nothing shameful in wanting a decent future for yourself."

Hannah wanted to comfort Rachel, wanted to smooth away the lines of pain and guilt and doubt ravaging the sensitive girl's face. "You've got such a bright future ahead. Nobody could ever blame you for the decision you made. And I . . . I'll always think of you as my own special angel, the one who answered my prayers. I'll never take for granted the gift you've given me, this chance to be a mom one more time when it seemed as if all hope was gone. You were my miracle, Rachel, you and Eleanor Rose. You even named her after my grandmother. It was as if . . . as if she was always meant to belong to me."

"I wanted it to seem like that. I wanted to believe that," Rachel confessed. "But somehow, no matter how hard I tried to think of Ellie as yours, I just couldn't chase away feeling like . . ."

She rolled her eyes heavenward. The agonized depths glinted with tears. Dread coiled in the pit of Hannah's stomach. She wanted to stay silent, but she couldn't. "Like what, Rachel?"

"Like I'd made a terrible mistake."

Hannah's blood chilled.

"I know I don't deserve Ellie," Rachel rushed on. "I gave her up. Abandoned her. I have no right to her anymore. I keep telling myself that you're her mama now. I just can't get my heart to believe it."

Did Rachel want Ellie back? Hannah reeled as the possibility crashed down on her. All this time she'd been trying to make amends, to pay for her mistake so many years ago. So many times, she tried to believe it was over, that she'd grieved enough, blamed herself enough, paid enough. She'd never dreamed she'd face any atonement as cruel as this one.

Rachel had said she didn't deserve Ellie. All Hannah had to do was agree. To let her know it was too late to change her mind. That Ellie was her daughter now. That she loved her. Becca loved her. And Sam . . .

Hannah almost cried out as she thought of him. Maybe she had done something terrible to deserve this depth of pain. But what crime had Sam ever committed except loving her? Loving Ellie?

Shouldn't she try to hang onto Ellie for his sake, if not her own? Didn't she owe it to Sam to . . .

To what?

Twist the knife deeper into Rachel's heart? Make her grieve forever for the baby she'd lost? Pay the horrible, endless price of blame and self-hatred Hannah had faced every day of her life for twenty-seven years, wondering about the life that had vanished along with the tiny bundle that had come from her body? Her future that could never be? Her heart that would always have an empty place she could never fill? Should Rachel play doting aunt in all the years to come, bringing presents, winning kisses all too brief, while Ellie was calling someone else "mama," running to someone else when she skinned her knee or got her first broken heart? What kind of punishment was that? For Ellie to become just another secret she'd hide away, carry with her like a stone in her heart?

Hannah closed her eyes, memories flooding back to her. Her parents' rage. The desperate race to the social worker's office, pleading with the stony-faced man to give her her baby back. The law said she could change her mind, didn't it? Only three weeks—it had only been three weeks.

Rachel had lasted two more.

Hannah looked down into Ellie's face, innocent as an angel's. The baby didn't know that her mother's heart was breaking. *Both* of her mothers' hearts.

Hannah dredged up the last bit of her strength, her voice a hoarse croak. "Do you want to . . . to hold her?" It was a mistake, intuition warned her. Letting her hold Ellie would only make Rachel want her more. If there was to be any chance of persuading her to stick with her first decision, leave the baby where she was, Hannah shouldn't let the girl get any closer to Ellie, see what an angel the baby was, how incredibly precious.

Rachel's gaze sprang up to hers, incredulous at the offer, so desperate Hannah felt an urge to snatch the baby close again. "Can I—you mean, you'd let me—?"

"Take her." Hannah carefully, tenderly laid Ellie in the crook of Rachel's arms.

The girl sobbed, laughed, kissed Ellie's cheek. She drew in deep breaths, taking in the sweet, clean baby scent of her. Ellie curled her little fingers in a strand of Rachel's hair.

"Do you remember me?" Rachel choked out. "I'm your mama. I didn't forget you. I couldn't forget you. I just kept loving you and loving you even when I was gone."

Hannah's throat constricted. *Yes, Rachel,* she thought, *and you would have kept on loving her year after year, birthday after birthday, forever. But you'd never have been able to hold her or tell her so yourself. You'd never be able to make her birthday cake, or teach her how to tie her shoes. When she said the word mama for the first time, you wouldn't be there. Another woman's face would light up. Another woman's eyes would fill with tears. And you'd never even know it had happened at all.*

It's not fair! Hannah wanted to scream. *Maybe I deserve this pain, but not Sam. Oh, God, not Sam!*

He'd never understand what they had to do. How in God's name could she explain it to him? Tell him why?

"I have to—" Rachel stammered. "I thought I could . . . could give her up. But I can't." She looked up, face mottled, tear-stained. "I can't live without her. It's like, like I can't breathe. Like someone ripped out my heart. You must hate me."

"No," Hannah choked out.

"I don't know what I'm going to tell my mom. And Dad—he's going to go crazy." Her chin jutted up, defiance showing through her tears. "But I don't care. If they don't want to love me anymore, they don't have to. But I . . . I love my baby. I love her. I want her. Is that such a terrible thing?"

"It's hard work, taking care of a little one," Hannah warned. "You won't be able to do things your friends are doing. Taking care of her at school will be tough. And you have to go to school so you'll be able to support yourself and Ellie, so both of you can have a decent life."

Rachel bit her lip, her face crumpling. "You don't think I can do it?"

It would be so easy, a voice in Hannah whispered, just plant a few more doubts, empathize with her but make the future look bleak. Not for Rachel. From the light in the girl's eyes, it was obvious that Rachel would be willing to face anything for her little daughter. No. Paint Ellie's future with shadows and doubt and give

Rachel glimpses of all the things her little daughter might have to do without. *That* might shake Rachel's determination to reclaim Ellie.

Rachel stared at her, eyes wide, so vulnerable, filled with questions and dread and self-doubt. "Don't you think I can take care of her?" she asked again.

Hannah swallowed hard. Sucked in a steadying breath. It took all her strength to tell the truth. "No. I think you *can*. If it's what you want."

For an instant, Rachel's eyes widened with hope, then she looked down at Ellie, crestfallen. "I don't deserve her. I left her in that basket, all alone. You'd be a better mom for Ellie. You'd never do what I did."

She looked so alone, woebegone, self-loathing digging its claws deep into her delicate features. "What kind of person abandons her little baby?" she asked, so lost.

"A person who is scared and desperate, a person who doesn't know what else to do."

"But you—look at everything you've done for Ellie. This room and . . . and the way you love her. For a whole month. I told you that you could keep her. I know it isn't fair to just come and take her back."

Hannah turned away, her eyes burning, her throat thick. She pressed her fist to her lips to keep from crying. *It isn't fair*, Hannah thought, imagining this room empty, silent, her arms aching again, with no baby to hold. The years stretching out the way they had before Ellie had come into her life—a giant blank canvas she had no idea how to fill.

Except it would be different, now. Because she'd made Sam want a different future, too. What had he said about Ellie? She'd be his second chance to get this "daddy" thing right. That he wouldn't be so afraid this time. He wouldn't miss all the things that really mattered because he was buried in his work.

She'd been lost and miserable in those weeks after Becca left home. What would it be like with Ellie gone?

"Rachel, will you give me just a little time? To break the news to Becca and . . . and Sam? It's going to be a . . . shock. We all love her."

"I'm sorry." Rachel broke down into tears. "I'm so sorry. I didn't mean to hurt anyone. Taking her back— it's not fair! I know it's not fair!"

"Maybe it's not fair," Hannah said softly. "But it's *right.*"

She knew that. And Rachel knew it, too.

Was it possible Hannah could get Becca and Sam to see it that way? If she could only help them to let go of the little baby they'd all claimed as their own. Work through the pain, the loss. But how? You couldn't give up a baby you loved without the loss breaking your heart.

It's impossible, Hannah thought.

Nobody knew that better than she did.

20

HANNAH CURLED UP in the rocking chair, Ellie in her arms, the house terrible in its silence. Her chest burned, raw, her eyes swollen from crying, her hands trembling as she stroked Ellie's plump cheek, the soft down curling on her head, her tiny rosebud lips that loved to suck on the end of Hannah's little finger.

"Your mama came back for you," she murmured, memorizing the exact color of Ellie's eyes, the way her long lashes looked as if fairies had dipped them in gold. "You can't be my little girl anymore. You belong with her. She loves you very much."

But not the way I love you, a voice inside Hannah protested. *She's young. She'll have other babies, other chances, a whole lifetime to fill up with children's laughter. You were my last chance. . . .*

But that didn't matter now that she'd run head on into this dilemma. She didn't have a choice.

"Oh, God, Ellie, what am I going to say to Sam? Losing you will break his heart." She shivered, glanced out the window. She could see Sam's truck in the driveway. He and Becca had gotten home a good twenty minutes ago, but neither one of them had come inside yet. Hannah knew she should go out and get them, break the hideous news to them. Stalling wasn't going to change anything. But somehow, she wanted to give them this little bit of extra time to be happy, to enjoy whatever it was they were doing, to believe life was wonderful and the four of them would be together always.

Just a little more time . . . so she could think of what to say to them, think of how to explain. They'd be so angry, so hurt, so confused. Like she was, Hannah thought miserably. Except she'd done something to deserve this. Sam and Becca—they'd done nothing at all.

She jumped at the sound of Reckless barking greeting, the back door opening.

"Hannah?" Sam called, his voice brimming with such excitement it was a knife in Hannah's heart. "Hannah, come on out back. And bring Ellie. Becca and I have a surprise for the two of you."

Hannah struggled to steady her voice. "Be right down."

There would be time enough to tell them after they showed off whatever the two of them had concocted. The challenge would be keeping them from guessing something was terribly wrong from the instant they saw her face.

Balancing Ellie in one arm, she stopped in the bathroom long enough to splash ice cold water on her face and scrub away the worst evidence of her crying jag. Then, she slipped her floppy garden hat from its hook on the wall. Hopefully the brim would shadow her face for the time being.

Hannah stepped out onto the back porch, the glare of sunlight blinding her tear-burned eyes for a moment in spite of the shade from her hat. She blinked hard, hearing voices from the backyard. Becca's, high pitched and eager, Sam's boyish with enthusiasm.

Oh, God, how can I do this? Hannah cried inwardly. *How can I tell them—*

"Mom? That you, Mom?" Becca yelled. "Hurry up! I can't wait!"

If only she knew what was coming, Hannah thought sadly, her daughter would be praying she'd never round the corner of the house.

Hannah forced her feet to move, felt as if she were breathing in broken glass as she stepped into the backyard, its familiar green sweep spreading out before her. Sheets rippled on the clothesline, just the way they had the day she'd first discovered Ellie. Flowers showed off bright colors. Becca's old fort stood guard over all. Lately, the old wooden structure had seemed as if it were just waiting, biding its time until another little girl climbed up its ladder to play make-believe.

Sam and Becca stood close together, their backs to the lilac garden, as if they were hiding something. Their eyes shone bright as stars. "We thought it was time we initiated Ellie fully into the family," Becca said.

Sam's voice choked. "I know you've waited a long time to fill this spot, Hannah."

They stepped aside. Hannah froze. Fresh-turned dark earth mounded in a circle around a hole into which the root ball of a tender little lilac bush had been placed. Heart-shaped leaves glowed spring green in the rays of the sun, some barely unfurled, three lavender blossoms bending its thin branches, beauty almost too heavy to hold.

"We know you like to 'tuck them in' yourself," Becca said. "So we got it this far and left the rest of the fun for you."

"Hand over my favorite daughter, Mom, and finish planting," Sam said, tugging Becca's hair. "This one's been giving me nothing but trouble since we climbed into the truck this morning."

She had to say something, Hannah thought wildly, hanging onto the baby for dear life. She had to tell them. But she felt that if she made a single sound she'd shatter into tiny pieces.

"Hannah?" Sam questioned, perplexed, his arms outstretched for Ellie. "Is something the matter?"

"She's just getting all choked up," Becca brushed his worries off. "You know how she always does. She's trying not to ball her eyes out. C'mon, Mom. Might as well surrender and get it over with. Ball away. You know you want to. Hey, I almost want to, too. A new lilac bush at last. Your mother's day garden is complete. And you never thought it would be."

"It's . . . it's beautiful," Hannah said.

"You better get those roots covered. It's not good to leave them open to the sun very long!" Becca said. But Sam was watching Hannah sharply with worried eyes. He wasn't buying for a minute Becca's explanation of Hannah's behavior.

Hannah forced a smile. Was she stalling a little longer or just doing what she had to? She had to finish planting the lilac bush, didn't she? Becca was right, the sooner the roots were covered, the better. She handed the baby to Sam, her throat closing with emotion at the tenderness in his touch, how at ease he'd become with Ellie, how warm and real and at peace. Hannah pressed the image in between the pages of her memory, wondering if she'd ever see the man she loved so much look this way again.

She knelt down on the ground, felt the earth give slightly beneath her knees. The garden was warming up, the dirt rich and moist from soaking up last winter's snow. Some people used garden gloves to keep their hands clean, but Hannah had never liked them. She loved the feel of the dirt on her hands, crumbly and cool, full of promise of growing things to come. The earth was alive, alive like the dreams they'd all had of years to come. Alive like the love they'd come to feel for the baby fate had dropped into their arms. Alive like the pain that would cut through them, the grief, the anger, the loss, when Ellie went away.

Hannah scooped the dirt around the lilac's roots. She'd planted so many hopes and dreams in this garden. None more precious than the one this tiny bush represented. But this dream had already withered away.

Even so, she tucked the plant in as tenderly as she could, gently burying the dream forever. Becca had the dented aluminum watering can waiting and ready, filled to the brim from the garden hose. Hannah tipped the can at an angle so that a soft rain of drops could fall on the plant.

"Do you like it? The color and everything? Dad and I couldn't decide. They've got some weird ones now. Pink and stuff, but I figured you'd want it to match ours. Yours and Daddy's and mine."

"It's . . . just right," Hannah said, setting the watering can back down. She wished she could just kneel there forever, dampness seeping through the denim of her jeans, the breeze buffing her cheeks dry, the old straw hat brim hiding from Becca and Sam the devastation searing through her. Anguish they would have to share.

Bracing herself with the smooth wood handle of the shovel Sam had left to one side, its blade thrust deep into the ground to hold it upright, Hannah climbed to her feet, then brushed the bits of grass and dirt off her jeans.

Nothing else to do now, nothing to say—except the truth.

"Thank you both. It was—" Her voice broke. "The

sweetest thing you've ever done for me. I'll never forget it. Never."

"I'll bet not. If Ellie's the same as her big sister was, she'll be wanting to pick handfuls of the flowers as soon as she can reach. Remember how we'd have to help Becca cut them with the clippers. She'd get so mad that she couldn't just snap their little heads off the way she could with the tulips and daffodils."

Hannah closed her eyes for a moment, her imagination filled with things that would never be. Ellie toddling about in a ruffled Easter dress, bunnies frolicking on her pinafore. A bonnet, white straw with clusters of silk flowers held on her curls by a fine elastic thread under her chin. Black patent leather Mary Janes, sparkling and new, the strap across her instep brushed by the deep ruffles on her little white anklets. And fingers in miniature white gloves curling ever so carefully around the twiglike stems of lilacs from the bush that belonged just to her.

There's still time, a voice inside her said. *Time to change your mind. You could convince Rachel to let Ellie go. You and Sam could fight her—in court, if you had to. But it would never get that far. If you just joined forces with Rachel's parents, pushed the girl, hard—she'd fall apart, she'd crumble underneath the pressure. Ellie could stay your little girl. Sam's little girl. Forever.*

No, Hannah whispered inside. She doesn't belong to you. She really never has.

"Can you two come inside for a little bit? There's something we need to talk about."

Lines carved deep in Sam's tanned brow. "Sure. Bec, grab the shovel and watering can. Your mom likes to keep them in order."

"Just leave them for now," Hannah said, earning a strange look from Sam. "I'll get them later. I just—" *Just want to get this over with. Can't bear the weight of carrying all this grief alone.*

"Okay. Whatever you say," Sam said. Hannah turned, trudged to the house, feeling like she was on her way to her own execution. She led them into the sun porch, sank down on the swing.

Sam settled into one wicker rocker, Becca in the other one. He retrieved Ellie's pacifier from the end of the ribbon attached to the front of her outfit by a fat fuzzy bumblebee and popped it into the baby's mouth.

"All right, Hannah," he said quietly. "What is it?"

Hannah swept the old hat off her head, played with a bit of thread where the stitching was coming apart. She looked up at Becca's curious face, then to Sam's somber one. "Something happened while you were gone."

Sam regarded her somberly. "Tell us about it."

"It's hard to." Hannah fought the tremor in her voice. "I know how much it will . . . will hurt you. And I don't want to do that, not ever."

"We know that. If it's bad news, better just get it over with, fast," Sam urged, bracing himself.

"I was changing Ellie and I heard someone at the door. I thought it was the two of you coming back, but it wasn't."

"Don't tell me that Blake guy is prowling around again." Sam bristled like a watchdog whose turf had been invaded. "What the hell was his excuse this time?"

"No. It wasn't Tony. It was . . . Ellie's mother."

Shocked silence fell over the room. Hannah could see Becca's mind racing with questions she was far too afraid to ask. But it was Sam's reaction that stunned her. Anger flared white hot in his eyes, surpassed only by a sharp blaze of . . . what was it? Fear?

"You're Ellie's mother," Sam bit out, fierce. "Not some irresponsible teenager who just dumped the kid like so much trash. If she comes back don't let her see the baby. She has no right after what she did."

Words struck Hannah like a blow. "Is that how you really feel?"

"Ellie's got a good home here. Parents who love her. A sister. This—whoever this girl is who gave birth to Ellie gave up her rights to Ellie when she left her."

"Four weeks, Sam," Hannah corrected softly. "Just four weeks. And I have a feeling she was trying to get back to Ellie a good part of that time."

"You don't know that! You can't possibly—besides, it doesn't matter a damn whether she was trying to come back or not. All that matters is that she left Ellie in the first place."

"Mom, who . . . who is she?" Becca asked, white-faced. "Who is Ellie's mom?"

"It's . . . Rachel," Hannah said.

"Rachel?" Becca cried out, disbelieving.

"Rachel Johnson?" Sam stared as if he'd been poleaxed.

"That's impossible," Becca gasped. "She's never even kissed a guy! Never wanted to, she's so shy! Did someone . . . force her to . . . you know?"

"No. She wanted to be like other girls just once. See what it was like to have a boyfriend. When the time came to say 'no,' I'm not sure she knew how. She's always been so timid, wanted so much to please anyone she cared about. I think things just got out of hand and she didn't know how to stop them."

Sam didn't want to feel empathy for the girl. He wanted to close out any feeling but a fierce, protective anger. Sam sighed. "Where's the father?"

"Out of the picture." Hannah grimaced. "He doesn't

have room in his life for Rachel or the baby. He's got important things to do with *his* life. Medical school at Harvard."

"Selfish son of a bitch. Like Rachel hasn't been working her whole damn life to play that violin she loves! You've always loved Rachel like she was one of your own. Tried to be there for her. Why the hell didn't she come to you for help?"

Hannah shrugged. "In a way she did, in the only way she knew how. She entrusted her baby to me. She left for Austria with the orchestra just a few days after Ellie was born. She's been trying to work up the courage and make arrangements to come back to Willowton ever since."

"*That's* why she came back to the States? Because of the baby?" Becca asked.

"It's only natural," Sam said, in spite of a flicker of unease in his eyes. "After everything she's been through. The strain must have been unbelievable."

"She didn't tell a soul, all those months," Hannah said. "She hid the pregnancy."

"How?" Becca shook her head in stunned amazement. "You can't just hide it when your stomach sticks out like you swallowed a basketball. Someone's bound to have noticed."

"Rachel has always been tiny. And she's always had a gift for blending into the scenery when she wants to. She's never been like you and Jana, Becca, demanding a share of the spotlight. Considering Rachel's personality and those baggy clothes you kids wear half the time, it's not so hard to see how she carried it off."

"Maybe she could hide being pregnant," Becca admitted. "But you can't have a baby in the middle of a dorm without somebody noticing!"

"She had the baby in a hotel, all alone."

Sam flinched. Becca's eyes widened. "Are you kidding?" Becca gasped. "How could she do that? It must've hurt so bad! And she couldn't have known what to do—I mean, *I* sure wouldn't have, and Rachel, well, she knew less than any of us about that kind of stuff. She thought you could get pregnant from French kissing until she was in eighth grade. Bet she'd *still* believe it if you hadn't had *the talk* with her at one of my slumber parties."

Hannah winced, remembering the earnest, wide-eyed girl perched on the end of her bed. Sam had been out of town on business, and Rachel had wandered up, away from the other girls. It had taken Hannah almost an hour to get Rachel to confide what had upset her so much. She'd been terrified that one of her friends was going to have a baby since the day the other girl had confided she'd been French kissed by the captain of the football team.

Hannah had been touched by Rachel's innocence, her compassion, her fear for her friend. In a teenage world where most kids were more worried about getting the newest designer jeans, or getting a date, she'd always seemed as if she belonged to a simpler, more wholesome time.

"What can we do to help Rachel now?" Sam asked. "Get her to a doctor? I don't know. It must have been such a relief to her, seeing her baby girl with you, just the way she'd wanted it. Given her a sense of closure about the baby. Comforted her to see with her own eyes that everything had turned out all right. Did you show her the nursery? She couldn't dream of a more perfect place for Ellie to grow up."

Hannah's eyes burned as he stroked one strong, brown hand across Ellie's downy hair.

"You told her we'll take good care of her, didn't you?

Would it help if I talked to her, too? Let her know that I feel the same way you do about raising Ellie? That she'll never want for anything. Especially not love?"

"I don't think that would make any difference, Sam."

"What do you mean, Mom?" Becca asked. "Don't you think Rachel will care about how Dad feels? I know Rachel's always been kind of shy around Dad. But she's like that with all guys—scared, you know. Not that it's any wonder. Her own dad blows up at her all the time."

"It's not that."

Sam scowled. "Then what is it? What are you saying?"

Hannah swallowed hard. "Rachel came back to the States because . . . she wants Ellie back."

"What the hell?" Sam choked out, stricken. He climbed to his feet, Ellie cradled close in his arms.

"She's taking Ellie back?" Becca cried. "But . . . but she can't do that, can she? The judge and that . . . that lawyer guy we saw at Antonio's—they gave Ellie to you. She can't just change her mind, can she?"

"She was under a lot of strain when she left the baby," Hannah tried to explain. "She's had time to think about it now. She realizes she made a mistake."

"No way." Sam shook his head, his arms tightening around Ellie. He shifted her, until she lay upright, her little cheek over his heart. "I'm sorry for Rachel. I am. I always liked the kid. But this isn't something you can . . . can just pretend never happened. What's she going to do with a baby? Her parents aren't likely to help her. She doesn't have any job skills. Hasn't finished school. And from what you said, the father doesn't want anything to do with her or the baby."

"That's right."

"So what's she plan to do?" Sam demanded, pacing

the tiny room. "Drag the kid back with her to campus? Stick Ellie in some college daycare program while she goes to class and works in some convenience store for minimum wage so she can buy diapers? Then she can take Ellie off and the two of them can live in poverty for the rest of their lives. Clothes from the Goodwill. Old shoes that don't fit. And at Christmas, Santa always somehow missing whatever hole in the wall they're living in."

Hannah fought to steady herself. It wasn't as if she didn't fear the same things. But uncertain as the future might be, it was for Rachel to decide. "Rachel will do everything she can for this baby."

"Well, that's not good enough!" Sam roared, startling a cry out of the baby curled against him. He stalked to the far corner of the room. Hannah saw his shoulders quiver. He turned back to her, his eyes on fire. "That's not good enough," he repeated. "Ellie is my daughter now. Mine. I won't let Rachel take her."

"Sam—"

"We'll fight this, Hannah. Surely the law will be on our side. We'll do whatever we have to do. Hire the best lawyers—" He stopped, stared at her, confused. She felt Becca's gaze on her as well, shocked at what she'd discovered about her friend, hurting and desperate as she saw how it was tearing her parents apart. If only Becca knew how much worse things could be.

"What . . . what is it?" Sam demanded. "You can't tell me you don't want to do whatever we have to to keep Ellie? I know how much this baby means to you."

"She means the world to me," Hannah confessed. "You know that. As for fighting for Ellie—I thought of that, too. Came up with a million reasons why she should belong to us, stay here, be our little girl."

"Then it's settled." Sam's jaw set like granite.

"No, Sam. We can't do it. Can't fight her."

"Why the hell not?"

"Rachel's just a baby herself. She got scared. Desperate. What if it had been Becca so scared and alone?"

"Becca would never do such a thing! She'd come to us! Wouldn't you, Becca?" Sam glared at Becca, demanding her agreement. Becca flushed, her gaze fluttering away. And Hannah knew that if Becca had ever been confronted with the situation Rachel had, it would've been hard for her to come forward as well. Hannah prayed Becca would have trusted her enough to ask for help in the end. But she knew the girl would have suffered in silence, alone and scared, before she had the courage to do so.

And if it would have been tough for Becca to be honest with Sam and Hannah, how impossible would it have seemed for Rachel to go to her own mom and dad? That was the danger Hannah had tried to caution Margo Johnson about so many times. When you reacted to a broken dish with the same intensity of fury you did to failing a class it taught kids to hide any mistake they made no matter what the cost. Made it impossible for them to turn to you. No matter what kind of trouble they were in, the thing they feared most of all was their parents' anger.

"Becca?" Sam demanded more stridently. Becca's flush deepened even more.

"I . . . I'd want to. I think I would . . ." she stammered, wanting to give him the answer he needed but trying hard to tell the truth. "But you're not anything like Rachel's mom and dad."

"Don't you see, Sam? Rachel didn't have parents who would support her no matter what. Try to understand."

"I'll *never* understand," he snarled. "How can you even think of letting her take Ellie back? You love this baby. So do I. We can give her everything she needs. Everything she wants. A home. Two parents to love her. A big sister and a yard to play in. Maybe Rachel *does* hurt like hell right now, missing her baby. But she'll get over it in time. She and Ellie will both be a hell of a lot better off in the end."

Hannah looked into his eyes, so stormy with rage and incredulity. So virulently determined it scared Hannah, made her wonder what he might say to the girl, might do. Her stomach churned, her hands trembled with terror and inevitability.

"I don't care what the excuse is," Sam said, and Hannah could see the effort it took him to crush the sympathy he felt for the girl. Sympathy that could cost him too much—the child he'd come to love.

"No decent mother would do what Rachel did." Sam glared into Hannah's face.

Hannah teetered on a blade edge of inevitability, terrified, wanting to scramble away from the precipice. There had to be another way, she thought desperately. Some way to ease Sam's fury, make him understand Rachel, without baring the truth that could only hurt him. A part of him was shattered already—that sensitive, deep hidden part of his spirit that had dared to love Ellie with all his heart. If she told him the truth, she'd kill a more vulnerable place still, lay waste to his love for *her.* Turn their marriage from a haven of love and trust into twenty-two years of lies.

"Tell me, damn it!" Sam demanded. "What kind of woman deserts her own baby?"

There was nothing left to do. Nothing left to say. Except the truth. Hannah's lungs burned. She dug her hands into the folds of her shirt to keep them from shaking.

"A woman like me," Hannah said hopelessly.

Sam's face crumpled in disgust. "Don't even try to excuse Rachel by claiming you might have done the same thing if you'd been backed against the wall that way, Hannah! All your life you've always been so damned sympathetic, putting yourself in everybody else's shoes. Well, sympathize with Rachel all you want, but don't even try to make me believe you'd ever desert your own baby. I don't believe it and neither does Becca. Nobody who knows you would, if they were in their right mind!"

"Dad's right, Mom. You never would."

Hannah hated the stark vulnerability in her daughter's eyes, the knowledge she was about to shake the foundations of everything Becca had always believed about her mother.

"Both of you, please. Just listen—"

"I said *don't*," Sam snapped. Becca jumped, startled, flashed eyes wide with alarm toward her father. "You won't do a damned thing except make me even madder than I already am."

"Don't?" Hannah gave a ragged laugh. "Don't what? Don't tell you the truth?"

"You never even dated before we met!" Sam scoffed. "Don't even try to make me believe—"

"I was seventeen," Hannah said dully. "There was a boy who . . . who'd just come to town."

Sam looked sick, like he wanted to retch, wanted to run. "I don't believe you!"

"Ohmigod!" Becca pressed her fingers to her lips. "That guy at Antonio's. That's why you didn't want me looking in your yearbook. You had a thing for him! But you didn't—you couldn't have had a baby. Not you."

Hannah sagged back into the porch swing, closed her eyes against the shock in Sam's eyes, the pain. "You thought I was so . . . so skittish with you because I'd never been with anybody before. I was scared because I *had,* and it had cost me so much. Turned my life upside down."

"I don't believe it," Sam denied, ashen-faced. "In all these years someone would have told me. *You* would have. You could never keep a secret. Besides, you lived here your whole life. A scandal like that—people would still gossip about it sometimes. I would've been bound to get wind of it."

"Nobody in Willowton ever knew. My parents sent me out to Oregon, to my aunt and uncle. I stayed with them until my baby was born."

"No," Becca whimpered, her face so pale, so wounded. "No, Mom."

"She was a little girl. So . . . so beautiful. With loads of dark hair and lashes so thick and black they made shadows on her cheeks. She had your nose, Becca, and my smile."

Sam had trusted her, Hannah thought in blind misery. And in one stroke she'd destroyed that trust more cruelly and completely than he could ever have imagined.

"What happened to her?" Becca asked tremulously. "Your . . . your baby?"

"I gave her up for adoption because my parents were pressuring me. I didn't know what else to do. When I realized what a terrible mistake I'd made, I tried to get her back, but it was too late. She'd gotten sick. The social worker told me it was her lungs." Hannah's voice dropped, low.

"Remember when you were little, Becca? And your asthma made it hard to breathe? You'd sit in the oxygen tent at the hospital and we'd make up stories about a magical cave all made of glass and the princess who was trapped inside it."

"But even though she was . . . was trapped, she had all kinds of adventures. Discovered a pirate's treasure. Made friends with a fierce dragon and went flying into the stars on his back."

Becca's eyes filled with tears. "I remember."

"That's how my . . . my little girl died. She couldn't breathe. They couldn't help her."

Sam turned away, and Hannah sensed his whole being pulsing with misery, hurt, betrayal.

"No wonder you were always so scared when I got sick," Becca said. "I remember the nurses would always tell you to go and . . . and get something to eat, or take a rest. Promised they'd watch me. But you'd never . . . never leave me."

"Becca?" Sam said. "Could you take Ellie? Leave your mother and me alone?"

Becca looked from one to the other, wary. "I don't . . . don't want to. I'm scared you'll—"

What? Hannah thought, heart squeezing in sympathy for her little girl. *Scared we'll talk? Say things we can never take back? That damage has already been done.*

"It's all right, sweetheart," she soothed. "Do what your daddy says. This has been a . . . a real shock to him."

"It's been a shock to me, too!" Becca burst out.

Hannah closed her eyes for a moment. "I know. But Daddy and I—we need to talk this out. Just the two of us. We'll come find you in a little bit."

Reluctantly, Becca gathered Ellie in her arms and trudged upstairs. Hannah could hear her crying. Silence fell over the sunny room. Deadly, sickening silence.

Hannah dreaded the moment Sam spoke.

"Who?" he demanded in a raspy voice. "Who did that to you? Got you pregnant? Tony Blake?"

Hannah wanted to close her eyes, block out the reactions streaking across Sam's features.

"All this time . . . the way he looked at you in the courtroom . . . the way he charged in playing hero . . . all this time, you both knew—"

"Sam, it was an accident. Complete coincidence. I never expected to see him again in my whole life. Never wanted to."

"God, I must have looked like a complete idiot. That bastard Blake—bet he had a hell of a good laugh after I was gone. Damned fool husband. Not a blasted clue what was going on."

"Sam—"

"You don't think I looked like an idiot? Hell, I was the only one who didn't know you two had slept together, conceived a child together. That Blake had known every inch of your body long before I even touched you."

"I was seventeen! I'd never even met you! It didn't mean anything—"

"If it didn't mean anything, then why didn't you just tell me about it?"

"Because I was afraid!" Hannah burst out. "Terrified! If you found out I'd given up my baby, I knew you'd never be able to forgive me! I needed you so much, Sam. Loved you so much. You'd started to . . . to trust me."

"*That* was a big mistake!"

A sob wrenched through Hannah. "You always thought I was perfect! I never said that I was! But now . . . how could I tell you that? I had to be perfect, completely flawless. One mistake, one scar, one little flaw and I was scared I'd break something inside you. That you'd shut that tiny window I'd managed to pry open, to slip into your heart."

"You're the one who lied to me!" Sam blazed. "Don't even try to turn this around, blame it on me."

"I'm not," Hannah exclaimed, then said more softly. "I'm not. I'm just trying to explain why I couldn't risk telling you the whole truth. Why I was so scared. Nobody's perfect, Sam. You're not perfect. Becca's not perfect. But then, I've never expected you to be. But I . . . I'm not perfect either. I'm just a woman, with fears and faults and secrets just like everyone else. That doesn't mean I don't love you!"

He turned his back on her, shoulders rigid, as if trying to wall her out. "Don't talk to me about love. You lied to me from the first day I met you."

"If I did, it was because I was terrified you couldn't love me. The real me. The me who makes mistakes, who doesn't always manage to do the right thing, even though I try. Please, Sam. Love me."

A ripple of emotion wracked his shoulders. Hannah watched him turn, walk away, complete destruction in his face.

She stared after him, her heart breaking. *Love me . . .* Her plea filled the silence. But he didn't even glance back.

She'd been right, all those years when she'd been so afraid. He loved a dream, a mirage, a perfect reflection in a mirror. Not the real Hannah he'd held in his arms.

Her secret was out.

She could never take it back.

She would never be "perfect" again.

21

WINDSHIELD WIPERS SWIPED drizzle from the window, the farm fields beyond seeming gray and dreary instead of bursting with new life. As long as she could remember, Hannah had been the one to point out the first tiny shoots of corn marching in green rows across the hills.

She'd point out new lambs and calves toddling after their mothers on wobbly legs. You couldn't love spring and not like rain, she'd explained when everyone else was grumbling about gray skies and chill drops that always seemed to slip beneath the collars of raincoats.

But today, Hannah's spirits were so dismal, the drumming of the rain raked at her nerves. Or maybe it wasn't the rain at all. Maybe it was the silence that filled the interior of the car—a stifling silence that felt so uncomfortable and strange because she'd never experienced it before. Not with Becca in the seat beside her.

One of Hannah's favorite things in the world had always been ferrying Becca here and there to school and to lessons, to friends' houses or the town nearby that was big enough to boast a mall. Becca had jokingly called it "mother-daughter bondage time," and Hannah had always laughed at the joke, but in a way it was true. Becca was held hostage for however long the trip took, and that was when some of their best talks had taken place.

That time, and bedtime, Hannah remembered with a twinge. Bedtime had always been her daughter's appointed time for asking impossible-to-answer questions about death and God and the meaning of the universe. Hannah had always wondered if Becca did it on purpose, figuring it was a better stalling technique than simply asking for a glass of water. Or had the child really been thinking such deep thoughts all day, and had only just figured out at bedtime how to put those questions into words?

She would have been grateful for one of those philosophical questions now. The questions that filled her daughter's eyes at the moment were far harder to answer, and more painful to consider.

She should be getting used to the silence, though, by now. The past two days had been as miserable as any she'd ever spent in her life.

Sam sleeping on the couch, not even trying to hide it from Becca. Becca looking as if she couldn't wait to get back to school and out of the line of fire. Not that Hannah could blame her. This break had been a disaster. First the upheaval over bringing Ellie into their family, then the trauma of tearing her out again. Worst still, finding out about the baby Hannah had had at seventeen, Becca discovering that her mother was guilty of something heinous years ago, that discovery changing everything.

It was one of the drawbacks of growing up, Hannah thought sadly. Facing the fact that your parents are only human.

She glanced over at Becca, mourning the dark circles under her daughter's eyes, the pensive curve to her mouth. Becca's good-bye to Sam had been tearful, and Hannah knew it had to have been one of the hardest things Sam had done, pretending to be "so busy with work" Hannah needed to drive Becca back to school alone. He'd claimed he'd figure construction bids at his office in the farmhouse. That way, he could watch Ellie as well.

He hadn't fooled Hannah for a minute. She knew he'd cleared his schedule the minute Becca agreed to let them take her back to college. Was the truth that he just didn't want to be alone in the car with Hannah on the ride home? Or was there another reason? In spite of all his hurt and anger and confusion, Sam still hadn't been able to help being chivalrous, offering Hannah the last few hours alone with their daughter?

Hannah wasn't sure if she should be grateful or furious. How did you explain to Becca what had happened between her parents? How could you reassure someone when you didn't have any idea what was going to happen next, if things could ever be healed again? How did you fill silence that seemed to press on your chest like a rock until you could barely breathe, let alone say the things you needed to say to reassure your little girl?

"You need to stop for anything?" Hannah asked, more to hammer at the barrier between them than ask the question. "Pop? A candy bar? Use the rest room?"

"No thanks. I'm fine."

Hannah grimaced. *Fine* was the one thing she was absolutely certain Becca was *not*. Silence started to fall again. She couldn't endure it.

"Becca, it's not going to go away if we don't talk about it."

Becca looked startled for a moment, flushed. "I didn't want to push you. There's a really pretty over-look right up ahead. The R.A.s took us there for a pic-nic during freshman orientation. Let's pull off for a minute. We won't be able to get out and stretch our legs, but it's still beautiful and quiet."

Hannah navigated the turn to the overlook Becca pointed out, then wound along the narrow gravel road. At the end, a stone barricade edged the broad plane of a bluff jutting out over a winding strip of river, a small town cradled in a hollow below. Roofs of every color sloped in every direction atop what looked like doll-houses, streets carving the town neatly into little square blocks. A church steeple pointed like a pale fin-ger against the gray sky.

Hannah put the car into park and turned off the engine, the windshield wipers stopping mid-swipe, rain pattering softly against the glass. The little town was everything she loved about Iowa—the warmth, the simplicity, the cherishing of family and tradition.

Most of the people had probably lived there forever, some still holding down farms their ancestors had won homesteading generations ago. It was the kind of place where everyone still met each other's eyes and said hello. Knew the names of not only the kids on their street, but the names of the dogs as well.

But warm and wonderful and seemingly safe as it was, people still made mistakes there, still had secrets, still grieved private losses. Still lost husbands they loved.

Hannah sighed, half turned toward Becca on the car seat. "I just want you to know how . . . how sorry I am that everything got so crazy. I wanted your break to be perfect."

"You want everything to be perfect. You practically make yourself sick trying to make it that way. No offense, Mom, but it's kind of silly. The best things aren't perfect at all."

Hannah shot her a quizzical glance. "What would cotton candy be like if it didn't stick to your fingers? And trees aren't nearly as pretty when they're all pruned and shaped like the ones kids draw in kindergarten—a big green lollipop with a straight brown trunk. The best trees are the twisty ones the wind has tangled all up, with knots where storms tore off limbs and places that are good for climbing."

"You're trying to make me feel better, baby."

"Maybe I'm just telling you the way it is. And I'm not a baby anymore, Mom. Even if I *was* acting like one."

"I know that."

"I was being a real spoiled brat. All judgmental about Rachel. I didn't even think about what she was going through. I've had lots of time to think the past few days, even when I didn't much want to."

Hannah looked into her daughter's face, saw something new there, unexpected. A sadder, wiser Becca where blind innocence had been. It hurt Hannah to see it. And yet, there was a new softness in her daughter's features as well, a kind of seriousness, a hint of compassion, as if she'd stumbled across something unexpected inside herself, as if it had deepened her to peer into other peoples' pain.

"I'm sorry, sweetheart. I know this has been tough on you."

"This isn't about me for once. This is about you, Mom."

Hannah swallowed hard. She hadn't realized how much her little girl had grown up. Becca had always been kindhearted, generous, but like most kids, the world had revolved around her—"crises according to Becca." Her understanding of people's pain and trouble, failings and triumphs limited by how they affected her life.

The Becca they'd left at college last fall would have been asking a hundred questions: *What'll happen if Dad moves out? Will I still get to see him? Where will I go for Christmas? Who gets to keep Reckless? When I get tickets for concerts at school, will you fight over who gets the best seats?*

This Becca was thinking about Hannah instead. It touched her, made her ache. She'd wanted to keep Becca safe a little longer, oblivious to grown-up hurts and disappointments and failures. She'd wanted Becca to be able to believe home would never change and her room would always be waiting for her, and if you tried your best, even if you failed, it was enough. But Becca had stumbled into the real world when Ellie came into their lives. And that day on the porch she'd plunged into reality so deep she'd never be completely oblivious to it again.

Becca plucked at a button on the front of her blouse. "Mom, do you remember when I used to get sick and you'd make me peppermint tea to settle my stomach?"

"I remember. But I can't say I can see what it has to do with anything right now."

Becca's eyes lit up, her mouth softened into a memory-filled smile. "You'd always put it in that little white teacup, the one your great-grandma brought over on the boat from Ireland. It was the only time anyone ever got to use it."

Hannah nodded, picturing a little Becca, pale and wan with whatever bug the kids had been passing around school. They'd tuck her up like a queen on the couch, pillows propping her up, a quilt bundled around her. Piles of books and games, crayons and coloring books littered the table. And flowers. Hannah had always filled a vase with flowers and put it where

Becca could see it, bright colors to remind her of how beautiful it would be outdoors when she could finally shed her nightgown and run off with the other girls.

Hannah couldn't count the number of times she'd fixed up the little white wooden tray for Becca—chicken noodle soup and soda crackers and the cup with peppermint tea. But the teacup and the tray had been tucked away for a very long time.

"You used to say the cup was magic," Hannah recalled.

"Well, it always made me feel better, just holding it in my hand. So I guess that's a kind of magic, don't you?"

"I suppose so."

"It had a chip in the rim, just a little one, from being jostled around so much. It crossed the ocean, and then made the journey on the trains and wagons and such to get all the way to Iowa. Lots of people would've thrown it away, called it 'broken,' but you don't even see the chip. You look right past it to see the little pink flower on the cup, the curve of the handle, the shape of the saucer. You see your great-grandma's hands holding it, cherishing it because it was like tasting home for her, the place she left with Great-grandpa the day after they were married."

Hannah smiled for the first time in two days, grateful that Becca had taken care to remember the family tales she'd tried to pass down to her. "And I thought you weren't paying attention all the times I told you that story."

"You love that cup, even though it isn't perfect. I just . . ." Becca hesitated. "Don't give up on Daddy, Mom. He just might surprise you."

"This isn't your father's fault. I'm the one who kept secrets. I didn't tell him—"

"Gee, after the way he acted when you finally *did*

tell him, I wonder why." Becca attempted to make a comical face.

Hannah chuckled.

"There, see!" Becca exclaimed. "You know it's true!"

Hannah shook her head in denial. "That's not why I laughed at all. I just haven't seen you make that face since you were about twelve."

"I'm not twelve anymore." Becca sobered. "And you aren't seventeen. Mom, do you *really* think you did something so terrible by giving up your baby?"

"Your daddy does. He's never gotten over the hurt from his mother leaving him."

"He was eight years old! It's a little bit different. Your baby never even would have remembered you. She would've had parents who adored her. A whole different life with a house and a backyard with a dog in it. Wasn't that what you were trying to give her when you offered her up for adoption?"

"I *think* so. I *hope* so. Hope I wasn't just scared and trying to run away from the trouble I'd gotten into. But I don't think your dad believes there is any good excuse for what I did."

"Well, Dad's never been pregnant and scared. I want to know what *you* think."

Hannah stared at her, astonished. What *did* she think about what had happened so many years ago? Now that she was older, wiser, had seen more of life? Had she been selfish or self*less*, giving up her baby? Was she a terrible person or had she just gotten caught in a painful trap, left with no good way to get out? Had she been wicked to make love with Tony? Or had she just been a naïve kid who'd bought the Romeo and Juliet myth hook, line and sinker and paid the price for it?

"Mom, you weren't the only girl in your class that got all crazy because of a boy that year, were you?"

"I suppose not." No, the hot romance between shy Hannah and the hunk of the month had been a major topic of gossip at Willowton High. But they hadn't been the *only* couple that set the cafeteria buzzing. The whole school had been filled with kids scrambling to get dates for the football games or the prom or senior skip day. The insides of the stalls in the girl's bathrooms had been full of graffiti. *Joanie loves Mitch. Scott and Sandy 4-ever. And hadn't there been about a half dozen girls claiming eternal passion for one of the starters on the football team?*

"You'd better believe plenty of those girls were steaming up car windows in some dark alley somewhere."

"Rebekah!" Hannah cried out, chagrined.

"Well, it's true! You just *think* you were the only one. You weren't. Guess I got to thinking about it when I couldn't sleep last night. Some of those girls just got lucky, plain and simple, and never got pregnant. Some were more street wise and used protection. Some got caught big time, and ran to some clinic or hid their pregnancies like you. But getting pregnant doesn't have anything to do with what kind of people they were. Good, bad, slutty or just believing in that whole Prince Charming thing."

"I guess I hadn't thought about it that way."

"I'm just saying that if it could happen to you and Rachel, it could happen to anybody. And that Rachel's getting pregnant doesn't make her a slut any more than *not* turning up pregnant makes a bitch queen a 'nice girl.' Rachel's still worth a hundred girls like that, baby or no baby." Becca's cheeks glowed with righteous indignation. "And so are you."

Hannah bit her bottom lip to keep it from trembling. Love for Becca filled her up inside, shoving back the hollow feeling of terror, the fear that she'd lost not only

Sam's love, but Becca's as well. "I was so . . . so scared you would hate me when you found out."

Becca hugged her, smiled. "Give me a little bit of credit, will you?" Then Becca drew away, her heart in her eyes. "How could I hate you, Mom? You're the one who taught me everything I know about love."

"Oh, Becca—" Hannah choked out, trying to find the words to tell her little girl just how much she loved her.

"You taught Daddy, too," she said. "Just give him a chance to remember."

"But if I'd never insisted on taking in Ellie, if I hadn't pushed so hard, wanted her so much—everything would still be fine. I wouldn't have hurt you. Broken your father's heart."

"If you hadn't taken Ellie in and loved her you wouldn't be *you*. I'm glad you did it, Mom. You remember when you first told me about finding Ellie, that she probably belonged to one of my friends?"

"I remember."

Eyes downcast, Becca shrugged in shame. "I wasn't thinking about how terrible whoever it was must feel. I wasn't thinking about what it would feel like to have a baby all by yourself or what it would be like to leave your baby in a basket and hope someone would take her in. I wasn't wondering what I could do to help my friend. I was just mad someone I knew would do such a thing, make me uncomfortable. I wanted to know who she was so I wouldn't have to talk to her again. So I could pretend I hadn't ever really liked her anyway." She winced, and Hannah could sense how scared Becca was, admitting her dark side to Hannah and herself. "I was just thinking about myself, not about Ellie or her mom or you."

Hannah wanted to comfort her, sooth the lines of

self-disgust from her forehead, ease the guilt that had obviously been gnawing inside Becca. "It's only natural to think about how things are going to affect us. And nobody likes change. Besides, you spend so much of your teenage years sure that you're bulletproof, immortal, that nothing bad can touch you or any of your friends—it's a nasty shock when you find out it's not true."

"Guess I know that now. Maybe I won't be so quick to judge other people until I know the whole story. I just want you to know I went over to see Rachel before I left. I told her—she's my friend, you know. I'll do whatever I can to help her. Remember when we were in sixth grade and for Mother's Day we made six 'get out of chore free' coupons for you? I gave her baby-sitting coupons. An unlimited supply."

Hannah's heart warmed, ached at the new wisdom, the deeper compassion in her daughter's eyes. "That kindness will mean everything to Rachel in the future."

Becca shrugged. "She's talking about transferring. It'd be too hard for her to be around the kids in concert orchestra—see them doing all kinds of cool stuff, knowing she could've been first chair but now, well, she can't be in the top orchestra at all. You can't go on tour if you've got a baby."

No, Hannah thought sadly. Rachel wouldn't be traveling anymore. She'd have to adjust her dreams now, widen the circle of her heart to include little Eleanor Rose. Hannah couldn't help wondering how Rachel would feel about the decision she'd made twenty-seven years from now.

Would she be glad she'd decided to take Ellie back into her life? Or would some part of her always wonder what it would have been like to study violin in Vienna? Maybe the truth was that there was no perfect answer when you were faced with a choice like that. But wasn't that one of the hard truths of anybody's life? That you had to choose one path or another. And once you did, the other path vanished? You could never find your way to it again.

"If she comes to my school, maybe I can baby-sit Ellie sometimes," Becca said. "Do you think Rachel would like that?"

Hannah smiled around the lump in her throat. "I'm proud of you, Becca. Rachel is going to need friends more than ever now."

Becca's eyes brightened with tears. "You didn't have them when you had your baby. You didn't have anyone."

"I could have told Josie any time over the years, but I chose not to. I was so ashamed. I couldn't even tell my grandma. Mom and Dad convinced me that she'd never look at me the same way again."

The enormity of it seemed to penetrate Becca. Fill her with visions of what it would be like if even the grandmother you adored might turn her back on you. "How do you think she would have felt?"

"Sad, probably. She'd know that a baby would make things so much harder for me, whether I decided to keep my little girl or not. But I don't think my grandma would have shut me out. She'd have loved me no matter what. I was just too scared to tell her."

"Like you're scared about Daddy now?" Becca asked.

"Yeah. Like I'm scared about your father now."

"Don't give up on him, Mom. He adores you."

But he's always thought I was perfect, Hannah thought, hugging her daughter tight.

And now, he knows I'm not.

Hannah felt Becca's warmth, the love of her little

girl. No, not a little girl any longer. Maybe Becca was right. Sam had had a nasty shock, finding out Hannah's secret that way, realizing that the big city lawyer he'd hated on sight had fathered a child with her.

And as if that wasn't miserable enough, he'd had to face the pain of giving up baby Ellie.

Time. Maybe all Sam needed was a little time to sort things through. Maybe he'd find a way to forgive her if she told him—told him how hard it was to sleep in their bed without him. Told him how he'd changed her life when he'd fallen in love with her so long ago, taught her to love the way he could make her body feel when he touched her—like she was beautiful, clean again, something to cherish instead of just thrown away.

When she got home, she'd tell him just how much she'd always loved him.

How he'd changed her life, given her the courage to hope for things she'd been certain she'd lost forever during those lonely months in the rain-swept Oregon hills.

A husband who could love her forever, a baby she'd never have to let go.

A home filled with laughter and warmth, love and tears, with someone who'd reach out to hold her when she cried. Even if he didn't know who her tears were for.

Tears for the child she'd given up long before she'd lost herself in Sam O'Connell's star-blue eyes.

Tears for the Hannah who could have run into his arms without any shadows or doubts, without any guilt or fear.

The Hannah she might have been.

Twilight veiled the night in soft lavender, a few brash stars winking here and there in the sky. The rain had finally surrendered about an hour from home. Hannah hoped it would turn out to be a good omen. She'd spent most of the return trip composing speeches, figuring out just what she needed to say to Sam when she got back to the farmhouse. Even the weariness and stiff muscles from the nearly seven hour round-trip drive hadn't been able to dampen her determination to get it right this time.

There were plenty of tangles to face when she got home. Tangles as she tried to regain Sam's trust. Snags in returning Ellie to Rachel. Hannah wasn't naïve—she knew perfectly well she couldn't just hand the baby back to her mother. They'd need lawyers and court hearings and God knew what other hoops they'd have to jump through.

And, no matter how filled with regret Rachel was now, there was still no avoiding the fact that she'd left a baby alone in the backyard. Anything could have happened to Ellie: a stray dog could have mauled her, Hannah could have been away for the afternoon, failed to find Ellie until she was dehydrated. Rachel was over eighteen. An adult in the eyes of the court. How could the judge and police, the lawyers and social workers be made to understand how *young* Rachel was? How vulnerable? That you couldn't define "adult" by some arbitrary number of birthdays? Hannah had known kids who could've lived quite successfully on their own at fifteen, no problem. She'd known other kids who were still stumbling around blindly at twenty-four.

One thing she was certain of: she and Sam would be Rachel's only advocates in this. Margo and Hank Johnson would be little help to the girl, at least for now. Hank was hard-line, with a quick fuse, impatient with anything he saw as weakness. And Margo had never understood her shy, fragile, dreamer of a daughter. Even if she had, it would take time for anyone to adjust to the news that her teenage daughter had had a baby in secret, and you'd never suspected a thing. Maybe Rachel's troubles would stir up some strength in Margo, some protectiveness of her daughter. Maybe working through things with the baby would somehow set them both on the road to an understanding they'd never had. But that would take time. And time was the one thing Rachel didn't have.

She was in trouble and needed help now. One of the things Hannah had always loved best about Sam was his determination to offer the underdog a helping hand. And God knew, Rachel was definitely in need of support. Maybe his desire to help Rachel would help melt his fury toward Hannah. Maybe if they had to work together he'd see how sorry Hannah was for hurting him, how very much she loved him. Maybe he could even start to trust her again, just a little.

Becca seemed to have faith that everything would turn out for the best, Hannah thought with a surge of hope. She was sure that Sam would fight his way through his anger and sense of betrayal. Hannah knew one thing for certain. She was going to do everything in her power to convince him to try.

She loved him.

Not with that fresh hot flare of infatuation she'd felt at nineteen that people raved about. Raging hormones, racing pulses, hands so restless and hungry they had to devour every curve and plane of his body. What she felt for Sam was miles deeper, mountains stronger, a love so deep it was as if her spirit and Sam's had joined together in a single river, flowed through the years together, until she couldn't tell where he ended and she began.

How had they lost that closeness during the months of their estrangement? Why had she felt compelled to pull back? Turn away? Hide her tender, vulnerable places from him in spite of the fact that she needed him more than ever. His touch to make her feel whole, the admiring light in his eyes to make her feel beautiful, the cocky edge to his grin that made him look so young and handsome and happy. Happy, with a joy Hannah held even more precious because Sam made certain she knew that she was the one who had brought that emotion back into his life.

What had made her pull away? Her illness and pain? Not wanting him to see her that way—weak and pale, unable to respond to his touch no matter how much she loved him, no matter how much she wanted to give him the physical loving he'd needed? She'd despaired so deeply inside when her body wouldn't obey her, wouldn't be coaxed by him, wouldn't respond.

She'd been ashamed. Afraid of what he would think of her. Maybe she was the one who hadn't trusted *him* enough to tell him the truth about what was happening, not only to her body, but her spirit every time she failed him in their bed.

Afraid to tell him anything at all, because if she did she might have to delve deeper, to the source of her pain, her confusion, the baby she'd had as a scared teenage girl, the guilt she'd felt about giving her baby up. The blame she'd layered on herself when she'd gone back to reclaim her child, discovering that her baby had died. And the fear that she was being punished for what she'd done, keeping her child a secret. That the price fate demanded was a cradle empty after Becca, a womb that wouldn't shelter another child, hopes for a big family that wouldn't be realized.

The surgery, the hysterectomy had ended any last, faint bit of hope she had managed to cling to, bringing all those memories, all those feelings, the guilt, the grief, the loss flooding back, sharper than ever before.

She turned and glimpsed the Johnson house to her left, wondered if Rachel had worked up the courage to tell her parents about her baby. Wondered how Hank and Margo were taking the news. Hannah knew one thing for certain—the scene with Rachel's father would be plenty ugly. Maybe if she and Sam went over with Rachel, kept things from getting too far out of control . . .

Angry as Sam was with Hannah, surely he'd be willing to do that. He'd had more than his share of ugly scenes with his own father during the years old Mr. O'Connell had been drinking. Hannah shuddered. But had any of those scenes been as painful as the one between her and Sam two days before? Could anyone have hurt Sam more deeply? Broken faith with him more completely? Not just keeping secrets about the past, but ushering them under Sam's very roof?

Hannah pulled up in front of the farmhouse, heart hammering. One thing Sam O'Connell had never been good at was hiding his feelings. At least she'd have some idea exactly what she was facing the moment she got inside the house and took one good look at his face.

Hannah grabbed her purse and swung her legs out of the car, then made her way up the sidewalk. She opened the door, rehearsing what she was going to say. "Sam?" she called out as she entered the kitchen and shut the door behind her. "Sam, where are you?"

She heard footsteps coming toward the kitchen. Oddly light, soft ones rather than the clumping sounds of Sam's work boots.

"Hannah?" Josie's voice. Tentative. Filled with sympathy. Hannah's stomach curled in on itself, tight with dread.

"Josie—" Hannah fought to keep her voice steady as

her friend rounded the corner and entered the room, baby Ellie cradled in her arms. "Where's Sam?"

Josie couldn't meet her eyes. Her voice quavered. "I'm so . . . so sorry, Hannah."

"About what?" Hannah demanded, alarmed. "Where's Sam?"

"He called me this morning. Asked if I could come over here, look after Ellie. He had some things he had to take care of. I just thought he—I mean, I only wanted to help. I didn't know what he was going to do."

Hannah tried to suck in a deep breath, couldn't. "Josie, do what? Tell me!"

Stricken eyes met hers at last. "He's gone, Hannah."

Tears seared Hannah's eyes, her nails digging deep into the soft skin of her palms. "No! No, Sam wouldn't—"

"He left a letter. Said he needed time to think. When he left he was . . . was carrying a suitcase. My God, Hannah! What happened between you two?"

Hannah clamped her hand over her mouth, trying not to retch, trying not to scream. The words raged on, echoing inside her again and again. *He's gone . . .*

She barely felt Josie's hand on her arm, guiding her to a chair. Hannah sank down so woodenly she doubted she would have noticed if she'd sat down on broken glass.

"Hannah?" Josie prodded. "I know you two have been having some problems, but—separating? Nobody in the world would have been able to make me believe that would ever happen to you guys."

"I just hope it's only temporary. That he doesn't want it forever."

"No way, Hannah! He adores you! I wish Tom thought I was half as perfect as Sam thinks you are! You should hear him talk about you! You both might as well still be nineteen and crazy in love, the way he goes on about you!"

Hannah leaned her head back, the ceiling swimming before her tear-filled eyes. "He hasn't changed. I'm the one who . . . who made a mess of things."

"You?" Josie gasped. "Come on, Hannah! You've never done anything in your life that could make Sam want to leave you."

"You're wrong. I was wrong. I don't know how to fix it." She told Josie all that had happened, saw her friend's face change like quicksilver, from shock to sympathy.

"And all this time, you've been living with this guilt alone?" Josie mourned. "And as if things weren't hard enough, I dragged Tony Blake back into your life. I'm sorry. So sorry."

"How could you have known? It was my choice not to tell Sam. And in the end, it was my choice to finally tell him the truth. Why we had to give Ellie's mother a second chance. Even if Tony had never set foot in Willowton, I would have had to tell Sam what I'd done."

"But Tony Blake—I know he made it worse! Why did he have to come back here?"

"His mother—"

"He hasn't given a damn about her since I came to Willowton eleven years ago. Forgive me if I don't buy the devoted son routine."

"Everyone has regrets, Josie. Maybe he finally realized his mom won't be here forever, that she needed him. Or maybe he'd finally grown up enough to realize what it was like for me when he deserted me and the baby. Maybe part of him wanted to say he was sorry, make sure I was all right. Or maybe he wanted to find out about his daughter."

"Nowhere in sight when he could've actually made himself useful, but once the hard decisions are made, the tough work is finished, then he appears like magic to make everyone feel sorry for him."

"Tony used to be pretty self-centered, I admit that. But he did try to help with Ellie."

"From the sound of things he did plenty more than that." Josie raged. "He should've handed the case off to someone else when I asked him to help. Made his excuses. Shouldn't it have occurred to the jerk that you wouldn't want to relive the hell he put you through? And as for Sam—the man thinks you're an angel. Did Tony expect Sam to welcome him with open arms?"

"There's no reason Tony would expect to meet Sam at all!" Hannah protested. "Tony came to Willowton to take care of his mother. That doesn't mean it had anything at all to do with me."

"Yeah, well, I guess you'll find out exactly how deep Tony Blake is in all this misery soon enough, now that Sam is gone."

Hannah flinched, remembering the unsettling tenderness in Tony's eyes, the self-deprecating jokes about how he should have married her when he had the chance. Things that had fed her uncertainty about Sam even just a little. Now the whole thing made her feel sick to her stomach. "Oh, Josie. What am I going to do?"

"I don't know."

"The letter—where is it?"

"On your bed. Do you want me to come with you?"

"No. Just wait here. Please . . . wait." Numbly Hannah made her way up to the bedroom. She winced as she saw the white pages filled by Sam's bold scrawl. She picked them up, sank down on the bed and read:

Dear Hannah,
      Contacted a lawyer for Rachel—

Hannah stopped, read the words again, her heart squeezing. A lawyer for Rachel? That was the last thing she'd have expected Sam to be worrying about right now, angry and disillusioned as he must be. His kindness made her ache to throw her arms around him, tell him how special he was. She blinked tears from her eyes and read on.

Tom says she's going to need a good lawyer if she's to have any hope of getting custody of Ellie. She'll have to prove fitness as a parent, take parenting classes under the supervision of social services. Worst of all, she's going to have to face charges of child endangerment since she did leave Ellie unattended. The lawyer said there's no guarantee which way the court will end up ruling, but that our support of her case might help. I've talked to Rachel, told her she was welcome to move into the farmhouse for the time being, so she can be with her baby while she's going through all this. It'll be good for her and she'll be some company for you. I hate to think of you in the house alone.

I have to get away for a while. Think. If you need me, I'll be staying at the office. Take care of yourself and Rachel and Ellie. I want you to know I'm keeping in touch with Becca. She must be so confused right now. When the time is right, I'll let you know what I've figured out.

                                                                              Sam

Hannah stared at his signature, the first time since they started dating he hadn't written "love" in front of his name. The letter was warm, caring, full of help and compassion for Rachel and little Ellie. It was kind to Hannah, too. More than she had a right to hope for after the way she'd hurt him. Far less than she'd needed—reassurance that he still loved her, planned to come back to her once his pain had dulled with time.

She heard Reckless bark, then moments later, floorboards creak, someone mounting the stairs.

"Josie?" Hannah croaked, her throat hoarse with pain.

"No," a small voice said. "She's still downstairs. It's me. Rachel."

The girl wandered into the opening of the door, hesitated there for a long moment, her face white and strained, her eyes red and swollen. Thin hands clutched the brand new suitcase her parents had gotten her last year for graduation. Hannah winced. A bright airline tag with words in German was still fastened around the suitcase's handle.

"Mr. O'Connell said it was okay for me to stay here for a while," Rachel explained, fidgeting with the suitcase handle as if she were half-afraid Hannah would turn her away.

She gave the girl a big hug. Rachel felt so small and fragile, like a bird battered by a raging storm. For just an instant, Rachel melted into Hannah's arms with a tiny sigh, as if she had suddenly found safe harbor. Fierce protectiveness surged through Hannah, and she tightened her arms around Rachel for a moment longer, felt unexpected tears push at the backs of her eyes. It would probably do them both good to have a nice long cry, release at least some of the crushing tension they'd been suffering. But if Hannah indulged in tears herself, Rachel was certain to wonder why. Not that Hannah could avoid the inevitable. When Sam didn't come home, Rachel would know something was wrong. And if she discovered the rift between Hannah and Sam, Rachel would be sure to lay the blame squarely on her own fragile shoulders. There was no way in the world Hannah was going to burden the poor girl with any more guilt.

Hannah patted Rachel gently on the back three times, then with a parting squeeze, let her go.

"You know, from the time you were little, I always wished I could scoop you up and keep you here with me. This is your home for as long as you want to stay. Becca's room is empty. You can stay there. Or we could move a bed into the nursery if you'd rather, so you can be closer to Ellie."

Rachel sniffled, eyes stark in her ashen face. "Thank you. I'd like to be able to . . . to stay with Ellie. Ever since I left her, I keep waking up in the middle of the night, thinking I hear her crying. Now I'll be able to peek into her cradle, and know she's all right."

Hannah remembered all too well that sinking, suffocating feeling—hearing your baby cry, waking up to find your arms empty, your heart torn. What would it have been like if she could have had the same opportunity Rachel would—to hold her little girl again? Know her tiny daughter was safe, loved? That no one could ever take her away? But there were no guarantees yet that Rachel would find a happy ending. There were far too many barriers she'd have to cross before Ellie was forever safe in her arms.

Still, the one thing Rachel did have was hope. Hope and the freedom to gather Ellie close whenever she wanted, kiss her downy little head, explain to the baby how much her mama had missed her while she'd been gone. That not a day had passed without loving her. Heartbroken and guilt-stricken, miserable and neck deep in trouble as Rachel was, for a moment, Hannah envied her.

Rachel dragged her suitcase inside, her gaze roaming around the familiar room with the aura of a child running fingers over the folds of a beloved security blanket, quietly comforting herself, catching her breath, trying to assure herself that the worst was over.

"I don't know where I would have gone if Mr. O'Connell hadn't come through," she confessed. "My dad was . . . is . . . um, madder than I've ever seen him before. And my mom—" Rachel's voice broke, and she fought hard to steady it. "Mom was even worse. She cried. I'd never seen her cry before."

Painful as that was, it gave Hannah hope for the future. That Margo would wade through her own hurt and humiliation and come to understand the depth of her daughter's pain.

"They'll get over it. Give them time." Hannah prayed "time" had even half the healing power she kept trying to convince herself it did.

Tears welled in Rachel's eyes, rolled down her cheeks. "Dad would have hit me if Mom and Mr. O'Connell hadn't stopped him."

Hannah stared at her, stunned. "Sam—Sam was at your house?"

"I kept trying to get up the nerve to talk to my parents alone, tell them about Ellie. He saw me out in my yard and stopped to tell me about the lawyer he got for me. I hadn't been able to tell Mom and Dad yet. He asked if I wanted him to come with me."

Hannah closed her eyes. She could imagine what Sam's offer had meant to Rachel. What it would have meant to Hannah herself to have Sam's strength to lean on during that fateful day so many years ago when she'd gone into her father's den and faced her own parents alone.

"I'm in a lot of trouble." She picked at the bright red

luggage tag, daunted. "But he said that both of you would try to help me. I wish there was something I could do to help you, too."

"Help us? We're doing just fine. You're not to worry about anything except yourself and that beautiful baby girl of yours." Hannah forced an encouraging smile. She hadn't fooled Rachel for a moment.

The girl's too-sensitive mouth twisted in misery. "I saw the suitcase in Mr. O'Connell's car. Is he leaving because of me?"

"Because of you?" Hannah flinched, the image of that suitcase in Sam's car unbearably painful. Sam, hurting so badly he couldn't even stand to be in the same house with her, talk to her, try to work things out.

"Because I'm trying to take Ellie back, and he already loves her? Because he can't stand to be in the house with me?"

"No."

Rachel stared at her, disbelieving. The girl had enough real guilt to deal with, Hannah thought. She didn't need to carry any that didn't belong to her.

"Sam and I have . . . have some things we need to work out. Problems that are just between the two of us. Things that have nothing at all to do with you. He needs some time away from me." Hannah was surprised at how much the admission hurt.

Rachel peered at her, wide-eyed. "I always thought you were—you seemed so perfect for each other. I'm sorry."

"I am, too," Hannah said.

"He looked so . . . so strange when he left," Rachel said. "Where is he going?"

"He's staying at his office for now."

Hannah looked out the window. He'd worked so

hard to get everything in place here—lawyers and living accommodations. Company for her and classes for Rachel to attend. He'd spelled out everything so carefully in his letter. Everything except what mattered to Hannah most. Was he ever coming back?

She'd gone through the motions, sent a worried Josie back home to her baby and the husband whose love she didn't doubt. She settled Rachel in Ellie's nursery, let the girl take over the nightly baby chores Hannah had found so precious. There was nothing more for Hannah to do. Becca was gone, Sam gone, Ellie belonged to someone else. She paced the floor, hands idle, heart aching until she couldn't avoid going to bed any longer.

Her throat burned as she finally closed the bedroom door behind her. Hannah spread her fingers upon the quilt that had covered them both again for those few precious nights.

She cried inside, picturing his eyes, the stubborn angle of his jaw, his hands, callused and deft from years of hard work, tender and sensitive from old heartaches and new joys.

Come home, Sam, she pleaded inside. *Please let me know everything is going to be all right.*

But the room was silent, the night empty. Hannah hugged Sam's pillow tight, burying her face against its softness so she could breathe in his scent, stifle her tears, pray that he would come back to her, and that someday, somehow, she'd see what she longed for more than anything in the world—forgiveness in Sam's sky-blue eyes.

22

HANNAH PACED THE KITCHEN, her stomach in knots, her nerves wound so tight she feared they'd snap every time the phone rang. She'd nearly dropped the kitchen phone into Reckless's water bowl in her haste to answer it early that morning, and twice this afternoon she'd knocked the phone off the old-fashioned child's desk it sat on in the living room.

Three people had wanted to side the farmhouse, another had wanted to scrub her carpet for free if she'd just let them demonstrate their fancy new vacuum cleaner. Becca had called twice and Margo Johnson once. Rachel's mother had been shattered, angry, hurt, looking for someone to blame. She'd demanded to know why Hannah hadn't told her about Rachel the moment she'd found out the truth. Then, Margo had broken down in tears, wanting to know why Rachel hadn't come to her, while at the same time, saying it was best if Rachel didn't come home because of her father.

Hannah had felt sorry for Margo, hoped that somehow the woman would rise to the occasion this time, be able to help her daughter. And yet, it wasn't Hannah's fault Rachel hadn't gone straight to her mother. Margo Johnson had closed the doors between Rachel and herself long before Hannah had found little Ellie in the basket. All Hannah could do was be there for both Margo and Rachel, help them however she could.

But the most disturbing phone call by far had come twenty minutes ago—Tony Blake announcing that he was on his way to the farmhouse. He had something vital to tell her.

Hannah poured herself a glass of water and swallowed it in a long gulp. She didn't think she could handle any more bad news at the moment. She'd tried to put Tony off, stall him for however long she could. But a word or two about legal problems and Rachel being in deep trouble had been enough to get Hannah to cave.

Tony was the last person she wanted to see at the moment, considering the shape she was in. But he'd promised to help. Hannah owed it to Rachel to at least go through the motions. She didn't want to antagonize one of the people they'd need on their side if Rachel was to regain custody of her little girl.

Hannah packed a ham sandwich for Rachel and bottles and sun block for Ellie, then sent the two of them off to the park saying she wanted the house quiet when Tony arrived. Rachel didn't need to hear some of the things Tony might have to say. The poor girl already blamed herself too much as it was for all that had happened.

Too restless to stay indoors where every tabletop or expanse of wall seemed to hold pictures of Sam and Becca and her in happier times, Hannah strayed out into the front yard in an effort to calm her jangling nerves before Tony arrived. She pulled a few weeds from the bed where roses were loosing their lush perfume into the air, then strayed to the roses that were putting on a show.

She leaned close to fronds of hot pink roses climbing in blossom-heavy tangles up the sides of the white painted arbor. "Sometimes I wish you could just wall the whole place in," she said to the flowers. "Like the brambles in the fairy tale *Briar Rose*. Sam would be sure to come home then, fight his way through to me. He never could resist a damsel in distress. Look what he's done for Rachel—"

Hannah pressed her fingers against her chest, touching the place where Sam's selflessness made her ache. She heard Tony's car pull to a stop, the car door slam. Resigned that there was no way she was going to get out of this meeting, she straightened and squared her shoulders.

"Still talking to flowers, Hannah?" Tony observed, the lightness of his words belied by the deep lines etched in his forehead. "You know, even back in high school I never saw you go outside when you didn't say something to at least one bush or tree or flower. I can imagine you've got plenty to say right now."

Hannah didn't like the probing light in his eyes, as if he intended to pry the truth from her, whether she wanted to confide in him or not. "I don't understand," she tried to demur.

"You look like you haven't slept in three days. Of course, I can't say as I blame you, all things considered. You've got quite a mess on your hands."

"Things are a little complicated at the moment, but they'll get straightened out again." Hannah gave a dismissive shrug.

But Tony didn't seem as willing to let her off the hook so easily. "The judge wasn't amused when the Johnson girl's mother reported her daughter was staying at your house. The cops are wondering why you didn't call them the moment you realized who'd left the baby in your backyard. And I'm trying to figure out just why your husband thought he needed to hire another lawyer."

"It's hard to explain." Hannah felt like dropping from exhaustion just thinking of how tangled everything had gotten.

"I've got nothing but time," Tony said. "I cleared the rest of the afternoon and dumped my whole schedule until tomorrow so I can help you, Hannah. I'm not going anywhere until you and I get this disaster with Rachel figured out."

Terrific, Hannah thought grimly. What could be more miserable than having Tony hovering around at the moment? She tried to find a polite way of telling him she'd rather he head back to the office and pick up his busy schedule right where he'd left off. "Tony, I—"

Tony raised one hand in protest, as if he knew exactly what she was going to say. "Listen to me, Hannah! I'm not blind and I'm not stupid. Obviously this whole thing just blew up in your face. The girl coming back, demanding her kid. Sam diving into the situation, head first, stirring everything up with the courts. I've got to tell you, he didn't do you any favors."

Irritation nipped at Hannah. "This isn't about me anymore."

Tony swore. "It's not about you? You're the only one I care about in this whole damned mess. You and what's best for that little girl. I know how much you love Ellie, Hannah. I've seen the way you look at her.

And there's no way in hell I'm handing her over to someone else just because Sam O'Connell doesn't want to be bothered by two A.M. feedings. How irresponsible does O'Connell think I am? Does he really think I'd help give Ellie to some scatterbrained kid who can barely wipe her own nose let alone take care of the needs of a baby? No way!"

"Tony—"

"Rachel Johnson abandoned her baby," Tony insisted, his face rock hard, unyielding. "There's positively no excuse for what she did."

Hannah bristled instinctively, the days of strain scraping her nerves raw. "Oh, I understand now. There's no excuse for the girl to panic and run away from the situation. But the boy who got her pregnant—he can do whatever he wants. Turn his back, walk away, and pretend as if nothing's happened."

Tony stared, taken aback by the edge of bitterness in her voice. After a moment, he grimaced. "Point taken. But even if that's true, there is still something that you need to know. For your own protection, Hannah. And for Ellie's."

"And what is that?" Hannah said wearily, hoping maybe once Tony said whatever he was so determined to say, she'd be able to convince him to leave.

"You remember what I said about Sam? That he didn't want the baby?" Tony said eagerly. "Hannah, Sam is doing everything in his power to make sure the court takes that baby out of your home for good. He hired a lawyer for the girl, entered a statement on her behalf. I'm betting he didn't bother mentioning that to you."

Hannah swallowed hard, amazed again at Sam's generosity of spirit. She knew just how much it had cost him to give the courts the very things they would need to whisk Ellie out of his life.

"Hannah, you can't let O'Connell do this to you—take your baby away," Tony insisted.

"As a matter of fact, I'm the one who decided Ellie's mother deserved a second chance if she wanted one," Hannah revealed. "Sam . . . Sam didn't want to give Ellie up at first. But once I told him exactly what it feels like to be scared and pregnant and all alone, he changed his mind."

"Told him?" Tony choked out, stunned. "You told him—"

"Everything." If she lived a thousand years, Hannah knew she'd never forget the pain those revelations had caused Sam. Dealing wounds that would never heal, crushing his image of her, everything he'd believed about her, about the two of them together. Once broken, there was no way to put those pieces together again.

"My God, Hannah!" A light sparked in Tony's eyes. "You told him! About us—you and me. About our baby? No wonder O'Connell was lashing out, then! But you said if he ever found out, he'd never forgive you."

"I don't know if he will," Hannah admitted.

"Then why did you—" Tony stopped. He caught Hannah's hands, held them fast even when she made a halfhearted effort to tug them away. "Hannah, I know this is hard for you, but it will be better in the long run, O'Connell knowing the truth. I'll need to talk to both of you—as Ellie's guardian ad litem. When will O'Connell be back?" Was it Hannah's imagination, or did Tony almost look as if he were looking forward to it?

Hannah flushed, looked down at her hands. She tugged more insistently until Tony let her go. "I don't know when Sam will be back."

"I can wait. He'll have to come home eventually."

Hannah squirmed inwardly, trapped. "I haven't seen him since I took Becca back to school yesterday morning."

"What? You mean O'Connell didn't spend last night here with you?"

Hannah's cheeks burned, her stomach clenching. "It was a shock to him—finding out about what I'd done. He just couldn't face—"

"You mean the bastard left you? Alone? And you so broken up over losing little Ellie?"

"No!" Hannah bit out hastily. "He just—he needs a little time to sort things through."

"Then he's a damned fool!" Tony burst out. "*I* wouldn't leave you this way! I'm not moving from this house until I know you're settled and happy the way you deserve to be. If O'Connell is too stupid to realize how fine you are, then he doesn't deserve you as his wife! If you were mine, every single day I'd make sure you knew just how precious you were."

Hannah stared, taken aback at Blake's impassioned words.

"Hannah, maybe . . . maybe you feel strongly about helping Ellie's mother. You've always been too kind-hearted for your own good. But that doesn't mean you can't have other babies to fill your arms."

"No," Hannah said, old pain and loss flooding through her, but not quite so sharp-edged this time. "I can't have children anymore."

"You're not too old, Hannah! I know other women who put off having a family until their forties."

"I was sick. The doctors said performing a hysterectomy was their only choice."

Tony shrugged. "It doesn't matter! With my job in the courts handling child welfare cases, I'm almost always one of the first people to know when those kids need someone to love them. A mother like you."

"That's . . . kind, Tony," Hannah said, confused. "But I know Sam won't be willing to take the risk again, after the way things turned out this time."

"Fine, then. Let him go off to his corner and sulk about how badly he was burned. How terrible you were not to tell him about an affair that was over years before he even met you. If O'Connell is too stupid to realize how lucky he is to have you in his life, then let him find out just how much he likes it without you!"

Hannah shook her head, the picture Tony painted filling her with horror, loss.

"*Yes*, Hannah!" Tony recaptured her hands, and this time held on with a fierceness that startled her. "You say that O'Connell's run out on you? Well, fine, then. Obviously he doesn't want the same things you do. I saw in that courtroom just how desperately you want more children in your life. I could give you those children."

"Wh—what?"

"Hannah, people change. Sometimes they don't want the same things. It doesn't mean anyone's terrible or wrong, it just means maybe it's time to make a change."

"You're not making any sense."

"I'm trying to tell you how I feel. That after all those years wandering around, making money, gaining respect in my profession, doing the rounds of society parties with wives I thought were perfect for the kind of life I wanted, I saw you again and realized somehow I'd gotten everything wrong. I had everything. But I didn't have the one thing that really mattered."

Hannah shook her head, so uncomfortable she could barely speak. "No, Tony . . . don't—"

"You told Sam the truth, it's time I told you. I

haven't been able to stop thinking about you since I saw you in the courthouse, about how things might have been if you and I had stayed together. The kids we would have had. The life we should have had together."

"The life we should have had together?" Hannah echoed with a ragged laugh. "If you'd stayed in Willowton you would have been miserable. You would have ended up hating me."

"I'll take you to the city—buy you the kind of house you deserve. Build you whatever you want! You can furnish it with everything bright and new, not worn out hand-me-downs. Sam wants out—then let him go. We can make a new start, Hannah."

Hannah stared at Tony. *Oh, God,* Hannah thought. This is what those searching looks of his had meant, what his touches had hinted at. Hopes that they could be together? In the weeks when her relationship with Sam had been so troubled had she somehow given Tony false hope?

Not entirely false, she reminded herself ruthlessly. Hadn't there been times she'd imagined what it would have been like for the two of them to be together?

His face was so intent, his mind obviously racing so far ahead he couldn't even see what was right in front of him. She should have been frustrated, disgusted. Instead she felt sad, resigned.

"Make a new start?" Hannah said. "We never had an old start. Tony, we've never wanted the same things. Not even when we were in high school."

"But it's different, now. Don't you see, Hannah? We could be good together."

"For how long? A month? A year? Even less time than that? Until things got too quiet, too routine, and you started getting restless again?"

"You think you know me, but you don't. If you'd give me a chance—"

"I remember my grandmother always had an old Irish saying. 'Faraway hills are green.' All your life, you've longed for those hills, Tony, while I wanted to stay right where I am."

"You don't know that! You've never even tried any-place else. Hell, O'Connell couldn't even bother building you your own house—someplace shining and fresh with everything new."

"You think Sam wouldn't have built me the finest house in Willowton if I'd have let him? Sam may not always have liked the old plumbing in this house, the cracks he had to patch in the walls, the trick heating vent in our bedroom. But the one thing he understood from the first moment he stepped into this house was that to me it would always be *home*," she said with anguished tenderness. "That was a good enough reason for him to stay here, too."

Tony's eyes flashed with impatience. "Well then, where is he now? Why isn't he here with you when you need him most? He heard something he didn't like and he just washed his hands of the whole situation."

"He *didn't* just wash his hands of the whole situation. No, he stepped in and did all the practical things I hadn't even thought of to help Ellie's mother. He offered her a place to stay with us, so she could get to know her baby again. He talked to her parents, so she didn't have to face that alone. He hired her a lawyer to help cut through the legal mess she's facing."

And then he put his suitcase in his truck and disappeared, Hannah couldn't bring herself to say.

"Then why isn't he here if he's such a damned saint?"

"Sam's never been a saint. Just a man. A good man.

He needs a little time to sort things out! God knows I should give it to him! It's my fault he didn't know I'd had a baby before I met him. It's my fault he didn't realize who you are. Sam's so honest. So proud. When I think about how he must have felt when he found out the truth, it makes me sick!"

"What about you, Hannah?" Tony challenged. "Did you ever stop to wonder why you didn't tell him about us? Because you knew he'd react just the way he did—as if you were soiled goods. As if those few months you and I spent together mattered more than the twenty-two years you two were married."

Hannah flinched as his jab hit its mark. "I wasn't honest with him. I don't blame him."

"Of course not. You've never blamed anybody except yourself for anything. You didn't blame me for walking out on you—"

"You'd made it clear you weren't staying in Willowton."

"And now it's not O'Connell's fault he's taken off just when you need him most."

"Sam was there when I needed him most. He was patient, so patient when I was too ashamed to even look another man in the face. Gentle when I wanted to shy away. I'd made up my mind I'd never take chances again. That it was too dangerous to love someone. When I found out my baby had died, I figured I didn't deserve a second chance at being a mother, and that there wasn't a man on earth who would want me as his wife."

"I did that to you? Made you feel that way?" Tony looked sick.

"No, Tony. *I'm* the only one who could make myself feel like that. It was my choice. The defense I used to protect myself from ever feeling the kind of pain and loss I felt when you and our baby slipped out of my life. But Sam . . . Sam made me believe I might actually be able to hope for something more."

"Let me show you the kind of life I can give you! Remember how it felt that spring in the stables? We couldn't keep our hands off each other."

"Not necessarily a good thing," Hannah tried to lighten things up. "Isn't that what got us in trouble?"

"Give me just one chance to prove it wasn't a bad thing—what was between us. Let me show you just how good it can be." His arms shot out, and he caught her, hard against him, his mouth coming down on hers in a practiced, searching kiss, the one final argument he hoped she couldn't resist.

To fight him would only make him believe she was responding to him. Instead, Hannah just went limp, not fighting, not moving, just waiting for him to realize it was hopeless and give up.

She felt him get more desperate, a frustrated groan rising in his throat. He pulled away, his cheeks hot, his jaw clenched, his eyes registering defeat.

He peered into her eyes with that sharp, probing gaze of a lawyer, trying to peel back layers of deception to find the raw truth. He didn't like the truth he saw. "There's no hope for us, Hannah, is there?"

"I'm sorry, Tony," Hannah said.

He stared at her, disappointment bitter in his eyes. But even though Hannah had always hated to see anyone hurting, she didn't let his expression disturb her too much. Before the week was out, Tony would be turning his gaze away from Willowton and the nostalgia that had brought him here. His eyes would be back on Grandma's "faraway hills."

Silence fell, the awkward moments seeming to stretch out forever. Hannah's lips stung from the kiss that hadn't fired anything inside her but sympathy for this man who was so worldly, so rich, so handsome. He'd learned everything in his executive lifestyle except how to be happy.

"Well, then," Tony said. "I'll probably head back to Chicago. Found a suitable nurse two weeks ago, but I wanted to see how things turned out between you and me."

"I thought you needed to talk to Sam and me."

"That'll keep. Just call whenever it would be convenient for the two of you to come in. I'll do whatever I can to help Rachel get custody of her baby."

"Thank you for that."

Tony shrugged one broad shoulder. "I figure, then we'll be even. Debts paid. The past all settled."

"I'd like that."

"Maybe you could check in on my mother once in a while. She'll be lonely once I'm gone. Maybe you're right about me, after all. Not fitting in here. Things haven't exactly worked out the way I planned. I figure I'll head back to the city." Tony forced a chuckle. "So, what about it? Would you mind stopping by to see my mother? She always loved you."

"I'd be happy to visit her," Hannah said.

"I'd get her a place in the city where she could be close by, but she'd be miserable away from this one-horse town. It is the one place in all those years of traveling with the air force that mom managed to think of as home." He smiled a little, and Hannah saw a hint of the boy she'd fallen head over heels for years ago. "Some people are just crazy that way."

Hannah smiled. "I suppose some of us are."

Tony went to the front door, and into the sunshine, Hannah following behind. She stood on the porch as he strode down the walk, the edges of the old slate stones already softened by the first shoots of lavender.

At the arbor Tony stopped, turned back to look, his eyes taking in the white clapboard walls, the wooden shutters, Hannah silhouetted against the bright green front door.

Hannah supposed he realized the truth the same as she did. There was nothing more to say.

At least not to Tony.

She ran into the house, scooped up her keys and started back out the door.

"Wait!"

Hannah stopped, turned to see Rachel slipping sheepishly from the backyard.

"What are you doing here?" Hannah asked, surprised.

"I was so nervous about what Mr. Blake would say, I couldn't stand it. Instead of going to the park, Ellie and I camped out back. There's a flat rock behind that big fallen oak tree in the ravine. You can pretty much see the driveway and all of the backyard from there, but nobody can see you." Rachel's cheeks washed pink. "That's where I watched until you took Ellie inside the day that I left her."

Hannah smiled. She knew just the place. "You *were* there! Thank God! That's one of the questions you are going to have to answer in the custody hearings—show that Ellie was never out of your sight, was never in any danger. But you're going to have to prove it, Rachel. Did you see anything special? Different from other days? It's important."

"There were sheets on the line, but then, you've hung out sheets for as long as I can remember. And I would know that even if I'd left Ellie alone." Rachel frowned a moment, then brightened. "The flowers! When you came outside you didn't stop to talk to the flowers. You didn't even look at them. You looked so sad. I'd never seen you like that before."

Hannah grinned, remembering Tony remarking on the way she talked to flowers moments before. With his word on the subject, too, surely they'd have to believe Rachel.

"I felt like someone was watching me," Hannah exclaimed. "I should have checked. You were hidden away where you and Becca used to set traps for unicorns when you were little."

"Yeah. I watched until you took her into the house, then sneaked through the ravine to those empty lots way on the other side. I was too scared to come into your lane. It's a dead end, no easy way out if things didn't go the way I wanted them to. Besides, everybody in the neighborhood knows me. If someone had seen me, it would have been impossible to explain since I was supposed to be away at school."

It was true, thought Hannah. One of the things she loved best about the neighborhood was that everyone knew each other, looked out for each other. She'd wondered why Ellie's mother hadn't just left the baby on the front porch. Now that made perfect sense. Rachel had known she'd come out to gather the laundry from the line. She'd been able to watch over Ellie until the baby was safe in Hannah's arms.

"What did Mr. Blake say when he was here?" Rachel asked. "Will I get to keep my baby?"

"With proof you didn't leave until she was safe in my hands? Absolutely!" Hannah said with new confidence. "It may not be easy, Rachel, and it may take some time. But I know you'll be the one baking Ellie's birthday cakes and holding her hand on the first day of school. Mr. Blake is going to try to help you. We all are. And we aren't going to stop until you've gotten through school, gotten a job you'll love, have a way to build a good life for you and your little girl."

"I thought I might . . . might teach music. It's not Carnegie Hall, but—remember my old orchestra teacher? Mr. Binns? He changed my life. Gave me something to love, to block out the way other kids teased me. If I could give that to someone else, wouldn't that be almost better than playing on stage?"

"You'll be a wonderful teacher. And who knows? Cities have orchestras. You could play in one of them for a while. And as Ellie grows up—well, if you keep studying hard, maybe you'll go back to Vienna when you're my age. It'll be brand new, an adventure."

Rachel's eyes filled with tears. "You make me feel like . . . like maybe I haven't ruined everything. Maybe my life won't be like Dad said—a disaster forever because I had my baby."

"That's one of the most wonderful things about being human, Rachel. You make mistakes, but sometimes you can fix things. Things can work out even better than you'd ever dreamed. I hope it works out that way for me."

For the very first time, Rachel seemed to notice the car keys Hannah held. "Where are you going?"

"I have to go to Sam. Talk to him. I wanted to give him what he asked for. Time to think. The space he needed. But I can't wait any longer. There are so many things I need to say to him."

"You're going down to his shop, then?" Rachel fidgeted with the soft yarn fringe on Ellie's blanket. "He said . . . he said he wanted to finish something before Ellie and I left. He didn't say what."

"That's so like Sam," Hannah said. Whenever things got hard or rough or painful he'd always flung himself into work with a fury to block out emotions he didn't want to feel. Make himself so busy he couldn't stop to think.

Hannah hugged Rachel, dropped a quick kiss on the girl's forehead and on Ellie's chubby cheek. "Don't worry," she told them. "Everything is going to be fine."

She rushed to the car, climbed in and started the ignition, and as she pulled out of the driveway, she prayed that she was right.

She didn't know if Sam would understand. She didn't know if he would care. She didn't know if he would ever be able to forgive her, forget. Give their love another chance.

But one thing Hannah did know for certain was this: Sam O'Connell was going to hear just how much she loved him.

What if he walks away? a voice inside her questioned. Hannah's stomach churned. She pressed one fist to her mouth, trying to choke back the panic the thought of Sam leaving had stirred up inside her. She'd lived through loss before, she told herself. She'd survived when Tony had deserted her, and when her baby had been taken from her arms.

She'd survive if Sam left her, too.

But it would be the hardest thing she had ever had to do.

23

IT WAS NO USE.

Sam tossed the freshly turned leg into the box of scrap wood in the corner, and brushed the wood shavings from hands nicked and bleeding. He grabbed a white cloth handkerchief from his back pocket and wrapped it around his finger, swearing under his breath.

"Fine," he snapped at the half-finished project before him. "I give up. My concentration's shot. I'm going to lose a finger if I keep it up." He touched the miniature rocker he'd made for the child-size rocking chair he'd been putting together for Ellie and sighed.

What the hell would it matter if he lost his whole damned hand? It couldn't hurt any worse than losing his heart. And losing Hannah was like having it torn right out of him, leaving him hopeless and numb and hurting so bad he could hardly breathe.

Sam ran his hand through his hair and trudged out of the shop area into the offices beyond. Sunday—there wasn't a soul around. It was silent. Dead. Computer screens vacant black eyes, chairs empty, tools all stacked neatly. He'd always loved this place from the day he'd first walked through the door, saw the echoing warehouse space, the sunny rooms where the shop offices would be.

He'd been so young, so naïve, so eager to prove himself. But even he had never guessed how the place would get into his blood. Every stick of trim, desk, sawhorse and rack of supplies tangible evidence that he'd left behind all the old labels that had haunted him. Here, he wasn't just a drunk's worthless son, a kid whose mother had abandoned him. Here he could stand on his own two feet, be his own man.

He'd drawn so much strength from this place. He'd only wished he had someone to share those feelings with. Wished Hannah could be more a part of it, understand he'd been able to build all this because of her. Maybe it didn't seem very romantic, the way a woman would see it. There weren't flowers here or midnight glasses of champagne or love letters under the pillow. But in a way, this place was his own unique love song to Hannah, built of wood shavings and bricks, hammers and blueprints and hard-won self-reliance. This place had made possible all the gifts he'd been able to give her through the years. The most precious one of all: time with Becca.

Again, today, he'd found just what he needed here. He'd always figured he was part wolf—needed to burrow into his den when he was wounded.

Here, he usually managed to block out most of the things that had troubled him. It hadn't mattered here that his mother had dumped him or his father was a drunk. All that had mattered was the fact that he was good with his hands, had a gift for seeing things that didn't exist and building them. When other people couldn't imagine a house or a building, he already had it pictured perfectly in his mind—complete with patio furniture and icy pitchers of lemonade sweating in the summer sun.

Yeah, he'd been damned good at imagining things his whole life. But he'd been so careful not to let himself imagine this. Hannah slipping away from him.

Sam stalked to his office, the desk piled with plans and figures, orders for materials and payroll numbers. All the things he'd depended on to distract him from his deepest fears. Frames of every size and shape jostled for space on the credenza that abutted the office's rear wall, a storage unit for forms and supplies he needed close to hand.

But he'd never much given a damn what was inside the long chest. It was the images the frames held that had filled him with determination, made him work harder, strive to do better.

Hannah. Becca. His two girls, he'd always called them. They smiled out at him in vivid Kodak color. Becca astride a fat, cream-colored pony at the county fair. Hannah stretched out, dozing on the quilt at their favorite picnic spot. Becca and Hannah and half a dozen neighbor kids perched on the massive wall of the snow fort they'd spent three school snow days building. Rachel was somewhere in that throng, Sam remembered. Her arms weren't waving in triumph. She wasn't striking some comical pose. She crowded close to Hannah, hands shoved behind her back, head dipped, shy in front of the camera.

A wedding picture stood in a silver frame, Hannah looking as warm and vibrant as one of the lilies that grew tall in her gardens. Beside that image, another one dwarfed by the size of all the other pictures. This frame fit in the palm of Sam's hand. He picked up the scarred wooden frame it seemed as if he'd had forever, and he held to the light the first picture of Hannah he'd ever taken.

Wistful, woebegone, she sat on the edge of a bluff at the park he'd taken her to for a picnic. He'd caught her unawares, but the picture of her at that instant had seared itself into his heart. He'd fallen in love with her at that moment. Wanted to wipe away the lost angel sadness he saw in her beautiful face. He'd never known what she was thinking about at the moment he'd snapped the picture. Now, he knew what had haunted her eyes, saddened her mouth, made her look so fragile and alone even in a raucous bunch of college kids. Now he knew why he'd instinctively wanted so much to protect her.

He'd wanted her to trust him. To tell him what was hurting her. He wanted to be her knight in shining armor, rush into the dragon fire to save her. But he'd failed her when he'd left the house. He'd left her in her own private hell to burn. And now, it was too late to change it.

He heard a key rattle in the front door. He swore, cursing himself for giving his secretary a key so she could open the office when he was away and his job foremen keys so they could get to the tool room. He caught a glimpse of his reflection in the glass of one of the frames, his face haggard and lined deep with misery. What the hell excuse could he think up to explain the rotten shape he was in?

He heard footsteps. Tried to paste a smile onto his lips. He could see for himself it was a grotesque failure. Unfortunately, he still had to greet whoever it was. He turned around. His heart slammed into his ribs hard, then seemed to stop beating.

"Hannah." He choked out her name, his hand closing so tight on the small picture frame, its rough edges cut into his palm. *Oh, God*, Sam thought, his mouth going dry. She'd been disgusted enough to come find him. Must want to get it over with. To tell him— It hurt so much he couldn't even put it into words.

"You know, I haven't been down here since before . . . before I got sick," Hannah said in a small voice as she wandered to the credenza, trailed her fingertips over the corners of frames, along the edges of the pictures that captured the only joy in Sam's life. "And before that, well, I can't remember the last time."

"You were busy with Becca." Sam dismissed it.

"Yes. Busy." She sounded disappointed. The pallor of her face terrified him. What was she doing, touching the pictures, staring at them, her lashes hiding her eyes, keeping him from guessing—what? Why she'd followed him here? Sam grimaced. It wasn't as if he were too dense to figure it out.

"I tried to give you the time you needed," she said. "You were so patient with me when I was going through everything with the surgery and being sick. I don't know how you did it, Sam. I . . . guess I'm not as understanding as you are. I couldn't wait any longer to talk to you."

Talk? Wasn't that what had rammed this red hot poker into the middle of his chest? Wasn't that what had tortured him until he couldn't close his eyes without imagining Hannah in Tony Blake's arms? Loving him. Touching him. Responding to him the way Sam had always believed she only responded to him.

But that wasn't the worst of the nightmares that had turned the past few nights into hell. The worst was the memory of Hannah's eyes when he'd raged at her, the grief in them, the pain, the inevitability, as if she believed she'd deserved it—all his anger and betrayal and fear.

Soon he'd be able to add another image to his gallery of horrors. Hannah giving him exactly what he deserved, telling him she hated him for letting her down. Telling him she'd never forgive him for hurting her. Sam winced, picturing all too clearly the sharp light in eyes that had always been so warm, so welcoming. Eyes that had always shone at him with love. Now they'd be changed, be like his mother's had been. Sick with disgust, disappointment, dismissal. Dark with revulsion because Hannah had finally seen whatever it was that had made Sam's own mother hate him.

But hadn't he earned it this time? He'd raged at Hannah, forgetting all about the fragile, shy girl he'd fallen in love with. He'd let his pride get so burned he lashed out instead of trying to protect her.

"I suppose we'd better get this over with," Sam said, his gut burning with shame.

"Get this over with?" Hannah echoed, turning to face him. His knees almost buckled when he saw the dark circles under eyes raw from crying. Her mouth was soft and bruised and sad, but she was still the most beautiful thing Sam had ever set eyes on.

In that instant, it seemed impossible to imagine that she'd ever belonged to him at all. "You'll be wanting me out of the house."

Hannah's eyes widened, glistened with a sheen of tears. "Will I?" she asked in a tight little voice.

Didn't he owe her the truth? "I failed you, Hannah."

"*You* failed *me?*"

Sam shoulders slumped. "That's why I . . . I couldn't face you."

"Sam, I—"

"I guess I figured you wouldn't want me around home."

"How could you think that?" Hannah exclaimed,

her face so stunned it almost made Sam dare to hope. Even so, she needed to see his behavior for exactly what it was.

"I screwed up, Hannah. Just the way I screwed up the day my mother left."

"What in the world are you talking about?" Hannah asked, her face ice white, her eyes dark with pain and confusion.

"The day my mother left, she wanted me to . . . to wear this stupid shirt she'd gotten me. The other kids made fun of me, so I ruined it on purpose, tore it and stained it by dragging it across my bike chain."

"Oh, Sam. You were just being a little boy. Your mother didn't leave you because you wrecked one shirt." She laid a hand on his arm so gently he had to stifle a moan.

She'd comforted him so many times in the twenty-two years they'd been married. Tiny touches that soothed the ragged places in his soul, smiles so tender they warmed the cold places in his heart, a faith in him that shone from her eyes and strengthened him, made him want to be a better man than he was—the kind of man who could half deserve her. But he'd lost any right to that comfort by the way he had torn into her on the sun porch five days ago.

"I'm not an idiot. I know she didn't leave because of one lousy shirt, even if I did believe that when I was a kid. But she had some reason for leaving me, Hannah. There had to be some flaw that she could see, something so ugly it made her leave me behind."

"It wasn't your fault that she left you, Sam. You didn't do anything to deserve what she did to you. You were a little boy who loved your mother and she let you down."

Sam swore, bitterly. "I guess we have something in

common then, my mother and I. She let me down when I needed her and I did the same thing to you. I let you down when you told me about Blake."

"It's not the same thing at all!" Hannah cried. "You were an innocent little boy who deserved your mother's love. You did nothing wrong, Sam. And as for Tony Blake—you did nothing wrong there, either. You trusted me. And you found out in the most painful way possible that I'd lied to you. It's no wonder you were hurt by it. You got angry."

"Angry?" Sam gave a raw laugh. "I was a first-rate bastard."

"But it's no wonder—"

"What? That I could be selfish as hell? Throw away twenty-two years of love and marriage and trust because I was hurt? My pride was wounded? I never stopped for a minute to imagine what it must have been like for you all those years when nobody knew about what you'd been through. Facing your little girl's birthday every year, never being able to cry." Sam's eyes burned fiercely. He clenched his fists in self-disgust. "You should have been able to cry with me."

His voice cracked, his throat raw. "All I ever wanted was to be strong for you, Hannah. Your knight in shining armor. First sign of a real dragon and I ran."

"Are you still running, Sam?"

He winced at the vulnerability in her voice, those eyes so filled with everything good and warm and fine.

"If you're here now, if we can face the dragon down together, that's all that really matters."

He was almost afraid to hope. "Do you mean it, Hannah?"

"It was so . . . so stupid. When we were there on the sun porch. I said everything except the things that really mattered. I'm going to say them now."

"I'm listening. I promise I won't walk away."

"Everything I went through—being alone, pregnant, giving my baby away. Finding out she was lost forever—I never thought I'd survive it. But I figured I deserved the pain I felt for what I'd done. When I went to college, the one thing I was certain of was this. I'd survive. But happiness? Love? Those were beyond my reach."

"Hannah, you didn't do anything a million other kids hadn't done. You got caught. You did the best you could."

Her smile warmed him. "Becca said almost the same thing. I just want you to know what you gave me when you loved me, Sam. A new beginning. A chance for the kind of love I'd stopped believing could ever exist for me. You were so patient, so caring. I was so scared of being hurt, but I couldn't help myself. I loved you so much."

Sam's face contorted in anguish, disbelief. "Why? I've never been able to figure out why."

Hannah cradled his jaw in her hand, her palm so warm, so gentle. "You made me laugh when I'd forgotten how to smile. When I tried to hide away inside myself you wouldn't let me slip away. You came after me with that grin of yours, those eyes that had seen enough pain to understand it in me."

"Remember the picture I took—that first one?" Sam pointed to the frame he'd held awhile before. "You reminded me of those flowers we studied in botany— the ones that withered up if you touched them too roughly. I had no idea how strong you were. You looked so sad that day. Now I know why."

Hannah's face clouded, sorrow she could finally share. "It was my baby's birthday. That was one of the reasons I got up the nerve to go out with you. I thought you'd keep my mind off it, at least a little bit. Figured you'd be all groping hands and cocky jokes, easy to shove away. I never expected to fall in love with you. But you were so gentle with me, Sam. So tender. You made me feel . . . safe when I hadn't felt that way in a very long time."

Sam's throat constricted with emotion, and he grasped her hand, holding on, tight. "Did I ruin it, Hannah?" he rasped. "Things got so rough between us, so strained for so long. It was hell feeling you pull away. Tell me I haven't lost you."

"I could never leave you, Sam. You refused to leave me."

"I don't understand."

"In that bleak shadow life that I'd gone to. You pulled me back into the sunshine and showed me flowers again and made me lie on my back on a green hillside and count the stars in the sky. There were so many of them, some bright, some tiny, some lost and tumbling from the heavens. Like people . . . like me. You reached up to catch me. Made me feel like it mattered to you that I find some way to shine again. Maybe not the way I did before, but a new way." Her voice softened, her eyes saddened. "If only I hadn't gotten it all wrong."

The joy surging through Sam froze. "Wrong?"

"I thought I had to be perfect. You always said that I was. And I'm not. I make mistakes, get petty and angry and afraid. I'll disappoint you. Sometimes I don't know where to turn, what to say."

Sam shook his head in disbelief. "You thought I expected you to be what? Some sort of saint? I've always loved the woman in you. Your humanity. I always knew it was as hard for you to do the right thing as it was for anyone else. The miracle was that you did it anyway. You made it look easy, Hannah. But I was never fool enough to think it really was."

Sam drew her close, held her against the beat of his heart. "When I said you were perfect, I meant you were perfect for *me*, Hannah. Just the way you are. Not some sort of angel."

He could feel her shoulders shaking, knew she was trying not to cry. "I was afraid that if you knew about the baby—you wouldn't love me," she admitted brokenly.

"Oh, God, Hannah!"

"That was the one thing you could never forgive—leaving a child behind. I thought you'd think I was like your mother. That I didn't care about my baby. Didn't want her." Tears flowed down her cheeks. "But I loved her, Sam. Wanted her so much."

"I know, love," Sam hushed her. "I know."

"I was just so scared. I didn't know . . . know what to do. There was no one I could talk to." She raised her face to look at him. "Sam, would you . . . would you have hated me if I'd told you when we first fell in love?"

Sam hesitated, thinking hard, knowing they both needed the truth. "I don't know what I would have done then," Sam said slowly. "My mother hurt me so much. I was so raw. Not to mention I was young and stupid. Saw everything in black and white. I know better now. There are a million shades of gray. I can't say what I would have done then. I can only tell you about how I feel now. You're the best thing that ever happened to me, Hannah."

"Oh, Sam," she whispered, but he laid his fingers on her lips, wanting so much for her to listen, trying so hard to find the right words to tell her what she'd given him for so long.

"When I was lost and so damned tired of wandering, you gave me a home, Hannah. Not a house. A place to live. A home is so much more. Someone glad to see me when I came home at night. Eyes that lit up whenever they saw me. Hands to touch me in ways no one had ever touched me before. It's not about sex, Hannah. It was about being . . . cherished. Wanted. Welcomed. It was the luckiest day of my life when you welcomed me into your heart."

He gathered her to him again, kissing her face, her cheeks, her eyelids, her hair. Tasted tears, and didn't know if they were Hannah's or his own.

"I guess realizing what you went through got me thinking about other things, too. I can't forget Mom left me, but listening to you makes me think that maybe, just maybe, I don't know everything that happened way back then. How desperate she might have been. How badly it might have hurt her to have to leave me. She had no money, no skills. How was she supposed to take care of two kids? Trisha was always the fragile one, sensitive. Tiny for her age with these big, haunted eyes. In some ways, a lot like Rachel. She was already terrified when Dad went off on his binges. I remember I found her once, hiding under the basement stairs. Couldn't get her to talk for a week." He flinched inwardly, probing the old pain. "When I think of my little sister sleeping on cement floors, cleaning up after Dad, living on potato chips and Twinkies—" Sam stopped, cleared his throat, then met Hannah's eyes with an honesty that touched her to the core. "If Mom could only take one of us—I'm glad she took Trisha."

Hannah cradled his face in her hands. "That's so like you, Sam. Wanting to spare your baby sister from everything you saw. I hope she was happy. But I know . . . know that what you suffered made you the man you are. And I love that man. With all my heart."

Sam stood before her, soul stripped bare, needing to say it all just one time. Things he'd never put into words. "I just—sometimes I can't help wondering why she never even tried to contact me, you know? See if I was all right."

Hannah fretted her bottom lip. He could see she was wanting to comfort him, but she loved him too much to brush off his question with platitudes. "It was wrong of your mother not to make sure you were safe. I can't pretend to understand what she did, Sam. But it might have made sense in her own mind. Maybe your mother thought you would never forgive her, and that's why she didn't contact you. God knows, she would never forgive herself."

"Maybe. Maybe she grieved over it like you grieved over your little girl, Hannah, but felt helpless to change it. I'd like to believe that. It's equally possible she was glad to be rid of me and never thought of me again. Either way, I'll never know. Maybe it's time to stop tearing myself up, wondering what the answer is. Maybe it's finally time to let it go."

Hannah glowed, her eyes filled with such love, such respect, it humbled him. "You make me so proud, Sam."

It was the first time anyone had said that to him. His heart welled up with pleasure. "Do you think I'd be crazy if . . . if sometime I tried to find Trisha? I'd at least like to know that my baby sister is all right."

"No. I don't think you'd be crazy. Whatever you want to do, Sam, I support you, with all my heart."

"I've always thought I got cheated somehow, because of my mother. That I didn't get the love I deserved. But now, I figure everyone only gets so much love poured into their life. When you loved me,

Hannah, I got more love than most people get in a lifetime. All I've ever wanted was you, Hannah. Just the way you are. The instant I touched your hand, I was home." Sam gave a ragged laugh. "I know I acted like an idiot, but I was so damned scared."

"Of what?"

Sam's cheeks darkened, saying the words aloud a physical pain. "I was afraid you wanted him. Would have chosen him if you'd had a choice."

He didn't know what he expected. But surely not laughter. That rare, silvery sound that was Hannah's own, a sound he'd never hoped to hear again. Her eyes shone for him, only for him. "I would have chosen you," she said, such certainty in her voice it made his pulses leap. "I *did* choose you. *Tonight.*"

"By coming here?" Sam asked.

"No," Hannah said, grinning. "By turning Tony Blake down flat."

"You mean the guy made a pass at you?" Sam roared, jealousy flaring. "I knew it!"

"He promised me wealth and all the babies I could want. Life in the big city and fancy clothes and cars. Everything *he* thought I should want. You know better. I want patchwork quilts and our iron bed with the rails all bent from my great-grandmother pulling on them in childbirth. I want my Mother's Day garden with lilacs and my porch swing to dream on. I told Tony Blake exactly what I told you. I choose you, Sam. Always you. Only you."

Sam laughed, lifting her up by the waist, swinging her around in a joyous circle. "Hannah," he murmured over and over again. "Oh, Hannah!"

He drifted her feet back to the ground, startled by the suddenly pensive light in her eyes. "What is it, love?" he asked.

"I *am* sorry, Sam. So sorry about everything that happened. Not telling you about my past, and about losing Ellie when you started to love her."

Sam glanced down, drew in a steadying breath. "Do you want another baby, Hannah?" he asked. "I won't lie to you. It scares me. But . . . if it's what you want, maybe we could find another baby, adopt her . . ."

Hannah smiled tenderly, and he knew she understood him, down to his very soul. "I didn't know what to do with myself once Becca left," she admitted. "I thought having Ellie in our lives would fix that. But it wasn't fair. Babies grow up. Go away. That's the way it's meant to be. I just need to find some new way to fill up that empty space."

"How can I help you do that, Hannah?" he asked earnestly.

"I have to do it myself, Sam."

"Tell me, Hannah. Tell me what you dream."

"I was thinking—maybe I don't need babies of my own anymore. Maybe . . . I could help girls like Rachel—teach them what they need to know to keep their babies if that's what they want. Or, if they make the decision to give their babies up, help the girls to heal. Maybe that's what this whole thing was about. All the pain, the memories, the confusion. Reliving what I went through years ago. Maybe it was a way to bring me full circle. To show me a place to belong now that my own little girl doesn't need me anymore."

"Becca will always need you. And so will I."

Hannah kissed Sam's cheek, slipped her arms around his waist.

Sam made a face. "She'll be so relieved to hear we've finally—what was it she said last time she called—'quit acting stupid!' "

Hannah laughed, thinking of her little girl—no, a

grown woman now, with a life of her own, adventures just beginning.

Adventures, Hannah thought. Maybe it wasn't too late to begin some of her own. She trailed her fingertips down his chest, touching him the way she knew always made him catch fire. "There's one more thing I want, Sam. So much."

His eyes twinkled wickedly. She tingled all over, felt the rush of excitement she'd lost for so long. She'd never take that desire for granted again.

"Besides making love until neither one of us can move?" Sam teased. "We aren't as young as we used to be, you know."

"Speak for yourself. Here, with you, I almost feel like I'm Becca's age. Young in a way I've never felt before. I was born old, Sam. Now, maybe it's my turn to be a child. I want to discover everything, have adventures. Stay up dancing with you until dawn."

"Hannah, you don't have to change for me."

Hannah shook back her hair, smiling. "I want to get to know you the way I should have years ago when I got too wrapped up in proving I was a decent mother. I guess I didn't realize that somehow, part of me stopped worrying about being a good wife at the same time."

"No, Hannah. Never."

But she wouldn't be dissuaded. She peered up at him, so solemn it made him ache. "Tell me honestly, Sam. Promise. No more secrets between us."

"Promise," he said.

"Didn't you ever feel left out—just a little? Didn't you wish I'd . . . I'd come down here to the shop, see everything you were trying to build. Get excited over the things that made up your day?"

He flushed, looked down. "I was a selfish bastard."

She hooked her finger under his jaw, urged him to

meet her eyes. "Now I'm going to be selfish—with our time, together. I promise I'll do better."

"Just be yourself, Hannah. My Hannah. I love you just the way you are."

Sam kissed her, held her. Hannah nibbled at his ear. "Sam, speaking of being more adventurous . . . I was thinking maybe we could start right now. You know, just to make sure I don't get cold feet."

"What did you have in mind?"

"Do you know we've never made love on that couch?" She pointed to the one he'd spent the most miserable night of his life on just the night before. What a terrific way to drive out those painful memories.

Sam laughed, loving her. "One last question, Hannah. Tell me the truth. It's about your Mother's Day garden. We can take Ellie's lilac out. I just don't want it to hurt you, make you sad."

"No. I want to remember Ellie forever. What she gave us. Something most people never get in a lifetime."

"What's that?" Sam asked tenderly.

"A chance to find out just how lucky we are."

**Visit the Simon & Schuster
romance Web site:**

www.SimonSaysLove.com

**and sign up for our
romance e-mail updates!**

Keep up on the latest
new romance releases,
author appearances, news, chats,
special offers, and more!
We'll deliver the information
right to your inbox—if it's new,
you'll know about it.

POCKET BOOKS

2800.02

Return to
a time of romance...

SONNET
BOOKS

Where today's

hottest romance authors

bring you vibrant

and vivid love stories

with a dash of history.

PUBLISHED BY POCKET BOOKS